THE FORT

BERNARD CORNWELL

The Fort

HarperCollins*Publishers*

HarperCollins*Publishers*
77–85 Fulham Palace Road,
Hammersmith, London W6 8JB

www.harpercollins.co.uk

Published by HarperCollins*Publishers* 2010
1

Map © Garry Gates 2010

A catalogue record for this book
is available from the British Library

ISBN: 978–0–00–733172–7

While some of the events and characters are based on historical incidents
and figures, this novel is entirely a work of fiction.

Set in Meridien by Palimpsest Book Production Limited,
Falkirk, Stirlingshire

Printed and bound in Great Britain by
Clays Ltd, St Ives plc

THE FORT
*is dedicated, with great admiration, to
Colonel John Wessmiller, US Army (Retired)
who would have known just what to do.*

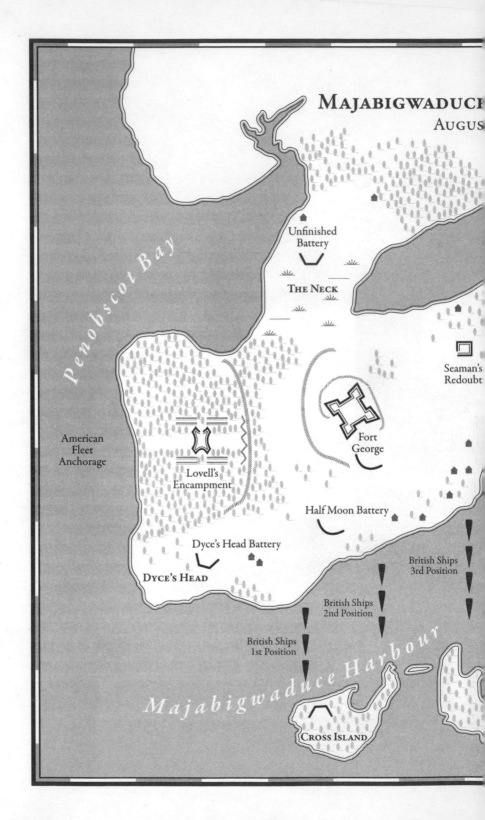

MAJABIGWADUC
AUGUS

Unfinished
Battery

THE NECK

Penobscot Bay

Seaman's
Redoubt

American
Fleet
Anchorage

Fort
George

Lovell's
Encampment

Half Moon Battery

Dyce's Head Battery

DYCE'S HEAD

British Ships
3rd Position

British Ships
2nd Position

British Ships
1st Position

Majabigwaduce Harbour

CROSS ISLAND

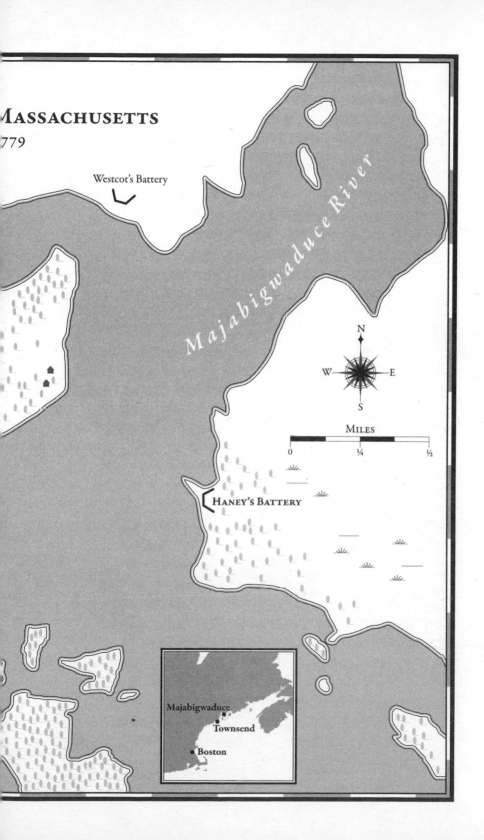

MASSACHUSETTS
1779

Westcot's Battery

Majabigwaduce River

N
W   E
S

MILES
0   ¼   ½

HANEY'S BATTERY

Majabigwaduce
Townsend
Boston

A voice in the darkness, a knock at the door,
And a word that shall echo for evermore!
For, borne on the night-wind of the Past,
Through all our history, to the last,
In the hour of darkness and peril and need,
The people will waken and listen to hear
The hurrying hoof-beats of that steed,
And the midnight message of Paul Revere.

From Henry Longfellow's
The Midnight Ride of Paul Revere

Slowly and sadly we laid him down,
From the field of his fame fresh and gory;
We carved not a line, and we raised not a stone,
But we left him alone with his glory.

From Charles Wolfe's
The Burial of Sir John Moore after Corunna

A NOTE ON NAMES
AND TERMS

In 1779 there was no state of Maine, it was then the eastern province of Massachusetts. Some place names have also changed. Majabigwaduce is now called Castine, Townsend is Bucks Harbor, and Falmouth is Portland, Maine. Buck's plantation (properly Plantation Number One) is Bucksport, Orphan Island is Verona Island, Long Island (in the Penobscot River) is now Islesboro Island, Wasaumkeag Point is now Cape Jellison and Cross Island is today called Nautilus Island.

The novel frequently refers to 'ships', 'sloops', 'brigs', and 'schooners'. They are all, of course, ships in the same way that they are all boats, but properly a ship was a large, square-rigged, three-masted vessel like a frigate (think of the USS *Constitution*) or a ship of the line (like HMS *Victory*). Nowadays we think of a sloop as a single-masted sailboat, but in 1779 it denoted a three-masted vessel that was usually smaller than a ship and distinguished by having a flush main deck (thus no raised poop deck). Sloops, like ships, were square rigged (meaning they carried rectangular sails hung from crosswise yards). A brig, or brigantine, was also a large square-rigged sailing vessel, but with only two masts. Schooners, like brigs, carried two masts, but were rigged with fore-and-aft sails which, when hoisted, lie along the centre line of the vessel rather than across it. There were variations, such as brig-sloops, but at Penobscot Bay, in 1779, there were only ships, sloops, brigs and schooners. With the exception of the *Felicity* all the names of the boats are taken from history.

Most of the characters in the novel existed. The only fictional names are those of any character whose surname begins with F (with the exception of Captain Thomas Farnham, RN), and the names of British privates and non-commissioned officers (with the exception of Sergeant Lawrence, Royal Artillery).

Excerpt of letter from the Massachusetts Council, to Brigadier-General Solomon Lovell, July 2nd, 1779:

You will in all your operations consult with the Commander of the fleet that the Naval Force may cooperate with the troops under your command in Endeavoring to Captivate Kill or Destroy the whole force of the Enemy there both by sea & land. And as there is good reason to believe that some of the Principal men at Majorbagaduce requested the enemy to come there and take possession you will be peculiarly careful not to let any of them escape, but to secure them for their evil doings . . . We now commend you to the Supream being Sincerely praying him to preserve you and the Forces under your Command in health and safety, & Return you Crowned with Victory and Laurels.

From a postscript to Doctor John Calef's Journal, 1780, concerning Majabigwaduce:

To this new country, the Loyalists resort with their families . . . and find asylum from the tyranny of Congress, and their taxgatherers . . . and there they continue in full hope, and pleasant expectation, that they may soon re-enjoy the liberties and privileges which would be best secured to them by the . . . British Constitution.

Letter from Captain Henry Mowat, Royal Navy, to Jonathan Buck, written aboard HMS *Albany*, Penobscot River, June 15th, 1779:

Sir, Understanding that you are at the head of a Regiment of the King's deluded Subjects on this River and parts adjacent and that you hold a Colonel's Commission under the influence of a body of men termed the General Congress of the United States of America, it therefore becomes my duty to require you to appear without loss of time before General McLean and the commanding Officer of the King's Ships now on board the Blonde off of Majorbigwaduce with a Muster Roll of the People under your direction.

ONE

There was not much wind so the ships headed sluggishly upriver. There were ten of them, five warships escorting five transports, and the flooding tide did more to carry them northwards than the fitful breeze. The rain had stopped, but the clouds were low, grey and direful. Water dripped monotonously from sails and rigging.

There was little to see from the ships, though all their gunwales were crowded with men staring at the river's banks that widened into a great inland lake. The hills about the lake were low and covered with trees, while the shoreline was intricate with creeks, headlands, wooded islands and small, stony beaches. Here and there among the trees were cleared spaces where logs were piled or perhaps a wooden cabin stood beside a small cornfield. Smoke rose from those clearings and some men aboard the ships wondered if the distant fires were signals to warn the country of the fleet's arrival. The only people they saw were a man and a boy fishing from a small open boat. The boy, who was named William Hutchings, waved excitedly at the ships, but his uncle spat. 'There come the devils,' he said.

The devils were mostly silent. On board the largest warship, a 32-gun frigate named *Blonde*, a devil in a blue coat and an oilskin-covered cocked hat lowered his telescope. He frowned thoughtfully at the dark, silent woods past which his ship slid. 'To my mind,' he said, 'it looks like Scotland.'

'Aye, it does,' his companion, a red-coated devil, answered cautiously, 'a resemblance, certainly.'

'More wooded than Scotland, though?'

'A deal more wooded,' the second man said.

'But like the west coast of Scotland, wouldn't you say?'

'Not unlike,' the second devil agreed. He was sixty-two years old, quite short, and had a shrewd, weathered face. It was a kindly face with small, bright blue eyes. He had been a soldier for over forty years and in that time had endured a score of hard-fought battles that had left him with a near-useless right arm, a slight limp, and a tolerant view of sinful mankind. His name was Francis McLean and he was a Brigadier-General, a Scotsman, commanding officer of His Majesty's 82nd regiment of foot, Governor of Halifax, and now, at least according to the dictates of the King of England, the ruler of everything he surveyed from the *Blonde*'s quarterdeck. He had been aboard the frigate for thirteen days, the time it had taken to sail from Halifax in Nova Scotia, and he felt a twinge of worry that the length of the voyage might prove unlucky. He wondered if it might have been better to have made it in fourteen days and surreptitiously touched the wood of the rail. A burnt wreck lay on the eastern shore. It had once been a substantial ship capable of crossing an ocean, but now it was a ribcage of charred wood half inundated by the flooding tide that carried the *Blonde* upriver. 'So how far are we now from the open sea?' he asked the blue-uniformed captain of the *Blonde*.

'Twenty-six nautical miles,' Captain Andrew Barkley answered briskly, 'and there,' he pointed over the starboard bow and past the lion-crested cathead from which one of the frigate's anchors was suspended, 'is your new home.'

McLean borrowed the captain's glass and, using his awkward right arm as a rest for the tubes, trained the telescope forrard.

4

For a moment the small motions of the ship defeated him so that all he glimpsed was a blur of grey clouds, dark land and sullen water, but he steadied himself to see that the Penobscot River widened to make the great lake that Captain Barkley called Penobscot Bay. The bay, McLean thought, was really a great sea loch, which he knew from his study of Barkley's charts was some eight miles from east to west and three miles from north to south. A harbour opened from the bay's eastern shore. The mouth of the harbour was edged by rocks, while on its northern side was a hill crowned thick with trees. A settlement stood on the southern slope of that hill; over a score of wooden homes and barns were set among patches of corn, plots of vegetables and piles of timber. A handful of fishing boats was anchored in the harbour, along with one small brig that McLean assumed was a trading vessel. 'So that's Majabigwaduce,' he said softly.

'Back topsails!' the captain called, 'order the fleet to heave to. I shall trouble you to signal for a pilot, Mister Fennel!'

'Aye aye, sir!'

The frigate suddenly seethed with men running to release sheets. 'That's Majabigwaduce,' Barkley said in a tone that suggested the name was as risible as the place.

'Number one gun!' Lieutenant Fennel shouted, provoking another rush of men who ran to the forward starboard cannon.

'Do you have any idea,' McLean asked the captain, 'what Majabigwaduce signifies?'

'Signifies?'

'Does the name mean anything?'

'No idea, no idea,' Barkley said, apparently irritated by the question. 'Now, Mister Fennel!'

The gun, charged and wadded, but without any shot, was fired. The recoil was slight, but the sound of the gun seemed hugely loud and the cloud of smoke enveloped half the *Blonde*'s deck. The gunshot faded, then was echoed back from the shore before fading a second time.

'We shall discover something now, won't we?' Barkley said.

'What is that?' McLean enquired.

'Whether they're loyal, General, whether they're loyal. If they've been infected by rebellion then they'll hardly supply a pilot, will they?'

'I suppose not,' McLean said, though he suspected a disloyal pilot could well serve his rebellious cause by guiding HMS *Blonde* onto a rock. There were plenty of those breaking the bay's surface. On one, not fifty paces from the frigate's port gunwales, a cormorant spread its dark wings to dry.

They waited. the gun had been fired, the customary signal requesting a pilot, but the smoke prevented anyone aboard from seeing whether the settlement of Majabigwaduce would respond. The five transport ships, four sloops and frigate drifted upriver on the tide. The loudest noise was the groan, wheeze and splashing from the pump aboard one of the sloops, HMS *North*. The water spurted and gushed rhythmically from an elm spigot set into her hull as sailors pumped her bilge. 'She should have been broken up for firewood,' Captain Barkley said sourly.

'There's no patching her?' McLean asked.

'Her timbers are rotten. She's a sieve,' Barkley said dismissively. Small waves slapped the *Blonde*'s hull, and the blue ensign at her stern stirred slow in the fitful wind. Still no boat appeared and so Barkley ordered the signal gun fired a second time. The sound echoed and faded again and, just when Barkley was considering taking the flotilla into the harbour without the benefit of a pilot, a seaman hailed from the foremast top. 'Boat coming, sir!'

When the powder smoke cleared, the men on *Blonde* saw a small open boat was indeed tacking out from the harbour. The south-west breeze was so light that the tan-coloured sails hardly gave the boat any headway against the tide, and so a young man was pulling on two long oars. Once in the wide bay he shipped the oars and sheeted his sails hard so that

6

the small boat beat slowly up to the flotilla. A girl sat at the tiller and she steered the little craft against the *Blonde*'s starboard flank where the young man leaped nimbly onto the boarding steps that climbed the tumblehome. He was tall, fair-haired, with hands calloused and blackened from handling tarred rigging and fishing nets. He wore homespun breeches and a canvas jacket, had clumsy boots and a knitted hat. He climbed to the deck, then called down to the girl. 'You take good care of her, Beth!'

'Stop gawping, you puddin'-headed bastards!' the bosun roared at the seamen staring at the fair-haired girl who was using an oar to push her small craft away from the frigate's hull. 'You're the pilot?' the bosun asked the young man.

'James Fletcher,' the young man said, 'and I guess I am, but you don't need no pilot anyways.' He grinned as he walked towards the officers at the *Blonde*'s stern. 'Any of you gentlemen have tobacco?' he asked as he climbed the companionway to the poop deck. He was rewarded with silence until General McLean reached into a pocket and extracted a short clay pipe, its bowl already stuffed with tobacco.

'Will that do?' the general asked.

'That'll do just perfect,' Fletcher said appreciatively, then prised the plug from the bowl and crammed it into his mouth. He handed the empty pipe back to the general. 'Haven't had tobacco in two months,' he said in explanation, then nodded familiarly to Barkley. 'Ain't no real dangers in Bagaduce, Captain, just so long as you stand off Dyce's Head, see?' He pointed to the tree-crowned bluff on the northern side of the harbour entrance. 'Rocks there. And more rocks off Cross Island on the other side. Hold her in the channel's centre and you'll be safe as safe.'

'Bagaduce?' General McLean asked.

'That's what we call it, your honour. Bagaduce. Easier on the tongue than Majabigwaduce.' The pilot grinned, then spat tobacco juice that splattered across the *Blonde*'s holy-stoned planking. There was silence on the quarterdeck as the officers regarded the dark stain.

'Majabigwaduce,' McLean broke the silence, 'does it mean anything?'

'Big bay with big tides,' Fletcher said, 'or so my father always said. 'Course it's an Indian name so it could mean anything.' The young man looked around the frigate's deck with an evident appreciation. 'Day of excitement, this,' he remarked genially.

'Excitement?' General McLean asked.

'Phoebe Perkins is expecting. We all thought the baby would have dropped from her by now, but it ain't. And it'll be a girl!'

'You know that?' General McLean asked, amused.

'Phoebe's had six babes already and every last one of them a girl. You should fire another gun, Captain, startle this new one out of her!'

'Mister Fennel!' Captain Barkley called through a speaking trumpet, 'sheet in, if you please.'

The *Blonde* gathered way. 'Take her in,' Barkley told the helmsman, and so the *Blonde*, the *North*, the *Albany*, the *Nautilus*, the *Hope*, and the five transports they escorted came to Majabigwaduce. They arrived safe in the harbour and anchored there. It was June 17th, 1779 and, for the first time since they had been driven from Boston in March, 1776, the British were back in Massachusetts.

Some two hundred miles west and a little south of where the devils arrived, Brigadier-General Peleg Wadsworth paraded his battalion on the town common. Only seventeen were present, not one of whom could be described as correct. The youngest, Alexander, was five, while the oldest were the twelve-year-old Fowler twins, Rebecca and Dorcas, and they all gazed earnestly at the brigadier, who was thirty-one. 'What

I want you to do,' the general said, 'is march forward in single file. On the word of command you stop. What is the word of command, Jared?'

Jared, who was nine, thought for a second. 'Halt?'

'Very good, Jared. The next command after that will be "prepare to form line", and you will do nothing!' The brigadier peered sternly at his diminutive troops who were in a column of march facing northwards. 'Understand? You do nothing! Then I'm going to shout that companies one, two, three and four will face left. Those companies,' and here the general walked down the line indicating which children comprised the leading four companies, 'are the left wing. What are you, Jared?'

'The left wing,' Jared said, flapping his arms.

'Excellent! And you,' the general paced on down the rest of the line, 'are companies five, six, seven and eight, the right wing, and you will face right. I shall then give the order to face front and you turn. Then we counter-wheel. Alexander? You're the colour party so you don't move.'

'I want to kill a redcoat, Daddy,' Alexander pleaded.

'You don't move, Alexander,' the colour party's father insisted, then repeated all he had said. Alexander was holding a long stick that, in the circumstances, substituted for the American flag. He now aimed this at the church and pretended to shoot redcoats and so had to be chivvied back into the column that singly and generally agreed that they understood what their erstwhile schoolmaster wanted them to do. 'Now remember,' Peleg Wadsworth encouraged them, 'that when I order counter-wheel you march in the direction you're facing, but you swing around like the arm of a clock! I want to see you turn smoothly. Are we all ready?'

A small crowd had gathered to watch and advise. One man, a visiting minister, had been appalled to see children so young being taught the rudiments of soldiery and had chided General Wadsworth on the matter, but the brigadier had assured the

9

man of God that it was not the children who were being trained, but himself. He wished to understand precisely how a column of companies deployed into a regimental line that could blast an enemy with musket fire. It was hard to advance troops in line because a long row of men inevitably straggled and lost its cohesion, to avoid which men must advance in companies, one behind the other, but such a column was fatally vulnerable to cannon-fire and quite unable to use most of its muskets, and so the art of the manoeuvre was to advance in column and then deploy swiftly into line. Wadsworth wanted to master the drill, but because he was a general of the Massachusetts Militia, and because the militia were mostly on their farms or in their workshops, Wadsworth was using children. The leading company, which would normally hold three ranks of thirty or more men each, was today comprised of Rebecca Fowler, aged twelve, and her nine-year-old cousin, Jared, both of whom were bright children and, Wadsworth hoped, capable of setting an example that the remaining children would copy. The manoeuvre he was attempting was difficult. The battalion would march in column towards the enemy and then halt. The leading companies would turn to face one way, the rearward companies turn to face the opposite direction and then the whole line would counter-wheel about the colours in a smooth pivot until commanded to halt. That would leave the first four companies facing away from the enemy and Wadsworth would need to order those eight children to about turn, at which point the whole formidable battalion would be ready to open fire against the enemy. Wadsworth had watched British regiments perform a similar manoeuvre on Long Island and he had reluctantly admired their precision and seen for himself the swiftness with which they had been transformed from a column into a long line that had unleashed a torrent of musketry on the American forces.

'Are we ready?' Wadsworth asked again. If he could explain

the system to children, he had decided, then teaching the state militia should be easy enough. 'Forward march!'

The children marched creditably well, though Alexander kept skipping to try and match steps with his companions. 'Battalion!' Wadsworth called, 'Halt!'

They halted. So far so good. 'Battalion! Prepare to form line! Don't move yet!' He paused a moment. 'The left wing will face left! The right wing will face right, on my word of command. Battalion! Face front!'

Rebecca turned right instead of left and the battalion milled about in a moment of confusion before someone's hair was pulled and Alexander began shouting bang as he shot imaginary redcoats coming from the Common Burying Ground. 'Counter-wheel, march!' Wadsworth shouted, and the children swivelled in different directions and by now, the general thought despairingly, the British troops would have hammered two slaughterous volleys into his regiment. Perhaps, Wadsworth thought, using the children from the school where he had taught before becoming a soldier was not the best way to develop his mastery of infantry tactics. 'Form line,' he shouted.

'The way to do it,' a man on crutches offered from the crowd, 'is company by company. It's slower, General, but slow and steady wins the day.'

'No, no, no!' someone else chimed in. 'First company front right marker to step one pace left and one pace forward, and he becomes left marker, raises his hand, and the rest fall in on him. Or her, in your regiment, General.'

'Better company by company,' the crippled man insisted, 'that's how we did it at Germantown.'

'But you lost at Germantown,' the second man pointed out.

Johnny Fiske pretended to be shot, staggered dramatically and fell down, and Peleg Wadsworth, he found it hard to think of himself as a general, decided he had failed to explain the manoeuvre properly. He wondered whether he would ever need to master the intricacies of infantry drill. The French had joined America's struggle for freedom and had sent an army across the Atlantic and the war was now being fought in the southern states very far from Massachusetts.

'Is the war won?' a voice interrupted his thoughts and he turned to see his wife, Elizabeth, carrying their one-year-old daughter, Zilpha, in her arms.

'I do believe,' Peleg Wadsworth said, 'that the children have killed every last redcoat in America.'

'God be praised for that,' Elizabeth said lightly. She was twenty-six, five years younger than her husband, and pregnant again. Alexander was her oldest, then came three-year-old Charles and the infant Zilpha, who stared wide-eyed and solemn at her father. Elizabeth was almost as tall as her husband who was putting notebook and pencil back into a uniform pocket. He looked good in uniform, she thought, though the white-faced blue coat with its elegant buttoned tail was in desperate need of patching, but there was no blue cloth available, not even in Boston, at least not at a price that Peleg and Elizabeth Wadsworth could afford. Elizabeth was secretly amused by her husband's intense, worried expression. He was a good man, she thought fondly, as honest as the day was long and trusted by all his neighbours. He needed a haircut, though the slightly ragged dark locks gave his lean face an attractively rakish look. 'I'm sorry to interrupt the war,' Elizabeth said, 'but you have a visitor.' She nodded back towards their house where a man in uniform was tethering his horse to the hitching post.

The visitor was thin with a round, bespectacled face that was familiar to Wadsworth, but he could not place the man who, his horse safely tied, took a paper from his tail-coat pocket and strolled across the sunlit common. His uniform was pale brown with white facings. A sabre hung by leather straps from his sword belt. 'General Wadsworth,' he said as he came close, 'it is good to see you in health, sir,' he added, and for a second Wadsworth flailed desperately as he tried to match a name to the face, then, blessedly, the name came.

'Captain Todd,' he said, hiding his relief.

'Major Todd now, sir.'

'I congratulate you, Major.'

'I'm appointed an aide to General Ward,' Todd said, 'who sends you this.' He handed the paper to Wadsworth. It was a single sheet, folded and sealed, with General Artemas Ward's name inscribed in spidery writing beneath the seal.

Major Todd looked sternly at the children. Still in a ragged line, they stared back at him, intrigued by the curved blade at his waist. 'Stand at ease,' Todd ordered them, then smiled at Wadsworth. 'You recruit them young, General?'

Wadsworth, somewhat embarrassed to have been discovered drilling children, did not answer. He had unsealed the paper and now read the brief message. General Artemas Ward presented his compliments to Brigadier-General Wadsworth and regretted to inform him that a charge had been laid against Lieutenant-Colonel Paul Revere, commanding officer of the Massachusetts' Artillery Regiment, specifically that he had been drawing rations and pay for thirty non-existent men, and General Ward now required Wadsworth to make enquiries into the substance of the allegation.

Wadsworth read the message a second time, then dismissed the children and beckoned Todd to walk with him towards the Burying Ground. 'General Ward is well?' he asked politely. Artemas Ward commanded the Massachusetts Militia.

'He's well enough,' Todd answered, 'other than some pains in the legs.'

'He grows old,' Wadsworth said, and for a dutiful moment the two men exchanged news of births, marriages, illnesses and deaths, the small change of a community. They had paused in the shade of an elm and after a while Wadsworth gestured with the letter. 'It seems strange to me,' he said carefully, 'that a major should bring such a trivial message.'

'Trivial?' Todd asked sternly, 'we are talking of peculation, General.'

'Which, if true, will have been recorded in the muster returns. Does it require a general to inspect the books? A clerk could do that.'

'A clerk has done that,' Todd said grimly, 'but a clerk's name on the official report bears no weight.'

Wadsworth heard the grimness. 'And you seek weight?' he asked.

'General Ward would have the matter investigated thoroughly,' Todd answered firmly, 'and you are the Adjutant-General of the Militia, which makes you responsible for the good discipline of the forces.'

Wadsworth flinched at what he regarded as an impertinent and unnecessary reminder of his duties, but he let the insolence pass unreproved. Todd had the reputation of being a thorough and diligent man, but Wadsworth also recalled a rumour that Major William Todd and Lieutenant-Colonel Paul Revere nurtured a strong dislike of each other. Todd had served with Revere in the artillery, but had resigned in protest at the regiment's disorganization, and Wadsworth suspected that Todd was using his new position to strike at his old enemy, and Wadsworth liked it not. 'Colonel Revere,' he spoke mildly, though with deliberate provocation, 'enjoys a reputation as a fine and fervent patriot.'

'He is a dishonest man,' Todd retorted vehemently.

'If wars were fought only by the honest,' Wadsworth said, 'then we would surely have perpetual peace?'

'You're acquainted with Colonel Revere, sir?' Todd asked.

'I cannot claim more than an acquaintance,' Wadsworth said.

Todd nodded, as if that was the proper answer. 'Your reputation, General,' he said, 'is unassailable. If you prove peculation, then not a man in Massachusetts will dispute the verdict.'

Wadsworth glanced at the message again. 'Just thirty men?' he asked dubiously. 'You've ridden from Boston for such a small affair?'

'It's not far to ride,' Todd said defensively, 'and I have business in Plymouth, so it was convenient to wait on you.'

'If you have business, Major,' Wadsworth said, 'then I won't detain you.' Courtesy demanded that he at least offered Todd some refreshment and Wadsworth was a courteous man, but he was annoyed at being implicated in what he strongly suspected was a private feud.

'There is talk,' Todd remarked as the two men walked back across the common, 'of an attack on Canada.'

'There is always talk of an attack on Canada,' Wadsworth said with some asperity.

'If such an attack occurs,' Todd said, 'we would want our artillery commanded by the best available man.'

'I would assume,' Wadsworth said, 'that we would desire that whether we march on Canada or not.'

'We need a man of probity,' Todd said.

'We need a man who can shoot straight,' Wadsworth said brusquely and wondered whether Todd aspired to command the artillery regiment himself, but he said nothing more. His wife was waiting beside the hitching post with a glass of water that Todd accepted gratefully before riding south towards Plymouth. Wadsworth went indoors and showed Elizabeth the letter. 'I fear it is politics, my dear,' he said, 'politics.'

'Is that bad?'

'It is awkward,' Wadsworth said. 'Colonel Revere is a man of faction.'

'Faction?'

'Colonel Revere is zealous,' Wadsworth said carefully, 'and his zeal makes enemies as well as friends. I suspect Major Todd laid the charge. It is a question of jealousy.'

15

'So you think the allegation is untrue?'

'I have no opinion,' Wadsworth said, 'and would dearly like to continue in that ignorance.' He took the letter back and read it again.

'It is still wrongdoing,' Elizabeth said sternly.

'Or a false allegation? A clerk's error? But it involves me in faction and I dislike faction. If I prove wrongdoing then I make enemies of half Boston and earn the enmity of every freemason. Which is why I would prefer to remain in ignorance.'

'So you will ignore it?' Elizabeth asked.

'I shall do my duty, my dear,' Wadsworth said. He had always done his duty, and done it well. As a student at Harvard, as a schoolteacher, as a captain in Lexington's town troop, as an aide to General Washington in the Continental Army and now as a brigadier in the militia. But there were times, he thought, when his own side was far more difficult than the British. He folded the letter and went for his dinner.

Majabigwaduce was a hump of land, almost an island, shaped like an anvil. From east to west it was just under two miles long, and from north to south rarely more than half a mile wide, and the ridge of its rocky hump climbed from the east to the west where it ended in a blunt, high, wooded bluff that overlooked the wide Penobscot Bay. The settlement lay on the ridge's southern side, where the British fleet lay in the harbour's anchorage. It was a village of small houses, barns and storehouses. The smallest houses were simple log cabins, but some were more substantial dwellings of two storeys, their frames clad in cedar shingles that looked silver in the day's watery sunlight. There was no church yet.

The ridge above the village was thick with spruce, though to the west, where the land was highest, there were fine maples, beech and birch. Oaks grew by the water. Much of the land about the settlement had been cleared and planted

16

with corn, and now axes bit into spruce trees as the redcoats set about clearing the ridge above the village.

Seven hundred soldiers had come to Majabigwaduce. Four hundred and fifty were kilted highlanders of the 74th, another two hundred were lowlanders from the 82nd, while the remaining fifty were engineers and gunners. The fleet that had brought them had dispersed, the *Blonde* sailing on to New York and leaving behind only three empty transport ships and three small sloops-of-war whose masts now dominated Majabigwaduce's harbour. The beach was heaped with landed supplies and a new track, beaten into the dirt, now ran straight up the long slope from the water's edge to the ridge's crest. Brigadier McLean climbed that track, walking with the aid of a twisted blackthorn stick and accompanied by a civilian. 'We are a small force, Doctor Calef,' McLean said, 'but you may rely on us to do our duty.'

'Calf,' Calef said.

'I beg your pardon?'

'My name, General, is pronounced calf.'

'I do pray your pardon, Doctor,' McLean said, inclining his head.

Doctor Calef was a thickset man a few years younger than McLean. He wore a low crowned hat over a wig that had not been powdered for weeks and which framed a blunt face distinguished by a determined jaw. He had introduced himself to McLean, offering advice, professional help and whatever other support he could give. 'You're here to stay, I trust?' the doctor demanded.

'Decidedly, sir, decidedly,' McLean said, digging his stick into the thin soil, 'oh, indeed we mean to stay.'

'To do what?' Calef asked curtly.

'Let me see now,' McLean paused, watching as two men stepped back from a half-felled tree that toppled, slowly at first, then crashed down in an explosion of splintering branches, pine needles and dust. 'My first duty, Doctor,' he said, 'is to prevent

17

the rebels from using the bay as a haven for their privateers. Those pirates have been a nuisance.' That was mild. The American rebels held all the coastline between Canada and New York except for the beleaguered British garrison in Newport, Rhode Island, and British merchant ships, making that long voyage, were ever at risk from the well-armed, fast-sailing rebel privateers. By occupying Majabigwaduce the British would dominate Penobscot Bay and so deny the rebels its fine anchorage, which would become a base for Britain's Royal Navy. 'At the same time,' McLean continued, 'I am ordered to deter any rebel attack on Canada and thirdly, Doctor, I am to encourage trade here.'

'Mast wood,' Calef growled.

'Especially mast wood,' McLean agreed, 'and fourthly we are to settle this region.'

'Settle it?'

'For the crown, Doctor, for the crown.' McLean smiled and waved his blackthorn stick at the landscape. 'Behold, Doctor Calef, His Majesty's province of New Ireland.'

'New Ireland?' Calef asked.

'From the border of Canada and eighty miles southwards,' McLean said, 'all New Ireland.'

'Let's trust it's not as papist as old Ireland,' Calef said sourly.

'I'm sure it will be God-fearing,' McLean said tactfully. The general had served many years in Portugal and did not share his countrymen's distaste for Roman Catholics, but he was a good enough soldier to know when not to fight. 'So what brought you to New Ireland, Doctor?' he asked, changing the subject.

'I was driven from Boston by damned rebels,' Calef said angrily.

'And you chose to come here?' McLean asked, unable to hide his surprise that the doctor had fled Boston to this fog-ridden wilderness.

'Where else could I take my family?' Calef demanded, still

18

angry. 'Dear God, General, but there's no legitimate government between here and New York! In all but name the colonies are independent already! In Boston the wretches have an administration, a legislature, offices of state, a judiciary! Why? Why is it permitted?'

'You could have moved to New York?' McLean suggested, ignoring Calef's indignant question, 'or to Halifax?'

'I'm a Massachusetts man,' Calef said, 'and I trust that one day I will return to Boston, but a Boston cleansed of rebellion.'

'I pray so too,' McLean said. 'Tell me, Doctor, did the woman give birth safely?'

Doctor Calef blinked, as if the question surprised him. 'The woman? Oh, you mean Joseph Perkins's wife. Yes, she was delivered safely. A fine girl.'

'Another girl, eh?' McLean said, and turned to gaze at the wide bay beyond the harbour entrance. 'Big bay with big tides,' he said lightly, then saw the doctor's incomprehension. 'I was told that was the meaning of Majabigwaduce,' he explained.

Calef frowned, then made a small gesture as if the question was irrelevant. 'I've no idea what the name means, General. You must ask the savages. It's their name for the place.'

'Well, it's all New Ireland now,' McLean said, then touched his hat. 'Good day, Doctor, I'm sure we shall talk further. I'm grateful for your support, grateful indeed, but if you'll excuse me, duty calls.'

Calef watched the general limp uphill, then called to him. 'General McLean!'

'Sir?' McLean turned.

'You don't imagine the rebels are going to let you stay here, do you?'

McLean appeared to consider the question for a few seconds, almost as though he had never thought about it before. 'I would think not,' he said mildly.

19

'They'll come for you,' Calef warned him. 'Soon as they know you're here, General, they'll come for you.'

'Do you know?' McLean said, 'I rather think they will.' He touched his hat again. 'Good day, Doctor. I'm glad about Mrs Perkins.'

'Damn Mrs Perkins,' the doctor said, but too softly for the general to hear, then he turned and stared southwards down the long bay, past Long Island, to where the river disappeared on its way to the far off sea, and he wondered how long before a rebel fleet appeared in that channel.

That fleet would appear, he was sure. Boston would learn of McLean's presence, and Boston would want to scour this place free of redcoats. And Calef knew Boston. He had been a member of the General Assembly there, a Massachusetts legislator, but he was also a stubborn loyalist who had been driven from his home after the British left Boston. Now he lived here, at Majabigwaduce, and the rebels were coming for him again. He knew it, he feared their coming, and he feared that a general who cared about a woman and her baby was a man too soft to do the necessary job. 'Just kill them all,' he growled to himself, 'just kill them all.'

Six days after Brigadier-General Wadsworth had paraded the children, and after Brigadier-General McLean had sailed into Majabigwaduce's snug haven, a captain paced the quarter-deck of his ship, the Continental Navy frigate *Warren*. It was a warm Boston morning. There was fog over the harbour islands, and a humid south-west wind bringing a promise of afternoon thunder.

'The glass?' the captain asked brusquely.

'Dropping, sir,' a midshipman answered.

'As I thought,' Captain Dudley Saltonstall said, 'as I thought.' He paced larboard to starboard and starboard to larboard beneath the mizzen's neatly furled spanker on its long boom. His long-chinned face was shadowed by the forrard peak of his cocked hat, beneath which his dark eyes looked sharply from the multitude of ships anchored in the roads to his crew who, though short-handed, were swarming over the frigate's deck, sides and rigging to give the ship her morning scrub. Saltonstall was newly appointed to the *Warren* and he was determined she should be a neat ship.

'As I thought,' Saltonstall said again. The midshipman, standing respectfully beside the larboard aft gun, braced his leg against the gun's carriage and said nothing. The wind was fresh enough to jerk the *Warren* on her anchor cables and make her shudder to the small waves that flickered white across the harbour. The *Warren*, like the two nearby vessels that also belonged to the Continental Navy, flew the red- and white-striped flag on which a snake surmounted the words 'Don't Tread on Me'. Many of the other ships in the crowded harbour flew the bold new flag of the United States, striped and starred, but two smart brigs, both armed with fourteen six-pounder cannons and both anchored close to the *Warren*, flew the Massachusetts Navy flag that showed a green pine tree on a white field and bore the words 'An Appeal to Heaven'.

'An appeal to nonsense,' Saltonstall growled.

'Sir?' the midshipman asked nervously.

'If our cause is just, Mister Coningsby, why need we appeal to heaven? Let us rather appeal to force, to justice, to reason.'

'Aye aye, sir,' the midshipman said, unsettled by the captain's habit of looking past the man he spoke to.

'Appeal to heaven!' Saltonstall sneered, still gazing past the midshipman's ear towards the offending flag. 'In war, Mister Coningsby, one might do better to appeal to hell.'

The ensigns of other vessels were more picaresque. One low-slung ship, her masts raked sharply aft and her gun ports painted black, had a coiled rattlesnake emblazoned on her ensign, while a second flew the skull and crossbones, and a third showed King George of England losing his crown to

21

a cheerful looking Yankee wielding a spiked club. Captain Saltonstall disapproved of all such home-made flags. They made for untidiness. A dozen other ships had British flags, but all those flags were being flown beneath American colours to show they had been captured, and Captain Saltonstall disapproved of that too. It was not that the British merchantmen had been captured, that was plainly a good thing, nor that the flags proclaimed the victories because that too was desirable, but rather that the captured ships were now presumed to be private property. Not the property of the United States, but of the privateers like the low-slung, raked-masted, rattle-snake-decorated sloop.

'They are pirates, Mister Coningsby,' Saltonstall growled.

'Aye aye, sir,' Midshipman Fanning replied. Midshipman Coningsby had died of the fever a week previously, but all Fanning's nervous attempts to correct his captain had failed and he had abandoned any hope of being called by his real name.

Saltonstall was still frowning at the privateers. 'How can we find decent crew when piracy beckons?' Saltonstall complained, 'tell me that, Mister Coningsby!'

'I don't know, sir.'

'We cannot, Mister Coningsby, we cannot,' Saltonstall said, shuddering at the injustice of the law. It was true that the privateers were patriotic pirates who were fierce as wolves in battle, but they fought for private gain, and that made it impossible for a Continental warship like the *Warren* to find good crew. What young man of Boston would serve his country for pennies when he could join a privateer and earn a share of the plunder? No wonder the *Warren* was short-handed! She carried thirty-two guns and was as fine a frigate as any on the American seaboard, but Saltonstall had only men enough to fight half his weapons, while the privateers were all fully manned. 'It is an abomination, Mister Coningsby!'

'Aye aye, sir,' Midshipman Fanning said.

'Look at that!' Saltonstall checked his pacing to point a finger at the *Ariadne*, a fat British merchantman that had been captured by a privateer. 'You know what she was carrying, Mister Coningsby?'

'Black walnut from New York to London, sir?'

'And she carried six cannon, Mister Coningsby! Nine-pounder guns! Six of them. Good long nine-pounders! Newly made! And where are those guns now?'

'I don't know, sir.'

'For sale in Boston!' Saltonstall spat the words. 'For sale, Mister Coningsby, in Boston, when our country has desperate need of cannon! It makes me angry, Mister Coningsby, it makes me angry indeed.'

'Aye aye, sir.'

'Those cannon will be melted down for gew-gaws. For gew-gaws! It makes me angry, upon my soul, it does.' Captain Saltonstall carried his anger to the starboard rail where he paused to watch a small cutter approach from the north. Its dark sails first appeared as a patch in the fog, then the patch took shape and hardened into a single-masted vessel about forty feet long. She was not a fishing boat, she was too narrow for such work, but her gunwales were pierced with tholes showing that she could ship a dozen oars and so be rowed on calm days and Saltonstall recognized her as one of the fast messenger boats used by the government of Massachusetts. A man was standing amidships with cupped hands, evidently shouting his news to the moored vessels through which the cutter slid. Saltonstall would dearly have liked to know what the man shouted, but he considered it was beneath his dignity as a Continental Navy captain to make vulgar enquiries, and so he turned away just as a schooner, her gunwales punctu-ated by gunports, gathered way to pass the *Warren*. The schooner was a black-hulled privateer with the name *King-Killer* prominent in white paint at her waist. her dirt-streaked sails were sheeted in hard to beat her way out of the harbour.

She carried a dozen deck guns, enough to batter most British merchantmen into quick surrender, and she was built for speed so that she could escape any warship of the British navy. Her deck was crowded with men while at her mizzen gaff was a blue flag with the word Liberty embroidered in white letters. Saltonstall waited for that flag to be lowered in salute to his own ensign, but as the black schooner passed she offered no sign of recognition. A man at her taffrail looked at Saltonstall, then spat into the sea and the *Warren*'s captain bridled, suspecting an insult. He watched her go towards the fog. The *King-Killer* was off hunting, going across the bay, around the northern hook of Cape Cod and out into the Atlantic where the fat British cargo ships wallowed on their westward runs from Halifax to New York.

'Gew-gaws,' Saltonstall growled.

A stub-masted open barge, painted white with a black stripe around its gunwale, pushed off from the Castle Island quay. A dozen men manned the oars, pulling hard against the small waves, and the sight of the barge made Captain Saltonstall fish a watch from his pocket. He clicked open the lid and saw that it was ten minutes past eight in the morning. The barge was precisely on time, and within an hour he would see it return from Boston, this time carrying the commander of the Castle Island garrison, a man who preferred to sleep in the city. Saltonstall approved of the Castle Island barge. She was smartly painted and her crew, if not in real uniform, wore matching blue shirts. There was an attempt at order there, at discipline, at propriety.

The captain resumed his pacing, larboard to starboard, starboard to larboard.

The *King-Killer* vanished in the fog.

The Castle Island barge threaded the anchorage. A church bell began to toll.

Boston harbour, a warm morning, June 23rd, 1779.

*   *   *

24

The paymaster of His Majesty's 82nd Regiment of Foot strode west along Majabigwaduce's ridge. From behind him came the sound of axes striking trees, while all around him was fog. A thick fog. Every morning since the fleet had arrived there had been fog. 'It will burn off,' the paymaster said cheerfully.

'Aye, sir,' Sergeant McClure answered dully. The sergeant had a picquet of six men from the 82nd Foot, the Duke of Hamilton's regiment and so known as the Hamiltons. McClure was thirty, older by far than his men and twelve years older than the paymaster, a lieutenant, who led the picquet at a fast, enthusiastic pace. His orders were to establish a sentry post at the peninsula's western heights from where a lookout could be kept on the wide Penobscot Bay. If any enemy was to come, then the bay was their likeliest approach. The picquet was in thick woodland now, dwarfed by tall, dark, fog-shrouded trees. 'The brigadier, sir,' Sergeant McClure ventured, 'said there might be rebels here.'

'Nonsense! There are no rebels here! They have all fled, Sergeant!'

'If you say so, sir.'

'I do say so,' the young officer said enthusiastically, then stopped suddenly and pointed into the underbrush. 'There!'

'A rebel, sir?' McClure asked dutifully, seeing nothing worthy of note among the pines.

'Is it a thrush?'

'Ah,' McClure saw what had interested the paymaster and looked more closely, 'it's a bird, sir.'

'Strangely, Sergeant, I was apprised of that fact,' the lieutenant said happily. 'Note the breast, Sergeant.'

Sergeant McClure dutifully noted the bird's breast. 'Red, sir?'

'Red indeed. I congratulate you, Sergeant, and does it not put you in mind of our native robin? But this fellow is larger, much larger! Handsome fellow, isn't he?'

25

'Want me to shoot him, sir?' McClure asked.

'No, Sergeant, I merely wish you to admire his plumage. A thrush is wearing his majesty's red coat, would you not consider that an omen of good-fortune?'

'Oh, aye, sir, I would.'

'I detect in you, Sergeant, a lack of zeal.' The eighteen-year-old lieutenant smiled to show he was not serious. He was a tall lad, a full head above the stocky sergeant, and had a round, eager and mobile face, a smile quick as lightning, and shrewdly observant eyes. His coat was cut from expensive scarlet cloth, faced with black and bright with buttons that were rumoured to be made of the finest gold. Lieutenant John Moore was not wealthy, he was a doctor's son, but everyone knew he was a friend of the young Duke's, and the Duke was said to be richer than the next ten richest men in all Scotland, and a rich friend, as everyone also knew, was the next best thing to being wealthy oneself. The Duke of Hamilton was so rich that he had paid all the expenses of raising the 82nd Regiment of Foot, buying them uniforms, muskets and bayonets, and rumour said his grace could prob-ably afford to raise another ten such regiments without even noticing the expense. 'Onwards,' Moore said, 'onwards, ever onwards!'

The six privates, all from the Lowlands of Scotland, did not move. They just gazed at Lieutenant Moore as though he were a strange species from some far-off heathen country.

'Onwards!' Moore called again, striding fast once more through the trees. The fog muffled the harsh sound of the axes coming from where Brigadier McLean's men were clearing the ridge so that their planned fort would have open fields of fire. The 82nd's picquet, meanwhile, was climbing a gentle slope that levelled onto a wide plateau of thick under-growth and dark firs. Moore trampled through the brush, then again stopped abruptly. 'There,' he said, pointing, *'Thalassa, Thalassa.'*

'The lassie?' McClure asked.

'You have not read Xenophon's *Anabasis*, Sergeant?' Moore asked in mock horror.

'Is that the one after Leviticus, sir?'

Moore smiled. '*Thalassa*, Sergeant, *Thalassa*,' he said in mock reproof, 'was the cry of the ten thousand when at last, after their long march, and after their dark ordeals, they came to the sea. That's what it means! The sea! The sea! And they shouted for joy because they saw their safety in the gentle heaves of its bosom.'

'Its bosom, sir,' McClure echoed, peering down a sudden steep bluff, thick with trees, to glimpse the cold sea through the foliage and beneath the drifting fog. 'It's not very bosomy, sir.'

'And it is across that water, Sergeant, from their lair in the black lands of Boston, that the enemy will come. They will arrive in their hundreds and in their thousands, they will prowl like the dark hordes of Midian, they will descend upon us like the Assyrian!'

'Not if this fog lasts, sir,' McClure said, 'the buggers will get lost, sir.'

Moore, for once, said nothing. He was gazing down the bluff. It was not quite a cliff, but no man could climb it easily. An attacker would need to drag himself up the two hundred feet by pulling on the straggly saplings, and a man using his hands to keep his footing could not use his musket. The beach, just visible, was brief and stony.

'But are the buggers coming, sir?' McClure asked.

'We cannot say,' Moore said distractedly.

'But the brigadier thinks so, sir?' McClure asked anxiously. The privates listened, glancing nervously from the short sergeant to the tall officer.

'We must assume, Sergeant,' Moore said airily, 'that the wretched creatures will resent our presence. We make life difficult for them. By establishing ourselves in this land of soured milk and bitter honey we deny their privateers the harbours they require for their foul depredations. We are a thorn in their side, we are inconvenient, we are a challenge to their quietude.'

McClure frowned and scratched his forehead. 'So you're saying the buggers will come, sir?'

'I bloody hope so,' Moore said with sudden vehemence.

'Not here, sir,' McClure said confidently. 'Too steep.'

'They'll want to land somewhere in range of their ships' cannons,' Moore said.

'Cannons, sir?'

'Big metal tubes which expel balls, Sergeant.'

'Oh, thank you, sir. I was wondering, sir,' McClure said with a smile.

Moore tried and failed to suppress a smile. 'We shall be plied with shot, Sergeant, have no doubt of that. And I've no doubt ships could spatter this slope with cannon fire, but how would men climb it into our musket fire? Yet even so, let's hope they land here. No troops could climb this slope if we're waiting at the top, eh? By God, Sergeant, we'll make a fine cull of the rebellious bastards!'

'And so we will, sir,' McClure said loyally, though in his sixteen years of service he had become used to brash young officers whose confidence exceeded their experience. Lieutenant John Moore, the sergeant decided, was another such, yet McClure liked him. The paymaster possessed an easy authority, rare in a man so young, and he was reckoned to be a fair officer who cared about his troops. Even so, McClure thought, John Moore would have to learn some sense or else die young.

'We shall slaughter them,' Moore said enthusiastically, then held out his hand. 'Your musket, Sergeant.'

McClure handed the officer his musket and watched as Moore laid a guinea on the ground. 'The soldier who can fire faster than me will be rewarded with the guinea,' Moore said.

'Your mark is that half-rotted tree canted on the slope, you see it?'

'Aim at the dead bent tree.' McClure explained to the privates. 'Sir?'

'Sergeant?'

'Won't the sound of muskets alarm the camp, sir?'

'I warned the brigadier we'd be shooting. Sergeant, your cartridge box, if you please.'

'Be quick, lads,' McClure encouraged his men. 'Let's take the officer's money!'

'You may load and prime,' Moore said. 'I propose to fire five shots. If any of you manage five before me, then you will take the guinea. Imagine, gentlemen, that a horde of malodorous rebels are climbing the bluff, then do the king's work and send the wretches to hell.'

The muskets were loaded; the powder, wadding and shot were rammed down the barrels, the locks were primed and the frizzens closed. The clicks of the flints being cocked seemed oddly loud in the fog-shrouded morning.

'Gentlemen of the 82nd,' Moore demanded grandly, 'are you ready?'

'The buggers are ready, sir,' McClure said.

'Present!' Moore ordered, 'fire!'

Seven muskets coughed, blasting evil-smelling powder smoke that was far thicker than the swirling fog. The smoke lingered as birds fled through the thick trees and gulls called from the water. Through the echo of the shots McClure heard the balls ripping through leaves and clattering on the stones of the small beach. The men were tearing open their next cartridges with their teeth, but Lieutenant Moore was already ahead. He had primed the musket, closed the frizzen and now dropped the heavy stock to the ground and poured in the powder. He pushed the cartridge paper and ball into the muzzle, whipped the ramrod up, slid it down hard, pulled it free with the ringing sound of metal on metal, then jammed the ramrod into the turf, tossed the gun up to his shoulder, cocked, and fired.

No one had yet beaten Lieutenant John Moore. Major Dunlop had timed Moore once and, with disbelief, had announced that the lieutenant had fired five shots inside sixty seconds. Most men could manage three shots a minute with a clean musket, a few could shoot four rounds, but the doctor's son, friend of a duke, could fire five. Moore had been trained in musketry by a Prussian, and as a boy he had practised and practised, perfecting the essential soldier's skill, and so certain was he of his ability that, as he loaded the last two shots, he did not even bother to look at his borrowed weapon, but instead smiled wryly at Sergeant McClure. 'Five!' Moore announced, his ears ringing with the explosions. 'Did any man defeat me, Sergeant?'

'No, sir. Private Neill managed three shots, sir, the rest did two.'

'Then my guinea is safe,' Moore said, scooping it up.

'But are we?' McClure muttered.

'You spoke, Sergeant?'

McClure stared down the bluff. The smoke was clearing and he could see that the canted tree, just thirty paces away, was unscarred by any musket ball. 'There's precious few of us, sir,' he said, 'and we're all alone here and there's a lot of rebels.'

'All the more to kill,' Moore said. 'We shall take post here till the fog lifts, Sergeant, then look for a better vantage point.'

'Aye, sir.'

The picquet was posted; their task to watch for the coming of an enemy. That enemy, the brigadier had assured his officers, would come. Of that McLean was sure. So he cut down trees and plotted where the fort must be.

To defend the king's land from the king's enemies.

Excerpt of letter from the Massachusetts Council, to the Continental Navy Board in Boston, June 30th, 1779:

Gentlemen: The General Assembly of this State have determined on an Expedition to Penobscot to Dislodge the Enemy of the United States lately enter'd There who are said to be committing Hostilities on the Good People of this State . . . fortifying themselves at Baggobagadoos, and as They are supported by a Considerable Naval Force, to Effect our Design, it will be expedient to send there, to aid our Land Operations a Superior Naval Force. Therefore . . . we write you . . . requesting you to aid our Designs, by adding to the Naval Force of this State, now, with all Possible Speed preparing, for an expedition to Penobscot; the Continental Frigate now in this Harbour, and the other armed Continental vessells here.

Excerpts from the Warrant of Impressment issued to Masschusetts Sheriffs, July 3rd, 1779:

You are hereby authorized and Commanded taking with you such Assistance as you judge proper, forthwith to take seize and impress any able-bodied Seamen, or Mariner which you shall

31

find in your Precinct . . . to serve on board any of the Vessels entered into the Service of this State to be employed in the proposed expedition to Penobscot . . . You are hereby Authorized to enter on board and search any Ship or Vessel or to break open and search any Dwelling house or other building in which you shall suspect any such Seamen or Mariners to be concealed.

Excerpt from a letter sent by Brigadier-General Charles Cushing to the Council of the State of Massachusetts, June 19th, 1779

I have Issued orders to the officers of my Brigade requiring them to inlist men agreeable thereto. I would inform your Honors that at present there seems no prospect of getting one man as the Bounty offered is in the Esteem of the people inadequate.

TWO

Lieutenant-Colonel Paul Revere stood square in the Boston Armory yard. He wore a light blue uniform coat faced in brown, white deerskin breeches, knee boots, and had a naval cutlass hanging from a thick brown belt. His wide-brimmed hat was made of felt, and it shadowed a broad, stubborn face that was creased in thought. 'You making that list, boy?' he demanded brusquely.

'Yes, sir,' the boy answered. He was twelve, the son of Josiah Flint who ruled the armory from his high-backed, well-padded chair that had been dragged from the office and set beside the trestle table where the boy made his list. Flint liked to sit in the yard when the weather allowed so he could keep an eye on the comings and goings in his domain.

'Drag chains,' Revere said, 'sponges, searchers, relievers, am I going too fast?'

'Relievers,' the boy muttered, dipping his pen into the inkwell.

'Hot today,' Josiah Flint grumbled from the depths of his chair.

'It's summer,' Revere said, 'and it should be hot. Rammers, boy, and wad hooks. Spikes, tompions, linstocks, vent-covers. What have I forgotten, Mister Flint?'

'Priming wires, Colonel.'

'Priming wires, boy.'

'Priming wires,' the boy said, finishing the list.

'And there's something else in the back of my mind,' Flint said, frowning, then thought for a moment before shaking his head. 'Maybe nothing,' he said.

'You hunt through your pa's supplies, boy,' Revere said, 'and you make piles of all those things. We need to know how many we've got. You note down how many and then you tell me. Off you go.'

'And buckets,' Josiah Flint added hurriedly.

'And buckets!' Revere called after the boy. 'And not leaking buckets either!' He took the boy's vacated chair and watched as Josiah Flint bit into a chicken leg. Flint was an enormous man, his belly spilling over his belt, and he seemed intent on becoming even fatter because whenever Revere visited the arsenal he found his friend eating. He had a plate of cornbread, radishes and chicken that he vaguely gestured towards, as if inviting Colonel Revere to share the dish.

'You haven't been given orders yet, Colonel?' Flint asked. His nose had been shattered by a bullet at Saratoga just minutes before a cannonball took away his right leg. He could no longer breathe through his nose and so his breath had to be drawn past the half-masticated food filling his mouth. It made a snuffling sound. 'They should have given you orders, Colonel.'

'They don't know whether they're pissing or puking, Mister Flint,' Revere said, 'but I can't wait while they make up their minds. The guns have to be ready!'

'No man better than you, Colonel,' Josiah Flint said, picking a shred of radish from his front teeth.

'But I didn't go to Harvard, did I?' Revere asked with a forced laugh. 'If I spoke Latin, Mister Flint, I'd be a general by now.'

'*Hic, haec, hoc,*' Flint said through a mouthful of bread.

'I expect so,' Revere said. He pulled a folded copy of the *Boston Intelligencer* from his pocket and spread it on the table, then took out his reading glasses. He disliked wearing them for he suspected they gave him an unmilitary appearance, but he needed the spectacles to read the account of the British incursion into eastern Massachusetts. 'Who would have believed it,' he said, 'the bastard redcoats back in New England!'

'Not for long, Colonel.'

'I hope not,' Revere said. The Massachusetts government, learning that the British had landed men at Majabigwaduce, had determined to send an expedition to the Penobscot River, to which end a fleet was being gathered, orders being sent to the militia and officers being appointed. 'Well, well,' Revere said, peering at the newspaper. 'It seems the Spanish have declared war on the British now!'

'Spain as well as France,' Flint said. 'The bloodybacks can't last long now.'

'Let's pray they last long enough to give us a chance to fight them at Maja.' Revere paused, 'Majabigwaduce,' he said. 'I wonder what that name means?'

'Just some Indian nonsense,' Flint said. 'Place Where the Muskrat Pissed Down its Legs, probably.'

'Probably,' Revere said distantly. He took off his glasses and stared at a pair of sheerlegs that waited to lift a cannon barrel from a carriage rotted by damp. 'Have they given you a requisition for cannon, Mister Flint?'

'Just for five hundred muskets, Colonel, to be rented for a dollar each to the militia.'

'Rented!'

'Rented,' Flint confirmed.

'If they're to kill the British,' Revere said, 'then money shouldn't come into it.'

'Money always comes into it,' Flint said. 'There are six new British nine-pounders in Appleby's yard, but we can't touch them. They're to be auctioned.'

35

'The Council should buy them,' Revere said.

'The Council don't have the money,' Flint said, stripping a leg-bone of its flesh, 'not enough coinage to pay the wages, rent the privateers, purchase supplies and buy cannon. You'll have to make do with the guns we've got.'

'They'll do, they'll do,' Revere said grudgingly.

'And I hope the Council has the sense to appoint you to command those guns, Colonel!'

Revere said nothing to that, merely stared at the sheer-legs. He had an engaging smile that warmed men's hearts, but he was not smiling now. He was seething.

He was seething because the Council had appointed the commanders of the expedition to rout the British from Majabigwaduce, but so far no man had been named to lead the artillery and Revere knew that cannons would be needed. He knew too that he was the best man to command those cannon, he was indeed the commanding officer of the Bay of Massachusetts State Artillery Regiment, yet the Council had pointedly refrained from sending him any orders.

'They will appoint you, Colonel,' Flint said loyally, 'they have to!'

'Not if Major Todd has his way,' Revere said bitterly.

'I expect he went to Harvard,' Flint said, *'hic, haec, hoc.'*

'Harvard or Yale, probably,' Revere agreed, 'and he wanted to run the artillery like a counting-house! Lists and regulations! I told him, make the men gunners first, then kill the British, and after that make the lists, but he didn't listen. He was forever saying I was disorganized, but I know my guns, Mister Flint, I know my guns. There's a skill in gunnery, an art, and not everyone has the touch. It doesn't come from book-learning, not artillery. It's an art.'

'That's very true,' Flint wheezed through a full mouth.

'But I'll ready their cannon,' Revere said, 'so whoever commands them has things done properly. There may not be enough lists, Mister Flint,' he chuckled at that, 'but they'll

36

have good and ready guns. Eighteen-pounders and more! Bloodyback-killers! Guns to slaughter the English, they will have guns. I'll see to that.'

Flint paused to release a belch, then frowned. 'Are you sure you want to go to Maja, whatever it is?'

'Of course I'm sure!'

Flint patted his belly, then put two radishes into his mouth. 'It ain't comfortable, Colonel.'

'What does that mean, Josiah?'

'Down east?' Flint asked. 'You'll get nothing but mosquitoes, rain and sleeping under a tree down east.' He feared that his friend would not be given command of the expedition's artillery and, in his clumsy way, was trying to provide some consolation. 'And you're not as young as you were, Colonel!'

'Forty-five's not old!' Revere protested.

'Old enough to know sense,' Flint said, 'and to appreciate a proper bed with a woman inside it.'

'A proper bed, Mister Flint, is beside my guns. Beside my guns that point towards the English! That's all I ask, a chance to serve my country.' Revere had tried to join the fighting ever since the rebellion had begun, but his applications to the Continental Army had been refused for reasons that Revere could only suspect and never confirm. General Washington, it was said, wanted men of birth and honour, and that rumour had only made Revere more resentful. The Massachusetts Militia was not so particular, yet Revere's service so far had been uneventful. True, he had gone to Newport to help evict the British, but that campaign had ended in failure before Revere and his guns arrived, and so he had been forced to command the garrison on Castle Island and his prayers that a British fleet would come to be battered by his cannon had gone unanswered. Paul Revere, who hated the British with a passion that could shake his body with its pure vehemence, had yet to kill a single redcoat.

'You've heard the trumpet call, Colonel,' Flint said respect-fully.

'I've heard the trumpet call,' Revere agreed.

A sentry opened the armory gate and a man in the faded blue uniform of the Continental Army entered the yard from the street. He was tall, good-looking and some years younger than Revere who stood in wary greeting. 'Colonel Revere?' the newcomer asked.

'At your service, General.'

'I am Peleg Wadsworth.'

'I know who you are, General,' Revere said, smiling and taking the offered hand. He noted that Wadsworth did not return the smile. 'I hope you bring me good news from the Council, General?'

'I would like a word, Colonel,' Wadsworth said, 'a brief word.' The brigadier glanced at the monstrous Josiah Flint in his padded chair. 'A word in private,' he added grimly.

So the trumpet call would have to wait.

Captain Henry Mowat stood on Majabigwaduce's beach. He was a stocky man with a ruddy face now shadowed by the long peak of his cocked hat. His naval coat was dark blue with lighter blue facings, all stained white by salt. He was in his forties, a lifelong sailor, and he stood with his feet planted apart as though balancing on a quarterdeck. His dark hair was powdered and a slight trail of the powder had sifted down the spine of his uniform coat. He was glaring at the longboats that lay alongside his ship, the *Albany*. 'What the devil takes all this time?' he growled.

His companion, Doctor John Calef, had no idea what was causing the delay on board the *Albany* and so offered no answer. 'You've received no intelligence from Boston?' he asked Mowat instead.

'We don't need intelligence,' Mowat said brusquely. He was the senior naval officer at Majabigwaduce and, like Brigadier

McLean, a Scotsman, but where the brigadier was emollient and soft-spoken, Mowat was famed for his bluntness. He fidgeted with the cord-bound hilt of his sword. 'The bastards will come, Doctor, mark my word, the bastards will come. Like flies to dung, Doctor, they'll come.'

Calef thought that likening the British presence at Majabigwaduce to dung was an unfortunate choice, but he made no comment on that. 'In force?' he asked.

'They may be damned rebels, but they're not damned fools. Of course they'll come in force.' Mowat still gazed at the anchored ship, then cupped his hands. 'Mister Farraby,' he bellowed across the water, 'what the devil is happening?'

'Roving a new sling, sir!' the call came back.

'How many guns will you bring ashore?' the doctor enquired.

'As many as McLean wants,' Mowat said. His three sloops of war were anchored fore and aft to make a line across the harbour's mouth, their starboard broadsides facing the entrance to greet any rebel ship that dared intrude. Those broadsides were puny. HMS *North*, which lay closest to Majabigwaduce's beach, carried twenty guns, ten on each side, while the *Albany*, at the centre, and the *Nautilus*, each carried nine cannons in their broadsides. An enemy ship would thus be greeted by twenty-eight guns, none throwing a ball larger than nine pounds, and the last intelligence Mowat had received from Boston indicated that a rebel frigate was in that harbour, a frigate that mounted thirty-two guns, most of which would be much larger than his small cannon. And the rebel frigate *Warren* would be supported by the privateers of Massachusetts, most of whose craft were just as heavily gunned as his own sloops of war. 'It'll be a fight,' he said sourly, 'a rare good fight.'

The new sling had evidently been roved because a nine-pounder gun barrel was being hoisted from the *Albany*'s deck and gently lowered into one of the waiting longboats. Over a ton of metal hung from the yardarm, poised above the heads of the pigtailed sailors waiting in the small boat below. Mowat was bringing his port broadsides ashore so the guns could protect the fort McLean was building on Majabigwaduce's crest. 'If you abandon your portside guns,' Calef enquired in a puzzled tone, 'what happens if the enemy passes you?'

'Then, sir, we are dead men,' Mowat said curtly. He watched the longboat settle precariously low in the choppy water as it took the weight of the cannon's barrel. The carriage would be brought ashore in another boat and, like the barrel, be hauled uphill to the site of the fort by one of the two teams of oxen that had been commandeered from the Hutchings farm. 'Dead men!' Mowat said, almost cheerfully, 'but to kill us, Doctor, they must first pass us, and I do not intend to be passed.'

Calef felt relief at Mowat's belligerence. The Scottish naval captain was famous in Massachusetts, or perhaps infamous was a better word, but to all loyalists, like Calef, Mowat was a hero who inspired confidence. He had been captured by rebel civilians, the self-styled Sons of Liberty, while walking ashore in Falmouth. His release had been negotiated by the leading citizens of that proud harbour town, and the condition of Mowat's release had been that he surrender himself next day so that the legality of his arrest could be established by lawyers, but instead Mowat had returned with a flotilla that had bombarded the town from dawn to dusk and, when most of the houses lay shattered, he had sent shore parties to set fire to the wreckage. Two thirds of Falmouth had been destroyed to send the message that Captain Mowat was not a man to be trifled with.

Calef frowned slightly as Brigadier McLean and two junior officers strolled along the stony beach towards Mowat. Calef still had doubts about the Scottish brigadier, fearing that he was too gentle in his demeanour, but Captain Mowat evidently had no such misgivings because he smiled broadly as McLean approached. 'You've not come to pester me,

McLean,' he said with mock severity, 'your precious guns are coming!'

'I never doubted it, Mowat, never doubted it,' McLean said, 'not for a moment.' He touched his hat to Doctor Calef, then turned back to Mowat. 'And how are your fine fellows this morning, Mowat?'

'Working, McLean, working!'

McLean gestured at his two companions. 'Doctor, allow me to present Lieutenant Campbell of the 74th,' McLean paused to allow the dark-kilted Campbell to offer the doctor a small bow, 'and Paymaster Moore of the 82nd.' John Moore offered a more elegant bow, Calef raised his hat in response and McLean turned to gaze at the three sloops with the longboats nuzzling their flanks. 'Your longboats are all busy, Mowat?'

'They're busy, and so they damn well should be. Idleness encourages the devil.'

'So it does,' Calef agreed.

'And there was I seeking an idle moment,' McLean said happily.

'You need a boat?' Mowat asked.

'I'd not take your matelots from their duties,' the brigadier said, then looked past Mowat to where a young man and woman were hauling a heavy wooden rowboat down to the incoming tide. 'Isn't that the young fellow who piloted us into the harbour?'

Doctor Calef turned. 'James Fletcher,' he said grimly.

'Is he loyal?' McLean asked.

'He's a damned light-headed fool,' Calef said, and then, grudgingly, 'but his father was a loyal man.'

'Then like father, like son, I trust,' McLean said and turned to Moore. 'John? Ask Mister Fletcher if he can spare us an hour?' It was evident that Fletcher and his sister were planning to row to their fishing boat, the *Felicity*, which lay in deeper water. 'Tell him I wish to see Majabigwaduce from the river and will pay for his time.'

Moore went on his errand and McLean watched as another cannon barrel was hoisted aloft from the *Albany*'s deck. Smaller boats were ferrying other supplies ashore; cartridges and salt beef, rum barrels and cannonballs, wadding and rammers, the paraphernalia of war, all of which was being hauled or carried to where his fort was still little more than a scratched square in the thin turf of the ridge's top. John Nutting, a Loyalist American and an engineer who had travelled to Britain to urge the occupation of Majabigwaduce, was laying out the design of the stronghold in the cleared land. The fort would be simple enough, just a square of earthen ramparts with diamond-shaped bastions at its four corners. Each of the walls would be two hundred and fifty paces in length and would be fronted by a steep-sided ditch, but even such a simple fort required firesteps and embrasures, and needed masonry magazines that would keep the ammunition dry, and a well deep enough to provide plentiful water. Tents housed the soldiers for the moment, but McLean wanted those vulnerable encampments protected by the fort. He wanted high walls, thick walls, walls manned by men and studded by guns, because he knew that the south-west wind would bring more than the smell of salt and shellfish. It would bring rebels, a swarm of them, and the air would stink of powder-smoke, of turds and of blood.

'Phoebe Perkins's child contracted a fever last night,' Calef said brutally.

'I trust she will live?' McLean said.

'God's will be done,' Calef said in a tone that suggested God might not care very much. 'They've named her Temperance.'

'Temperance! Oh dear, poor girl, poor girl. I shall pray for her,' McLean said, and pray for ourselves too, he thought, but did not say.

Because the rebels were coming.

*   *   *

42

Peleg Wadsworth felt awkward as he led Lieutenant-Colonel Revere into the shadowed vastness of one of the armory's stores where sparrows bickered in the high beams above boxes of muskets and bales of cloth and stacks of iron-hooped barrels. It was true that Wadsworth outranked Revere, but he was almost fifteen years younger than the colonel and he felt a vague inadequacy in the presence of a man of such obvious competence. Revere had a reputation as an engraver, as a silversmith and as a metal-worker, and it showed in his hands that were strong and fire-scarred, the hands of a man who could make and mend, the hands of a practical man. Peleg Wadsworth had been a teacher, and a good one, but he had known the scorn of his pupils' parents who reckoned their children's futures lay not with grammar or in fractions, but in the command of tools and the working of metal, wood or stone. Wadsworth could construe Latin and Greek, he was intimate with the works of Shakespeare and Montaigne, but faced with a broken chair he felt helpless. Revere, he knew, was the opposite. Give Revere a broken chair and he would mend it competently so that, like the man himself, it was strong, sturdy and dependable.

Or was he dependable? That was the question that had brought Wadsworth to this armory, and he wished that the errand had never been given him. He felt tongue-tied when Revere stopped and turned to him at the storeroom's centre, but then a scuffling sound from behind a pile of broken muskets gave Wadsworth a welcome distraction. 'We're not alone?' he asked.

'Those are rats, General,' Revere said with amusement, 'rats. They do like the grease on cartridges, they do.'

'I thought cartridges were stored in the Public Magazine?'

'They keep enough here for proofing, General, and the rats do like them. We call them redcoats on account they're the enemy.'

'Cats will surely defeat them?'

'We have cats, General, but it's a hard-fought contest. Good American cats and patriot terriers against dirty British rats,' Revere said. 'I assume you want reassurance on the artillery train, General?'

'I'm sure all is in order.'

'Oh, it is, you can rely on that. As of now, General, we have two eighteen-pounders, three nine-pounders, one howitzer, and four little ones.'

'Small howitzers?'

'Four-pounder cannons, General, and I wouldn't use them to shoot rats. You need something heavier-built like the French four-pounders. And if you have influence, General, which I'm sure you do, ask the Board of War to release more eighteen-pounders.'

Wadsworth nodded. 'I'll make a note of that,' he promised.

'You have your guns, General, I assure you,' Revere said, 'with all their side arms, powder and shot. I've hardly seen Castle Island these last few days on account of readying the train.'

'Yes, indeed, Castle Island,' Wadsworth said. He towered a head over Revere, which gave him an excuse not to meet the colonel's eyes, though he was aware that Revere was staring at him intently as if daring Wadsworth to give him bad news. 'You command at Castle Island?' Wadsworth asked, not because he needed confirmation, but out of desperation to say anything.

'You didn't need to come here to find that out,' Revere said with amusement, 'but yes, General, I command the Massachusetts Artillery Regiment and, because most of our guns are mounted on the island, I command there too. And you, General, will command at Majajuce?'

'Majajuce?' Wadsworth said, then realised Revere meant Majabigwaduce. 'I am second in command,' he went on, 'to General Lovell.'

'And there are British rats at Majajuce,' Revere said.

44

'As far as we can determine,' Wadsworth said, 'they've landed at least a thousand men and possess three sloops-of-war. Not an over-large force, but not risible either.'

'Risible,' Revere said, as if amused by the word. 'But to rid Massachusetts of those rats, General, you'll need guns.'

'We will indeed.'

'And the guns will need an officer in command,' Revere added pointedly.

'Indeed they will,' Wadsworth said. All the senior appointments of the expedition that was being hurriedly prepared to evict the British from Majabigwaduce had been made. Solomon Lovell would command the ground forces, Commander Dudley Saltonstall of the Continental Frigate *Warren* would be the naval commander, and Wadsworth would be Lovell's deputy. The troops, drawn from the militias of York, Cumberland and Lincoln counties, had their commanding officers, while the adjutant-general, quartermaster-general, surgeon-general and brigade majors had all received their orders, and now only the commander of the artillery train needed to be appointed.

'The guns will need an officer in command,' Revere pressed Wadsworth, 'and I command the Artillery Regiment.'

Wadsworth gazed at a ginger-coloured cat washing itself on top of a barrel. 'No one,' he said carefully, 'would deny that you are the man best qualified to command the artillery at Majabigwaduce.'

'So I can expect a letter from the Board of War?' Revere said.

'If I am satisfied,' Wadsworth said, nerving himself to raise the matter that had brought him to the armory.

'Satisfied about what, General?' Revere asked, still looking up into Wadsworth's face.

Peleg Wadsworth made himself look into the steady brown eyes. 'A complaint was made,' he said, 'concerning the Castle Island ration demands, a matter of surplus, Colonel . . . '

'Surplus!' Revere interrupted, not angrily, but in a tone

suggesting he found the word amusing. He smiled, and Wadsworth found himself unexpectedly warming to the man. 'Tell me, General,' Revere went on, 'how many troops you'll be taking to Majajuce.'

'We can't be certain,' Wadsworth said, 'but we expect to take an infantry force of at least fifteen hundred men.'

'And you've ordered rations for that many?'

'Of course.'

'And if only fourteen hundred men report for duty, General, what will you do with the surplus ration?'

'It will be accounted for,' Wadsworth said, 'of course.'

'This is war!' Revere said energetically. 'War and blood, fire and iron, death and damage, and a man can't account for everything in war! I'll make as many lists as you like when the war is over.'

Wadsworth frowned. Doubtless it was war, yet the Castle Island garrison, like Lieutenant-Colonel Revere himself, had yet to fire a shot at the enemy. 'It is alleged, Colonel,' Wadsworth said firmly, 'that your garrison was comprised of a fixed number of men, yet the ration demands consistently cited thirty non-existent gunners.'

Revere gave a tolerant smile, suggesting he had heard all this before. 'Consistently,' he said derisively, 'consistently, eh? Long words don't kill the enemy, General.'

'Another long word,' Wadsworth said, 'is peculation.'

The accusation was now open. The word hung in the dusty air. It was alleged that Revere had ordered extra rations that he had then sold for personal gain, though Wadsworth did not articulate that full accusation. He did not need to. Colonel Revere looked up into Wadsworth's face, then shook his head sadly. He turned and walked slowly to a nine-pounder cannon that stood at the back of the storehouse. The gun had been captured at Saratoga and Revere now stroked its long barrel with a capable, broad-fingered hand. 'For years, General,' he spoke quietly, 'I have pursued and promoted the cause of liberty.' He was staring down at the royal cipher on the gun's breech. 'When you were learning books, General, I was riding to Philadelphia and New York to spread the idea of liberty. I risked capture and imprisonment for liberty. I threw tea into Boston Harbour and I rode to warn Lexington when the British started this war. That's when we first met, General, at Lexington.'

'I remember it...' Wadsworth began.

'And I risked the well-being of my dear wife,' Revere interrupted hotly, 'and the welfare of my children to serve a cause I love, General.' He turned and looked at Wadsworth who stood in the buttress of sunlight cast through the wide-open door. 'I have been a patriot, General, and I have proved my patriotism...'

'No one is suggesting...'

'Yes, they are, General!' Revere said with a sudden passion. 'They are suggesting I am a dishonest man! That I would steal from the cause to which I have devoted my life! It's Major Todd, isn't it?'

'I'm not at liberty to reveal...'

'You don't need to,' Revere said scathingly. 'It's Major Todd. He doesn't like me, General, and I regret that, and I regret that the Major doesn't know the first thing he's talking about! I was told, General, that thirty men of the Barnstable County Militia were being posted to me for artillery training and I ordered rations accordingly, and then Major Fellows, for his own reasons, General, for his own good reasons held the men back, and I explained all that, but Major Todd isn't a man to listen to reason, General.'

'Major Todd is a man of diligence,' Wadsworth said sternly, 'and I am not saying he advanced the complaint, merely that he is a most efficient and honorable officer.'

'A Harvard man, is he?' Revere asked sharply.

Wadsworth frowned. 'I cannot think that relevant, Colonel.'

'I've no doubt you don't, but Major Todd still misunderstood

47

the situation, General,' Revere said. He paused, and for a moment it seemed his indignation would burst out with the violence of thunder, but instead he smiled. 'It is not peculation, General,' he said, 'and I don't doubt I was remiss in not checking the books, but mistakes are made. I concentrated on making the guns efficient, General, efficient!' He walked towards Wadsworth, his voice low. 'All I have ever asked, General, is for a chance to fight for my country. To fight for the cause I love. To fight for my dear children's future. Do you have children, General?'

'I do.'

'As do I. Dear children. And you think I would risk my family name, their reputation, and the cause I love for thirty loaves of bread? Or for thirty pieces of silver?'

Wadsworth had learned as a schoolmaster to judge his pupils by their demeanour. Boys, he had discovered, rarely looked authority in the eye when they lied. Girls were far more difficult to read, but boys, when they lied, almost always looked uncomfortable. Their gaze would shift, but Revere's gaze was steady, his face was earnest, and Wadsworth felt a great surge of relief. He put a hand inside his uniform coat and brought out a paper, folded and sealed. 'I had hoped you would satisfy me, Colonel, upon my soul, I had hoped that. And you have.' He smiled and held the paper towards Revere.

Revere's eyes glistened as he took the warrant. He broke the seal and opened the paper to discover a letter written by John Avery, deputy-secretary of the Council of State, and countersigned by General Solomon Lovell. The letter appointed Lieutenant-Colonel Paul Revere as the commander of the artillery train that was to accompany the expedition to Majabigwaduce, where he was ordered to do all in his power to 'captivate, kill or destroy the whole force of the enemy'. Revere read the warrant a second time, then wiped his cheek. 'General,' he said, and his voice had a catch in it, 'this is all I desire.'

'I am pleased, Colonel,' Wadsworth said warmly. 'You will receive orders later today, but I can tell you their gist now. Your guns should be taken to the Long Wharf ready for embarkation, and you should withdraw from the public magazine whatever gunpowder you require.'

'Shubael Hewes has to authorize that,' Revere said distractedly, still reading the warrant.

'Shubael Hewes?'

'The Deputy Sheriff, General, but don't you worry, I know Shubael.' Revere folded the warrant carefully, then cuffed at his eyes and sniffed. 'We are going to captivate, kill and destroy them, General. We are going to make those red-coated bastards wish they had never sailed from England.'

'We shall certainly dislodge them,' Wadsworth said with a smile.

'More than dislodge the monsters,' Revere said vengefully, 'we shall slaughter them! And those we don't kill, General, we'll march through town and back just to give folk a chance to let them know how welcome they are in Massachusetts.'

Wadsworth held out his hand. 'I look forward to serving with you, Colonel.'

'I look forward to sharing victory with you, General,' Revere said, shaking the offered hand.

Revere watched Wadsworth leave, then, still holding the warrant as though it were the holy grail, went back to the courtyard where Josiah Flint was stirring butter into a dish of mashed turnips. 'I'm going to war, Josiah,' Revere said reverently.

'I did that,' Flint said, 'and I was never so hungry in all my born days.'

'I've waited for this,' Revere said.

'There'll be no Nantucket turnips where you're going,' Flint said. 'I don't know why they taste better, but upon my soul you can't trump a turnip from Nantucket. You think it's the salt air?'

'Commanding the state's artillery!'

'You ever travelled down east? It ain't a Christian place, Colonel. Fog and flies is all it is, fog and flies, and the fog chills you and the flies bite like the very devil.'

'I'm going to war. It's all I ever asked! A chance, Josiah!' Revere's face was radiant. He turned a full triumphant circle, then slammed his fist onto the table. 'I am going to war!'

Lieutenant-Colonel Paul Revere had heard the trumpet and he was going to war.

James Fletcher's boat buffeted against the outgoing tide, pushed by a convenient south-west wind that drove the *Felicity* upriver past Majabigwaduce's high bluff. The *Felicity* was a small boat, just twenty-four feet long, with a stubby mast from which a faded red sail hung from a high gaff. The sun sparkled prettily on the small waves of Penobscot Bay, but behind the *Felicity* a bank of thick fog shrouded the view towards the distant ocean. Brigadier McLean, enthroned on a tarry heap of nets in the boat's belly, wanted to see Majabigwaduce just as the enemy would first see it, from the water. He wanted to put himself in his enemy's shoes and decide how he would attack the peninsula if he were a rebel. He stared fixedly at the shore, and again remarked how the scenery put him in mind of Scotland's west coast. 'Don't you agree, Mister Moore?' he asked Lieutenant John Moore who was one of two junior officers who had been ordered to accompany the brigadier.

'Not dissimilar, sir,' Moore said, though abstractedly, as if he merely essayed a courtesy rather than a thoughtful response.

'More trees here, of course,' the brigadier said.

'Indeed, sir, indeed,' Moore said, still not paying proper attention to his commanding officer's remarks. Instead he was gazing at James Fletcher's sister, Bethany, who had the tiller of the *Felicity* in her right hand.

McLean sighed. He liked Moore very much, considering the young man to have great promise, but he understood too that any young man would rather gaze at Bethany Fletcher than make polite conversation to a senior officer. She was a rare beauty to find in this distant place. Her hair was pale gold, framing a sun-darkened face given strength by a long nose. Her blue eyes were trusting and friendly, but the feature that made her beautiful, that could have lit the darkest night, was her smile. It was an extraordinary smile, wide and generous, that had dazzled John Moore and his companion, Lieutenant Campbell, who also gaped at Bethany as though he had never seen a young woman before. He kept plucking at his dark kilt as the wind lifted it from his thighs.

'And the sea monsters here are extraordinary,' McLean went on, 'like dragons, wouldn't you say, John? Pink dragons with green spots?'

'Indeed, sir,' Moore said, then gave a start as he belatedly realized the brigadier was teasing him. He had the grace to look abashed. 'I'm sorry, sir.'

James Fletcher laughed. 'No dragons here, General.'

McLean smiled. He looked at the distant fog. 'You have much fog here, Mister Fletcher?'

'We gets fog in the spring, General, and fog in the summer, and then comes the fog in the fall and after that the snow, which we usually can't see because it's hidden by fog,' Fletcher said with a smile as wide as his sister's, 'fog and more fog.'

'Yet you like living here?' McLean asked gently.

'God's own country, General,' Fletcher answered enthusiastically, 'and God hides it from the heathen by wrapping it in fog.'

'And you, Miss Fletcher?' McLean enquired of Bethany. 'Do you like living in Majabigwaduce?'

'I like it fine, sir,' she said with a smile.

'Don't steer too close to the shore, Miss Fletcher,' McLean said sternly. 'I would never forgive myself if some disaffected person was to take a shot at our uniforms and struck you instead.' McLean had tried to dissuade Bethany from accompanying the reconnaissance, but he had not tried over-enthusiastically, acknowledging to himself that the company of a pretty girl was a rare delight.

James Fletcher dismissed the fear. 'No one will shoot at the *Felicity*,' he said confidently, 'and besides, most folks round here are loyal to his majesty.'

'As you are, Mister Fletcher?' Lieutenant John Moore asked pointedly.

James paused, and the brigadier saw the flicker of his eyes towards his sister. Then James grinned. 'I've no quarrel with the king,' he said. 'He leaves me alone and I leave him alone, and so the two of us rub along fair enough.'

'So you will take the oath?' McLean asked, and saw how solemnly Beth gazed at her brother.

'Don't have much choice, sir, do I? Not if I want to fish and scratch a living.'

Brigadier McLean had issued a proclamation to the country about Majabigwaduce, assuring the inhabitants that if they were loyal to his majesty and took the oath swearing to that loyalty, then they would have nothing to fear from his forces, but if any man refused the oath, then the proclamation promised hard times to him and his family. 'You do indeed have a choice,' McLean said.

'We were raised to love the king, sir,' James said.

'I'm glad to hear it,' McLean said. He gazed at the dark woods. 'I understood,' the brigadier went on, 'that the authorities in Boston have been conscripting men?'

'That they have,' James agreed.

'Yet you have not been conscripted?'

'Oh, they tried,' James said dismissively, 'but they're leery of this part of Massachusetts.'

'Leery?'

'Not much sympathy for the rebellion here, General.'

'But some folk here are disaffected?' McLean asked.

'A few,' James said, 'but some folk are never happy.'

'A lot of folks here fled from Boston,' Bethany said, 'and they're all loyalists.'

'When the British left, Miss Fletcher? Is that what you mean?'

'Yes, sir. Like Doctor Calef. He had no wish to stay in a city ruled by rebellion, sir.'

'Was that your fate?' John Moore asked.

'Oh no,' James said, 'our family's been here since God made the world.'

'Your parents live in Majabigwaduce?' the brigadier asked.

'Father's in the burying ground, God rest him,' James said.

'I'm sorry,' McLean said.

'And Mother's good as dead,' James went on.

'James!' Bethany said reprovingly.

'Crippled, bedridden and speechless,' James said. Six years before, he explained, when Bethany was twelve and James fourteen, their widowed mother had been gored by a bull she had been leading to pasture. Then, two years later, she had suffered a stroke that had left her stammering and confused.

'Life is hard on us,' McLean said. He stared at a log house built close to the river's bank and noted the huge heap of firewood stacked against one outer wall. 'And it must be hard,' he went on, 'to make a new life in a wilderness if you are accustomed to a city like Boston.'

'Wilderness, General?' James asked, amused.

'It is hard for the Boston folk who came here, sir,' Bethany said more usefully.

'They have to learn to fish, General,' James said, 'or grow crops, or cut wood.'

'You grow many crops?' McLean asked.

'Rye, oats and potatoes,' Bethany answered, 'and corn, sir.'

'They can trap, General,' James put in. 'Our dad made a fine living from trapping! Beaver, marten, weasels.'

'He caught an ermine once,' Bethany said proudly.

'And doubtless that scrap of fur is around some fine lady's neck in London, General,' James said. 'Then there's mast timber,' he went on. 'Not so much in Majabigwaduce, but plenty upriver and any man can learn to cut and trim a tree. And there are sawmills aplenty! Why there must be thirty sawmills between here and the river's head. A man can make scantlings or staves, boards or posts, anything he pleases!'

'You trade in timber?' McLean asked.

'I fish, General, and it's a poor man who can't keep his family alive by fishing.'

'What do you catch?'

'Cod, General, and cunners, haddock, hake, eel, flounder, pollock, skate, mackerel, salmon, alewives. We have more fish than we know what to do with! And all good eating! It's what gives our Beth her pretty complexion, all that fish!'

Bethany gave her brother a fond glance. 'You're silly, James,' she said.

'You are not married, Miss Fletcher?' the general asked.

'No, sir.'

'Our Beth was betrothed, General,' James explained, 'to a rare good man. Captain of a schooner. She was to be married this spring.'

McLean looked gently at the girl. 'Was to be?'

'He was lost at sea, sir,' Bethany said.

'Fishing on the banks,' James explained. 'He got caught by a nor'easter, General, and the nor'easters have blown many a good man out of this world to the next.'

'I'm sorry.'

'She'll find another,' James said carelessly. 'She's not the ugliest girl in the world,' he grinned, 'are you?'

The brigadier turned his gaze back to the shore. He sometimes allowed himself the small luxury of imagining that no enemy would come to attack him, but he knew that was unlikely. McLean's small force was now the only British presence between

54

the Canadian border and Rhode Island and the rebels would surely want that presence destroyed. They would come. He pointed south. 'We might return now?' he suggested, and Bethany obliged by turning the *Felicity* into the wind. Her brother hardened the jib, staysail and main so that the small boat tipped as she beat into the brisk breeze and sharp dashes of spray slapped against the three officers' red coats. McLean looked again at Majabigwaduce's high western bluff that faced onto the wide river. 'If you were in command here,' he asked his two lieutenants, 'how would you defend the place?' Lieutenant Campbell, a lank youth with a prominent nose and an equally prominent Adam's apple, swallowed nervously and said nothing, while young Moore just leaned back on the heaped nets as though contemplating an afternoon's sleep. 'Come, come,' the brigadier chided the pair, 'tell me what you would do.'

'Does that not depend on what the enemy does, sir?' Moore asked idly.

'Then assume with me that they arrive with a dozen or more ships and, say, fifteen hundred men?'

Moore closed his eyes, while Lieutenant Campbell tried to look enthusiastic. 'We put our guns on the bluff, sir,' he offered, gesturing towards the high ground that dominated the river and harbour entrance.

'But the bay is wide,' McLean pointed out, 'so the enemy can pass us on the farther bank and land upstream of us. Then they cross the neck,' he pointed to the narrow isthmus of low ground that connected Majabigwaduce to the mainland, 'and attack us from the landward side.'

Campbell frowned and bit his lip as he pondered that suggestion. 'So we put guns there too, sir,' he offered, 'maybe a smaller fort?'

McLean nodded encouragingly, then glanced at Moore. 'Asleep, Mister Moore?'

Moore smiled, but did not open his eyes. '*Wer alles verteidigt, verteidigt nichts,*' he said.

55

'I believe *der alte Fritz* thought of that long before you did, Mister Moore,' McLean responded, then smiled at Bethany. 'Our paymaster is showing off, Miss Fletcher, by quoting Frederick the Great. He's also quite right, he who defends everything defends nothing. So,' the brigadier looked back to Moore, 'what would you defend here at Majabigwaduce?'

'I would defend, sir, that which the enemy wishes to possess.'

'And that is?'

'The harbour, sir.'

'So you would allow the enemy to land their troops on the neck?' McLean asked. The brigadier's reconnaissance had convinced him that the rebels would probably land north of Majabigwaduce. They might try to enter the harbour, fighting their way through Mowat's sloops to land troops on the beach below the fort, but if McLean was in command of the rebels he reckoned he would choose to land on the wide, shelving beach of the isthmus. By doing that, the enemy would cut him off from the mainland and could assault his ramparts safe from any cannon-fire from the Royal Navy vessels. There was a small chance that they might be daring and assault the bluff to gain the peninsula's high ground, but the bluff's slope was dauntingly steep. He sighed inwardly. He could not defend everything because, as the great Frederick had said, by defending everything a man defended nothing.

'They'll land somewhere, sir,' Moore answered the brigadier's question, 'and there's little we can do can stop them landing, not if they come in sufficient force. But why do they land, sir?'

'You tell me.'

'To capture the harbour, sir, because that is the value of this place.'

'Thou art not far from the kingdom of heaven, Mister Moore,' McLean said, 'and they do want the harbour and they will come for it, but let us hope they do not come soon.'

'The sooner they come, sir,' Moore said, 'the sooner we can kill them.'

'I would wish to finish the fort first,' McLean said. The fort, which he had decided to name Fort George, was hardly begun. The soil was thin, rocky and hard to work, and the ridge so thick with trees that a week's toil had scarcely cleared a sufficient killing ground. If the enemy came soon, McLean knew, he would have small choice but to fire a few defiant guns and then haul down the flag. 'Are you a prayerful man, Mister Moore?' McLean asked.

'Indeed I am, sir.'

'Then pray the enemy delays,' McLean said fervently, then looked to James Fletcher. 'Mister Fletcher, you would land us back on the beach?'

'That I will, General,' James said cheerfully.

'And pray for us, Mister Fletcher.'

'Not sure the good Lord listens to me, sir.'

'James!' Bethany reproved her brother.

James grinned. 'You need prayers to protect yourself here, General?'

McLean paused for a moment, then shrugged. 'It depends, Mister Fletcher, on the enemy's strength, but I would wish for twice as many men and twice our number of ships to feel secure.'

'Maybe they won't come, sir,' Fletcher said. 'Those folks in Boston never took much note of what happens here.' Wisps of fog were drifting with the wind as the *Felicity* ran past the three sloops of war that guarded the harbour entrance. James Fletcher noted how the three ships were anchored fore and aft so that they could not swing with the tide or wind, thus allowing each sloop to keep its broadside pointed at the harbour entrance. The ship nearest the beach, the *North*, had two intermittent jets of water pulsing from its portside, and James could hear the clank of the elmwood pumps as men thrust at the long handles. Those pumps rarely stopped, suggesting the *North* was an ill-found ship, though her guns were doubtless efficient enough to help protect the harbour mouth and, to protect that entrance even further, red-coated Royal Marines were hacking at the thin soil and rocks of Cross Island, which edged the southern side of the channel. Fletcher reckoned the marines were making a battery there. Behind the three sloops and making a second line across the harbour, were three of the transport ships that had carried the redcoats to Majabigwaduce. Those transports were not armed, but their size alone made them a formidable obstacle to any ship that might attempt to pass the smaller sloops.

McLean handed Fletcher an oilcloth-wrapped parcel of tobacco and one of the Spanish silver dollars that were common currency, as payment for the use of his boat. 'Come, Mister Moore,' he called sharply as the paymaster offered Bethany an arm to help her over the uneven beach. 'We have work to do!'

James Fletcher also had work to do. It was still high summer, but the log pile had to be made for the winter and, that evening, he split wood outside their house. He worked deep into the twilight, slashing the axe down hard to splinter logs into usable firewood.

'You're thinking, James.' Bethany had come from the house and was watching him. She wore an apron over her grey dress.

'Is that bad?'

'You always work too hard when you're thinking,' she said. She sat on a bench fronting the house. 'Mother's sleeping.'

'Good,' James said. He left the axe embedded in a stump and sat beside his sister on the bench that overlooked the harbour. The sky was purple and black, the water glinted with little ripples of fading silver about the anchored boats; glimmers of lamplight reflected on the small waves. A bugle sounded from the ridge where two tented encampments housed the redcoats. A picquet of six men guarded the guns

58

and ammunition that had been parked on the beach above the tideline. 'That young officer liked you, Beth,' James said. Bethany just smiled, but said nothing. 'They're nice enough fellows,' James said.

'I like the general,' Bethany said.

'A decent man, he seems,' James said.

'I wonder what happened to his arm?'

'Soldiers, Beth. Soldiers get wounded.'

'And killed.'

'Yes.'

They sat in companionable silence for a while as the darkness closed slow on the river and on the harbour and on the bluff. 'So will you sign the oath?' Bethany asked after a while.

'Not sure I have much choice,' James said bleakly.

'But will you?'

James picked a shred of tobacco from between his teeth. 'Father would have wanted me to sign.'

'I'm not sure Father thought about it much,' Bethany said. 'We never had government here, neither royal nor rebel.'

'He loved the king,' James said. 'He hated the French and loved the king.' He sighed. 'We have to make a living, Beth. If I don't take the oath then they'll take the *Felicity* away from us, and then what do we do? I can't have that.' A dog howled somewhere in the village and James waited till the sound died away. 'I like McLean well enough,' he said, 'but . . .' He let the thought fade away into the darkness.

'But?' Bethany asked. Her brother shrugged and made no answer. Beth slapped at a mosquito. '"Choose you this day whom you will serve,"' she quoted, '"whether the gods which your father served that were on the other side of the flood, or . . ."' She left the Bible verse unfinished.

'There's too much bitterness,' James said.

'You thought it would pass us by?'

'I hoped it would. What does anyone want with Bagaduce anyway?'

Bethany smiled. 'The Dutch were here, the French made a fort here, it seems the whole world wants us.'

'But it's our home, Beth. We made this place, it's ours.' James paused. He was not sure he could articulate what was in his mind. 'You know Colonel Buck left?'

Buck was the local commander of the Massachusetts Militia and he had fled north up the Penobscot River when the British arrived. 'I heard,' Bethany said.

'And John Lymburner and his friends are saying what a coward Buck is, and that's just nonsense! It's all just bitterness, Beth.'

'So you'll ignore it?' she asked. 'Just sign the oath and pretend it isn't happening?'

James stared down at his hands. 'What do you think I should do?'

'You know what I think,' Bethany said firmly.

'Just 'cos your fellow was a damned rebel,' James said, smiling. He gazed at the shivering reflections cast from the lanterns on board the three sloops. 'What I want, Beth, is for them all to leave us alone.'

'They won't do that now,' she said.

James nodded. 'They won't, so I'll write a letter, Beth,' he said, 'and you can take it over the river to John Brewer. He'll know how to get it to Boston.'

Bethany was silent for a while, then frowned. 'And the oath? Will you sign it?'

'We'll cross that bridge when we have to,' he said. 'I don't know, Beth, I honestly don't know.'

James wrote the letter on a blank page torn from the back of the family Bible. He wrote simply, saying what he had seen in Majabigwaduce and its harbour. He told how many guns were mounted on the sloops and where the British were making earthworks, how many soldiers he believed had come to the village and how many guns had been shipped to the beach. He used the other side of the paper to make a rough map of the peninsula on which he drew the position of the fort and the place where the three sloops of war were anchored. He marked the battery on Cross Island, then turned the page over and signed the letter with his name, biting his lower lip as he formed the clumsy letters.

'Maybe you shouldn't put your name to it,' Bethany said.

James sealed the folded paper with candle-wax. 'The soldiers probably won't trouble you, Beth, which is why you should carry the letter, but if they do, and if they find the letter, then I don't want you blamed. Say you didn't know what was in it and let me be punished.'

'So you're a rebel now?'

James hesitated, then nodded. 'Yes,' he said, 'I suppose I am.'

'Good,' Bethany said.

The sound of a flute came from a house higher up the hill. The lights still shimmered on the harbour water and dark night came to Majabigwaduce.

Excerpts of a letter from the Selectmen of Newburyport, Massachusetts, to the General Court of Massachusetts, July 12th, 1779:

Last Friday one James Collins an Inhabitant of Penobscot on his way home from Boston went through this Town . . . upon Examination (we) find that he has been an Enemy to the united States of America . . . and that immediately after the British Fleet arrived at Penobscot this Collins . . . took Passage from Kennebeck to Boston . . . where he arrived last Tuesday, and as we apprehend got all the Intelligence he Possibly cou'd Relative to the movements of our Fleet and Army . . . (we) are suspicious of his being a Spy and have accordingly Secured him in the Gaol in this Town.

Order addressed to the Massachusetts Board of War, July 3rd, 1779:

Ordered that the Board of War be and hereby are directed to procure three hundred and fifty Barrels of Flour, One hundred and sixteen Barrels of Pork, One hundred and Sixty five Barrels of Beef, Eleven Tierces of Rice, Three hundred and Fifty bushels of Pease, five hundred and fifty two Gallons of Molasses, Two Thousand, One hundred and Seventy Six pound of Soap and Seven hundred and Sixty Eight pound of Candles being a deficient Quantity . . . on board the Transports for the intended Expedition to Penobscot.

THREE

On Sunday, 18th July, 1779, Peleg Wadsworth worshipped at Christ Church on Salem Street where the rector was the Reverend Stephen Lewis who, until two years before, had been a British army chaplain. The rector had been captured with the rest of the defeated British army at Saratoga, yet in captivity he had changed his allegiance and sworn an oath of loyalty to the United States of America, which meant his congregation this summer Sunday was swollen by townsfolk curious about how he would preach when his adopted country was about to launch an expedition against his former comrades. The Reverend Lewis chose his text from the Book of Daniel. He related the story of Shadrach, Meshach and Abednego, the three men who had been hurled into King Nebuchadnezzar's furnace and who, by God's saving grace, had survived the flames. For an hour or more Wadsworth wondered how the scripture was relevant to the military preparations that obsessed Boston, and even whether some ancient lingering loyalty was making the rector ambivalent, but then the Reverend Lewis moved to his final peroration. He told how all the king's men had assembled to watch the execution and instead they saw that 'the fire had no power'. 'The king's men,' the rector repeated fiercely, 'saw that "the fire had no power!" There is God's promise, in the twenty-seventh verse of the third chapter of Daniel! The fire set by the king's men had no power!' The Reverend Lewis stared directly at Wadsworth as he repeated the last two words, 'no power!', and Wadsworth thought of the redcoats waiting at Majabigwaduce and prayed that their fire would indeed have no power. He thought of the ships lying at anchor in Boston's harbour, he thought of the militia who were assembling at Townsend where the ships would rendezvous with the troops, and he prayed again that the enemy's fire would prove impotent.

After the service Wadsworth shook a multitude of hands and received the good wishes of many in the congregation, but he did not leave the church. Instead he waited beneath the organ loft until he was alone, then he went back up the aisle, opened a box pew at random, and knelt on a hassock newly embroidered with the flag of the United States. Around the flag were stitched the words 'God Watcheth Over Us' and Wadsworth prayed that was true, and prayed that God would watch over his family whom he named one by one: Elizabeth, his dear wife, then Alexander, Charles and Zilpha. He prayed that the campaign against the British in Majabigwaduce would be brief and successful. Brief because Elizabeth's next child was due within five or six weeks and he was afraid for her and wanted to be with her when the baby was born. He prayed for the men whom he would lead into battle. He mouthed the prayer, the words a half-formed murmur, but each one distinct and fervent in his spirit. The cause is just, he told God, and men must die for it, and he begged God to receive those men into their new heavenly home, and he prayed for the widows who must be made and the orphans who would be left. 'And if it please you, God,' he said in a slightly louder voice, 'let not Elizabeth be widowed, and permit my children to grow with a father in their house.' He wondered how many other such prayers were being offered this Sunday morning.

'General Wadsworth, sir?' a tentative voice spoke behind him.

Wadsworth turned to see a tall, slim young man in a dark green uniform coat crossed by a white belt. The young man looked anxious, worried perhaps that he had disturbed Wadsworth's devotions. He had dark hair that was bound into a short, thick pigtail. For a moment Wadsworth supposed the man had been sent to him with orders, then the memory of a much younger boy flooded his mind and the memory allowed him to recognize the man. 'William Dennis!' Wadsworth said with real pleasure. He did some quick addition in his head and realized Dennis must now be nineteen years old. 'It was eight years ago we last met!'

'I hoped you'd recollect me, sir,' Dennis said, pleased.

'Of course I remember you!' Wadsworth reached across the box pew to shake the young man's hand, 'and remember you well!'

'I heard you were here, sir,' Dennis said, 'so took the liberty of seeking you out.'

'I'm glad!'

'And you're a general now, sir.'

'A leap from school-mastering, is it not?' Wadsworth said wryly, 'and you?'

'A lieutenant in the Continental Marines, sir.'

'I congratulate you.'

'And bound for Penobscot, sir, as are you.'

'You're on the *Warren*?'

'I am, sir, but posted to the *Vengeance*.' The *Vengeance* was one of the privateers, a twenty-gun ship.

'Then we shall share a victory,' Wadsworth said. He opened the pew door and gestured towards the street. 'Will you walk with me to the harbour?'

'Of course, sir.'

'You attended service, I hope?'

'The Reverend Frobisher preached at West Church,' Dennis said, 'and I wanted to hear him.'

'You don't sound impressed,' Wadsworth said, amused.

'He chose a text from the Sermon on the Mount,' Dennis said, '"He maketh His sun to rise on the evil and the good, and sendeth rain on the just and on the unjust."'

'Ah!' Wadsworth said with a grimace. 'Was he saying that God is not on our side? If so, it sounds dispiriting.'

'He was assuring us, sir, that the revealed truths of our faith cannot depend on the outcome of a battle, a campaign or even a war. He said we cannot know God's will, sir, except for that part which illuminates our conscience.'

'I suppose that's true,' Wadsworth allowed.

'And he said war is the devil's business, sir.'

'That's certainly true,' Wadsworth said as they left the church, 'but hardly an apt sermon for a town about to send its men to war?' He closed the church door and saw that the wind-driven drizzle that had blown him uphill from the harbour had lifted and the sky was clearing itself of high, scudding clouds. He walked with Dennis towards the water, wondering when the fleet would leave. Commodore Saltonstall had given the order to set sail on the previous Thursday, but had postponed the departure because the wind had risen to a gale strong enough to part ships' cables. But the great fleet must sail soon. It would go eastwards, towards the enemy, towards the devil's business.

He glanced at Dennis. He had grown into a handsome young man. His dark green coat was faced with white and his white breeches piped with green. He wore a straight sword in a leather scabbard trimmed with silver oak leaves. 'I have never understood,' Wadsworth said, 'why the marines wear green. Wouldn't blue be more, well, marine?'

'I'm told that the only cloth that was available in Philadelphia, sir, was green.'

'Ah! That thought never occurred to me. How are your parents?'

'Very well, sir, thank you,' Dennis said enthusiastically. 'They'll be pleased to know I met you.'

68

'Send them my respects,' Wadsworth said. He had taught William Dennis to read and to write, he had taught him grammar in both Latin and English, but then the family had moved to Connecticut and Wadsworth had lost touch. He remembered Dennis well, though. He had been a bright boy, alert and mischievous, but never malevolent. 'I beat you once, didn't I?' he asked.

'Twice, sir,' Dennis said with a grin, 'and I deserved both punishments.'

'That was never a duty I enjoyed,' Wadsworth said.

'But necessary?'

'Oh, indeed.'

'Their conversation was constantly interrupted by men who wished to shake their hands and wish them success against the British. 'Give them hell, General,' one man said, a sentiment echoed by everyone who accosted the pair. Wadsworth smiled, shook offered hands and finally escaped the well-wishers by entering the Bunch of Grapes, a tavern close to Long Wharf. 'I think God will forgive us for crossing a tavern threshold on the Sabbath day,' he said.

'It's more like the army's headquarters these days,' Dennis said, amused. The tavern was crowded with men in uniforms, many of whom were gathered by a wall where notices had been tacked, so many notices that they overlapped each other. Some offered bounties to men willing to serve on privateers, others had been put there by Solomon Lovell's staff.

'We're to sleep aboard the ships tonight!' a man shouted, then saw Wadsworth. 'Is that because we're sailing tomorrow, General?'

'I hope so,' Wadsworth said, 'but make sure you're all aboard by nightfall.'

'Can I bring her?' the man asked. He had his arm around one of the tavern's whores, a pretty young red-haired girl who already looked drunk.

Wadsworth ignored the question, instead leading Dennis

69

to an empty table at the back of the room, which was alive with conversation, hope and optimism. A burly man in a salt-stained sailor's coat stood and thumped a table with his fist. He raised a tankard when the room had fallen silent. 'Here's to victory at Bagaduce!' he shouted. 'Death to the Tories, and to the day when we carry fat George's head through Boston on the point of a bayonet!'

'Much is expected of us,' Wadsworth said when the cheers had ended.

'King George might not oblige us with his head,' Dennis said, amused, 'but I'm sure we shall not disappoint the other expectations.' He waited as Wadsworth ordered oyster stew and ale. 'Did you know that folk are buying shares in the expedition?'

'Shares?'

'The privateer owners, sir, are selling the plunder they expect to take. I assume you haven't invested?'

'I was never a speculator,' Wadsworth said. 'How does it work?'

'Well, Captain Thomas of the *Vengeance*, sir, expects to capture fifteen hundred pounds' worth of plunder, and he's offering a hundred shares in that expectation for fifteen pounds apiece.'

'Good Lord! And what if he doesn't capture fifteen hundred pounds' worth of material?'

'Then the speculators lose, sir.'

'I suppose they must, yes. And people are buying?'

'Many! I believe the *Vengeance*'s shares are trading upwards of twenty-two pounds each now.'

'What a world we live in,' Wadsworth said, amused. 'Tell me,' he pushed the jug of ale towards Dennis, 'what you were doing before you joined the marines?'

'I was studying, sir.'

'Harvard?'

'Yale.'

'Then I didn't beat you nearly often enough or hard enough,' Wadsworth said.

Dennis laughed. 'My ambition is the law.'

'A noble ambition.'

'I hope so, sir. When the British are defeated I shall go back to my studies.'

'I see you carry them with you,' Wadsworth said, nodding towards a book-shaped lump in the tail of the lieutenant's coat, 'or is that the scriptures?'

'Beccaria, sir,' Dennis said, pulling the book out of his tail pocket. 'I'm reading him for pleasure, or should I say enlightenment?'

'Both, I hope. I've heard of him,' Wadsworth said, 'and very much want to read him.'

'You'll permit me to lend you the book when I've finished it?'

'That would be kind,' Wadsworth said. He opened the book, *On Crimes and Punishments* by Cesare Beccaria, newly translated from the Italian, and he saw the minutely written pencilled notes on the margins of almost every page, and he thought how sad it was that a sterling young man like Dennis should need to go to war. Then he thought that though the rain might indeed fall on the just and unjust alike, it was unthinkable that God would allow decent men who fought in a noble cause to lose. That was a comforting reflection. 'Doesn't Beccaria have strange ideas?' he asked.

'He believes judicial execution is both wrong and ineffective, sir.'

'Really?'

'He argues the case cogently, sir.'

'He'll need to!'

They ate, and afterwards walked the few paces to the harbour where the ships' masts made a forest. Wadsworth looked for the sloop that would carry him to battle, but he could not make the *Sally* out amongst the tangle of hulls and masts and rigging. A gull cried overhead, a dog ran along the wharf with

71

a cod's head in its mouth and a legless beggar shuffled towards him. 'Wounded at Saratoga, sir,' the beggar said and Wadsworth handed the man a shilling.

'Can I hail you a boat, sir?' Dennis asked.

'That would be kind.'

Peleg Wadsworth gazed at the fleet and remembered his morning prayers. There was so much confidence in Boston, so much hope and so many expectations, but war, he knew from experience, truly was the devil's business.

And it was time to go to war.

'This is not seemly,' Doctor Calef said.

Brigadier McLean, standing beside the doctor, ignored the protest.

'It is not seemly!' Calef said louder.

'It is necessary,' Brigadier McLean retorted in a tone harsh enough to startle the doctor. The troops had worshipped in the open air that Sunday morning, the Scottish voices singing strongly in the blustery wind that fetched slaps of rain to dapple the harbour. The Reverend Campbell, the 82nd's chaplain, had preached from a text in Isaiah: 'In that day the Lord with his sore and great and strong sword shall punish Leviathan,' a text that McLean accepted was relevant, but he wondered whether he had a sword strong and great and sore enough to punish the troops he knew would surely come to dislodge him. The rain was falling more steadily now, drenching the ridgetop where the fort was being made and where the two regiments paraded in a hollow square. 'These men are new to war,' McLean explained to Calef, 'and most have never seen a battle, so they need to learn the consequences of disobedience.' He walked towards the square's centre where a Saint Andrew's cross had been erected. A young man, stripped to the waist, was tied to the cross with his back exposed to the wind and rain.

A sergeant pushed a folded strip of leather between the

young man's teeth. 'Bite on that, boy, and take your punishment like a man.'

McLean raised his voice so that every soldier could hear him. 'Private Macintosh attempted to desert. In so doing he broke his oath to his king, to his country and to God. For that he will be punished, as will any man here who tries to follow his example.'

'I don't care if he's punished,' Calef said when the brigadier rejoined him, 'but must it be done on the Lord's day? Can it not wait till tomorrow?'

'No,' McLean said, 'it cannot.' He nodded to the sergeant. 'Do your duty.'

Two drummer boys would do the whipping while a third beat the strokes on his drum. Private Macintosh had been caught trying to sneak across the low, marshy neck that joined Majabigwaduce to the mainland. That was the only route off the peninsula, unless a man stole a boat or, at a pinch, swam across the harbour, and McLean had placed a picquet in the trees close to the neck. They had brought Macintosh back and he had been sentenced to two hundred lashes, the severest punishment McLean had ever ordered, but he had few enough men as it was and he needed to deter others from desertion.

Desertion was a problem. Most men were content enough, but there were always a few who saw the promise of a better existence in the vastness of North America. Life here was a great deal easier than in the Highlands of Scotland, and Macintosh had made his run and now he would be punished.

'One!' the sergeant called.

'Lay it on hard,' McLean told the two drummer boys, 'you're not here to tickle him.'

'Two!'

McLean let his mind wander as the leather whips criss-crossed the man's back. He had seen many floggings in his years of service, and had ordered executions too, because floggings and executions were the enforcers of duty. He saw many of the soldiers staring aghast at the sight, so the punishment was probably working. McLean did not enjoy punishment parades, no one in his right mind would, but they were unavoidable and, with luck, Macintosh would reform into a decent soldier.

And what Leviathan, McLean wondered, would Macintosh have to fight? A schooner captained by a loyalist had put into Majabigwaduce a week before with a report that the rebels in Boston were assembling a fleet and an army. 'We were told there were forty or more ships coming your way, sir,' the schooner's captain had told him, 'and they're gathering upwards of three thousand men.'

Maybe that was true and maybe not. The schooner's captain had not visited Boston, just heard a rumour in Nantucket, and rumour, McLean knew, could inflate a company into a battalion and a battalion into an army. Nevertheless he had taken the information seriously enough to send the schooner back southwards with a despatch to Sir Henry Clinton in New York. The despatch merely said that McLean expected to be attacked soon and could not hold out without reinforcements. Why, he wondered, had he been given so few men and ships? If the crown wanted this piece of country, then why not send an adequate force? 'Thirty-eight!' the sergeant shouted. There was blood on Macintosh's back now, blood diluted by rain, but still enough blood to trickle down and darken the waistband of his kilt. 'Thirty-nine,' the sergeant bellowed, 'and lay it on hard!'

McLean resented the time this punishment parade stole from his preparations. He knew time was short and the fort was nowhere near completed. The trench about the four walls was scarcely two feet deep, the ramparts themselves not much higher. It was an excuse for a fort, a pathetic little earthwork, and he needed both men and time. He had offered wages to any civilian who was willing to work and, when insufficient men came forward, he sent patrols to impress labour.

'Sixty-one!' the sergeant shouted. Macintosh was whimpering now, the sound stifled by the leather gag. He shifted his weight and blood squelched in one shoe, then spilt over the shoe's edge.

'He'll not take much more,' Calef growled. Calef was replacing the battalion surgeon who was sick with a fever.

'Keep going!' McLean said.

'You want to kill him?'

'I want the battalion,' McLean said, 'to be more frightened of the lash than of the enemy.'

'Sixty-two!' the sergeant shouted.

'Tell me,' McLean suddenly turned on the doctor, 'why is the rumour being spread that I plan to hang any civilian who supports the rebellion?'

Calef looked uncomfortable. He flinched as the whipped man whimpered again, then looked defiantly at the general. 'To persuade such disaffected people to leave the region, of course. You don't want rebels lurking in the woods hereabouts.'

'Nor do I want a reputation as a hangman! We did not come here to persecute folk, but to persuade them to return to their proper allegiance. I would be grateful, Doctor, if a counter-rumour was propagated. That I have no intentions of hanging any man, rebel or not.'

'God's blood, man, I can see bone!' the doctor protested, ignoring McLean's strictures. The whimpers had become moans. McLean saw that the drummer boys were using less strength now, not because their arms were weakening, but out of pity, and neither he nor the sergeant corrected them.

McLean stopped the punishment at a hundred lashes. 'Cut him down, Sergeant,' he ordered, 'and carry him to the doctor's house.' He turned away from the bloody mess on the cross. 'Any of you who follow Macintosh's example will follow him here! Now dismiss the men to their duties.'

The civilians who had volunteered or been conscripted for labour trudged up the hill. One man, tall and gaunt, with wild dark hair and angry eyes pushed his way past McLean's aides to confront the general. 'You will be punished for this!' the man snarled.

'For what?' McLean enquired.

'For working on the Sabbath!' the man said. He towered over McLean. 'In all my days I have never worked on the Sabbath, never! You make me a sinner!'

McLean held his temper. A dozen or so other men had paused and were watching the gaunt man, and McLean suspected they would join the protest and refuse to desecrate a Sunday by working if he yielded. 'So why will you not work on a Sunday, sir?' McLean asked.

'It is the Lord's day, and we are commanded to keep it holy.' The man jabbed a finger at the brigadier, stopping just short of striking McLean's chest. 'It is God's commandment!'

'And Christ commanded that you render unto Caesar the things that are Caesar's,' McLean retorted, 'and today Caesar demands you make a rampart. But I will accommodate you, sir, I will accommodate you by not paying you. Work is paid labour, but today you will freely offer me your assistance which, sir, is a Christian act.'

'I will not . . .' the man began.

'Lieutenant Moore!' McLean raised his blackthorn stick to summon the lieutenant, though the gesture looked threatening and the gaunt man took a backwards step. 'Call back the drummer boys!' McLean called, 'I need another man whipped!' He turned his gaze back to the man. 'You either assist me, sir,' he said quietly, 'or I shall scourge you.'

The tall man glanced at the empty Saint Andrew's cross. 'I shall pray for your destruction,' he promised, but the fire had gone from his voice. He gave McLean a last defiant look, then turned away.

The civilians worked. They raised the wall of the fort another foot by laying logs along the low earthen berm. Some men cut down more trees, opening fields of fire for the fort, while others used picks and shovels to sink a well in the fort's north-eastern bastion. McLean ordered one long spruce trunk to be trimmed and stripped of its bark, then a sailor from the *Albany* attached a small pulley to the narrow end of the trunk and a long line was rove through the pulley's block. A deep hole was hacked in the south-western bastion and the spruce trunk was raised as a flagpole. Soldiers packed the hole with stones and, when the pole was reckoned to be stable, McLean ordered the union flag to be hauled into the damp sky. 'We shall call this place . . . ' he paused as the wind caught the flag and stretched it into the cloud-shrouded daylight. 'Fort George,' McLean said tentatively, as if testing the name. He liked it. 'Fort George,' he announced firmly and took off his hat. 'God save the King!'

Highlanders of the 74th started on a smaller earthwork, a gun emplacement, which they made close to the shore and facing the harbour mouth. The soil was easier near the beach and they swiftly threw up a crescent of earth that they reinforced with stones and logs. Other logs were split to make platforms for the cannon that would face the harbour mouth. A similar battery was being constructed on Cross Island so that an enemy ship, daring the harbour mouth, would face Captain Mowat's three broadsides and artillery fire from the bastions on either side of the entrance.

The rain lifted and fog drifted over the wide river reach. The new flag flew bright above Majabigwaduce, but for how long, McLean wondered, for how long?

Monday dawned fine in Boston. The wind came from the south west and the sky was clear. 'The glass rises,' Commodore Saltonstall announced to General Solomon Lovell on board the Continental frigate *Warren*. 'We shall sail, General.'

'And God grant us a fair voyage and a triumphant return,' Lovell answered.

'Amen,' Saltonstall said grudgingly, then snapped out orders

77

that signals should be made ordering the fleet to raise anchor and follow the flagship out of the harbour.

Solomon Lovell, almost fifty years old, towered over the Commodore. Lovell was a farmer, a legislator and a patriot, and it was reckoned in Massachusetts that Solomon Lovell had been well named for he enjoyed a reputation as a wise, judicious and sensible man. His neighbours in Weymouth had elected him to the Assembly in Boston where he was well-liked because, in a fractious legislature, Lovell was a peace-maker. He possessed an unquenchable optimism that fairness and the willingness to see another man's point of view would bring mutual prosperity, while his height and strong build, the latter earned by years of hard labour on his farm, added to the impression of utter dependability. His face was long and firm-jawed, while his eyes crinkled with easy amusement. His thick dark hair greyed at the temples, giving him a most distinguished appearance, and so it was no wonder that his fellow lawmakers had seen fit to give Solomon Lovell high rank in the Massachusetts Militia. Lovell, they reckoned, could be trusted. A few malcontents grumbled that his military experience was next to nothing, but Lovell's supporters, and they were many, believed Solomon Lovell was just the man for the task. He got things done. And his lack of experience was offset by his deputy, Peleg Wadsworth, who had fought under General Washington's command, and by Commodore Saltonstall, the naval commander, who was an even more experienced officer. Lovell would never be short of expert advice to hone his solid judgement.

The great anchor cable inched on board. The sailors at the capstan were chanting as they tramped round and round. 'Here's a rope!' a bosun shouted.

'To hang the Pope!' the men responded.

'And a chunk of cheese!'

'To choke him!'

Lovell smiled approvingly, then strolled to the stern rail

78

where he stared at the fleet, marvelling that Massachusetts had assembled so many ships so quickly. Lying closest to the *Warren* was a brig, the *Diligent*, that had been captured from Britain's Royal Navy, and beyond her was a sloop, the *Providence*, which had captured her, both vessels with twelve guns and both belonging to the Continental Navy. Anchored behind them, and flying the pine-tree flag of the Massachusetts Navy, were two brigs, the *Tyrannicide* and *Hazard*, and a brigantine, the *Active*. All were armed with fourteen cannon and, like the *Warren*, were now fully manned because the General Court and the Board of War had given permission for press gangs to take sailors from Boston's taverns and from merchant vessels in the harbour.

The *Warren*, with its eighteen-pounder and twelve-pounder cannon, was the most powerful ship in the fleet, but a further seven ships could all match or outgun any one of the three British sloops that were reported to be waiting at Majabigwaduce. Those seven ships were all privateers. The *Hector* and the *Hunter* carried eighteen guns apiece, while *Charming Sally*, *General Putnam*, *Black Prince*, *Monmouth* and *Vengeance* carried twenty guns each. There were smaller privateers too, like the *Sky Rocket* with her sixteen guns. In all, eighteen warships would sail to Majabigwaduce and those vessels mounted more than three hundred cannon, while the twenty-one transport ships would carry the men, the supplies, the guns and the fervent hopes of Massachusetts. Lovell was proud of his state. It had made up the deficiencies in the supplies, and the ships now carried enough food to feed sixteen hundred men for two months. Why, there were six tons of flour alone! Six tons!

Lovell, thinking of the extraordinary efforts that had been made to provision the expedition, slowly became aware that men were shouting at the *Warren* from other ships. The anchor was still not raised, but the bosun ordered the seamen to stop their chant and their work. It seemed the fleet would not leave after all. Commodore Saltonstall, who had been standing by the frigate's wheel, turned and paced back to Lovell. 'It appears,' the commodore said sourly, 'that the commander of your artillery is not aboard his ship.'

'He must be,' Lovell said.

'Must?'

'The orders were plain. Officers were to be aboard last night.'

'The *Samuel* reports that Colonel Revere is not on board. So what shall we do, General?'

Lovell was startled by the question. He had thought he was being given information, not being asked to make a decision. He stared across the sun-sparkling water as though the distant *Samuel*, a brig that was carrying the expedition's cannon, might suggest an answer.

'Well?' Saltonstall pressed, 'do we sail without him and his officers?'

'His officers?' Lovell asked.

'It transpires,' Saltonstall appeared to relish delivering the bad news, 'that Colonel Revere allowed his officers to spend a last night ashore.'

'Ashore?' Lovell asked, astonished, then stared again at the distant brig. 'We need Colonel Revere,' he said.

'We do?' Saltonstall asked sarcastically.

'Oh, a good officer!' Lovell said enthusiastically. 'He was one of the men who rode to warn Concord and Lexington. Doctor Warren, God rest his soul, sent them, and this ship is named for Doctor Warren, is it not?'

'Is it?' Saltonstall asked carelessly.

'A very great patriot, Doctor Warren,' Lovell said feelingly.

'And how does that affect Colonel Revere's absence?' Saltonstall asked bluntly.

'It,' Lovell began and realized he had no idea what he could answer, and so he straightened and squared his shoulders. 'We shall wait,' he announced firmly.

'We shall wait!' Saltonstall called to his officers. He began pacing his quarter-deck again, starboard to larboard and larboard to starboard, occasionally shooting a malevolent look at Lovell as though the general were personally responsible for the missing officer. Lovell found the commodore's hostility uncomfortable and so turned to stare at the fleet again. Many ships had loosed their topsails and men now scrambled along the yards to furl the canvas.

'General Lovell?' a new voice disturbed him and Lovell turned to see a tall marine officer whose sudden presence made the general take an involuntary step backwards. There was an intensity in the marine's face, and a ferocity, that made the face formidable. Just to see this man was to be impressed. He was even taller than Lovell, who was not a short man, and he had broad shoulders that strained the green cloth of his uniform jacket. He was holding his hat respectfully, revealing black hair that was cropped short over most of his scalp, but that he had allowed to grow long at the back so he could wear a short pigtail that was hardened with tar. 'My name is Welch, sir,' the marine said in a voice deep enough to match his hard face, 'Captain John Welch of the Continental Marines.'

'I'm pleased to make your acquaintance, Captain Welch,' Lovell said, and that was true. If a man must sail into battle then he would pray to have a man like Welch at his side. The hilt of Welch's sabre was worn down by use and, like its owner, seemed made for the efficient use of pure violence.

'I've spoken to the commodore, sir,' Welch said very formally, 'and he gave his consent that my men should be at your disposal when not required for naval duties.'

'That's most encouraging,' Lovell said.

'Two hundred and twenty-seven marines, sir, fit for duty. Good men, sir.'

'I've no doubt.'

'Well-trained,' Welch went on, his unblinking gaze fixed on Lovell's eyes, 'and well-disciplined.'

'A most valuable addition to our force,' Lovell said, unsure what else he could say.

'I want to fight, sir,' Welch said, as if he suspected Lovell might not use his marines.

'I am confident the opportunity will come,' Lovell said uneasily.

'I hope so, sir,' Welch said, then at last turned his gaze away from the general and nodded towards a fine-looking ship, the *General Putnam*, one of four privateers that had been commandeered by the Massachusetts Navy because their owners had baulked at volunteering their craft. The *General Putnam* carried twenty cannons, all of them nine-pounders, and she was reckoned one of the finest ships on the New England coast. 'We put a score of marines on the *Putnam*, sir,' Welch said, 'and they're led by Captain Carnes. You know him, sir?'

'I know John Carnes,' Lovell said, 'he captains the *Hector*.'

'This is his brother, sir, and a fine officer. He served under General Washington as a captain of artillery.'

'A fine posting,' Lovell said, 'yet he left it for the marines?'

'Captain Carnes prefers to see men up close as he kills them, sir,' Welch said evenly, 'but he knows his artillery, sir. He's a very competent gunner.'

Lovell understood immediately that Saltonstall had despatched Welch with the news, implicitly suggesting that Colonel Revere could be left behind and replaced by Captain Carnes, and Lovell bristled at the suggestion. 'We need Colonel Revere and his officers,' he said.

'I never suggested otherwise, sir,' Welch said, 'merely that Captain Carnes has an expertise that might be useful to you.'

Lovell felt acutely uncomfortable. He sensed that Welch had little faith in the militia and was trying to stiffen Lovell's force with the professionalism of his marines, but Lovell was determined that Massachusetts should reap the credit for the expulsion of the British. 'I'm sure Colonel Revere knows his business,' Lovell said stoutly. Welch did not reply to that, but stared at Lovell who again felt disconcerted by the intensity of the gaze. 'Of course, any advice Captain Carnes has . . . ' Lovell said, and let his voice tail away.

'I just wanted you to know we have an artilleryman in the marines, sir,' Welch said, then stepped a pace back and offered Lovell a salute.

'Thank you, Captain,' Lovell said, and felt relieved when the huge marine strode away.

The minutes passed. The church clocks in Boston struck the hour, the quarters and then the hour again. Major William Todd, one of the expedition's two brigade majors, brought the general a mug of tea. 'Newly made in the galley, sir.'

'Thank you.'

'The leaves captured by the brig *King-Killer*, sir,' Todd said, sipping his own tea.

'It's kind of the enemy to supply us with tea,' Lovell said lightly.

'Indeed it is, sir,' Todd said and then, after a pause, 'So Mister Revere is delaying us?'

Lovell knew of the antipathy between Todd and Revere and did his best to defuse whatever was in the major's mind. Todd was a good man, meticulous and hard-working, but somewhat unbending. 'I'm sure Lieutenant-Colonel Revere has very good cause to be absent,' he said firmly.

'He always does,' Todd said. 'In all the time he commanded Castle Island I doubt he spent a single night there. Mister Revere, sir, likes the comfort of his wife's bed.'

'Don't we all?'

Todd brushed a speck of lint from his blue uniform coat. 'He told General Wadsworth that he supplied rations for Major Fellows' men.'

'I'm certain he had cause for that.'

'Fellows died of the fever last August,' Todd then stepped a pace back in deference to the approach of the commodore.

Saltonstall glowered again at Lovell from beneath the peak of his cocked hat. 'If your damned fellow isn't coming,' Saltonstall said, 'then perhaps we might be allowed to get on with this damned war without him?'

'I'm sure Colonel Revere will be here very soon,' Lovell said emolliently, 'or we shall receive news of him. A messenger has been sent ashore, Commodore.'

Saltonstall grunted and walked away. Major Todd frowned at the retreating commodore. 'He takes after his mother's side of the family, I think. The Saltonstalls are usually most agreeable folk.'

Lovell was saved from responding by a hail from the brig *Diligent*. Colonel Revere, it seemed, had been sighted. He and three other officers were being rowed in the smart white-painted barge that served Castle Island, and the sternsheets of the barge, which was being rowed by a dozen blue-shirted men, were heaped high with baggage. Colonel Revere sat just forrard of the baggage and, as the barge came close to the *Warren* on its way to the brig *Samuel*, Revere waved up at Lovell. 'God speed us, General!' he shouted.

'Where have you been?' Lovell called sharply.

'A last night with the family, General!' Revere shouted happily, and then was out of earshot.

'A last night with the family?' Todd asked in wonderment.

'He must have misunderstood my orders,' Lovell said uncomfortably.

'I think you will discover, sir,' Todd said, 'that Colonel Revere misunderstands all orders that are not to his liking.'

'He's a patriot, Major,' Lovell reproved, 'a fine patriot!'

It took more time for the fine patriot's baggage to be hoisted aboard the brig, then the barge itself had to be readied for the voyage. It seemed Colonel Revere wished the Castle Island barge to be part of his equipment, for her oars were lashed to the thwarts and then she was attached by a towline to the *Samuel*. Then, at last, as the sun climbed to its height, the fleet was ready. The capstans turned again, the great anchors broke free and, with their sails bright in the summer sun, the might of Massachusetts sailed from Boston harbour.

To captivate, to kill and to destroy.

Lieutenant John Moore sat astride a camp stool, his legs either side of an empty powder barrel that served as a table. A tent sheltered him from a blustery west wind that brought spits of rain to patter hard on the yellowed canvas. Moore's job as paymaster for the 82nd Regiment bored him, even though the detailed work was done by Corporal Brown who had been a clerk in a Leith counting-house before becoming drunk one morning and so volunteering for the army. Moore turned the pages of the black-bound ledger that recorded the regiment's wages. 'Why is Private Neill having fourpence a week deducted?' Moore asked the corporal.

'Lost his boot-blacking, sir.'

'Boot-blacking cannot cost that much, surely?'

'Expensive stuff, sir,' Corporal Brown said.

'Plainly. I should buy some and resell it to the regiment.'

'Major Fraser wouldn't like that, sir, on account that his brother already does.'

Moore sighed and turned another stiff page of the thick paybook. He was supposed to check the figures, but he knew Corporal Brown would have done a meticulous job, so instead he stared out of the tent's open flaps to the western rampart of Fort George where some gunners were making a platform for one of their cannon. The rampart was still only waist high, though the ditch beyond was now lined with wooden spikes that were more formidable to look at than negotiate. Beyond the rampart was a long stretch of cleared ground studded with raw pine stumps. That land climbed gently to the peninsula's bluff where trees still stood thick and where tendrils of fog drifted through dark branches. Corporal Brown saw where Moore was looking. 'Can I ask you something, sir?'

'Whatever enters your head, Brown.'

The corporal nodded towards the timbered bluff that was little more than half a mile from the fort. 'Why didn't the brigadier make the fort there, sir?'

'You would have done so, Corporal, if you had command here?'

'It's the highest piece of land, sir. Isn't that where you make a fort?'

Moore frowned, not because he disapproved of the question, which, he thought, was an eminently sensible enquiry, but because he did not know how to frame the answer. To Moore it was obvious why McLean had chosen the lower position. It was to do with the interlocking of the ships' guns and the fort's cannon, with making the best of a difficult job, but though he knew the answer, he did not quite know how to express it. 'From here,' he said, 'our guns command both the harbour entrance and the harbour itself. Suppose we were all up on that high ground? The enemy could sail past us, take the harbour and village, and then starve us out at their leisure.'

'But if the bastards take that high ground, sir . . . ' Brown said dubiously, leaving the thought unfinished.

'If the bastards seize that high ground, Corporal,' Moore said, 'then they will place cannon there and fire down into the fort.' That was the risk McLean had taken. He had given the enemy the chance to take the high ground, but only so that he could do his job better, which was to defend the harbour. 'We don't have enough men,' Moore went on, 'to defend the bluff, but I can't think they'll land men there. It's much too steep.'

Yet the rebels would land somewhere. By leaning forward on his makeshift stool Moore could just make out the three sloops of war anchored in line across the harbour mouth. General McLean had suggested the enemy might try to attack that line, break it, and then land men on the beach below

86

the fort and Moore tried to imagine such a fight. He tried to turn the wisps of fog into powder smoke, but his imagination failed. The eighteen-year-old John Moore had never experienced battle, and every day he wondered how he would respond to the smell of powder and the screams of the wounded and the chaos.

'Lady approaching, sir,' Corporal Brown warned Moore.

'Lady?' Moore asked, startled from his reverie, then saw that Bethany Fletcher was approaching the tent. He stood and ducked under the tent flap to greet her, but the sight of her face tied his tongue, so he simply stood there, awkward, hat in hand, smiling.

'Lieutenant Moore,' Bethany said, stopping a pace away.

'Miss Fletcher,' Moore managed to speak, 'as ever, a pleasure.' He bowed.

'I was told to give you this, sir.' Bethany held out a slip of paper.

The paper was a receipt for corn and fish that James Fletcher had sold to the quartermaster. 'Four shillings!' Moore said.

'The quartermaster said you'd pay me, sir,' Bethany said.

'If Mister Reidhead so orders, then I shall obey. And it will be my pleasure to pay you, Miss Fletcher,' Moore said. He looked at the receipt again. 'It must have been a rare quantity of corn and fish! Four shillings' worth!'

Bethany bridled. 'It was Mister Reidhead who decided the amount, sir.'

'Oh, I am not suggesting that the amount is excessive,' Moore said, reddening. If he lost his composure when faced by a girl, he thought, how would he ever face the enemy? 'Corporal Brown!'

'Sir?'

'Four shillings for the lady!'

'At once, sir,' Brown said, coming from the tent, though instead of holding coins he brought a hammer and a chisel that he took to a nearby block of wood. He had one silver dollar that he laid on the timber, then he carefully placed the chisel's blade to make a single radial cut in the coin. The hammer smacked down and the coin leaped up from the chisel's bite. 'It's daft, sir, to slit a coin into five pieces,' Brown grumbled, replacing the dollar. 'Why can't we make four pieces worth one shilling and threepence each?'

'Because it's easier to cut a coin into four parts rather than five?' Moore asked.

'Of course it is, sir. Cutting into four only needs a wide chisel blade and two cuts,' Brown grumbled, then hammered another cut into the dollar, slicing away a wedge of silver that he pushed across the chopping block towards Bethany. 'There, miss, one shilling.'

Bethany took the sharp-edged slice. 'Is this how you pay the soldiers?' she asked Moore.

'Oh, we don't get paid, miss,' Corporal Brown answered, 'except in promissory notes.'

'Give Miss Fletcher the remainder of the coin,' Moore suggested, 'and she will have her four shillings and you need cut no more.' There was a shortage of coinage so the brigadier had decreed that each silver dollar was worth five shillings. 'Stop staring!' Moore called sharply to the gunners who had paused in their work to admire Beth Fletcher. Moore picked up the ravaged dollar and held it out to Bethany. 'There Miss Fletcher, your fee.'

'Thank you, sir.' Bethany put the shilling slice back on the block. 'So how many promissory notes do you have to write each week?' she asked.

'How many?' Moore was momentarily puzzled by the question. 'Oh, we don't issue notes as such, Miss Fletcher, but we do record in the ledger what wages are owed. The specie is kept for more important duties, like paying you for corn and fish.'

'And you must need a lot of corn and fish for two whole regiments,' she said. 'What is that? Two thousand men?'

'If only we were so numerous,' Moore said with a smile. 'In truth, Miss Fletcher, the 74th musters just four hundred and forty men and we Hamiltons number scarce half that. And we hear now that the rebels are readying a fleet and an army to assail us!'

'And you think that report is true?' Bethany asked.

'The fleet, perhaps, is already on its way.'

Bethany stared past the three sloops to where wisps of mist drifted across the wide Penobscot River. 'I pray, sir,' she said, 'that there will be no fighting.'

'And I pray otherwise,' Moore said.

'Really?' Bethany sounded surprised. She turned to look at the young lieutenant as if she had never really noticed him before. 'You want there to be a battle?'

'Soldiering is my chosen profession, Miss Fletcher,' Moore said, and felt very fraudulent as he said it, 'and battle is the fire in which soldiers are tempered.'

'The world would be better without such fire,' Bethany said.

'True, no doubt,' Moore said, 'but we did not strike the flint on the iron, Miss Fletcher. The rebels did that, they set the fire and our task is to extinguish the flame.' Bethany said nothing, and Moore decided he had sounded pompous. 'You and your brother should come to Doctor Calef's house in the evening,' he said.

'We should, sir?' Bethany asked, looking again at Moore.

'There is music in the garden when the weather permits, and dancing.'

'I don't dance, sir,' Bethany said.

'Oh, it is the officers who dance,' Moore said hastily, 'the sword dance.' He suppressed an urge to demonstrate a capering step. 'You would be most welcome,' he said instead.

'Thank you, sir,' Bethany said, then pocketed the ravaged dollar and turned away.

'Miss Fletcher!' Moore called after her.

She turned back. 'Sir?'

But Moore had no idea what to say, indeed he had surprised himself by calling after her in the first place. She was gazing at him, waiting. 'Thank you for the supplies,' he managed to say.

'It is business, Lieutenant,' Beth said evenly.

'Even so, thank you,' Moore said, confused.

'Does that mean you'd sell to the Yankees too, miss?' Corporal Brown asked cheerfully.

'We might give to them,' Beth said, and Moore could not tell whether she was teasing or not. She looked at him, gave a half-smile and walked away.

'A rare good-looking lassie,' Corporal Brown said.

'Is she?' Moore asked most unconvincingly. He was gazing down the slope to where the settlement's houses were spread along the harbour shore. He tried to imagine men fighting there, ranks of men blasting musket fire, the cannons thundering the sky with noise, the harbour filled with half-sunken ships, and he thought how sad it would be to die amidst that chaos without ever having held a girl like Bethany in his arms.

'Are we finished with the ledgers, sir?' Brown asked.

'We are finished with the ledgers,' Moore said.

He wondered if he really was a soldier. He wondered if he would have the courage to face battle. He stared after Bethany and felt lost.

'Reluctance, sir, reluctance. Gross reluctance,' Colonel Jonathan Mitchell, who commanded the Cumberland County militia, glared at Brigadier-General Peleg Wadsworth as though it was all Wadsworth's fault. 'Culpable reluctance.'

'You conscripted?' Wadsworth asked.

'Of course we goddamn conscripted. We had to conscript! Half the reluctant bastards are conscripted. We didn't get volunteers, just whining excuses, so we declared martial law, sir, and I sent troops to every township and rounded the bastards up, but too many ran and skulked, sir. They are reluctant, I tell you, reluctant!'

It had taken the fleet two days to sail to Townsend where the militia had been ordered to muster. General Lovell and Brigadier-General Wadsworth had been hoping for fifteen hundred men, but fewer than nine hundred waited for embarkation. 'Eight hundred and ninety-four, sir, to be precise,' Marston, Lovell's secretary, informed his master.

'Dear God,' Lovell said.

'It surely isn't too late to request a Continental battalion?' Wadsworth suggested.

'Unthinkable,' Lovell said instantly. The State of Massachusetts had declared itself capable of ejecting the British on its own, and the General Court would not look happily on a request for help from General Washington's troops. The Court, indeed, had been reluctant to accept Commodore Saltonstall's aid, except that the *Warren* was so obviously a formidable warship and to ignore its presence in Massachusetts waters would have been perverse. 'We do have the commodore's marines,' Lovell pointed out, 'and I'm assured the commodore will willingly release them to land service at Majabigwaduce.'

'We shall need them,' Wadsworth said. He had inspected the three militia battalions and had been appalled by what he found. Some men looked fit, young and eager, but far too many were either too old, too young or too sick. One man had even paraded on crutches. 'You can't fight,' Wadsworth had told the man.

'Which is what I told the soldiers when they came to get us,' the man said. He was grey-bearded, gaunt and wild-haired.

'Then go home,' Wadsworth said.

'How?'

'Same way you got here,' Wadsworth had said, despair making him irritable. A few paces down the line he found a curly-haired boy with cheeks that had never felt a razor. 'What's your name, son?' Wadsworth asked.

'Israel, sir.'

'Israel what?'

'Trask, sir.'

'How old are you, Israel Trask?'

'Fifteen, sir,' the boy said, trying to stand straighter. His voice had not broken and Wadsworth guessed he was scarcely fourteen. 'Three years in the army, sir,' Trask said.

'Three years?' Wadsworth asked in disbelief.

'Fifer with the infantry, sir,' Trask said. He had a sackcloth bag hanging at his back and a slender wooden pipe protruded from the bag's neck.

'You resigned from the infantry?' Wadsworth asked, amused.

'I was taken prisoner, sir,' Trask said, evidently offended by the question, 'and exchanged. And here I am, sir, ready to fight the syphilitic bastards again.'

If a boy had used that language in Wadsworth's classroom it would have provoked a caning, but these were strange times and so Wadsworth just patted the boy's shoulder before walking on down the long line. Some men looked at him resentfully and he supposed they were the men who had been pressed by the militia. Maybe two thirds looked healthy and young enough for soldiering, but the rest were miserable specimens. 'I thought you had a thousand men enrolled in Cumberland County alone?' Wadsworth remarked to Colonel Mitchell.

'Ha,' Mitchell said.

'Ha?' Wadsworth responded coldly.

'The Continental Army takes our best. We find a dozen decent recruits and the Continentals take six away and the other six run off to join the privateers.' Mitchell put a plug of tobacco in his mouth. 'I wish to God we had a thousand, but Boston doesn't send their wages and we don't have rations. And there are some places we can't recruit.'

'Loyalist places?'

'Loyalist places,' Mitchell had agreed grimly.

Wadsworth had walked on down the line, noting a one-eyed man who had some kind of nervous affliction that made his facial muscles quiver. The man grinned, and Wadsworth shuddered. 'Does he have his senses?' he asked Colonel Mitchell.

'Enough to shoot straight,' Mitchell said dourly.

'Half don't even have muskets!'

The fleet had brought five hundred muskets from the Boston Armory that would be rented to the militia. Most men at least knew how to use them because in these eastern counties folk expected to kill their own food and to skin the prey for clothing. They wore deerskin jerkins and trousers, deerskin shoes and carried deerskin pouches and packs. Wadsworth inspected them all and reckoned he would be lucky if five hundred would prove useful men, then he borrowed a horse from the parson and gave them a speech from the saddle.

'The British,' he called, 'have invaded Massachusetts! They must despise us, because they have sent few men and few ships! They believe we are powerless to evict them, but we are going to show them that Massachusetts men will defend their land! We will embark on our fleet!' He waved towards the masts showing above the southern rooftops. 'And we shall fight them, we shall defeat them and we shall evict them! You will return home with laurels on your brows!' It was not the most inspiring speech, Wadsworth thought, but he was encouraged when men cheered it. The cheer was late in starting, and it was feeble at first, but then the paraded ranks became enthusiastic.

The parson, a genial man about ten years older than Wadsworth, helped the brigadier down from the saddle. 'I trust they will have laurels on their brows,' the parson said, 'but most would prefer beefsteak in their stomachs.'

93

'I trust they find that as well,' Wadsworth said.

The Reverend Jonathan Murray took the horse's reins and led it towards his house. 'They may not look impressive, General, but they're good men!'

'Who needed pressing?' Wadsworth enquired drily.

'Only a few,' Murray answered. 'They worry about their families, their crops. Get them to Majabigwaduce and they'll serve willingly enough.'

'The blind, the halt and the lame?'

'Such men were good enough for our Lord,' Murray said, evidently seriously. 'And what if a few are half-blind? A man needs only one eye to aim a musket.'

General Lovell had quartered himself in the parson's ample house and, that evening, he convened all the senior officers of the expedition. Murray possessed a fine round table, made of maple wood, about which he normally led studies of the scripture, but which that night served to accommodate the naval and land commanders. Those who could not find a chair stood at the edges of the room, which was lit by eight candles in pewter sticks, grouped in the table's centre. Moths beat about the flames. General Lovell had taken the parson's high-backed chair and he gently rapped the table for silence. 'This is the first time,' Lovell said, 'that we've all gathered together. You probably all know each other, but permit me to make introductions.' He went around the table, naming Wadsworth first, then Commodore Saltonstall and the three colonels of the militia regiments. Major Jeremiah Hill, the expedition's adjutant-general, nodded solemnly as his name was pronounced, as did the two brigade majors, William Todd and Gawen Brown. The quartermaster, Colonel Tyler, sat next to Doctor Eliphalet Downer, the Surgeon General. 'I trust we won't require Doctor Downer's services,' Lovell said with a smile, then indicated the men who stood at the room's edges. Captain John Welch of the Continental Marines glowered next to Captain Hoysteed

Hacker of the Continental Navy who commanded the *Providence* while Captain Philip Brown commanded the brig *Diligent*. Six privateer captains had come to the house and Lovell named them all, then smiled at Lieutenant-Colonel Revere who stood beside the door. 'And last, but by no means least, our commander of the artillery train, Colonel Revere.'

'Whose services,' Revere said, 'I trust you will require!'

A murmur of laughter sounded in the room, though Wadsworth noticed the look of grim distaste on Todd's bespectacled face. The major glanced once at Revere, then studiously avoided looking at his enemy.

'I also requested the Reverend Murray to attend this council,' Lovell went on when the small laughter had subsided, 'and I now ask him to open our proceedings with a word of prayer.'

Men clasped their hands and bowed their heads as Murray entreated Almighty God to pour His blessings on the men and ships now assembled in Townsend. Wadsworth had his head bowed, but sneaked a sidelong look at Revere who, he noticed, had not lowered his head, but was staring balefully towards Todd. Wadsworth closed his eyes again. 'Give these men of Thy strength, Lord,' the Reverend Murray prayed, 'and bring these warriors safe home, victorious, to their wives, and to their children and to their families. We ask all this in Thy holy name, O Lord. Amen.'

'Amen,' the assembled officers echoed.

'Thank you, Reverend,' Lovell said, smiling happily. He took a breath and looked about the room, then stated the reason they were gathered together. 'The British have landed at Majabigwaduce, as you know, and our orders are to captivate, kill or destroy them. Major Todd, perhaps you will be good enough to tell us what we know of the enemy's dispositions?'

William Todd, his spectacles reflecting the candlelight, shuffled papers. 'We have received intelligence,' he said in his dry voice, 'from patriots in the Penobscot region. Notably

95

from Colonel Buck, but from others too. We know for certain that a considerable force of the enemy has landed, that they are guarded by three sloops of war, and that they are commanded by Brigadier-General Francis McLean.' Todd studied the earnest faces around the table. 'McLean,' he went on, 'is an experienced soldier. Most of his service was in the Portuguese employment.'

'A mercenary?' Commodore Saltonstall asked in a voice that reeked of scorn.

'I understand he was seconded to Portuguese service by the King of England,' Todd said, 'so no, not a mercenary. Of late he has been Governor of Halifax and is now entrusted with the forces at Majabigwaduce. My apprehension of him,' Todd leaned back as if to suggest that he was speculating now, 'is that he is an old man who was put out to pasture at Halifax and whose best days are, perhaps, behind him.' He shrugged as if to express uncertainty. 'He leads two regiments, neither of which has seen recent service. Indeed, his own regiment is newly raised and is therefore entirely inexperienced. The notional complement of a British regiment is one thousand men, but rarely do the real numbers exceed eight hundred, so a reasonable calculation suggests that our enemy comprises fifteen or sixteen hundred infantry with artillery support and, of course, the Royal Marines and the crews of the three ships.' Todd unrolled a large sheet of paper on which was drawn a crude map of Majabigwaduce and, as the men craned forward to see the plan, he showed where the defences were situated. He began with the fort, marked as a square. 'As of Wednesday,' he said, 'the walls were still low enough for a man to jump. The work goes slowly, we hear.' He tapped the three sloops that formed a barrier just inside the harbour entrance. 'Their broadsides face Penobscot Bay,' he said, 'and are supported by land batteries. There is one such battery here,' he pointed to Cross Island, 'and another on the peninsula here. Those two batteries will enfilade the harbour entrance.'

'None on Dyce's Head?' Hoysteed Hacker asked.

'Dyce's Head?' Lovell asked, and Hacker, who knew the coast well, pointed to the harbour's southern side and explained that the entrance was dominated by a high bluff that bore the name Dyce's Head. 'If I recall rightly,' Hacker went on, 'that ground is the highest on the whole peninsula.'

'We have not been informed of any batteries on Dyce's Head,' Todd said carefully.

'So they've surrendered the high ground?' Wadsworth asked in disbelief.

'Our information is some days old,' Todd warned.

'High ground,' Lovell said uncertainly, 'will be a splendid place for our guns.'

'Oh indeed,' Wadsworth said, and Lovell looked relieved.

'My guns will be ready,' Revere said belligerently.

Lovell smiled at Revere. 'Perhaps you will be good enough to tell our militia colonels what artillery support you will offer them?'

Revere straightened and William Todd stared fixedly at the table top. 'I have six eighteen-pounder cannon,' Revere said robustly, 'with four hundred rounds apiece. They're killers, gentlemen, and heavier than any guns I daresay the British have waiting for us. I have two nine-pounders with three hundred rounds apiece, and a pair of five-and-half-inch howitzers with one hundred rounds each.' John Welch looked startled at that, then frowned. He began to say something, but checked his words before they became intelligible.

'You had something to say, Captain?' Wadsworth interrupted Revere.

The tall marine in his dark green uniform was still frowning. 'If I were bombarding a fort, General,' he said, 'I'd want more howitzers. Lob bombs over the wall and kill the bastards from the inside. Howitzers and mortars. Do we have mortars?'

'Do we have mortars?' Wadsworth put the question to Revere.

Revere looked offended. 'The eighteen-pounders will topple their walls like the trumpets of Jericho,' he said, 'and to finish,' he looked at Lovell with some indignation as if offended that the general had permitted the interruption, 'we have four four-pounders, two of which are French metal and the equal of any six-pounder.'

Colonel Samuel McCobb, who led the Lincoln County militia, raised a hand. 'We can offer a field-mounted twelve-pounder,' he said.

'Most generous,' Lovell said, and then threw the discussion open, though in truth nothing was decided that evening. For over two hours men made suggestions and Lovell received each one with gratitude, but gave no opinion on any. Commodore Saltonstall agreed that the three British sloops must be destroyed so that his squadron could sail into the harbour and use their broadsides to bombard the fort, but he declined to suggest how soon that could be done. 'We must appraise their defences,' the commodore insisted grandly, 'I'm sure you all appreciate the good sense in a thorough reconnaissance.' He spoke condescendingly as if it offended his dignity as a Continental officer to be dealing with mere militia.

'We all appreciate the value of thorough reconnaissance,' Lovell agreed. He smiled benignly about the room. 'I shall inspect the militia in the morning,' he said, 'and then we shall embark. When we reach the Penobscot River we shall discover what obstacles we face, but I am confident that we shall overcome them. I thank you all, gentlemen, I thank you all.' And with that the council of war was over.

Some men gathered in the darkness outside the parson's house. 'They have fifteen or sixteen hundred men?' a militia officer grumbled, 'and we only have nine hundred?'

'You've also got the marines,' Captain Welch snarled from the shadows, but then, before anyone could respond, a shot sounded. Dogs began barking. Officers clutched their scabbards as they ran towards the lantern lights of Main Street where men were shouting, but no more musket shots sounded.

'What was it?' Lovell asked when the commotion had died down.

'A man from Lincoln County,' Wadsworth said.

'Fired his musket by mistake?'

'Shot off the toes of his left foot.'

'Oh dear, poor man.'

'Deliberately, sir. To avoid service.'

So now one less man would sail east, and too many of the remaining men were boys, cripples or old men. But there were the marines. Thank God, Wadsworth thought, there were the marines.

From a letter by John Brewer, written in 1779 and published in the *Bangor Whig and Courier*, August 13th, 1846:

'I then told the Commodore that . . . I thought that as the wind breezed up he might go in with his shipping, silence the two (sic) vessels and the six gun battery, and land the troops under cover of his own guns, and in half an hour make everything his own. In reply to which he hove up his long chin, and said, 'You seem to be damned knowing about the matter! I am not going to risk my shipping in that damned hole!'

Excerpts of a letter from John Preble to the Honourable Jeremiah Powell, President, Council Board of the State of Massachusetts Bay, July 24th, 1779:

I have been upon Command with the Indians five Weeks there is now there about 60 warriors the greater part firce for War and wait only for Orders to march and assist their Brothers the Americans. The Enemey coudent incurd their displeasure more than comming on their River or near it to fourtify they have declared to me they would Spil Every drop of their Blood in defence of their Land and Liberty they seem to be more and more Sensible of the diabollical intentions of the Enemy and the Justness of our Cause . . . This moment the Fleet appears in Sight which gives unival Joy to White and Black Soldiers Every one is Antious and desirious for action and I can acquaint your Honours that on my passage here in a burch Canoe the people at Naskeeg and up a long shore declared they were Ready . . . to fight for us altho they had taken the Oath of Fidelity to the British party.

FOUR

The fleet sailed eastwards, driven by a brisk south-westerly, though the privateers and naval ships, which were the quickest, had to shorten sail so that they did not out-race the lumbering transports. It took only a day's sailing to reach the Penobscot River, though it was a long day, dawn to dusk, that was livened when a strange sail was seen to the southward. Commodore Saltonstall ordered the *Hazard* and the *Diligent*, both brigantines and both fast sailors, to investigate the stranger. Saltonstall stayed inshore while the two brigs crammed on more sail and raced away southwards, leaving the fleet to creep up the coast past rocky headlands where the great seas broke white. Every few moments a thump would echo through a ship as her bows struck an errant tree trunk that had been floated down one of the rivers and had escaped the loggers at the river's mouth.

This was Commodore Saltonstall's first voyage in the *Warren* and he fussed over her trim, ordering ballast moved forrard to improve her performance. He twice ordered more sails set and let the frigate run at her full speed through the fleet. 'How is she?' he asked the helmsman during the second run and after Midshipman Fanning had supervised moving another half ton of ballast from the stern.

'She isn't bridling as much, sir. I reckon you tamed her.'

'Seven knots and a handful!' a seaman who had trailed a log line from the taffrail called. Men on the transport ships cheered at the fine sight of the frigate charging under full sail through the fleet.

'We might have tamed her upwind,' Saltonstall said wearily, 'but I dare say she'll need trimming again before she goes close.'

'I dare say she will, sir,' the helmsman agreed. He was an elderly man, barrel-chested, with long white hair twisted into a pigtail that reached his waist. His bare forearms were smothered with tattoos of fouled anchors and crowns, evidence that he had once sailed in Britain's Navy. He let go of the wheel, which spun clockwise, then checked itself and moved slowly back. 'See, sir? She's well liking it.'

'As I am,' Saltonstall said, 'but we can do better. Mister Coningsby! Another two hundred weight forrard! Lively now!'

'Aye aye, sir,' Midshipman Fanning said.

The *Hazard* and *Diligent* caught up with the fleet late in the afternoon. The *Diligent* shortened her sails as she slid to the leeward of the *Warren* and made her report on the strange sail that had been glimpsed to the south, 'She was the *General Glover* out of Marblehead, sir!' Captain Philip Brown hailed Saltonstall. 'A cargo vessel, sir, carrying baccy, rum and timber to France!'

'Take station!' Saltonstall shouted back and watched as the brig fell aft of him. Captain Brown, newly appointed to his command, had been First Lieutenant of the sloop *Providence* when it had captured the *Diligent* from the Royal Navy and his ship still bore the marks of that battle. Brown's old ship, the *Providence*, her hull similarly patched with new timber, now sailed at the van of Saltonstall's fleet where she flew the snake and stripe banner of the rebel navy.

The fleet was impressive, and had been joined by three more ships that had sailed direct to Townsend so that forty-two vessels, half of them warships, now sailed eastwards. Brigadier-General Lovell, gazing at the spread of sails from the afterdeck of the sloop *Sally*, was proud that his state, his country indeed, could assemble such a number of ships. The *Warren* was the largest, but a dozen other warships were almost as formidable as the frigate. The *Hampden*, which carried twenty-two guns and was thus the second most powerful ship in the fleet, had been sent by the state of New Hampshire and when she had arrived at Townsend she had sounded a salute, her nine-pounder guns thumping the air with their percussive greeting. 'I just wish we could encounter one of King George's ships now,' Solomon Lovell said, ''pon my word, but we'd give her a pounding!'

'So we would, by God's grace, so we would indeed!' the Reverend Jonathan Murray agreed wholeheartedly. Peleg Wadsworth had been somewhat surprised that the rector of Townsend had been invited to join the expedition, but it was evident that Murray and Lovell liked each other, and so the clergyman, who had appeared on board the *Sally* with a brace of large pistols belted at his waist, was now the expedition's chaplain. Lovell had insisted that they sail from Townsend in the sloop *Sally*, rather than in Saltonstall's larger frigate. 'It's better to be with the men, don't you think?' the brigadier enquired of Wadsworth.

'Indeed, sir,' Wadsworth agreed, though privately he suspected that Solomon Lovell found Commodore Saltonstall's company difficult. Lovell was a gregarious man while Saltonstall was reticent to the point of rudeness. 'Though the men do worry me, sir,' Wadsworth added.

'They worry you!' Lovell responded jovially. 'Now why should that be?' He had borrowed Captain Carver's telescope and was gazing seawards at Monhegan Island.

Wadsworth hesitated, not wanting to introduce a note of pessimism on a morning of bright sun and useful wind. 'We were expecting fifteen or sixteen hundred men, sir, and we have fewer than nine hundred. And many of those are of dubious usefulness.'

The Reverend Murray, clutching a wide-brimmed hat, made a gesture as if to suggest Wadsworth's concerns were misplaced. 'Let me tell you something I've learned,' the reverend said, 'in every endeavour, General Wadsworth, whenever men are gathered together for God's good purpose, there is always a core of men, just a core, that do the work! The rest merely watch.'

'We have enough men,' Lovell said, collapsing the telescope and turning to Wadsworth, 'which isn't to say I could not wish for more, but we have enough. We have ships enough and God is on our side!'

'Amen,' the Reverend Murray put in, 'and we have you, General!' He bowed to Lovell.

'Oh, you're too kind,' Lovell said, embarrassed.

'God in His infinite wisdom selects His instruments,' Murray said effusively, bowing a second time to Lovell.

'And God, I am sure, will send more men to join us,' Lovell went on hurriedly. 'I'm assured there are avid patriots in the Penobscot region, and I doubt not that they'll serve our cause. And the Indians will send warriors. Mark my words, Wadsworth, we shall scour the redcoats, we shall scour them!'

'I would still wish for more men,' Wadsworth said quietly.

'I would wish for the same,' Lovell said fervently, 'but we must make do with what the good Lord provides and remember that we are Americans!'

'Amen for that,' the Reverend Murray said, 'and amen again.'

The waist of the *Sally* was filled with four flat-bottomed lighters commandeered from Boston harbour. All the transports had similar cargoes. The shallow-draught boats were for landing the troops, and Wadsworth now gazed at those militia men who, in turn, watched the coast from the *Sally*'s portside rail. Tall plumes of smoke rose mysteriously from the dark wooded hills and Wadsworth had the uncomfortable feeling that the pillars of smoke were signal fires. Was the coast infested by loyalists who were telling the British that the Americans were coming?

'Captain Carver was grumbling to me,' Lovell broke into Wadsworth's thoughts. Nathaniel Carver was the *Sally*'s captain. 'He was complaining that the state commandeered too many transports!'

'We anticipated more men,' Wadsworth said.

'And I said to him,' Lovell went on cheerfully, 'how do you expect to convey the British prisoners to Boston without adequate shipping? He had no answer to that!'

'Fifteen hundred prisoners,' the Reverend Murray said with a chortle. 'They'll take some feeding!'

'Oh, I think more than fifteen hundred!' Lovell said confidently. 'Major Todd was estimating, merely estimating, and I can't think the enemy has sent fewer than two thousand! We'll have to pack two hundred prisoners into each and every transport, but Carver assures me the deck hatches can be battened down. My! What a return to Boston that will be, eh Wadsworth?'

'I pray for that day, sir,' Wadsworth said. Did the British really have fifteen hundred men, he wondered, and if they did then what possible reason could Lovell have for his optimism?

'It's just a pity we don't have a band!' Lovell said. 'We could mount a parade!' Lovell, a politician, was imagining the rewards of success: the cheering crowds, the thanks of the General Court and a parade like the triumphs of Ancient Rome where the captured enemy was marched through jeering crowds. 'I do believe,' the brigadier went on, leaning closer to Wadsworth, 'that McLean has brought most of Halifax's garrison to Majabigwaduce!'

'I'm certain Halifax is not abandoned, sir,' Wadsworth said.

'But under-defended!' Lovell said warmly. 'My word, Wadsworth, maybe we should contemplate a raid!'

'I suspect General Ward and the General Court might want to discuss the matter first, sir,' Wadsworth said drily.

'Artemas is a good, brave man, but we must look ahead, Wadsworth. Once we've defeated McLean what's to stop us attacking the British elsewhere?'

'The Royal Navy, sir?' Wadsworth suggested with a wry smile.

'Oh, we'll build more ships! More ships!' Lovell was unstoppable now, imagining his victory at Majabigwaduce expanding into the capture of Nova Scotia and, who knew, maybe all Canada? 'Doesn't the *Warren* look fine?' he exclaimed. 'Just look at her! Can there be a finer vessel afloat?'

At twilight the fleet turned into the vast mouth of the Penobscot River where it anchored off the Fox Islands, all except the *Hazard* and *Tyrannicide*, which were ordered to make a reconnaissance upriver. The two small brigs, both from the Massachusetts navy, sailed slowly northwards, using the long evening's gentle light to probe closer to Majabigwaduce, which lay a full twenty-six nautical miles from the open sea.

Commodore Saltonstall watched the two brigs until the gathering darkness hid their sails, then he took his supper on the quarterdeck beneath a sky bright with stars. His crew left him alone until one tall figure crossed to the commodore. 'A pot of wine, sir?'

'Captain Welch,' Saltonstall greeted the tall marine, 'I'm obliged to you.'

The two officers stood side-by-side at the *Warren's* taffrail. A violin sounded from the foredeck of the brig *Pallas*, which was anchored closest to the frigate. For a time neither the commodore nor the marine said anything, but simply listened to the music and to the gentle sound of waves slapping against the hull. 'So,' Saltonstall broke their companionable silence, 'what do you think?'

'The same as you I reckon, sir,' Welch said in his deep voice.

The commodore snorted. 'Boston should have demanded a Continental regiment.'

'That they should, sir.'

'But they want all the credit to go to Massachusetts! That's their idea, Welch. You mark what I say. There won't be many thanks offered to us.'

'But we'll do the work, sir.'

'Oh, we'll have to!' Saltonstall said. Already, in his brief tenure of command, the commodore had earned a reputation as a difficult and daunting figure, but he had struck up a friendship with the marine. Saltonstall recognized a fellow soul, a man who strove to make his men the best they could be. 'We'll have to do their work,' Saltonstall went on, 'if it can be done at all.' He paused, offering Welch a chance to comment, but the marine said nothing. 'Can it be done?' Saltonstall prompted him.

Welch stayed silent for a while, then nodded. 'We have the marines, sir, and I dare say every marine is worth two of the enemy. We might find five hundred militiamen who can fight. That should suffice, sir, if you can take care of their ships.'

'Three sloops of war,' Saltonstall said in a tone that suggested neither confidence nor pessimism about the prospects of destroying the Royal Navy squadron.

'My men will fight,' Welch said, 'and by Christ they'll fight like fiends. They're good men, sir, well-trained.'

'That I know,' Saltonstall said, 'but by God I won't let Lovell throw them away. You only fight ashore with my permission.'

'Of course, sir.'

'And if you get orders that make no sense, you refer them to me, you understand?'

'Perfectly, sir.'

'He's a farmer,' Saltonstall said scornfully, 'not a soldier, but a goddamned farmer.'

* * *

On board the *Sally*, in the captain's cramped cabin, the farmer was cradling a mug of tea laced with rum. Lovell shared the table with his secretary, John Marston, and with Wadsworth and the Reverend Murray who appeared to have been promoted to senior aide. 'We should reach Majabigwaduce tomorrow,' Lovell said, looking from face to face in the feeble light of the lantern that hung from a beam, 'and I assume the commodore will prevent the enemy ships from leaving the harbour and so obstructing us, in which case we should land immediately, don't you think?'

'If it's possible,' Wadsworth said cautiously.

'Let us be hopeful!' Lovell said. He dreamed of the victory parade in Boston and the vote of thanks from the legislature, but small doubts were creeping into his mind as he gazed at the crude map of Majabigwaduce's peninsula that was spread on the table where the remains of supper still lay. The *Sally*'s cook had produced a fine fish stew served with newly baked bread. 'We shall need to anchor off the land and launch the lighters,' Lovell said distractedly, then used a crust of corn-bread to tap the bluff at the western end of the peninsula. 'Can McLean really have left this height undefended?'

'Unfortified, certainly, if the reports are true,' Wadsworth said.

'Then we should accept his invitation, don't you think?'

Wadsworth nodded cautiously. 'We'll know more tomorrow, sir,' he said.

'I want to be ready,' Lovell said. He tapped the map again. 'We can't let our fellows sit idle while the commodore destroys the enemy shipping. We must put the men ashore fast.' Lovell gazed at the map as though it might provide some solution to the morrow's problems. Why had McLean not placed his fort on the high bluff? Was there a trap? If Lovell had been given the task of defending the peninsula he was sure he would have made a stronghold at the harbour's entrance, high on the point of land that dominated both the wide bay and the harbour, so why had McLean not done that? And McLean, Lovell reminded himself, was a professional soldier, so what did McLean know that Lovell did not? He felt a shiver of nervousness in his soul, then took comfort that he was not alone in his responsibility. Commodore Saltonstall was the naval commander, and Saltonstall's ships so outnumbered the enemy that surely no amount of professionalism could redress that imbalance. 'We must believe,' Lovell said, 'that our enemies are afflicted by over-confidence.'

'They are British,' the Reverend Murray said in agreement, 'and "pride goeth before destruction, and an haughty spirit before a fall." Proverbs eighteen,' he added helpfully, 'verse sixteen.'

'Words of wisdom,' Lovell said, 'and indeed they do underestimate us!' The general was staring at the map and searching for the optimism that had lightened his morning.

'They shall suffer for their arrogance,' Murray said, and raised a reverent hand, '"What is this thing that ye do? Will ye rebel against the king? Then answered I them, and said unto them, the God of Heaven, he will prosper us."' He smiled benignly. 'The words of the prophet Nehemiah, General.'

'He will indeed prosper us,' Lovell echoed, 'and perhaps you would lead us in prayer, Reverend?'

'Gladly.' The men bowed their heads as the Reverend Murray prayed that God would send a swift victory. 'May the forces of righteousness glorify Thy name, O Lord,' the Reverend Murray beseeched, 'and may we show magnanimity in the triumph that Thy words have promised us. We ask all this in Thy holy name, amen.'

'Amen,' Lovell said fervently, his eyes tight shut, 'and amen.'

'Amen,' Brigadier McLean muttered in response to the grace before supper. He had been invited to Doctor Calef's house, which lay two hundred yards east of Fort George. That name, he thought ruefully, was a grand name for a fort that was scarcely defensible. Captain Mowat had sent one hundred and eighty burly seamen to help the work, yet still the walls were only waist-high and a mere two cannons had been emplaced in the corner bastions.

'So the wretches are here?' Calef enquired.

'So we hear, Doctor, so we hear,' McLean responded. News of the enemy fleet's arrival had come from the river's mouth, brought by a fisherman who had fled the rebels so quickly that he had been unable to count the ships and could only say that there was a terrible lot of them. 'It seems they've sent a considerable fleet,' McLean commented, then thanked the doctor's wife who had passed him a dish of beans. Three candles lit the table, a finely polished oval of gleaming walnut. Most of the doctor's furniture had come from his Boston home and it looked strange here, much as if the contents of a fine Edinburgh mansion were to be moved to a Hebridean croft.

'Will they come tonight?' Mrs Calef enquired nervously.

'I'm assured no one can navigate the river in the dark,' McLean said, 'so no, ma'am, not this night.'

'They'll be here tomorrow,' Calef averred.

'So I expect.'

'In some force?' Calef asked.

'So the report said, Doctor, though I am denied any specific detail.' McLean flinched as he bit onto a grindstone chip trapped in the cornbread. 'Very fine bread, ma'am,' he said.

'We were maltreated in Boston,' Calef said.

'I am sorry to hear that.'

'My wife was insulted in the streets.'

McLean knew what was in Calef's mind, that if the rebels were to take Majabigwaduce then the persecution of the loyalists would start again. 'I regret that, Doctor.'

'I dare say,' Calef said, 'that if the rebels were to find me, General, they would imprison me.' The doctor was merely toying with his food, while his wife watched him anxiously.

'Then I must do my utmost,' McLean said, 'to keep you from imprisonment and your wife from insult.'

'Scourge them,' Calef said angrily.

'I do assure you, Doctor, that is our intent,' McLean said, then smiled at Calef's wife. 'These are very fine beans, ma'am.'

They ate mostly in silence after that. McLean wished he could offer a greater reassurance to the loyalists of Majabigwaduce, but the arrival of the rebel fleet surely meant an imminent defeat. His fort was unfinished. True he had made three batteries to cover the harbour entrance. There was one on Cross Island, the large Half Moon Battery down on the shore, and a third, much smaller, on the high bluff above the harbour mouth, but none of those batteries was a fort. They were emplacements for cannon that were there to fire at the enemy ships, but not one of the earthworks could withstand an assault by a company of determined infantry. There had simply not been enough time, and now the enemy was here.

Many years before, while fighting for the Dutch, McLean had been captured by the French and held prisoner. That had not been unpleasant. The French were generous and had treated him with courtesy. He wondered how the Americans would behave and feared, as he ate the tough, under-cooked beans, that he was about to find out.

Tomorrow.

Marine Lieutenant Downs of the *Tyrannicide* took men ashore on the northernmost of the Fox Islands. It was fully dark by the time their longboat grounded on a shingle beach beneath the black shapes of a half-dozen houses that stood on the higher ground. Small lights shone from behind shutters and around doorways and, as the marines dragged their boat higher up the beach, a voice hailed from the darkness. 'Who are you?'

'His Majesty's Royal Marines!' Downs called back. The Fox Islands were notorious for being loyalist and Downs did not want one of his men being killed or wounded by some malevolent Tory shooting out of the night. 'A relief fleet for Majabigwaduce!'

'What do you want here?' the voice called, still suspicious.

'Fresh water, news, a couple of women would be welcome too!'

Boots sounded on the shingle and a tall man emerged from the shadows. He carried a musket that he slung on his shoulder when he saw the dozen men about the longboat. He had noticed the white crossbelts, but in the dark of night he could not see that their coats were green and not red. 'Strange time to be looking for water,' he said.

'We're after water and news,' Downs said cheerfully. 'General McLean is still at Majabigwaduce?'

'No one's kicked him out yet.'

'Have you seen him?'

'I was there yesterday.'

'Then, sir, you will do me the honour of accompanying me to my ship,' Downs said. His marines, like those of the *Hazard*, had been sent to find men who had seen McLean's fortifications.

The islander took a pace backwards. 'What ship are you from?' he asked, still thoroughly suspicious.

'Take him,' Downs ordered and two of his marines seized the man, confiscated his musket and dragged him back to the longboat. 'Don't make a sound,' Lieutenant Downs warned the man, 'or we'll stove your skull in like an egg.'

'Bastards,' the man said, then grunted as a marine punched him in the belly.

'We are patriots,' Downs corrected him and, leaving two men to guard the prisoner, went to find more loyalists who could tell the expedition just what waited for them upriver.

Dawn brought a thick fog into which Lieutenant John Moore went with twenty men to the small battery that McLean had placed high on Majabigwaduce's bluff. The battery possessed

114

three six-pounder cannons mounted on naval carriages and served by sailors from HMS *North*, commanded by a midshipman who, to the eighteen-year-old Moore, looked no older than twelve or thirteen. 'I'm fifteen, sir,' the midshipman responded to Moore's enquiry, 'and three years in the Navy, sir.'

'I'm John Moore,' Moore introduced himself.

'Pearce Fenistone, sir, and honoured to make your acquaintance.' Fenistone's battery was no fortress, merely an emplacement for the guns. A space had been cleared in the trees, a patch of ground levelled, and a platform of split logs laid for the carriages. Four trees had been deliberately left unfelled and the gunners used their trunks as anchors for the cannons' breeching ropes and train-tackle. A ship's cannon was restrained by its breeching ropes, which were seized to the hull and stopped a gun recoiling across a deck, while the train-tackle was used to run the gun back into position, and Fenistone's men were using the tree trunks to tame their beasts. 'It does check the recoil, sir,' Fenistone said when Moore admired the ingenious arrangement, 'though we do get showered with pine needles every time we fire.' The battery had no parapet and its ready magazine was merely a shallow pit dug at the rear of the makeshift decking. Two gratings were piled with round shot beside which were piles of what looked like children's rope quoits. 'Ring-wadding, sir,' Fenistone explained.

'Ring-wadding?'

'The guns point downwards, sir, and the ring-wads hold the balls in the barrel. We'd look a little foolish if we loaded and the balls rolled out before we fired. It's most embarrassing when that happens.'

The battery had been placed above the harbour's mouth rather than at the western edge of the bluff. The six-pounders, which had been taken from the *North*'s portside broadside, were too light to have much effect at long range, but if the enemy ships attempted to enter the harbour they would be forced to sail beneath the three cannon that could fire down onto their decks. 'I'd wish for heavier metal, sir,' Fenistone said wistfully.

'And a proper fort to defend your guns?'

'In case their infantry attacks?' Fenistone asked. 'Well, fighting infantry isn't our job, sir, it's yours.' The midshipman smiled. For a fifteen-year-old, Moore thought, Fenistone was wonderfully confident. 'Captain Mowat gave us strict instructions what to do if we are attacked by land, sir,' he went on.

'Which is?'

'Spike the guns and run like buggery, sir,' Fenistone answered with a grin, 'and get the gunners back to the *North*, sir.' He slapped at a mosquito.

Moore looked down at Mowat's ships, which were wreathed in mist. The three sloops looked formidable enough in their line, though he knew they were lightly armed compared to most warships. Behind them, in a parallel line, were the three transport ships, which looked far larger and more threatening, but in truth were defenceless hulls, merely there to act as obstacles in the event the enemy managed to pierce Mowat's first line.

'Are they coming today, sir?' Fenistone asked anxiously.

'So we believe,' Moore said.

'We'll give them a warm British welcome, sir.'

'I'm sure you will,' Moore said with a smile, then beckoned at his men to stop gawping at the ships' guns and to follow him westwards through the trees.

He stopped at the brink of the bluff. Ahead of him was the wide Penobscot River beneath its thinning pall of fog. Moore stared southwards, but could see nothing stirring in the distant whiteness. 'So they are coming today, sir?' Sergeant McClure asked.

'We must assume so.'

'And our job, sir?'

'Is to take post here, Sergeant, in case the rascals attempt a landing.' Moore looked down the steep slope and thought the rebels would be foolish to attempt a landing on the narrow stony beach at the bluff's foot. He supposed they would land farther north, perhaps beyond the neck, and he wished he had been posted on the isthmus. There would be fighting and he had never fought; part of him feared that baptism and another part yearned to experience it.

'They'd be daft buggers to land here, sir,' McClure said, standing beside Moore and gazing down the precipitous slope.

'Let us hope they are daft buggers.'

'We'll shoot the bastards easy, sir.'

'If there are enough of us.'

'That's truc, sir.'

The fog thinned as the wind freshened. Lieutenant Moore had posted himself at the peninsula's south-western corner, at Dyce's Head, and as the sun climbed higher more and more men made their way to that vantage point to watch for the enemy. Brigadier McLean came, stumping with his stick along the narrow path between the pines, leading seven other red-coated officers who all stood gazing southwards down the river that sparkled so prettily under the summer sun. Still more officers arrived, and with them came civilians like Doctor Calef who stood close to the brigadier and tried to make small-talk. Captain Mowat was there with two other naval officers, all of them holding long telescopes though there was nothing to see. The river was empty.

'I forgot to ask you last night,' McLean said to Calef, 'how is Temperance?'

'Temperance?' Calef asked, puzzled, then remembered. 'Ah, she's recovering. If a baby survives a day of fever they usually recover. She'll live.'

'I'm glad,' McLean said. 'There are few things so distressing as a sick bairn.'

'You have children, General?'

'I never married,' McLean said, then doffed his hat as more

villagers came to the bluff with Colonel Goldthwait. Goldthwait was American and loyalist, a horse-breeder whose rank had been earned in the old Royal Militia. He feared that any rebel force in the river might persecute the loyalists and so he had brought his family to live under the protection of McLean's men. His two daughters had accompanied him to the bluff, along with Bethany Fletcher and Aaron Bank's twin daughters, and the presence of so many young women attracted the younger Scottish officers.

Lieutenant Moore steeled himself to approach Bethany. He took off his hat and offered a bow. 'Your brother isn't here?' he asked.

'He went fishing, Lieutenant,' Bethany lied.

'I thought no one was allowed to leave the peninsula?' Moore queried.

'James left before that order was given,' Bethany said.

'I pray he returns safely,' Moore said. 'If the rebels catch him, Miss Fletcher, I fear they might detain him.'

'If they catch you, Lieutenant,' Bethany said with a smile, 'they might detain you.'

'Then I must ensure I am not caught,' Moore said.

'Good morning, Miss Fletcher,' Brigadier McLean said cheerfully.

'Good morning, General,' Bethany said and lightened the brigadier's morning with her most dazzling smile. She felt awkward. Her pale-green linen dress was patched with common brown cloth and her bonnet was long-peaked and old-fashioned. The Goldthwait girls wore lovely cotton print dresses that they must have received from Boston before the British had withdrawn from that city. The British officers, Beth thought, must think her very plain.

Thomas Goldthwait, a tall and good-looking man dressed in the faded red coat of the old militia, took McLean aside. 'I wanted a word, General,' Goldthwait said. He sounded awkward.

'I'm at your service, sir,' McLean responded.

118

Goldthwait stared south for a brief while. 'I have three sons,' he said finally, still gazing southwards, 'and when you arrived, General, I gave them a choice.'

McLean nodded. '"Choose you this day whom you will serve?"' he guessed, quoting the scriptures.

'Yes,' Goldthwait said. He took a snuff box from a pocket and fiddled with its lid. 'I regret,' he went on, 'that Joseph and Benjamin chose to join the rebels.' He at last looked directly at McLean. 'That was not my wish, General, but I would wish you to know. I did not suggest that disaffection to them, and I assure you we are not a family attempting to ride two horses at the same time.' He stopped abruptly and shrugged.

'If I had a son,' McLean said, 'I would hope he would have the same loyalties as myself, Colonel, but I would also pray that he could think for himself. I assure you that we shall not think the less of you because of the folly of your sons.'

'Thank you,' Goldthwait said.

'We shall speak no more of it,' McLean said, then turned abruptly as Captain Mowat called that there were topsails visible.

And for a time no one spoke because there was nothing useful to say.

The enemy had come, the first evidence of their arrival a mass of topsails showing through the remnants of fog above a headland, but gradually, remorselessly, the fleet appeared in the channel beside Long Island and not one of the men or women watching could be anything but awed by the sight of so many sails, so many dark hulls, so many ships. 'It's an Armada,' Colonel Goldthwait broke the silence.

'Dear God,' McLean said softly. He gazed at the mass of shipping making slow progress in the small wind. 'Yet it's a brave sight,' he said.

'Brave, sir?' Bethany asked.

'It's not often you see so many ships together. You should remember this, Miss Fletcher, as a sight to describe to your

119

children.' He smiled at her, then turned to the three naval officers. 'Captain Mowat! Have you determined their number yet?'

'Not yet,' Mowat answered curtly. He was gazing through a telescope that was resting on a redcoat's shoulder. The enemy fleet had stayed close together as it cleared the treacherous ledges that lay beneath the waters east of Long Island, but now the ships were spreading and running before the wind towards the wide bay west of the peninsula. The warships, quicker than the transports, were stretching ahead and Mowat was making tiny adjustments to the glass as he tried to distinguish the different vessels, a task made difficult by the trees that obscured part of his view. He spent a long time staring at the *Warren*, counting her gunports and attempting to judge from the number of men visible on her deck how well she was manned. He grunted non-committally when his inspection was finished, then edged the glass leftwards to count the transports. 'As far as I can see, General,' he said at last, 'they have twenty transports. Maybe twenty-one.'

'Dear Lord above,' McLean said mildly, 'and how many warships?'

'About the same,' Mowat said.

'They do come in force,' McLean said, still mildly. 'Twenty transports, you say, Mowat?'

'Maybe twenty-one.'

'Time for some arithmetic, Paymaster,' McLean said to Lieutenant Moore. 'How many men did each of our transports carry?'

'Most of the men were in four of our transports, sir,' Moore said, 'so two hundred apiece?'

'So multiply that by twenty?'

There was a pause as every officer within earshot attempted the mental arithmetic. 'Four thousand, sir,' Moore said finally.

'Ah, you learned the same arithmetic as I did, Mister Moore,' McLean said, smiling.

'Dear God,' a highland officer gazed appalled at the size of the approaching fleet, 'in that many ships? They could have five thousand men!'

McLean shook his head. 'In the absence of our Lord and Saviour,' the brigadier said, 'I do believe they'd have trouble feeding that many.'

'Some of their ships are smaller than ours,' Mowat observed.

'And your conclusion, Mowat?' McLean asked.

'Between three and four thousand men,' Mowat said crisply. 'Enough, anyway. And the bastards have close to three hundred guns in broadside.'

'I see we shall be busy,' McLean said lightly.

'With your permission, General,' Mowat had finished his inspection and collapsed the glass, 'I'll return to the *Albany*.'

'Allow me to wish you joy of the day, Mowat,' McLean said.

'Let me desire the same for you, McLean,' Mowat replied, then paused to shake the brigadier's hand.

The three naval officers left to join their ships. McLean stayed on the bluff, saying little as he watched the enemy draw ever closer. It was a rough and ready rule of war that an attacker needed to outnumber a defender by three to one if an assault on a fort were to succeed, but Fort George was unfinished. The bastions were so low that a man could leap over them. The gun emplacements were scarcely begun. A thousand rebels would take the fort easily, and it was plain from the size of the fleet entering the bay that they must have brought at least two or three thousand men. 'We must do our best,' McLean finally said to no one in particular, then smiled. 'Ensign Campbell!' he called sharply. 'To me!'

Six kilted officers responded and Bethany looked puzzled. 'We are over-supplied with Campbells,' Moore said.

'The 74th has forty-three officers,' McLean explained more usefully, 'and comes from Argyle, Miss Fletcher, which is a place plentifully inhabited by Campbells. Twenty-three of the forty-three officers are named Campbell. Shout that name outside their tent lines, Miss Fletcher, and you can cause chaos.' The brigadier knew that every loyalist watching from the headland was sensing an approaching disaster and he was determined to show them confidence. 'It occurs to me,' he spoke to the six young kilted officers, 'that Sir Walter Raleigh played bowls as the Armada approached. We can match the English in insouciance, don't you think?'

'By playing bowls, sir?' one of the Campbells asked.

'I prefer swords to bowls,' McLean said, and drew his broadsword. His lamed right arm made drawing the weapon difficult and he had to use his left hand to help free the blade from its scabbard. He stooped and laid the sword on the turf.

Eleven other swords were placed on the ground. There were no musicians at Dyce's Head so the brigadier clapped his hands rhythmically and the six ensigns began to dance above the cross-laid blades. Some of the 74th's other officers sang as they clapped. They sang in Gaelic, and McLean joined in, smiling.

Bethany clapped with the other spectators. The ensigns danced, their feet close but never touching the swords. The Gaelic song finished, McLean indicated the defiant sword-dance could end and the boyish officers grinned as their audience applauded and the blades were retrieved. 'To your posts, gentlemen,' McLean said to his officers. 'Ladies and gentlemen,' he looked at the civilians, 'I cannot foretell what will happen now, but if you stay in your homes I am confident you will be treated with a proper civility.' He was not confident of that at all, but what else could he say? He turned to take one last look at the fleet. A splash and rumble of cable sounded clear across the water as the first ship dropped anchor. Its sails, loosened from the wind's grip, flapped wildly until men tamed the canvas onto the wide yards. A glint of light from the ship's afterdeck flashed bright in McLean's eyes and he knew a rebel was examining the shore with a telescope. He turned away, going back to his unfinished fort.

James Fletcher had spent the night on the Penobscot's eastern shore, the *Felicity* safe in a small cove. He watched the Massachusetts fleet appear from the south and he waited till the ships had almost reached Majabigwaduce before rowing out of the sheltered haven. Then the wind caught his mainsail and he could ship the oars and run before the breeze to where the fleet was anchoring. The transports had gone farthest north, anchoring west of the peninsula's bluff and, like the warships, well out of the range of any cannon the British might have ashore.

Fletcher headed for the largest of the warships, reckoning that would be the commander's vessel, but long before he reached the *Warren* he was intercepted by a guard boat manned by a dozen oarsmen and four green-jacketed marines. They hailed him and so he turned the *Felicity* into the wind and waited for the longboat to reach him. 'I've got news for the general,' he called to the marine officer.

'You'll have to see the commodore,' the marine insisted, and pointed to the *Warren*. Sailors on the frigate took the line Fletcher heaved, then he let the gaff fall and clambered up the frigate's side.

He stood on deck where a young and nervous midshipman arrived to be his escort. 'The commodore is busy, Mister Fletcher,' he explained.

'I'm sure he is.'

'But he will want to see you.'

'I hope so!' James said cheerfully.

The rebels' warships had anchored due west of the harbour mouth, which was filled by Captain Mowat's three sloops of war. Those sloops, anchored fore and aft to keep their starboard broadsides pointed towards the bay, had their gunports open and were flying the blue ensign at their sterns while at each masthead, three on each sloop, was the British flag. Twin pulses of white spurted rhythmically from the *North*'s flank and Fletcher grinned. 'They never stop pumping her,' he said.

'Her?'

'The *North*.' James pointed. 'The sloop closest to Dyce's Head, see? I reckon the rats have chewed clean through her bottom.'

Ensign Fanning gazed solemnly at the enemy ship. 'She's an old ship?' he guessed.

'Old and rotten,' James said, 'a pair of cannonballs through that hull will turn her into firewood.'

'You live here?' Fanning asked.

'All my life.'

Commodore Saltonstall ducked out of his cabin door, followed by a man James Fletcher knew well. John Brewer was a captain in the local militia, though he was so short of recruits that he had few men to command. It had been to Captain Brewer that James Fletcher had sent his map and letter, and Brewer now smiled at seeing him. 'You're welcome, young Fletcher!' Brewer gestured at the commodore. 'This is Captain Saltonstall. I daresay young James here has news for you, sir.'

'I do, sir,' James said eagerly.

Saltonstall seemed unimpressed. He looked once at James Fletcher, then turned to the portside rail where he stood for a long time gazing at Mowat's ships through a telescope. 'Mister Coningsby!' he snapped suddenly.

'Sir?' Midshipman Fanning responded.

'The bitter ends of number four's train-tackle look like a snake's honeymoon! See to it.'

'Aye aye, sir.'

Captain Brewer, a jovial man dressed in homespun and with an ancient broad-bladed cutlass strapped at his waist, grinned at Fletcher while Saltonstall continued to inspect the three ships that guarded the harbour's mouth. 'What is your name?' the commodore enquired brusquely.

James Fletcher decided the question was aimed at him. 'James Fletcher, sir. I live in Bagaduce.'

'Then come here, James Fletcher of Bagaduce,' Saltonstall demanded and James went to stand beside the commodore and, like him, gazed eastwards. To the left he could see the heavily wooded bluff that hid the fort from the commodore's view. Then came the three sloops with their combined broadsides of twenty-eight cannon and, just to their south, the guns on Cross Island. 'You live here,' Saltonstall said in a voice that suggested pity for such a fate, 'and I see three sloops and a battery, what am I missing?'

'Another battery on Dyce's Head, sir,' James said, pointing.

'Just as I told you, sir!' Brewer put in cheerfully.

Saltonstall ignored the militia captain. 'Of what strength?'

'I saw only three small guns being hauled up there, sir,' James said.

'Six-pounders, probably,' Brewer said.

'But they'll plunge their fire on us as we reach the harbour mouth,' Saltonstall observed.

'Reckon that's what they're up there for, sir,' James said, 'and there's another battery on the harbour shore.'

'So three batteries and three sloops,' Saltonstall said, collapsing the glass and turning to look at Fletcher. He did not seem to like what he saw. 'What water in the harbour?'

'What do you draw, sir?'

'Eleven feet, nine inches,' Saltonstall said. He was still talking to James, but now fixed his gaze just past James's head to stare at the poopdeck companionway.

'Plenty of water for you, sir,' James said with his customary cheerfulness.

'The tide?'

'Fifteen to eighteen feet, near enough,' James said, 'but even at low water you can pass her.' He pointed to the *Nautilus*,

125

the southernmost of Mowat's ships. 'You can get past her, sir, with ten feet to spare, and once you're inside you've not a care in the world.'

'Get past her?' Saltonstall asked scornfully.

'Plenty of room, sir.'

'And a battery not a hundred paces away?' Saltonstall asked harshly, meaning the guns on Cross Island. Those guns were just visible and behind them were tents for the gunners and a British flag high on a makeshift pole. 'And once I am inside,' he went on, 'how the devil do I get out?'

'Get out?' James asked, disconcerted by the commodore's evident dislike of him.

'I take your advice,' Saltonstall said sarcastically, 'and I sail into Majabigwaduce, but once there I am under the guns of their fort, am I not? And incapable of leaving?'

'Incapable, sir?' James said, nervous of the immaculate Saltonstall.

'For God's sake, you thickhead!' Saltonstall snapped. 'Any fool can sail into that harbour, but how the devil do you sail out again? Answer me that!'

'You don't need to come out, sir,' James said. The commodore was right, of course, that while it would be easy to use the prevailing wind to enter the harbour it would be a devilish business to tack out again, especially under fire from the fort's cannon.

'Oh, praise the Lord,' Saltonstall said, 'so I am just supposed to lie there, am I, allowing the shore batteries to reduce my ship to wreckage?'

'Lord love you, sir, no. You can sail on up into the Bagaduce River,' James said. 'Deep water there, sir, and long beyond the reach of any of their guns.'

'Must be thirty feet at low water up the river,' Brewer put in.

'Twenty, anyway,' James said.

'You seem to be damned knowing about the matter,' Saltonstall turned on Captain Brewer.

'I live here,' Brewer said.

'I am not going to risk my shipping in that damned hole,' Saltonstall said firmly, then turned away again to gaze at the defences.

'What damned hole, Commodore?' a bright voice interrupted.

Saltonstall turned to look at Peleg Wadsworth who had just arrived on board the frigate. 'Good morning, General,' the commodore grunted.

Brigadier Wadsworth looked happy. His concerns about the fitness of the militia had been dissipated by his first sight of the British defences, which had been visible from the *Sally*'s deck as it sailed north. Wadsworth had gazed through a telescope at the fort above the settlement and he had seen that the walls were pitifully low, confirming reports that the ramparts were unfinished. Two local men who had been brought to the fleet by marines from the *Tyrannicide* had also confirmed that McLean's works were far from completed and that the fort's guns were still not mounted. 'God has been good to us,' Wadsworth said, 'and the British are unprepared.' He smiled at Fletcher. 'Hello, young man, is that your boat tied alongside?'

'Yes, sir.'

'She looks a very trim craft,' Wadsworth said, then stepped alongside the commodore. 'General Lovell is determined to launch an assault this afternoon,' he told Saltonstall.

Saltonstall grunted again.

'And we beg the favour of your marines, sir.'

Saltonstall grunted a third time and then, after a pause, called aloud, 'Captain Welch!'

The tall marine stalked across the deck. 'Sir?'

'What kind of assault, General?' Saltonstall demanded.

'Straight at the bluff,' Wadsworth said confidently.

'There's a battery of guns on the bluff,' Saltonstall warned, then waved carelessly at Fletcher and Captain Brewer, 'they know.'

'Six-pounders probably,' Captain Brewer said, 'but aimed southwards.'

'The guns face the harbour mouth, sir,' James explained. 'They don't point at the bay,' he added.

'Then the guns shouldn't trouble us,' Wadsworth said cheerfully. He paused as if expecting agreement from the commodore, but Saltonstall just gazed past the brigadier, his long face somehow suggesting that he had better things to do than concern himself with Wadsworth's problems. 'If your marines take the right of the line,' Wadsworth suggested.

The commodore looked at Welch. 'Well?'

'It would be an honour, sir,' Welch said.

Saltonstall nodded. 'Then you can have my marines, Wadsworth,' he said. 'But take good care of them!' This was evidently a jest because the commodore gave a brief bark of laughter.

'I'm most grateful,' Wadsworth said heartily, 'and General Lovell asked me to enquire, Commodore, whether you plan an attack on their shipping?' Wadsworth asked the question with the utmost tact.

'You want it both ways, Wadsworth?' the commodore demanded fiercely. 'You want my marines to attack on land, but you'd deny me their service in an assault on the enemy shipping? So which do you want, land or sea?'

'I desire the cause of liberty to triumph,' Wadsworth said, knowing he sounded pompous.

Yet the words seemed to jar with the commodore who flinched, then looked at the three enemy sloops again. 'They're the cork in a bottle-neck,' he said. 'Not much of a cork, you might think, but a damned tight bottle. I can destroy their ships, Wadsworth, but at what price, eh? Tell me that! What price? Half our fleet?'

Captain Brewer and James Fletcher had stepped back respectfully, as if leaving the two senior officers to their discussion, while Captain Welch stood glowering beside the commodore. Wadsworth alone seemed at his ease. He smiled. 'Three ships can do that much damage?' he enquired of Saltonstall.

'Not their damned ships, but their damned fort and their damned batteries,' Saltonstall said. 'I sail in there, Wadsworth, and my fleet is under their fort's guns. We'll be pounded, man, pounded.'

'The fort hasn't mounted—' Captain Brewer began.

'I know how few guns they have!' Saltonstall turned angrily on Brewer, 'but that was yesterday. How many more today? Do we know? We do not! And how many field guns are concealed in the village there? Do we know? We do not. And once inside that damned bottle I can't get out unless I have an ebbing tide and an easterly wind. And no,' he looked sourly at James Fletcher, 'I am not minded to take my ship up a river where enemy field guns can be deployed. So, General,' he turned back to Peleg Wadsworth, 'do you wish to explain to the Navy Board the loss of yet another Continental frigate?'

'What I wish, Commodore,' Wadsworth still spoke respectfully, 'is for the enemy marines to be aboard their ships and not waiting for us on land.'

'Ah, that's different,' Saltonstall spoke grudgingly. 'You want me to engage their shipping. Very well. But I won't take my fleet into that damned hole, you understand? We'll engage them from without the harbour.'

'And I'm certain that threat alone will keep the enemy marines where we wish them to be,' Wadsworth said.

'Have you marked that chart for me?' Saltonstall turned on Captain Brewer.

'Not yet, sir.'

'Then do so. Very well, Wadsworth, I'll hammer the ships for you.'

Wadsworth stepped back, feeling rather as though he had waved a lit candle over an open barrel of gunpowder and had managed to survive without causing an explosion. He smiled at James Fletcher. 'Do I understand that you're familiar with Majabigwaduce, young man?' he asked.

'Bagaduce, sir? Yes, sir.'

'Then do me the honour of accompanying me. You too, Captain Welch? We must draw up orders.'

The *Felicity* was left tied to the *Warren* as James Fletcher was rowed with Wadsworth and Welch to the *Sally*, which, for the moment, acted as the army's headquarters. Wadsworth appraised James Fletcher and liked what he saw. 'So, Mister Fletcher,' he asked, 'why are you here?'

'To fight, sir.'

'Good man!'

The sun sparked off the water, it glittered. The expedition had come to Majabigwaduce and would go straight into battle.

Brigadier McLean had ordered every civilian to stay in their home because, if the rebels came, he did not want unnecessary casualties. Now he stood outside the long storehouse that had been built within the half-finished walls of Fort George. The garrison's precious supplies were in the long wooden building, all except the artillery's ammunition, which was buried in stone-lined pits just behind the unfinished ramparts. The union flag flapped noisily above the bastion nearest the harbour entrance. 'I think the wind's rising,' McLean remarked to Lieutenant John Moore.

'I believe it is, sir.'

'A wind to blow our enemy into the harbour,' McLean said.

'Sir?' Moore sounded plaintive.

'I know what you desire, John,' McLean said sympathetically.

'Please, sir.'

McLean paused as a sergeant bellowed at a private to extinguish his damned pipe. No smoking was allowed inside

Fort George because the ready magazines were not properly finished, and the powder-charges were protected from sparks and the weather by nothing more solid than number three sail canvas. 'You're our paymaster, Lieutenant,' McLean said teasingly, 'I can't afford to lose a good paymaster now, can I?'

'I'm a soldier, sir,' Moore said stubbornly.

McLean smiled, then relented. 'Take twenty men. And take Sergeant McClure. Report to Captain Campbell, that's Archibald Campbell. And John?'

John Moore, thus given permission to join the picquets on the bluff, turned a delighted face on the brigadier. 'Sir?'

'The duke won't thank me if you die. Take care.'

'I'm immortal, sir,' Moore said happily, 'and thank you, sir.'

Moore ran and McLean turned to greet Major Dunlop who was the senior officer of the 82nd and had replaced McLean as that battalion's commanding officer for as long as McLean had heavier responsibilities. The wind was brisk enough to blow Major Dunlop's cocked hat from his head. 'I'm sending Moore to join the picquets on the bluff, Dunlop,' McLean said as a sentry chased after the errant hat, 'I hope you have no objection?'

'None at all,' Dunlop said, 'but I doubt he'll see any action there.'

'I doubt it too, but it'll keep the young puppy happy.'

'That it will,' Dunlop agreed and the two men talked for a moment before the brigadier walked to the single twelve-pounder cannon that occupied the south-western bastion of Fort George. The blue-coated men of the Royal Artillery stood as the general approached, but he waved them back down. Their gun pointed towards the harbour mouth, its barrel aimed above the cannon in the Half Moon battery, which was dug into the shoreline. McLean looked across Mowat's ships to where he could just make out a handful of the enemy's warships, though by far the largest part of the enemy's fleet was hidden beyond the bluff.

'Will they come today, sir?' an artillery sergeant asked.

'What's your name, Sergeant?'

'Lawrence, sir.'

'Well, Sergeant Lawrence, I fear I cannot tell you what the enemy will do, but if I were in their shoes I'd certainly make an assault today.'

Lawrence, a broad-faced man in his thirties, patted the cascabel of his long-barrelled cannon. 'We'll give them a proper English welcome, sir.'

'And a proper Scottish one, too,' McLean said reprovingly.

'That as well, sir,' Lawrence responded stoutly.

The brigadier walked north along the rampart. It was a pitiable thing for a defence, no higher than a man's waist and protected by just two cannon and by a row of wooden spikes in the shallow ditch. McLean had made his dispositions, but he was too old and too experienced to deceive himself. The enemy had come in force. They outnumbered him in ships and men. He reckoned there were only two places they might come ashore. They would either batter their way into the harbour and land on the closest beach, or else put their men ashore at the neck. The companies he had sent to those places would doubtless give a good account of themselves, but eventually they would be forced to retreat into Fort George, and then the rebels would advance against the pathetic ramparts and his cannon would greet them, but what could two guns do against three thousand men or more?

'God's will be done,' McLean said.

By nightfall, he reckoned, he would be a prisoner. If he was lucky.

Lieutenant-Colonel Paul Revere sat in a corner of the *Sally*'s overcrowded stern cabin. It was dominated by an unlit black-lead stove around which the expedition's senior army officers were gathered. Captain Welch, whose marines would join the militia for the assault, was also present. General Lovell stood

132

on the bricks that surrounded the stove, but the cabin beams were so low that he was forced to stoop. A freshening wind buffeted the sloop, making her quiver and jerk on her anchor rode. 'General Wadsworth has good news,' Lovell opened the proceedings.

Wadsworth, even taller than Lovell, did not stand, but stayed seated on a sea-chest. 'We've been joined by forty-one Penobscot Indians,' he said. 'The enemy attempted to subvert the tribe with wampum and promises, but they are determined to fight for liberty.'

'Praise God,' the Reverend Jonathan Murray put in.

'And more Indians will come, I'm sure,' Wadsworth continued, 'and they're stout fellows.'

'They're damned savages,' someone muttered from the cabin's darkest corner.

Wadsworth pointedly ignored the comment and instead gestured to the good-looking young man who squatted at the cabin's edge, 'And Mister Fletcher was in Majabigwaduce just yesterday. He tells us the fort is far from finished, and that the enemy numbers less than a thousand men.'

'Praise be,' the reverend said.

'So this afternoon,' Lovell took over, 'Commodore Saltonstall will attack the enemy's ships!' He did not explain that the commodore had refused to sail his squadron into the harbour, but had rather elected to bombard the sloops with long-range gunfire. 'We pray for the navy's success,' Lovell continued, 'but we shan't leave all the fighting to them! We're going ashore, gentlemen. We shall attack the enemy with spirit!' The fierce look that accompanied these words was rather undercut by the general's cramped posture. 'Captain Welch will land on the right, leading his marines.'

'God bless them,' the reverend interjected.

'Colonel McCobb will detach two companies to support the marines,' Lovell said, 'while the rest of his splendid regiment will assault in the centre.'

133

Samuel McCobb, who commanded the Lincoln County militia, nodded. He had a lean, weatherbeaten face in which his eyes were very blue and against which his moustache was very white. He glanced at Captain Welch and seemed to approve of what he saw.

'The men of Cumberland County will attack on the left,' Lovell said, 'under Colonel Mitchell. Colonel Davis will assign boats to each transport, isn't that right, Colonel?'

'The orders are written,' Colonel Davis said curtly. He was one of Lovell's aides, responsible for liaising with the civilian skippers of the transports.

'And what about us?' a man of about Wadsworth's age asked. He wore homespun and deerskin, and had a strong, enthusiastic face darkened by the sun. 'You're not leaving the men of York County out of the game, are you, sir?'

'Ah, Major Littlefield,' Lovell acknowledged the man.

'Our fellows are eager to assault, sir, and they won't be happy being left aboard the ships,' Littlefield said.

'It's a question of boats and lighters,' Lovell replied. 'We don't have enough to land every man together, so the boats will return for the York County militia.'

'So be sure to have your fellows ready,' Colonel Davis said.

'And you make sure you leave some of the fighting for us!' Daniel Littlefield said, looking disappointed.

'We don't have enough landing boats?' Revere spoke for the first time. He sounded incredulous. 'Not enough boats?'

'Nowhere near,' Davis said brusquely, 'so we land what men we can, then the boats return for the rest.'

'So what about my guns?' Revere asked.

'General Wadsworth will command the attack,' Lovell responded, 'so perhaps he can answer Colonel Revere?'

Wadsworth smiled at the indignant-looking Revere. 'I am hoping, Colonel, that your guns will not be needed.'

'Not needed! I didn't bring them all the way here just to be ballast!'

'If our information is right,' Wadsworth said emolliently, 'then I trust we shall capture the bluff, and then advance straight on the fort.'

'With speed,' Welch insisted.

'Speed?' Lovell asked.

'The faster we go, the greater the shock,' Welch said. 'It's like prize-fighting,' he explained. 'We give the enemy a hard blow, then hit him again while he's dazed. Then hit him again. Keep him dazed, keep him off-balance and keep hitting.'

'Our hope,' Wadsworth said, 'is to advance with such fervour that we shall overrun the fort before the enemy gathers his wits.'

'Amen to that,' the Reverend Murray said.

'But if the fort is not captured immediately,' Wadsworth was talking to Revere again, 'then your guns shall be fetched ashore.'

'And any guns we capture,' Revere insisted, 'belong to the State of Massachusetts. Isn't that right?'

Captain Welch bridled at that, but said nothing.

'Of course,' Lovell said. 'Indeed, everything we capture shall belong to the great State of Massachusetts!' he beamed at the assembly.

'I believe, sir,' John Marston, the general's secretary, put in quietly, 'that the Council decreed that all plunder taken by privateers would be deemed as their private property.'

'Of course, of course!' Lovell said, disconcerted, 'but I'm sure there will be more than sufficient plunder to satisfy their investors.' He turned to the Reverend Murray. 'Chaplain? A word of prayer before we disperse?'

'Before you pray,' Captain Welch interrupted, 'one last thing.' He looked hard at the men commanding the militia. 'There's going to be noise and smoke and confusion. There will be blood and screams. There will be chaos and uncertainty. So have your men fix bayonets. You're not going to beat these bastards volley to volley, but sharp steel will scare the shit out of them. Fix bayonets and charge straight at the enemy. Shout as you charge and, believe me, they'll run.' He paused, his hard eyes looking at each of the militia commanders in turn who, all except for Major Daniel Littlefield who had nodded enthusiastic agreement, appeared somewhat daunted by the marine's grim words. 'Use sharp steel and blunt courage,' Welch growled, 'and we will win.' He said the last four words slowly, distinctly and with a grim emphasis.

The cabin stayed silent as the men contemplated the marine's words, then the Reverend Murray cleared his throat. 'Gentlemen,' he said, 'let us bow our heads.' He paused. 'O Lord,' he continued, 'Thou hast promised to cover us with Thy strong wings, so protect us now as we go . . .' He was interrupted by the sound of a cannon firing. The noise was sudden and shockingly loud. The echo of the gun rebounded back from the bluff, then the afternoon was riven by gunfire, by cannon after cannon and by echo after echo, and the rest of the prayer went unspoken as men hurried on deck to watch Commodore Saltonstall's warships make their first attack.

From the Oath demanded by Brigadier-General Francis McLean
of the inhabitants around the Penobscot River, July, 1779:

Calling the most great and sacred God to the truth of my
Intentions, I do most solemnly promise and swear that I will
bear true Allegiance and be a faithful subject to his most sacred
Majesty George the Third King of Great Britain France and
Ireland, and of the Colonies of N. America, Now falsely stiling
themselves the United States of America . . .

From the Proclamation to the inhabitants of the Penobscot
region, issued by Brigadier-General Solomon Lovell, July 29th,
1779:

I do hereby assure the Inhabitants of Penobscot and the
Country adjacent, that if they are found to be so lost to all the
virtues of good Citizens . . . by becoming the first to desert the
cause of Freedom of Virtue and of God . . . they must expect to
be the first also to experience the just resentment of this injured
and betrayed Country, in the condign punishment which their
treason deserves.

Excerpt of letter from Colonel John Frost, Massachusetts Militia, to the Council of Massachusetts, July 20th, 1779:

I would beg leave to inform your Honors In calling for Officers from the third Regiment in the Brigade to my Surprise I found that their was neither Officer in said Regiment . . . that had a Proper Commission the reason is all the Officers in said Regiment were Commissioned in the year 1776 with the Stile of George the Third King and Colonel Tristrum Jordan then commanded said Regiment but did not take proper care that the Commissions were altered agreable to an Act of this State . . . should be glad of your Honors Direction about the Affair and shall wait your Honors Orders.

FIVE

The *Tyrannicide*, flying the pine-tree flag of the Massachusetts Navy, was the first warship to engage the enemy. She came from the west, sliding before the freshening wind towards the harbour's narrow entrance. To the men watching from the shore it seemed she was determined to force that entrance by sailing into the small gap between HMS *Nautilus* and the battery on Cross Island, but then she swung to port so that she sailed northwards, parallel with the British sloops. Her forrard starboard gun opened the battle. The *Tyrannicide* was armed with six-pounders, seven in each broadside, and her first gun shrouded the brig in thick smoke. The ball struck the sea a hundred yards short of the *Nautilus*, bounced off a small wave, bounced a second time and then sank just as the whole British line disappeared behind its own smoke as Captain Mowat's ships took up the challenge. The *Hampden*, the big ship from New Hampshire, was next into action, her nine-pounders firing into the British smoke. All that Captain Salter of the *Hampden* could see of the three enemy sloops were their topmasts above the cloud. 'Batter them, boys!' he called cheerfully to his gunners.

The wind was brisk enough to shift the smoke quickly. Titus Salter watched as the *North* reappeared from the smoke cloud, then another stab of bright flame flashed from one of the British sloop's gunports and he heard the crash as her round shot struck the *Tyrannicide* ahead, then his view was again obscured by the grey, acrid smoke of his own guns. 'Reload!' a man bellowed. The *Hampden* sailed out of her smoke and Captain Salter cupped his hands and shouted. 'Hold your fire! Hold it!' A British round shot screamed close overhead, smacking a hole through the *Hampden*'s mizzen sail. 'Hold your damned fire!' Salter bellowed angrily.

A brig had suddenly appeared on the *Hampden*'s starboard quarter. She was a much smaller vessel, armed with fourteen six-pounders, and her skipper, instead of following the New Hampshire ship, was now overtaking her and so putting his ship between the *Hampden*'s guns and the British sloops. 'Damned fool,' Salter growled. 'Wait till she's clear!' he called to his gunners.

The brig, flying the pine-tree ensign of the Massachusetts Navy, was the *Hazard*, and her captain was vomiting from a stomach upset so her first lieutenant, George Little, was commanding her. He was oblivious to the *Hampden*, concerned only with taking his ship as close to the enemy as he could and then pounding the sloops with his seven-gun broadside. He wished the commodore had ordered a proper assault, an attack straight into the harbour mouth, but if he was ordered to restrict himself to a bombardment then he wanted his guns to do real damage. 'Kill the bastards!' he shouted at his gunners. Little was in his early twenties, a fisherman turned naval officer, a man of passion, a patriot, and he ordered his sheets released so that the power went from his sails and the *Hazard* slowed in the water to give her gunners a more stable platform. 'Fire, you bastards!' He gazed at the smoke cloud shrouding the British ship *Nautilus* and saw it infused with a red glow as a gun fired. The ball struck the *Hazard* low by the waterline, shuddering the hull. The ship shook again as her own guns fired, the noise seeming to fill the universe. 'Where the devil is the *Warren*?' Little protested.

'He's holding her back, sir,' the helmsman answered.

'For what?'

The helmsman shrugged. The gunners on the nearest six-pounder were swabbing out the barrel, propelling a jet of steam through the touch-hole that reminded Little of a whale spouting. 'Cover that touch-hole!' he screamed at them. The rush of air caused by a thrust swab could easily ignite powder residue and explode the rammer back into the gunner's guts. 'Use your thumb-stall, man,' he snarled at the gunner, 'and block the touch-hole when you swab!' He watched approvingly as the charge, wadding and shot were thrust efficiently down the cleared gun, then as the train-tackle ropes were hauled and the cannon run out. The wheels rumbled on the deck, the crew stepped aside, the gunner touched his linstock to the powder-filled quill and the gun belched its anger and smoke. Little was certain he heard the satisfying crunch of a shot striking home on the enemy. 'That's the way, boys!' he shouted, 'that's the only message the bastards understand! Kill them!' He could not keep still. He was shifting his weight from foot to foot, fidgeting, as if all his energy was frustrated by his inability to get closer to the hated enemy.

Captain Salter had now edged the *Hampden* ahead of the *Hazard* again. Earlier in the afternoon the commodore had toured the anchored fleet in the fast schooner *Rover* to shout his instructions to the captains who would engage the British. Aim for their anchor rodes, he had ordered, and Salter was doing his best to obey. His guns were loaded with bar and chain-shot, both designed to slash rigging and, though he doubted his gunners' accuracy in the smoke-shrouded afternoon, Salter understood what Saltonstall wanted. The three British sloops were held fore and aft by anchors to which spring-lines were attached, and by tightening or loosening the springs they could adjust their hulls to the wind or current and so keep their wall-like alignment across the harbour mouth. If a spring or an anchor-line could be severed then one of the enemy ships would swing like an opening gate, leaving a massive hole into which a rebel ship could sail to rake the sloops.

The chain-shot was two halves of a cannonball joined by a thick length of chain. When the shot flew it made a sudden sighing noise, like a scythe. The linked half-balls whirled as they flew, but they vanished into the smoke fog and Salter, staring hard at the mastheads, could see no sign that the scything chains were severing any lines. Instead the British gunners were returning the fire fast, keeping the smoke constant about their three hulls, and more fire, heavier fire, was thumping into the *Hampden* from the battery on Cross Island. The high bluff of the peninsula was also wreathed in yellow-grey smoke as the smaller battery on Dyce's Head joined in the fight.

The tide was flooding, drawing the ships closer to the harbour mouth, and Salter ordered his sheets tightened so that the *Hampden* could sail away from any danger of going aground. The Continental brig *Diligent*, with its puny three-pounders, sailed into the smoke cloud left by the *Hampden* and her small broadside spat towards the enemy. The *Hazard*, realizing the same danger of grounding, had gathered way and now crossed close behind Salter's stern. 'Where the devil is the *Warren*?' Lieutenant Little shouted across at Salter.

'Anchored still!' Salter called back.

'She's got eighteen-pounders! Why the devil isn't she battering the . . . ?'

Salter did not hear the last word because a six-pounder ball, fired from Dyce's Head, smacked into his deck and gouged long splinters from the planks before vanishing off the port-side. By a miracle no one was hurt. Two more ships were now following the *Diligent* into the smoke, their guns spitting fire and iron at the king's sloops. The noise was constant, a ceaseless ear-pounding percussion. Lieutenant Little was still shouting, but the *Hazard* had drawn away and Salter could not hear him over the sky-filling noise. A ball screamed overhead and Salter, looking up, was surprised to see a second hole in his mizzen sail. Another round shot cracked into the hull, shaking the big ship, and he listened for a scream, relieved when none sounded. The shifting smoke that hid the three British sloops was being constantly lit by gunflashes so that the grey cloud would glow for an instant, fade, then glow again. Glow after glow, relentless, flickering along the line of smoke, sometimes melding to a brighter red as two or three or four flames flared at once, and Salter recognized the skill that lay behind the frequency of those flashes. The gunners were fast. Mowat, he thought grimly, had trained his men well. 'Maybe the bastards will run out of ammunition,' he said to no one in particular, and then, as his ship turned west beneath Dyce's Head, he looked up to see redcoats among the trees on the high bluff. A puff of smoke lingered there, and Salter assumed a musket had been fired at his ship, but where the ball went he had no idea. Two more gouts of smoke showed among the trees, and then the *Hampden* was in open water, running down towards the anchored transports, and Salter wore ship to take the *Hampden* round again.

The *Hazard*'s carpenter, his trousers soaked to the waist, appeared from the after-hatch. 'We took a shot just under the waterline,' he reported to Lieutenant Little.

'How bad?'

'Nasty enough. Broke a pair of strakes. Reckon you'll need both pumps.'

'Plug it,' Little said.

'It killed a rat too,' the carpenter said, evidently amused.

'Plug it!' Little shouted at the man, 'because we're going round again. Double-shot the guns!' He called the last command down the deck, then turned an angry face on the helmsman. 'I want to get closer next time!'

'There are rocks off the entrance,' the helmsman warned.

'Closer, I said!'

'Aye aye, sir, closer it is, sir,' the helmsman said. He knew better than to argue, just as he knew better than to steer the ship any closer to Cross Island than he already had. He shifted a wad of tobacco in his mouth and spun the wheel to take the brig back southwards. A British round shot whipped just forrard of the *Hazard*'s jib-boom, skipped off a small wave, and finally splashed and sank a couple of hundred paces short of the anchored *Warren*.

Lieutenant John Moore watched from the height of Dyce's Head. The battle seemed very slow to him. The wind was brisk, yet the ships seemed to crawl across the smoke-shrouded water. The guns jetted smoke in huge billows through which the big ships moved with a stately grace. The noise was fearsome. At any one moment thirty or forty guns were being served and their reports elided into a rolling concussion louder and more prolonged than any thunder. The flames made the smoke momentarily lurid and Moore was suddenly besieged by the thought that hell itself would appear thus, yet for all the sound and fury there seemed to be little damage on either side. Mowat's three ships were immovable, their broadsides undiminished by the enemy fire, while the American ships sailed serenely through the splashes of the British bombardment. Some balls struck their targets; Moore distinctly heard the crash of splintering timber, yet he saw no evidence of damage and the scrubbed decks of the enemy ships appeared unstained by blood.

One enemy ship, larger than the rest, sailed close beneath Dyce's Head and Moore allowed his men to shoot their muskets down onto the enemy, though he knew the range was extreme and their hopes of hitting anything other than water were slim to nothing. He distinctly saw a man on the ship's afterdeck turn and gaze up at the bluff and Moore had the absurd instinct to wave at him. He checked himself. A sudden gust of stronger wind cleared the smoke from about the three Royal Navy sloops and Moore could see no injury to their hulls, while their masts still stood and their flags yet flew. A gun fired from the *Albany* and, just before the smoke obscured the ship again, Moore saw the water ahead of the gunport flatten and flee outwards in a fan pattern.

Nine enemy ships were attacking Mowat's line yet, to Moore's surprise, none tried to break that line. Instead they were circling and taking turns to hammer their broadsides at the sloops. Just behind Mowat's sloops, and anchored in a similar line, were the three big transport ships that had helped carry McLean's men to Majabigwaduce. Their crews leaned on their gunwales and watched the cannon smoke. Some enemy round shot, passing between the sloops, crashed into the transports whose job was to wait and see if any American ship succeeded in breaking through Mowat's line, then attempt to entangle that ship, but no enemy appeared willing to sail straight through the harbour mouth.

Lieutenant George Little wanted to sail into the harbour, but his orders were to stay west of the entrance and so he circled the *Hazard*, her sails banging like cannon-fire as he wore ship, then ran the small brig straight towards Cross Island. A cannonball, fired from the island's battery, screamed down the deck, just missing the helmsman. 'Waste of damned powder,' Little grumbled. 'Keep her steady.'

'Rock ledges ahead, sir.'

'Damn the ledges, damn you and damn the British. Get closer!'

The helmsman spun the wheel anyway, trying to take the *Hazard* north so her broadside could spit iron and defiance at the British sloops, but Little seized the wheel and turned it back. 'Get closer, I said!'

'Sweet Jesus Christ,' the helmsman said, surrendering the wheel.

Another round shot, heavy by its sound, smashed into the *Hazard*'s bows, then the ship shuddered and there was a grating sound as her hull struck a submerged rock. Little grimaced, then turned the wheel and the *Hazard* hesitated. The grinding noise continued deep below, but then the brig lurched and loosed herself from the rock and settled on her new course. 'Hands to the pumps!' Little called. 'And gunners! Aim well!' The guns crashed back against their breech ropes and the smoke blossomed, and a British ball struck the belaying pins aft of the forward mast and splintered them, and Little was bellowing at his gunners to reload.

High on the bluff Moore watched the small brig. For a moment he thought its captain intended to ram the *Nautilus*, but then the brig turned to sail into the smoke left by the guns of the *Black Prince*, a big privateer. The brig spat its fire and iron. 'A brave little ship,' Moore said.

'He gets any closer and he'll be selling his hull for firewood, sir,' Sergeant McClure said.

Moore watched the *Hazard* sail down the line. He saw round shot strike her hull, but her rate of fire never diminished. She turned west beneath him and Moore saw her gunners reloading. 'A terrier, that one,' he said.

'But we're not rats, sir, are we?'

'We are not rats, Sergeant,' Moore said, amused. Pearce Fenistone's small guns just behind the picquet fired, their balls slashing down at the enemy ships and their smoke filling the trees. The sun was low in the west now and made the smoke glow.

'Captain Campbell coming, sir,' McClure muttered in a low warning to Moore.

Moore turned to see the tall, kilted figure of Captain Archibald Campbell approaching from the north. Campbell, a highlander of the 74th, commanded all the picquets on the bluff.

'Moore,' he greeted the lieutenant, 'I think the Yankees plan to inconvenience us.'

'It's why they came, sir,' Moore replied happily.

Campbell blinked at the younger man as if suspecting he was being mocked. He flinched as the nearest cannon recoiled, its noise huge among the trees. The three guns' breech ropes had been seized to the pine trees and every shot provoked a rain of needles and cones. 'Come and look,' Campbell ordered, and Moore followed the lanky highlander back along the bluff's top to a place where a gap in the trees offered a view of the wider bay.

The enemy's transport ships were anchored in the bay, which was being whipped into white scudding waves by the brisk wind. The gaggle of ships was well out of range of any cannon McLean might have positioned on the high ground. 'See?' Campbell pointed at the fleet and Moore, shading his eyes against the setting sun, saw longboat's nestling against the hulls of the transports.

Moore took a small telescope from a pocket and opened its tubes. It took a moment to train and focus the glass, then he saw men in green coats clambering down into one of the longboats. 'I do believe,' he said, still gazing at the sight, 'that they plan to call on us.'

'I don't have a glass,' Campbell said resentfully.

Moore took the hint and offered the glass to the captain who took an age to adjust the lenses. Campbell, like Moore, saw the men filling the small boats. He saw, too, that they were carrying muskets. 'You think they'll attack us?' he asked, sounding surprised at such a thought.

'I think we'd best assume so,' Moore suggested. It was possible that the men were being redistributed among the transport ships, but why do that now? It seemed far more likely that the Americans planned a landing.

'Bring your fellows here,' Campbell ordered.

The American warships were still shooting at Mowat's sloops, though their fire was desultory now and none, not even the *Hazard*, was venturing close to the harbour mouth. Two of the attacking ships had already sailed out of range and dropped their anchors. Moore brought his men to join the rest of Campbell's picquets just as the longboats left the shelter of the transports' hulls and pulled towards the shore. The sun was very low now, dazzling the redcoats among the bluff's trees. 'They're coming!' Captain Campbell sounded astonished.

'Are the men's muskets loaded, Sergeant?' Moore asked McClure.

'Aye, sir.'

'Leave the muskets uncocked,' Moore ordered. He did not want a shot wasted by a careless man accidentally pulling the trigger.

'Ensign Campbell, John Campbell!' Captain Campbell shouted, 'run back to the fort and tell the brigadier the rascals are coming!'

The kilted ensign left and Moore watched the approaching boats, noting that they were having a hard time in the rising wind. The bay's waves were short and sharp, smacking hard against the big rowboats to smother their oarsmen and passengers with spray.

'McLean had best send reinforcements,' Campbell said nervously.

'We can see those fellows off,' Moore responded, surprised at how confident he felt. There were some eighty redcoats on the bluff and the enemy, he guessed, numbered at least two hundred men, but those two hundred had to clamber up the bluff and the first fifty or sixty feet were so steep that no man could climb and use a musket at the same time. After that the slope flattened somewhat, but it was still precipitous and the redcoats, positioned at the summit, could fire down at men struggling up the hill. A last flurry of cannon-fire sounded from the south, the thunder echoing briefly, and Moore, without asking for orders from Campbell, leaped a few paces down the upper slope to a place where he could see the attackers more clearly.

'We'll wait for the brigadier's reinforcements,' Campbell called reprovingly.

'Of course, sir,' Moore said, hiding his disdain for the tall highlander. Campbell had sent the ensign back to the fort, but that was a journey of almost three quarters of a mile, much of it through tangling undergrowth, and McLean's reinforcements had to make the same journey back. By the time they arrived the Yankees would long have landed. If the Americans were to be stopped then Campbell's men must do the job, but Moore sensed his commander's nervousness. 'Bring the men down here, Sergeant,' he called to McClure and, ignoring Archibald Campbell's plaintive enquiry as to what he thought he was doing, led McClure and the other Hamiltons north along the bluff's shoulder. They were at the place where the easier upper slope ended, just above the steepest part of the hill, and Moore was positioning his men so that they would be directly above the beach to which the Americans rowed. He was feeling a sudden excitement. He had dreamed of battle for so long and now it was imminent, though it was nothing like his dreams. In those dreams he was on a wide open field and the enemy was in dense ranks beneath their flags, and cavalry was on the flanks, and bands were playing and Moore had often imagined surviving the enemy volleys until he ordered his own men to fire back, but instead he was scrambling through bushes and watching a flotilla of large longboats pull hard for the shore.

Those boats were close now, not more than a hundred paces from the narrow beach where the short, wind-driven waves broke white. Then a gun sounded. Moore saw a cloud of smoke appear amidships on one of the transport ships and realized it had been a small cannon aboard that ship. The round shot crashed noisily through the bluff's trees, startling birds into the evening sky, and Moore thought the single shot must presage a bombardment, but no more guns fired. Instead

149

two flags broke from the ship's yardarm and the longboats suddenly rested their oars. The boats wallowed in the turbulent water, then began to turn around. They were going back.

'God damn them,' Moore said. He watched the boats turn clumsily and realized the Americans had abandoned their plans. 'Give them a volley,' he ordered McClure. The range was long, but Moore's frustration seethed in him. 'Fire!' he snapped at the sergeant.

The Hamiltons cocked their muskets, aimed, and let loose a ragged volley. The musket sound stuttered in the trees. Moore was standing to one side and was certain he saw a man in the nearest rowboat thrown violently forward. 'Hold your fire!' Campbell shouted angrily from the summit.

'We hit a man,' Moore told McClure.

'We did?' the sergeant sounded disbelieving.

'One less rebel, Sergeant,' Moore said, 'God damn their disloyal souls.'

The wind carried the musket smoke away and the sun, which had momentarily been obscured by a ribbon of cloud above the bay's western shore, suddenly flared bright and dazzling. There was a silence, except for the rush of wind and the fret of breaking waves.

A cheer sounded as the sun set. Brigadier McLean had led his officers down to the shore and along the beach to a place just beyond the Half Moon Battery and there, within easy earshot of the three Royal Navy sloops, he saluted them. To McLean, watching from the low unfinished ramparts of Fort George, it had appeared that the Americans had tried to enter the harbour, but had been repulsed by Mowat's guns, and so McLean wanted to thank the navy. His officers faced the ships, raised their hats and McLean led them in three heartfelt cheers.

The Union flag still flew above Fort George.

*   *   *

'An Indian named John,' Wadsworth said.

'What was that? Who?' General Lovell had been whispering to his secretary and missed his deputy's words.

'The man who died, sir. He was an Indian named John.'

'And then there were forty,' a man spoke from the cabin's edge.

'Not one of ours, then,' Saltonstall said.

'A brave man,' Wadsworth said, frowning at both comments. The Indian had been struck by a musket ball the previous evening, just after the assault boats had turned away from the shore. A small volley of musketry had crackled from the woods on the bluff and, though the range was far beyond any hope of accuracy, the British ball had struck the Indian in the chest, killing him in seconds. Wadsworth, on board the *Sally*, had seen the survivors climb aboard, their coats spattered with John's blood.

'Just why did we abandon last night's landing?' Saltonstall asked dourly. The commodore had tipped his chair back so that he looked at the army officers down his long nose.

'The wind was too strong,' Lovell explained, 'and we discerned that we should have difficulties returning the boats to the transports to embark the second division.'

The leaders of the expedition were meeting for a council of war in the commodore's cabin on board the *Warren*. Twenty-one men crowded about the table, twelve of them captains of the warships while the rest were majors or colonels from the militia. It was Monday morning, the wind had dropped, there was no fog and the skies above Penobscot Bay were clear and blue. 'The question,' Lovell opened the proceedings by tapping a long finger against the commodore's polished table, 'is whether we should exert our full force against the enemy today.'

'What else?' Captain Hallet, who commanded the Massachusetts Navy brigantine, *Active*, asked.

'If the ships were to assault the enemy vessels,' Lovell

suggested diffidently, 'and we were to land the men, I think God would prosper our endeavours.'

'He surely would,' the Reverend Murray said confidently.

'You want me to enter the harbour?' Saltonstall asked, alarmed.

'If that is necessary to destroy the enemy shipping?' Lovell responded with a question.

'Let me remind you,' the commodore let his chair fall forward with a sharp bang, 'that the enemy presents a line of guns supported by batteries and beneath the artillery of a fortress. To take ships into that damned hole without a reconnaissance would be the very height of madness.'

'Fighting madness,' someone muttered from the after part of the cabin, and Saltonstall glared at the officers there, but made no comment.

'You are suggesting, perhaps, that we have not reconnoitered sufficiently?' Lovell still spoke in questions.

'We have not,' Saltonstall said firmly.

'Yet we know where the enemy guns are situated,' Wadsworth said, just as firmly.

Saltonstall glared at the younger brigadier. 'I take my fleet into that damned hole,' he said, 'and I get tangled with their damned ships and all you have is a mess of wreckage, maybe ablaze, and all the while the damned enemy is pouring shot at us from their land batteries. You wish to explain to the Navy Board that I lost a precious frigate at the insistence of the Massachusetts Militia?'

'God will watch over you,' the Reverend Murray assured the commodore.

'God, sir, is not manning my guns!' Saltonstall snarled at the clergyman. 'I wish to God He were, but instead I have a crew of pressed men! Half the bastards have never seen a gun fired!'

'Let us not be heated,' Lovell put in hastily.

'Would it help, Commodore, if the battery on Cross Island were to be removed?' Wadsworth asked.

'Its removal is essential,' Saltonstall said.

Lovell looked helplessly at Wadsworth who began to think what troops he could use to assault the island, but Captain Welch intervened. 'We can do that, sir,' the tall marine said confidently.

Lovell smiled in relief. 'Then it seems we have a plan of action, gentlemen,' he said, and so they did. It took an hour of discussion to resolve the plan's details, but when the hour was over it had been decided that Captain Welch would lead over two hundred marines to attack the British battery on Cross Island and while that operation was being conducted the warships would again engage the three sloops so that their guns could not be trained on Welch's men. At the same time, to prevent the British from sending reinforcements south across the harbour, General Lovell would launch another attack on the peninsula. Lovell offered the plan for the council's approval and was rewarded with unanimous consent. 'I feel confident,' Lovell said happily, 'supremely confident, that Almighty God will shower blessings on this day's endeavours.'

'Amen,' the Reverend Murray said, 'and amen.'

Captain Michael Fielding sought out General McLean shortly after dawn. The general was seated in the new sunlight outside the large store-hut that had just been completed inside the fort. A servant was shaving McLean who smiled ruefully at Fielding. 'Shaving's difficult with a gimped right arm,' the general explained.

'Lift your chin, sir,' the servant said, and there was no talking for a moment as the razor scraped up the general's neck.

'What's on your mind, Captain?' McLean asked as the razor was rinsed.

'An abatis, sir.'

'An excellent thing to have on your mind,' McLean said lightly, then was silent again as the servant towelled his face.

'Thank you, Laird,' he said as the cloth was taken from his neck. 'Have you breakfasted, Captain?'

'Thin commons, sir.'

McLean smiled. 'I'm told the hens have begun to lay. Can't have you fellows starving. Laird? Be a good fellow and see if Graham can conjure up some poached eggs.'

'Aye, sir,' the servant gathered his bowl, towel, razor and strop, 'and coffee, sir?'

'I shall promote you to colonel if you can find me coffee, Laird.'

'You promoted me to general yesterday, sir,' Laird said, grinning.

'I did? Then give me cause to preserve your exalted rank.'

'I shall do my best, sir.'

McLean led Fielding to the fort's western rampart that faced towards the high wooded bluff. It was ridiculous to call it a rampart, for it was still unfinished and a fit man could leap it easily. The ditch beyond was shallow and the pointed stakes in its bed would hardly delay the enemy for a moment. Mclean's men had begun work to heighten the wall at dawn, but the general knew he needed another week's uninterrupted labour simply to make the ramparts high enough to deter an attack. He used his stick to help himself up the mound of logs and hard-packed soil that formed the rampart and stared across the harbour, beyond Mowat's flotilla, to where the enemy warships were anchored in the bay. 'No fog this morning, Captain.'

'None, sir.'

'God smiles on us, eh?'

'He is an Englishman, sir, remember?' Fielding suggested with a smile. Captain Michael Fielding was also an Englishman, an artilleryman in a dark blue coat. He was thirty years old, fair-haired, blue-eyed and disconcertingly elegant, looking as if he would be far more at home in some London salon than in this American wilderness. He was the epitome of the kind

154

of Englishman McLean instinctively disliked. He was too languid, too superior and too handsome, but to McLean's surprise Captain Fielding was also efficient, cooperative and intelligent. He led fifty gunners and commanded a strange assortment of cannon: six-pounders, nine-pounders and twelve-pounders, some on field carriages, a few on garrison carriages and the rest on naval trucks. The guns had been scraped together from the depots in Halifax to form makeshift batteries, but then, McLean thought, everything about this expedition was makeshift. He did not have enough men, enough ships or enough guns.

'Aye,' McLean said wistfully, 'I would like an abatis.'

'If you can lend me forty men, sir?' Fielding suggested.

McLean thought about the request. He had almost two hundred men scattered in a picquet line guarding those places where the Yankees might attempt a landing. He reckoned the enemy's approach to the bluff the previous evening had been just that, a bluff. They wanted him to think they would assault the peninsula's western end, but he was certain they would choose either the harbour or the neck, and the neck was by far the likeliest landing place. Yet he had to guard all the possible landing places, and the picquets watching the shore consumed almost a third of his men. The rest were labouring to deepen the fort's well and raise the fort's walls, but if he were to grant Fielding's request then he must detach some of those men, which meant slower progress on the vital ramparts. Yet the abatis was a good idea. 'Will forty men be enough?'

'We'd need an ox-team too, sir.'

'Aye, you will,' McLean said, but his ox-teams were busy hauling material from the harbour's beach where most of Fielding's guns were still parked.

McLean glanced at the twin bastions that flanked the fort's western wall. So far he only had two guns mounted, which was a paltry defence. It would be easy enough to bring more guns into the fort, but the wall was now just at the height where those guns needed platforms, and platforms took time and men. 'Where would you place the abatis?' he asked.

Fielding nodded westwards. 'I'd cover that approach, sir, and the northern side.'

'Aye,' McLean agreed. An abatis curving around the west and north of the fort would obstruct any Yankee attack from either the bluff or the neck.

'Much of the timber's already cut, sir,' Fielding said, attempting to persuade McLean.

'So it is, so it is,' McLean said distractedly. He beckoned the Englishman off the wall and across the ditch so they were out of earshot of the working parties that laid logs on top of the rampart. 'Let me be frank with you, Captain,' McLean said heavily.

'Of course, sir.'

'There are thousands of the rebel rascals. If they come, Captain, and they will come, then I must suppose that two or three thousand will attack us. You know what that means?'

Fielding was silent for a few seconds, then nodded. 'I do, sir.'

'I've seen enough war,' McLean said ruefully.

'You mean, sir, we can't stand against three thousand men?'

'Oh, we can stand, Captain. We can give them a bloody nose, right enough, but can we defeat them?' McLean turned and gestured at the half-finished wall. 'If that rampart was ten feet high I could die of old age inside the fort, and if we had a dozen guns mounted then I daresay we could defeat ten thousand men. But if they come today? Or tomorrow?'

'They'll overrun us, sir.'

'Aye, they will. And that's not cowardice speaking, Captain.'

Fielding smiled. 'No one, sir, can accuse General McLean of cowardice.'

'I thank you, Captain,' McLean said, then stared west towards the high ground. The ridge rose gently, studded with

156

the stumps of felled trees. 'I'm being candid with you, Captain,' he went on. 'The enemy is going to come, and we're going to show defiance, but I don't want a massacre here. I've seen that happen. I've seen men enraged to fury and seen them slaughter a garrison, and I did not come here to lead good young Scotsmen to an early grave.'

'I understand you, sir,' Fielding said.

'I hope you do.' McLean turned to look north where the cleared ground dropped away to the woods that screened the wide neck. That was where he thought his enemy would appear. 'We'll do our duty, Captain,' he said, 'but I'll not fight to the last man unless I see a chance of defeating the rascals. Enough mothers in Scotland have lost their sons.' He paused, then gave the artillery officer a smile, 'but I'll not surrender too easily either, so this is what we'll do. Make your abatis. Start on the northern side, Captain. How many field-mounted guns do you have?'

'Three nine-pounders, sir.'

'Put them just outside the fort on the north-eastern corner. You have case shot?'

'Plenty, sir, and Captain Mowat's sent some grape.'

'Well and good. So if the enemy comes from the north, which I think they will, you can give them a warm welcome.'

'And if they come this way, sir?' Fielding asked, pointing to the high western bluff.

'We lose our gamble,' McLean admitted. He hoped he had judged the tall Englishman right. A foolish man might construe the conversation as cowardice, even treasonable cowardice, but McLean reckoned Fielding was subtle and sensible enough to understand what had just been said. Brigadier Francis McLean had seen enough war to know when fighting was pointless, and he did not want hundreds of needless deaths on his conscience, but nor did he want to hand the rebels an easy victory. He would fight, he would do his duty, and he would cease to fight when he saw that defeat was inevitable. McLean turned back towards the fort, then suddenly remembered a matter that needed to be aired. 'Have your rogues been stealing potatoes from Doctor Calef's garden?' he asked.

'Not that I know of, sir.'

'Well someone has, and the doctor's not happy!'

'Isn't it early for potatoes, sir?'

'That won't stop them! And doubtless they taste well enough, so tell your fellows I'll be flogging the next man caught stealing the doctor's potatoes. Or anyone else's vegetables for that matter. Dear me, I do despair of soldiers. You could march them through heaven and they'd steal every last harp.' McLean gestured towards the fort. 'Now let's see if those eggs are cooked.'

There was a chance, McLean thought, just a slender chance that a rebel attack could be repulsed and Fielding's proposed abatis would increase that chance a little. An abatis was simply an obstacle of rough timber; a line of big branches and untrimmed trunks. An abatis could not stop an assault, but it would slow an enemy attack as men sought a way through the tangle of timber and, as the Yankees bunched behind the web of branches, Fielding's guns could hammer them with case shot like giant shotguns. McLean would place the three nine-pounders on his right flank so that as the enemy came around the open space at the end of the abatis they would advance straight into the cannon-fire, and raw troops, inexperienced in war, would be cowed by such concentrated artillery fire. Maybe, just maybe, the abatis would give the guns time enough to persuade the enemy not to press home their attack. That was a slim chance, but if the Yankees came from the west, from the bluff, then McLean reckoned there was no chance at all. He simply did not have enough artillery and so he would greet them with shots from the two guns emplaced on the western ramparts and then submit to the inevitable.

Laird had poached eggs waiting on a table set in the open air. 'And you have fried potatoes, sir,' he said happily.

'Potatoes, Laird?'

'New little potatoes, sir, fresh as daisies. And coffee, sir.'

'You're a rogue, Laird, you're an unprincipled damned rogue.'

'Yes, sir, I am, sir, and thank you, sir.'

McLean sat to his breakfast. He looked up at the flag that flew so bright in the day's new light and wondered what flag would fly there as the sun set. 'We must do our best,' he told Fielding, 'and that's all we can do. Our best.'

The marines would be attacking the British battery on Cross Island, which meant General Wadsworth could not use them in the assault on the bluff. 'That really doesn't signify,' Solomon Lovell had declared. 'I'm sure the marines are very fine fellows,' he had told Wadsworth, 'but we Massachusetts men must do the work! And we can do the work, upon my soul, we can!'

'Under your inspired leadership, General,' the Reverend Murray chimed in.

'Under God's leadership,' Lovell had said reprovingly.

'The good Lord chooses His instruments,' Murray said.

'So this will be a victory for the militia alone,' Lovell had told Wadsworth.

And Wadsworth thought that perhaps Lovell was right. He felt that hope as he stood on the afterdeck of the sloop *Bethaiah* and listened to Major Daniel Littlefield talk to the men of the York County militia. 'The redcoats are just boys!' Littlefield told his men, 'and they're not trained to fight the way we fight. Remember all those evenings on the training field? Some of you groused about that, you'd rather have been drinking Ichibod Flander's spruce beer, but you'll thank me when we're ashore. You're trained! And you're better than any damned redcoat! They're not cunning like you are,

159

they don't shoot as straight as you do, and they're frightened! Remember that! They're frightened young boys a long way from home.' Littlefield grinned at his men, then pointed at a bearded giant who crouched in the front row of his assembled troops. 'Isaac Whitney, you tell me this. Why do British soldiers wear red?'

Whitney frowned. 'Maybe so the blood don't show?'

'No!' Littlefield cried. 'They wear red to make themselves easy targets!' The men laughed. 'And you're all good shooters,' Littlefield went on, 'and today you shoot for liberty, for your homes, for your wives, for your sweethearts, and so that none of us has to live under a foreign tyranny!'

'Amen to that,' a man called.

'No more taxes!' another man shouted.

'Amen to that!' Littlefield said. The York County captain exuded confidence, and Wadsworth, watching and listening, felt immensely cheered. The militia was under strength and too many of its men were greybeards or else hardly men at all, yet Daniel Littlefield was inspiring them. 'We're going ashore,' Littlefield said, 'and we have to climb that rare steep slope. See it, boys?' He pointed to the bluff. 'It'll be a hard enough climb, but you'll be among trees. The redcoats can't see you among the trees. Oh, they'll shoot, but they won't be aiming, and you just climb, boys. If you don't know where to go, follow me. I'll be going straight up that slope and at the top I'm going to shoot some of those red-coated boys all the way back across the ocean. And remember,' he paused, looking earnestly at his men one by one, 'remember! They're much more frightened of you than you are of them. Oh, I know they look very fine and fancy on parade, but it's when you're in the woods and the guns begin to speak that a soldier earns his pay, and we're the better soldiers. You hear that? We're the better soldiers, and we're going to kick their royal backsides from here to kingdom come!' The men cheered that sentiment. Littlefield waited for the cheer to stop. 'Now, boys, go clean your guns, oil your locks and sharpen your bayonets. We have God's great work to do.'

'A fine speech,' Wadsworth congratulated the major.

Littlefield smiled. 'A true speech, sir.'

'I never doubted it.'

'Those redcoats are just frightened boys,' Littlefield said, looking towards the bluff where, he assumed, the British infantry was waiting among the trees. 'We magnify the enemy, sir. We think because they wear red coats that they must be ogres, but they're just boys. They march very prettily, and they know how to stand in a straight line, but that doesn't make them soldiers! We'll beat them. You were at Lexington, I think?'

'I was.'

'Then you saw the redcoats run!'

'I saw them retreat, yes.'

'Oh, I don't deny they're disciplined, sir, but you still beat them back. They're not trained for this sort of fight. They're trained to fight big battles in open land, not to be murdered in the undergrowth, so don't you have any doubts, sir. We shall win.'

And the major was right, Wadsworth reflected, the redcoats were trained to fight great battles where men had to stand in the open and exchange musket volleys. Wadsworth had seen that at Long Island and he had reluctantly admired the enemy's iron discipline, but here? Here among Majabigwaduce's dark trees? The discipline would surely be eroded by fear.

The British battery atop the bluff bellowed noise and smoke. It was invisible from the *Bethaiah* because the redcoats had positioned it to fire south towards the harbour entrance rather than west towards the anchored transports. The guns were shooting towards the *Hampden*, which was again cannonading the British sloops. The *Tyrannicide* and *Black Prince* sailed behind the New Hampshire ship, their job to distract the

British and keep the Royal Marines on board the sloops. Wadsworth wondered how well the guns on the heights of Dyce's Head were protected. 'Your task,' he said to Littlefield, 'is merely to threaten the enemy. You understand that?'

'A demonstration, sir, to dissuade the enemy from reinforcing Cross Island?'

'Precisely.'

'But if we perceive an opportunity?' Littlefield asked with a smile.

'It would certainly be a blessing to the commodore if we could destroy those guns,' Wadsworth said, nodding towards the fog of powder smoke lingering around the bluff.

'I make no promises, sir,' Littlefield said, 'but I reckon my men will feel happier with God's good earth under their feet. Let me sniff the enemy, sir. If they're few, then we'll make them fewer still.'

'But no undue risks, Major,' Wadsworth said sternly. 'We'll land in force tomorrow. I don't want to lose you this evening!'

'Oh, you won't lose me!' Littlefield said with amusement. 'I intend to watch the very last redcoat leave America, and I'll help him on his way with a boot up his royal backside.' He turned back to his men. 'Right, you rogues! Into the boats! We've got redcoats to kill!'

'Be careful, Major,' Wadsworth said, and immediately regretted the words because, to his ears, they sounded weak.

'Don't you worry, sir,' Littlefield said, 'we're going to win!'

And Wadsworth believed him.

That afternoon as the American ships again closed on the harbour mouth and opened fire against the three British vessels, Marine Captain Welch was on board the Continental sloop *Providence*, which was leading the two Massachusetts Navy brigs, the *Pallas* and *Defence*. The wind was light and the three small ships were all under oars. 'We call it the white ash wind,' Hoysteed Hacker, the captain of the *Providence*, told Welch.

The ash oars were monstrously long and very awkward to pull, but the navy crew worked enthusiastically to drive the sloop southwards against the flooding tide. They were rowing towards the channel that ran south of Cross Island. 'There's a rock right in the damned centre of the channel,' Hacker said, 'and no one knows how deep it lies. But the tide will help us once we're in the channel.'

Welch nodded, but said nothing. He was gazing back north. The American ships were again bombarding the three British sloops who were now firing back, blanketing their hulls in grey-white smoke. More smoke shrouded the northern side of Cross Island where the British battery was hammering its shot at the attacking Americans. Further north Welch could see the longboats pulling away from the transport ships. Good. The British must know why the *Providence*, *Pallas* and *Defence* were working their way around Cross Island, but they dared not send reinforcements across the harbour, not while a major attack threatened the bluff. 'We land soon,' Welch growled at his men as the oarsmen turned the sloop into the narrow channel, 'and we fix bayonets, and we go fast! You understand? We go fast!'

But just then a grinding noise sounded deep in the *Providence*'s hull and the sloop jarred to an instant stop. 'Rock,' Hoysteed Hacker explained laconically.

So the marines, over two hundred of them, could not go fast, because they had to wait while the tide lifted the *Providence*'s hull over the sunken rock. Welch simmered. He wanted to kill, he wanted to fight, and instead he was stranded in the channel and all he could see now was the wooded hump of Cross Island with the smoke discolouring the sky above. The sound of the guns was incessant, a melding thunder, and sometimes amidst that devil's drum roll would come the crunch of a shot striking timber. Welch fidgeted. He imagined redcoats being ferried across the harbour, and still the *Providence* could make no headway.

163

'Damn it!' Welch burst out.

'Tide's rising,' Hoysteed Hacker said. He was a large man, as tall as Welch, whose broad shoulders strained the seams of his naval uniform. He had a heavy face, thick-browed and lantern-jawed, with a ragged scar on the left cheek. The scar had been caused by a boarding pike wielded by a British sailor on HMS *Diligent*, the brig Hacker had captured. That sailor had died, gutted by Hacker's heavy cutlass, and the *Diligent* was now anchored in Penobscot Bay and flying the ensign of the Continental Navy. Hoysteed Hacker was not going to be intimidated by Welch's impatience. 'Can't hurry the tide,' he said.

'How long, for God's sake?'

'Long as it takes.'

They had to wait half an hour, but at last the *Providence*'s keel cleared the sunken rock and the sloop pulled on towards a small stony beach. Her bows touched the land and were held there by the light wind. The two smaller brigs grounded on either side and green-coated marines leaped into the water and waded ashore, carrying cartridge cases and muskets above their heads. Welch was leading one company while Captain Davis, who still wore the blue coat of the Continental Army rather than marine green, led the other. 'Let's go,' Welch said.

The marines fixed bayonets. The trees muffled the sound of the battery's guns only three hundred yards to the north. The British had posted no sentinels on the island's southern side, but Welch knew they would have seen the masts above the trees and he supposed they would be turning a cannon to face the expected attack. 'Make it quick!' Welch shouted as he led the way.

Two hundred and twenty marines went into the trees. They advanced in rough order, their bayonets glinting in the lowering sun that flickered through the thick pines. They climbed the island's slope, breasted the summit, and there, below them and just visible through the thick trunks, was a small encampment on the beach. There were four tents, a flagpole, and the battery where blue and red coats showed, and Welch, seeing the enemy close, felt the rage of battle rise in him, a rage fed by his hatred of the British. No gun faced him. The damned enemy was still firing at the American ships. He would teach them to kill Americans! He slid the naval cutlass from its scabbard, screamed a war shout and led the charge down the hill.

Twenty-two artillerymen manned the battery and twenty Royal Marines guarded them. They heard the enemy marines shouting, they saw the reflected sunlight glinting from the long blades, and the artillerymen ran. They had longboats beached close to the battery, and they abandoned the guns, abandoned everything, and sprinted for their boats. They shoved the three boats off the shingle and scrambled aboard just as the American marines burst from the trees. One boat was slow. It was afloat, but when the two men who had been pushing its bows tumbled over the gunwale, the boat grounded again. A gunner sergeant jumped out and heaved at the boat afresh, and a voice shouted a warning as a tall marine ran into the shallows. The sergeant heaved again at the boat's bows, then his coat was seized and he was flung back towards the beach. The longboat floated free and its oarsmen pulled desperately, turning and driving the boat towards the *Nautilus*, the nearest British sloop. The green-coated marines fired at the rowers. Musket balls thumped into the gunwales, an oarsman let go of his loom to clap a hand on an arm suddenly bright with blood, then a volley of musketry banged from the *Nautilus*'s forecastle and the balls whistled about the marines' heads.

The blue-coated artillery sergeant took a swing at Welch who blocked the fist with his left hand and, in a rage, slashed his cutlass at the sergeant's neck. The blade bit home, Welch sawed it, and blood sprayed high. Welch was still screaming. Red misted his vision as he grabbed the wounded man's hair and pulled him onto the newly sharpened blade, and there was still more blood jetting now, and the gunner sergeant was making a choking, gurgling noise and Welch, his green coat darkened with spatters of British blood, was grunting as he tried to slice the blade deeper still. The tide diluted the blood, and then the sergeant fell and the shallow water momentarily clouded around his twitching body. Welch put a boot on the man's head and forced him under water. He held the dying man there until the body was still

More muskets fired from the *Nautilus*, though the Royal Marines on the sloop's forecastle were shooting at long musket range and none of the Americans on Cross Island's beach was hit. The *Nautilus*'s broadside faced west, and no guns could be levered around to face the beach and so the Royal Marines shot muskets instead. 'Into the battery!' Captain Davis called. The captured battery faced north-west and a low hump of rocky land protected it from the *Nautilus* so that the rebels were safe enough when they were within its low breastworks. They discovered four guns in the emplacement. Two still had barrels too hot to touch from firing at the American ships, but the other pair had yet to be mounted on their carriages, which stood forlorn beside a rough pit that had been dug as a ready magazine. Captain Davis traced a finger over the royal cipher on one of the umounted barrels and thought it was kind of King George to provide guns for liberty. Men plundered the tents. There were blankets, bone-handled knives, a fragment of mirror and a walnut case that held three ivory-handled razors. There was a Bible, evidently much-thumbed, two packs of playing cards and a set of scrimshaw dice. There was an open barrel of salt pork, a box of ship's biscuits and two small casks of rum. Beside the guns were the mallets and iron spikes that should have been used to make the cannon useless, but the speed of the attack had driven the British off before the guns could be spiked.

The British flag still flew. Welch hauled it down and, for the first time that day, a smile showed on his blood-streaked face. He folded the flag carefully, then beckoned to one of his sergeants. 'Take this rag back to the *Providence*,' he ordered, 'and ask Captain Hacker for the loan of a boat and crew. He expects to be asked. Then take the flag to General Lovell.'

'To General Lovell?' the sergeant asked, surprised. 'Not to the commodore, sir?' Commodore Saltonstall was the marine's commander, not the brigadier.

'Take it to General Lovell,' Welch said. 'That flag,' he pointed over the rocky hump of land where, in the evening light, the flag above Fort George just showed, 'that flag will belong to the marines.' He looked down at the folds of sun-faded cloth in his big hands, then, with a shudder, spat on the flag. 'Tell General Lovell this is a gift.' He thrust the flag into the sergeant's hands. 'You got that? Tell him it's a gift from the marines.'

Because Welch reckoned Brigadier-General Goddamned Solomon Lovell needed to know who was going to win this campaign. Not Lovell's militia, but the marines. The marines, the best, the winners. And Welch would lead them to victory.

From a Petition signed by thirty-two officers belonging to the American warships in Penobscot Bay and sent to Commodore Saltonstall, July 27th, 1779:

> *To the Honorable the Commodore and Commander in Chief of the Fleet . . . we your petitioners strongly Impress'd with the importance of the Expedition, and earnestly desire to render our Country all the Service in our power Wou'd represent to your Honor, that the most spedy Exertions shou'd be used to Accomplish the design we came upon. We think Delays in the present Case are extremely dangerous: as our Enemies are daily Fortifying and Strengthening themselves . . . We don't mean to Advise, or Censure Your past Conduct, But intend only to express our desire of improving the present Opportunity to go Immediately into the Harbour, and Attack the Enemys Ships.*

From the Journal of Sergeant William Lawrence, Royal Artillery, July 13th, 1779:

> *The night is thought by our enemy to be the most Favorable time for storming Encampments . . . and None are so ready of*

taking that Advantage than his Majesty's subjects now in Rebellion, who in the Open field tremble for a British soldier.

From General Lovell's orderly book, July 24th, 1779, Head-Quarters on board the Transport *Sally*:

The Officers will be careful that every man is compleatly Equipt in Arms and Ammunition and that they have drink in their Canteens and a Morcel for their Pockets . . . the General flatters himself that should there be an Opportunity he will have the utmost exertions of every Officer and Soldier not only to maintain, but to add new Lustre to the Fame of the Massachusetts Militia.

SIX

The daylight was fading. The western sky glowed red and its light was reflected in lurid, shifting ripples across the bay. The rebel ships had been firing at the three British sloops, but, just as on the previous day, none had tried to pierce Mowat's line and so enter the harbour. They fired from a distance, aiming at the lingering cloud of red-touched, mast-pierced powder-smoke that shrouded the king's ships.

A cheer sounded from the rebel ships when they saw the flag taken down on Cross Island. Every man knew what that meant. The British had lost the battery to the south of the harbour entrance and the Americans could now make their own battery there, a battery that would be close to Mowat's line and could hammer his three ships mercilessly. The southern bulwark of the harbour, Cross Island, was captured and, as the sun leaked scarlet fire across the west and as the rebel ships still pounded their shots towards the distant sloops, Major Daniel Littlefield's militia was being rowed towards the northern bulwark.

That bulwark was Dyce's Head, the high rocky bluff on which the redcoats waited and from where the battery of six-pounders fired down at the bombarding ships. The evening was so calm that the smoke of the guns hung in the trees, indeed there was scarce enough breeze to move the American ships that belched flame, bar shot, chain shot and round shot towards Mowat's three sloops, but a vagary of that small wind, a sudden stirring of the summer air, lasted just long enough to blow the smoke away from HMS *Albany* that lay at the centre of Mowat's line and the Scottish captain, standing on his afterdeck, saw the longboats pulling away from the American transports and heading towards the bluff. 'Mister Frobisher!' Mowat called.

The *Albany*'s first lieutenant, who was supervising the starboard guns, turned towards his captain. 'Sir?'

A shot whistled overhead. Bar or chain shot, Mowat reckoned from the sound. The rebels seemed to have been aiming at his rigging mostly, but their gunnery was poor and none of the sloops had suffered significant damage. A few shrouds and halliards had been parted, and the hulls were scarred, but the sloops had lost neither men nor weapons. 'There are launches approaching the shore,' Mowat called to Frobisher, 'd'you see them?'

'Aye aye, sir, I see them!'

Frobisher tapped a gun captain on the shoulder. The gunner was a middle-aged man with long grey hair twisted into a pigtail. He had a scarf wrapped about his ears. He saw where Frobisher was pointing and nodded to show he understood what was wanted. His cannon, a nine-pounder, was already loaded with round shot. 'Run her out!' he ordered, and his crew seized the train-tackle and hauled the cannon so that the muzzle protruded from the gunwale. He shouted at his gun-deafened men to turn the heavy carriage, which they did with long spikes that gouged Mowat's carefully holy-stoned deck. 'Don't suppose we'll hit the buggers,' the gun captain said to Frobisher, 'but we might make 'em wet.' He could no longer see the rebel rowboats because the vagary of wind had died and thick pungent smoke was again enveloping the *Albany*, but he reckoned his cannon was

172

pointed in the right general direction. The gun captain thrust a thin spike through the touch-hole to pierce the canvas powder bag in the breech, then slid a portfire, a quill filled with finely mealed powder, into the hole he had made. 'Stand back, you bastards!' he bellowed and touched fire to the quill.

The gun shattered the evening air with its noise. Smoke, thick as a London fog, billowed and stank. A flame stabbed the smoke, lighting it and fading instantly. The gun leaped back, its truck wheels screaming until the breech ropes were snatched bar-tight to check the recoil. 'Swab out!' the gun captain shouted, plunging his leather-protected thumb onto the touch-hole.

'Give those launches one more shot,' Frobisher shouted over the noise of the guns, 'then aim at their ships again.'

'Aye aye, sir!'

The cannons had been firing at the American ships that manoeuvred three-quarters of a mile to the west. The launches were about the same distance away, so the gun captain had not needed to change his barrel's very slight elevation. He had used a fourth-weight charge, two and a quarter pounds of powder, and the round shot left the muzzle travelling at nine hundred and eighty feet every second. The ball lost some speed as it covered the four thousand three hundred feet before striking the water, but it had taken the shot less than five seconds to cover that distance. It slapped onto a wave, ricocheted shallowly upwards and then, trailing a shower of spray, it struck Major Littlefield's longboat plumb amidships.

To General Wadsworth, watching from the *Bethaiah*, it seemed as if the leading longboat simply disintegrated. Strakes of wood flew in the air, a man turned end over end, there was a flurry of white water and then nothing but floating oars, shattered scraps of timber and men struggling to stay afloat. The other longboats went to the rescue, pulling swimmers from the water as a second round shot splashed harmlessly nearby.

The longboats had stopped pulling for the bluff now. Wadsworth had expected them to land and then return to collect more men, indeed he had planned to go ashore with that second group, but instead the rowboats turned and headed back towards the transports. 'I hope Littlefield's not wounded,' Wadsworth said.

'Take more than a round shot to put the major down, sir,' James Fletcher commented cheerfully. Fletcher was now attached to Wadsworth's staff as an unofficial aide and local guide.

'I must assume Littlefield decided not to land,' Wadsworth said.

'Hard to fight when you're wet as a drowned rat, sir.'

'True,' Wadsworth said with a smile, then consoled himself that the threat to the bluff appeared to have achieved its purpose, which was to prevent the British sending reinforcements or a counter-attacking force to Cross Island.

The light faded fast. The eastern sky was already dark, though no stars yet showed, and the gunfire died with the day. The American warships sailed slowly back to their anchorage while Mowat's men, unscarred by the evening's duel, secured their guns. Wadsworth leaned on the *Bethaiah*'s gunwale and looked down at the shadowy boats as they approached the sloop. 'Major Littlefield!' he hailed. 'Major Littlefield!' he called again.

'He's drowned, sir,' a voice called back.

'He's what?'

'He and two other men, sir. Lost, sir.'

'Oh, dear God,' Wadsworth said. On shore, at the top of the bluff, a fire showed through the trees. Someone brewing tea, maybe, or cooking a supper.

And Major Littlefield was dead.

'Tragic,' General Lovell said when Wadsworth told him the news of Daniel Littlefield's death, though Wadsworth was not entirely sure that his commanding officer had listened to what he said. Lovell, instead, was examining a British flag that had been brought on board the *Sally* by a squat marine sergeant. 'Isn't it splendid!' Lovell exclaimed. 'We shall present it to the General Court, I think. A first trophy, Wadsworth!'

'The first of many that your Excellency will send to Boston,' the Reverend Jonathan Murray observed.

'It's a gift from the marines,' the sergeant put in stolidly.

'So you said, so you said,' Lovell said with a hint of testiness, then he smiled, 'and you must render Captain Welch my sincerest gratitude.' He glanced at the table that was covered with papers. 'Lift those documents a moment, Marston,' he ordered his secretary and, when the table was clear of paper, ink and pens, he spread the flag beneath the gently swinging lanterns. It was dark now, and the cabin was lit by four lanterns. ''Pon my soul!' Lovell stood back and admired the trophy, 'but this will look impressive in Faneuil Hall!'

'You might think of sending it to Major Littlefield's wife,' Wadsworth said.

'To his wife?' Lovell asked, evidently puzzled by the suggestion. 'What on earth would she want with a flag?'

'A reminder of her husband's gallantry?'

'Oh, you'll write to her,' Lovell said, 'and assure her that Major Littlefield died for the cause of liberty, but I can't think that she needs an enemy flag. Really I can't. It must go to Boston.' He turned to the marine sergeant. 'Thank you, my fine fellow, thank you! I shall make certain the commodore knows of my approbation.'

Lovell had summoned his military family. John Marston, the secretary, was writing in the orderly book, Wadsworth was leafing through the militia rosters, while Lieutenant-Colonel Davis, the liaison officer for the transport ships, was tallying the small craft available for a landing. The Reverend Murray was beaming helpfully, while Major Todd was cleaning a pistol with a scrap of flannel. 'You did send my orders to the Artillery Regiment?' Lovell demanded of Todd.

'Indeed, sir,' Todd said, then blew on the pistol's frizzen to clear some dust.

'Colonel Revere understands the need for haste?'

'I made that need abundantly clear, sir,' Todd said patiently. Lieutenant-Colonel Revere had been commanded to take guns to the newly-captured Cross Island that would now be defended by a garrison of sailors from the *Providence* and *Pallas* under the command of Hoysteed Hacker.

'So Colonel Revere's cannons should be active by dawn?' Lovell asked.

'I see no reason why not,' Wadsworth said.

'And that should dispose of the enemy shipping,' Lovell said happily, 'and so open the path to our success. Ah, Filmer! Thank you!'

Filmer, a servant, had brought supper of bacon, beans and cornbread, which Lovell and his companions ate at the table where the captured flag made a convenient napkin for the general's greasy hands. 'The marines are back on their ships?' Lovell asked.

'They are, sir,' Wadsworth answered.

'Though I suppose we must beg the commodore for their use again,' Lovell said resignedly.

'They are formidable,' Wadsworth said.

Lovell looked mischievous, a small half-smile on his usually solemn face. 'Did you hear that the naval officers sent the commodore a letter? Dear me! They chided him for not sailing into the harbour! Can you believe such a thing?'

'The letter shows admirable zeal, sir,' Wadsworth said evenly.

'And it must have caused him embarrassment!' Lovell said, plainly pleased with that thought. 'Poor man,' he added dutifully, 'but perhaps the remonstrance will spur him to a greater effort?'

'One prays so,' the Reverend Murray said.

'Let us pray it doesn't make him more obstinate in his dealings,' Wadsworth said, 'especially as we shall need his marines when we attack in earnest.'

'I suppose we will need them,' Lovell said grudgingly, 'if the commodore is agreeable, of course.'

'It means using a dozen longboats to land all his marines,' Davis said, 'and we already lack sufficient boats.'

'I do dislike the idea of landing piecemeal,' Lovell said, evidently toying with the idea of attacking without the marines and so keeping all the glory of victory to the militia.

'Why not use one of the smaller schooners?' Wadsworth suggested. 'I've seen them being rowed. I'm sure we could take one close enough inshore, and a schooner could carry at least a hundred men.'

Davis considered that solution, then nodded. 'The *Rachel* doesn't draw much,' he said.

'And we do need the marines,' Wadsworth said pointedly.

'I suppose we do, yes,' Lovell allowed. 'Well, we shall request their assistance.' He paused, tapping his knife against the pewter plate. 'When we capture the fort,' he said ruminatively, 'I don't want any redcoats escaping north across the isthmus. We should put a force to the north there? A blocking force?'

'Use the Indians?' Major Todd suggested, his spectacles reflecting the lantern-light. 'The British are scared of our savages.'

'They're much too valuable as fighters,' Wadsworth said hastily, 'I want them in the assault.'

'Valuable, maybe, when they're sober,' Major Todd said with a visible shudder, 'but they were inebriated again this morning.'

'The Indians?' Lovell asked. 'They were drunk?'

'Insensible, sir. The militiamen give them rum as an amusement.'

'The devil is in our midst,' Murray said darkly, 'and must be extirpated.'

'He must indeed, Chaplain,' Lovell said and looked at Marston, 'so add a command in tonight's daily orders. No man is to supply rum to the Indians. And, of course, add a mention regretting the death of Major . . . ' he paused.

'Littlefield,' Wadsworth said.

'Littlefield,' Lovell went on as if there had been no pause. 'Poor Littlefield. He came from Wells, did he not? A fine town. Perhaps his men can block the isthmus? Oh, and Marston, make some acknowledgement of the marines, will you? We must give praise where it's due, especially if we're to request the use of them again.' He mopped the grease on his plate with a piece of bread and put it into his mouth just as a hard knock sounded on the cabin door. Before anyone could respond the door was thrust open to reveal an indignant Lieutenant-Colonel Revere who came to the table's end and stared at Lovell who, his mouth full, could only wave a genial greeting.

'You ordered me to go ashore with the guns,' Revere said accusingly.

'So I did,' Lovell managed to say through his mouthful, 'so I did. Are they emplaced already?'

'You can't mean me to go ashore,' Revere said, with evident indignation. He gave his enemy, Major Todd, a dispassionate glance, then looked back to the general.

Lovell gazed at the commander of his artillery train with some bemusement. 'We need guns on Cross Island,' he said finally, 'and a new battery. Your task, surely, is to emplace them?'

'I have duties,' Revere said forcefully.

'Yes, Colonel, of course you do,' Lovell said.

'Your duty is to establish a battery on the island,' Wadsworth said forcibly.

'I can't be everywhere,' Revere declared to Lovell, ignoring Wadsworth, 'it isn't possible.'

'I believe my orders were explicit,' the general said, 'and required you to take the necessary guns ashore.'

'And I tell you I have responsibilities,' Revere protested.

178

'My dear Colonel,' Lovell said, leaning back from the table, 'I want a battery on Cross Island.'

'And you shall have one!' Revere said firmly. 'But it isn't a colonel's job to clear ground, to dig magazines or to cut down trees to clear fields of fire!'

'No, no, of course not,' Lovell said, flinching from Revere's anger.

'It is a colonel's job to establish and to command a battery,' Wadsworth said.

'You'll have your battery!' Revere snarled.

'Then I shall be satisfied,' Lovell said soothingly. Revere stared at the general for a brief moment and then, with a curt nod, turned and left. Lovell listened to the heavy footsteps climb the companionway, then let out a long breath. 'What on earth provoked that display?'

'I can't say,' Wadsworth answered, as puzzled as Lovell.

'The man is a troublemaker,' Todd said acidly, throwing an accusing look at Wadsworth who he knew had cleared Revere's appointment to command the artillery.

'A misunderstanding, I'm sure,' Lovell said, 'he's a very fine fellow! Didn't he ride to warn you at Lexington?' he asked the question of Wadsworth.

'He and at least twenty others,' Todd answered before Wadsworth could respond, 'and who do you suppose was the one rider who failed to reach Concord? Mister Revere,' he stressed the 'mister' maliciously, 'was captured by the British.'

'I do remember Revere bringing us warning that the regulars were coming,' Wadsworth said, 'he and William Dawes.'

'Revere was captured by the British?' Lovell asked. 'Oh, poor fellow.'

'Our enemies let him go, sir,' Todd said, 'but kept his horse, thus showing a nice appreciation of Mister Revere's value.'

'Oh, come now, come,' Lovell chided his brigade-major. 'Why do you dislike him so?'

Todd took off his spectacles and polished them with the

edge of the flag. 'It seems to me, sir,' he said, and the tone of his voice indicated he had taken the general's question with great seriousness, 'that the essentials of military success are organization and co-operation.'

'You're the most organized man I know!' Lovell put in.

'Thank you, sir. But Colonel Revere, sir, resents being under command. He believes, I assume, that he should command. He will go his own way, sir, and we shall go ours, and we shall receive neither co-operation nor organization.' Todd carefully hooked the spectacles back over his ears. 'I served with him, sir, in the artillery, and there was constant abrasion, irritation and conflict.'

'He's efficient,' Lovell said uncertainly, then more vigorously, 'everyone assures me he's efficient.'

'In his own interests, yes,' Todd said.

'And he knows his guns,' Wadsworth asserted.

Todd looked at Wadsworth and paused before speaking. 'I do hope so, sir.'

'He's a patriot!' Lovell said in a tone of finality. 'No one can deny that! Now, gentlemen, back to work.'

The moon was full and its light whispered silver across the bay. The tide was ebbing to carry the Penobscot's waters out to the wide Atlantic while on Cross Island the rebels were digging a new emplacement for the guns that would hammer Mowat's ships.

And on the bluff the redcoat picquets waited.

General McLean had been inordinately grateful for the two days' respite the rebels had granted him. The enemy fleet had arrived on Sunday, now it was late on Tuesday evening and there had still been no attack on Fort George, which had given him the opportunity to emplace two more guns and to raise the parapet by another two feet. He knew only too well how vulnerable his position was. He was resigned to that. He had done his best.

That night he stood at Fort George's gate that was nothing more than a brushwork barricade that could be pulled aside by the two sentries. He gazed southwards, admiring the sheen of moonlight on the harbour water. It was a pity that the artillerymen had been driven from their battery on Cross Island, but McLean had always known that position was indefensible. *Wer alles verteidigt, verteidigt nichts.* Making that battery had consumed men and time that might have been better spent on strengthening Fort George, but McLean did not regret it. The battery had done its work, deterring the American ships from entering the harbour and thus buying the last two days, but now, McLean supposed, the rebel ships would make their assault and with them would come the rebel infantry.

'You look pensive, sir,' Lieutenant Moore joined the general in the gateway.

'Aren't you supposed to be asleep?'

'I am, sir. This is but a dream.'

McLean smiled. 'When are you on duty?'

'Another two hours yet, sir.'

'Then you might accompany me,' the general suggested and led the way eastwards. 'You heard the enemy approached the bluff again?'

'Major Dunlop told me, sir.'

'And withdrew again,' McLean said, 'which suggests to me they are trying to deceive us.'

'Or lack the nerve to make an assault, sir?'

McLean shook his head. 'Never under-estimate an enemy, Lieutenant. Treat every foe as though he holds the winning cards and then, when his hand is declared, you won't be unpleasantly surprised. I think our enemy means us to believe he will assault the bluff, and so force us to commit troops there, while in truth he plans to land elsewhere.'

'Then post me elsewhere, sir.'

'You will stay on the bluff,' McLean said firmly. The general

181

had decided to thicken the picquet line facing north towards the marshy isthmus that joined Majabigwaduce to the mainland, for he still believed that to be the likeliest enemy approach. That picquet line should delay the rebels, and the tangle of the abatis would hold them for a few more moments, but inevitably they would break both those defences and charge the fort. 'If the enemy does land on the neck,' he told Moore, 'then I shall recall your picquet and you'll help defend the fort.'

'Yes, sir,' Moore said resignedly. He feared battle and he wanted battle. If the main fight tomorrow, if a fight even came tomorrow, was to be at the neck then Moore wanted to be there, but he knew he would not change McLean's mind, and so did not try.

The two men, one so young and the other a veteran of Flanders and Portugal, walked the path just north of the Hatch cornfield. Lamplight glowed bright from the windows of Doctor Calef's house, their destination. The doctor must have seen them approach in the moonlight because he threw open his door before McLean could knock. 'I have a house full of women,' the doctor greeted them morosely.

'Some men are more blessed than others,' McLean said. 'Good evening to you, Doctor.'

'There's tea, I believe,' Calef said, 'or something stronger?'

'Tea would be a pleasure,' McLean said.

A dozen women were gathered in the kitchen. The doctor's wife was there, as were Colonel Goldthwait's two daughters, the Banks girls and Bethany Fletcher. They sat on chairs and stools about the big table, which was covered with scraps of cloth. It was evident that the evening gathering was ending, because the women were stowing their work into bags. 'A sewing circle?' McLean asked.

'War doesn't stop a woman's work, General,' Mrs Calef answered.

'Nothing does,' McLean said. The women appeared to have been making and mending clothes for children, and McLean remembered his own mother joining just such a group every week. The women would talk, tell stories and sometimes sing as they darned and stitched. 'I'm glad you're all here,' McLean said, 'because I came to warn the good doctor that I expect a rebel attack tomorrow. Ah, thank you,' this last was to the maid who had brought him a mug of tea.

'You're sure about tomorrow?' Doctor Calef asked.

'I cannot speak for the enemy,' McLean said, 'but if I were in his shoes then I would come tomorrow.' In truth, had McLean been in the enemy's shoes, he would have attacked already. 'I wished to tell you,' he went on, 'that in the event of an assault you must stay indoors.' He looked at the anxious lamplit faces around the table. 'There's always a temptation to witness a fight, but in the confusion, ladies, a face seen through smoke can be mistaken for an enemy. I have no reason to believe the rebels will want to capture any of your houses, so you should be safe inside your own walls.'

'Wouldn't we be safer inside the fort?' Doctor Calef asked.

'The very last place to be,' McLean said firmly. 'Please, all of you, stay home. This is excellent tea!'

'If the rebels . . . ' Mrs Calef began, then thought better of what she had been about to say.

'If the rebels capture the fort?' McLean suggested helpfully.

'They'll find all those sworn oaths,' Mrs Calef said.

'And take revenge,' Jane Goldthwait, whom everyone called Lil for a reason long forgotten, added.

'Mister Moore,' McLean looked at the young lieutenant, 'if it looks likely that the fort will fall, then you will be responsible for burning the oaths.'

'I'd rather be killing the enemy on the ramparts, sir.'

'I am sure you would,' McLean said, 'but you will destroy the oaths first. That's an order, Lieutenant.'

'Yes, sir,' Moore said in a chastened voice.

Over six hundred local people had come to Majabigwaduce and signed the oath of loyalty to King George, and Lil Goldthwait was right, the rebels would want revenge on those folk. Dozens of families who lived about the river had already been forced from their homes in and near Boston and now they faced yet another eviction. McLean smiled. 'But we place the carriage in front of the horses, ladies. The fort has not fallen and, I can assure you, we shall do our utmost to repel the enemy.' That was not true. McLean had no wish to stand to the last man. Such a defence would be heroic, but utterly wasteful.

'There are men here who would willingly man the walls with you,' Doctor Calef said.

'I am grateful,' McLean replied, 'but such an action would expose your families to the enemy's anger and I would rather that did not happen. Please, all of you, remain in your homes.'

The general stayed to finish his tea, then he and Moore left. They stood a moment in the doctor's garden and watched the flicker of moonlight on the harbour. 'I think there'll be a fog tomorrow,' McLean said.

'The air's warm,' Moore said.

McLean stepped aside as a group of women came from the house. He bowed to them. The Banks girls, both young, were walking back to their father's house on the western side of the village beneath the fort, while Bethany Fletcher was going directly down the hill to her brother's house. 'I haven't seen your brother lately, Miss Fletcher,' McLean said.

'He went fishing, sir,' Bethany said.

'And hasn't returned?' Moore asked.

'He's sometimes away for a week,' Bethany said, flustered.

'Mister Moore,' McLean said, 'do you have time to escort Miss Fletcher safely home before you report for duty?'

'Yes, sir.'

'Then pray do so.'

'I'm safe, sir,' Bethany said.

'Indulge an old man's wishes, Miss Fletcher,' the general said, then bowed, 'and I bid you a good night.'

Moore and Bethany walked downhill in silence. It was not

far to the small house. They stopped by the woodpile, both feeling awkward. 'Thank you,' Bethany said.

'My pleasure, Miss Fletcher,' Moore said, and did not move.

'What will happen tomorrow?' Bethany asked.

'Maybe nothing.'

'The rebels won't attack?'

'I think they must,' Moore said, 'but that is their decision. They should attack soon.'

'Should?' Bethany asked. The moonlight glossed her eyes silver.

'We sent for reinforcements,' Moore said, 'though whether any such will come, I don't know.'

'But if they attack,' Bethany said, 'there will be a fight?'

'It's why we're here,' Moore said and felt his heart give a lurch at the thought that tomorrow he would discover what soldiering really was, or perhaps the lurch came from gazing at Bethany's eyes in the moonlight. He wanted to say things to her, but he felt confused and tongue-tied.

'I must go indoors,' she said. 'Molly Hatch is sitting beside my mother.'

'Your mother is no better?'

'She will never be better,' Bethany said. 'Goodnight, Lieutenant.'

'Your servant, Miss Fletcher,' Moore said, bowing to her, but even before he straightened she was gone. Moore went to collect his men who would take over the picquet duty on Dyce's Head.

Dawn was fog-shrouded, though from the new battery on Cross Island the British ships were clearly visible. The closest, HMS *Nautilus*, was now only a quarter-mile from the big guns that Revere's men had taken ashore. Those men had worked all night and they had worked well. They had cut a path through the trees of Cross Island and dragged a pair of eighteen-pounder cannon, one twelve-pounder and a five-and-a-half inch howitzer to the island's summit where the rocky land made a perfect artillery platform. More trees had been felled to open a field of fire for the cannon and in the dawn Captain Hoysteed Hacker, whose sailors were armed with muskets to protect the gunners, gazed at the three British sloops. The furthest away, the *North*, was a grey shape in the grey fog and mostly hidden by the bulk of the other two sloops, but the closest, *Nautilus*, was clearly visible. Her figurehead was a bare-chested sailor whose blond hair was wreathed with seaweed. 'Aren't we supposed to be turning that ship to splinters?' Hacker asked the artillery officer. The gunners were standing about their formidable weapons, but no man seemed to be either loading or aiming the guns.

'We lack wadding,' Lieutenant Philip Marett, a cousin of Colonel Revere and the officer commanding the battery, explained.

'You what?'

Marett looked sheepish. 'We seem to lack ring-wadding, sir.'

'The round shot is the wrong size too,' a sergeant said grimly.

Hacker scarcely believed what he was hearing. 'The round shot? Wrong size?'

The sergeant demonstrated by lifting a round shot and pushing it into the barrel of one of the two eighteen-pounders. One of his men rammed the shot, thrusting the ball up the long gun, which, because it was mounted on the highest point of Cross Island, was aimed slightly downwards so that it pointed at the bows of the *Nautilus*. The gunner pulled the rammer clear and stepped aside. Hacker heard a slight noise from the gun. The rumbling, metal on metal, became louder as the ball rolled slowly down the barrel and then, pathetically, dropped from the muzzle to thump onto the pine needles that coated the ground. 'Oh God,' Hacker said.

186

'There must have been confusion in Boston,' Marett said helplessly. He pointed to a neat pyramid of round shot. 'It seems they're for twelve-pounders,' he went on, 'and even if we could wad them the windage would make it near useless.' Windage was the tiny gap between a missile and the cannon's barrel. All guns suffered from windage, but if the gap was too great then much of the gun's propellant would waste itself around the ball's edges.

'You've sent for Colonel Revere?'

Marett's eyes darted around the cleared space as if searching for somewhere to hide. 'I'm sure there's eighteen-pounder ammunition on the *Samuel*, sir,' he said evasively.

'Suffering Christ,' Hacker said savagely, 'it'll take two hours to fetch it downriver!' The *Samuel* was anchored well to the north, a long way from the creek south of Cross Island.

'We could open fire with the twelve-pounder,' Marett suggested.

'You have wadding for that?'

'We could use turf?'

'Oh for God's sake, let's do it properly,' Hacker said, then had a sudden inspiration. 'The *Warren* mounts eighteen-pounders, doesn't she?'

'I don't know, sir.'

'She does, and she's a hell of a lot closer than the *Samuel*! We'll ask her for ammunition.'

Hoysteed Hacker's inspiration proved a happy one. Commodore Saltonstall snorted derision when he heard of the request for ammunition, but he acceded to it, and Captain Welch sent to the *General Putnam* and ordered Captain Thomas Carnes to assemble a work-party of marines to carry the necessary wadding and round shot ashore. Carnes, before he joined the marines, had served in Colonel Gridley's Artillery Regiment and afterwards commanded a battery of the New Jersey Artillery in the Continental Army and he was a cheerful, energetic man who rubbed his hands with delight

187

when he saw how close the *Nautilus* lay to the guns. 'We can use the twelve-pounder shot in the eighteens,' he declared.

'We can?' Marett asked.

'We'll double-shot,' Carnes said. 'Load an eighteen-pound ball by the charge and wad a twelve on top. We're going to splinter that nearest ship, boys!' He watched the Massachusetts gunners, all imbued now with enthusiasm from Carnes's energy, load and lay the cannon. Carnes stooped by the barrel and peered along its upper side. 'Aim slightly higher,' he said.

'Higher?' Marett asked. 'You want us to aim for the masts?'

'A cold barrel shoots low,' Carnes said, 'but as it heats up she'll shoot true. Lower her elevation after three shots, and take it one degree lower than you reckon necessary. I don't know why, but round shot always rises from a barrel. It's just a fraction, but if you compensate then you'll hit true and hard when the guns are hot.'

The sun was glowing bright in the fog when, at last, the battery opened fire. The two big eighteen-pounders were the ship-killers and Carnes used them to shoot at the *Nautilus*'s hull while the twelve-pounder fired bar shot at her rigging and the howitzer lobbed shells over the *Nautilus* to ravage the decks of the *North* and *Albany*.

The guns recoiled hard and far on the rocky ground. They needed realigning after each shot, and every discharge filled the space between the cleared trees with thick powder smoke that lingered in the still air. The smoke thickened the fog to such an extent that aiming was impossible until the view cleared, and that necessity slowed the rate of fire, but Carnes heard the satisfying crunch of round shots striking timber. The British could not return the fire. The *Nautilus* had no bow chasers, and her broadside of nine cannon was aimed west towards the harbour approach. Captain Tom Farnham, who commanded the *Nautilus*, might have warped his ship around to face Cross Island, but then Mowat would have lost a third of the cannons guarding the channel, and so the sloop had to endure.

The commodore, satisfied that the battery was at last in action, sent an order that Carnes and his handful of marines were to return to their ships, but before he left Carnes used a small telescope to stare at the *Nautilus* and saw the holes ripped in her bows. 'You're hitting her hard, Captain!' he told Marett. 'Remember! Aim low at this range and you'll sink that bastard by noon! Good day to you, sir!' This last greeting was to Brigadier-General Lovell who had come to watch the new battery in action.

'Good morning! Good morning!' Lovell beamed at the gunners. ''Pon my word, but you're hitting that ship hard, lads!' He borrowed Carnes's telescope. 'My word, you've knocked an arm off that ugly figurehead! Well done! Keep going and you'll sink her soon enough!'

The *Nautilus* was still afloat an hour before noon when Colonel Revere arrived with eighteen-pounder ammunition from the *Samuel*. He came in his smart white-painted barge that belonged to the Castle Island garrison and which Revere had commandeered for the expedition. Revere ordered sailors from the *Providence* to carry the round shot to the battery, then strode uphill to discover General Lovell still standing beside the guns. The fog had lifted and the general was peering through a glass that he rested on a gunner's shoulder. 'Colonel!' he greeted Revere cheerfully, 'I see we're striking hard!'

'What the devil do you mean, the wrong ammunition?' Revere ignored Lovell and challenged Captain Marett who pointed to the twelve-pounder round shot and began a halting explanation of his difficulties, but Revere brushed him aside. 'If you brought the wrong round shot,' he said, 'then you're to blame.' He watched as the gunners hauled one of the huge eighteen-pounders back into place. The gunner squinted down the barrel, then used a long-handled maul to drive a wedge deeper under the breech. The wedge slightly lifted the rear of the barrel, so lowering the muzzle and the gunner, satisfied with the angle, nodded at his crew to reload the cannon.

'They must be suffering, Colonel,' Lovell said happily, 'I can see distinct damage to her hull!'

'What are you doing?' Revere again ignored Lovell, rounding on Marett instead. The Colonel had peered down the barrel and had not liked what he saw. 'Are you shooting at the water, Captain? What's the use of shooting into the water?'

'Captain Carnes—' Marett began.

'Captain Carnes? Is he an officer in this regiment? Sergeant! I want the barrel raised. Loosen the breech wedge by two degrees. Good day, General,' he at last greeted Lovell.

'I came to congratulate the gunners,' Lovell said.

'We're just doing our duty, General,' Revere said briskly and again crouched behind the gun after the sergeant had loosened the wedge. 'Much better!'

'I trust you'll be at the Council of War this afternoon?' Lovell said.

'I shall be there, General. What are you waiting for?' This last was to the gunners. 'Give the bastards some iron pills!'

The sergeant had pierced the powder bag with a spike and now inserted the portfire. 'Stand back!' he shouted, then, satisfied that the space behind the gun was clear, he touched the burning slow-fuse to the portfire. There was a hiss, a puff of smoke from the touch-hole, then the gun roared and smoke billowed to fill the sky around the battery. The cannon leaped back, its wheels bouncing off the stony soil.

The shot flew down the *Nautilus*'s deck and narrowly missed her masts, though it passed close enough to shatter a stand of boarding pikes at the base of the mainmast before smacking harmlessly into the beach of the peninsula. A sailor on the sloop twisted and fell, scrabbling at his throat, and Captain Farnham saw blood where a splinter from a shattered pike-shaft had speared into the man's gullet. 'Get him below,' he ordered.

The surgeon's assistant tried to withdraw the splinter, but the man convulsed before he could slide it free. Blood spilt across the dark lower deck, the man's eyes widened to stare vacantly at the deck above, then he made a choking, gurgling noise and more blood welled from his throat and mouth. He convulsed again, then went still. He was dead, the first man killed on board the sloop. The surgeon himself was wounded, his thigh pierced by a sharp blade of wood driven from the hull by one of the earlier shots. Six men were in the sick bay, all of them similarly injured by splinters. The surgeon and his assistant were pulling the wood fragments free and bandaging the wounds, and all the while waiting for the dreaded hammer blow of the next shot to smash into the hull. The ship's carpenter was hammering wedges and caulking into the damaged bows, and the ship's pumps were clattering constantly as men tried to stop the water rising in the bilge.

'I do believe,' Captain Farnham said after another eighteen-pounder shot had screamed just above his deck, 'that they've lifted their aim. They're trying to dismast us now.'

'Better that than hulling us, sir,' his first lieutenant observed.

'Indeed,' Farnham said with evident relief, 'oh indeed.' He aimed his glass out of the harbour and saw, to his further relief, that the rebel warships showed no sign of readying themselves for another attack.

'Signal from the *Albany*, sir!' a midshipman called. 'Prepare to move ship, sir!'

'That's hardly a surprise, is it?' Farnham said.

Colonel Revere's battery on Cross Island had started its day in confusion, but now it had succeeded in one ambition. The three British sloops that barred the harbour entrance were being driven away eastwards.

And the door to Majabigwaduce had been opened.

General McLean stood on Dyce's Head and stared towards the enemy battery on Cross Island. He could see nothing of the rebel guns because their smoke shrouded the clearing the rebels had made on the island's summit, but he recognized the damage that had been done to his defences. Yet he could never have spared enough men to garrison Cross Island properly. Its fall had been inevitable. 'The wretched Yankees have done well,' he said grudgingly.

'A slow rate of fire,' Captain Michael Fielding observed.

Yet if the rebel gunners were slightly slower than Fielding's men of the Royal Artillery, they had still unblocked the harbour. Captain Mowat had sent a young lieutenant ashore who discovered McLean on the high bluff. 'The captain regrets, sir, that he must move the sloops away from the enemy guns.'

'Yes, he must,' McLean agreed, 'indeed he must.'

'He proposes to make a new line at the harbour's centre, sir.'

'Give Captain Mowat my best wishes,' McLean said, 'and thank him for informing me.' The three sloops and their attendant transport ships were already moving slowly eastwards. Captain Mowat had marked their new anchorage with buoys made from empty barrels and McLean could see that their new position was not nearly as formidable as their old. The ships would now make a line well to the east of the harbour entrance, no longer a cork in a tight bottle-neck, but halfway inside the bottle, and their retreat would surely invite an attack by the enemy fleet. That was a pity, McLean thought, but he understood that Mowat had no choice but to retreat now that the rebels possessed Cross Island.

The brigadier had gone to the bluff to see whether Fielding's twelve-pounders could be deployed to shoot down at the new rebel battery on Cross Island. The small six-pounders on the bluff were already firing at the rebel position, but they were puny cannons and, besides, the new enemy battery lay in the island's centre and was shooting down a corridor of cleared trees and that corridor pointed northwards. The guns themselves were hidden from Dyce's Head, lying to the north-west of the enemy battery, and Midshipman Fenistone's three guns were spitting their small balls into Cross Island's trees in optimistic hope of hitting whatever was hidden by the smoke and the foliage. 'I'm not sure we gain much by using twelve-pounders, sir,' Fielding said, 'except to cause more damage to those trees.'

McLean nodded, then walked a few paces westwards to gaze at the enemy shipping. He was astonished that the Americans had made no move to attack him. He had expected the rebel warships to be at the harbour entrance, adding their fire to the new battery, and that rebel infantry would already be assaulting him, but the anchored fleet lay peacefully under the sun. He could see clothes hung out to dry on lines slung between the transport ships' masts. 'My worry,' he said to Fielding, 'is that if we put twelves here we won't have time to withdraw them when the enemy attacks.'

'Without horse teams,' Fielding agreed, 'we won't.'

'I do miss my horses,' McLean said gently. He took off his cocked hat and stared ruefully at the inner leather band, which was coming apart. His white hair lifted in a sudden waft of wind. 'Well,' he said, 'I dare say we can afford to lose a trio of six-pounders, but I won't abide the loss of any twelves.' McLean turned and gazed at the smoke enveloping Cross Island, then carefully replaced his hat. 'Leave the twelves at the fort,' he decided, 'and thank you, Captain.' He turned as footsteps sounded loud among the trees. Lieutenant Caffrae, a Hamilton, was running towards the general. 'More bad news, I suspect,' McLean said.

Caffrae, a lithe and energetic young man, was panting as he stopped in front of McLean. 'The rebels have landed men north of the neck, sir.'

'Have they indeed! Are they advancing?'

Caffrae shook his head. 'We saw about sixty men in boats, sir. They landed out of sight, sir, but they're in the trees beyond the marsh.'

'Just sixty men?'

'That's all we saw, sir.'

'Major Dunlop is apprised?'

'He sent me to tell you, sir.'

'The devil moves in a mysterious way,' McLean said. 'Is he trying to make us stare northwards while he attacks here? Or is that the advanced guard of his real attack?' He smiled at the breathless Caffrae whom he considered one of his best young officers. 'We'll have to wait and see, but the onslaught must come soon. Well, I'm going back to the fort and you, Caffrae, are going to tell Major Dunlop that I'll reinforce his picquet on the neck.'

On board the sloops the sailors readied to drop anchors for their new position. The guns on Cross Island still pounded the *Nautilus* where men bled and died. North of the isthmus the rebels began making an earthwork where cannon could command the redcoats' escape route from Majabigwaduce. It was Tuesday, July 27th, and the ring around Fort George was closing tight.

'I believe I can say with great confidence,' Lovell addressed the Council of War in the commodore's cabin aboard the *Warren*, 'that we have achieved splendid things! Noble things!' The general was at his most avuncular, smiling at the men crowded about the table and along the cabin's sides. 'Now we must go on to achieve our larger designs. We must captivate, kill and destroy the tyrant!'

For a while the council indulged itself in pleasurable contemplation of the capture of Cross Island, a victory that surely presaged a greater triumph on the northern side of the harbour. Compliments were offered to the marines in the person of Captain Welch who said nothing, but just stood behind Saltonstall's chair and looked grim. The commodore, also silent, appeared bored. Once or twice he deigned to incline his head when Lovell directed a question at him, but for the most part he appeared to be aloof from the matters under discussion. Nor did he seem in the least abashed by the petition sent to him by thirty-two officers from the rebel warships that had respectfully requested that the commodore should destroy or capture the three British sloops without any more delay. The letter had been couched in the politest terms, but no amount of courtesy could hide that the petition was a bitter criticism of Saltonstall's leadership. Nearly all of the men who had signed that letter were in the cabin, but Saltonstall pointedly ignored them.

'I assume, gentlemen, we are agreed that we must make our assault soon?' Lovell asked.

Voices murmured their assent. 'Tonight, go tonight,' George Little, first lieutenant of the *Hazard*, suggested forcibly.

'Wait too long,' Colonel Jonathan Mitchell, commander of the Cumberland County militia, said, 'and they'll have their damned fort finished. The sooner we attack, the sooner we go home.'

'Wait too long,' George Little warned, 'and you'll see British reinforcements coming upriver.' He pointed out of the cabin's wide stern windows. The ebbing tide had turned the *Warren* on her anchor cable and the windows now looked towards the south-west. The sun was setting there, glossing the waters of Penobscot Bay into slithering patterns of red and gold.

'Let us not anticipate such things,' Lovell said.

Wadsworth thought such things were worth anticipating, especially if they lent haste to the job at hand. 'I would suggest, sir,' he said warmly, 'that we make our assault tonight.'

'Tonight!' Lovell stared at his deputy.

'We have a full moon,' Wadsworth said, 'and with some small luck the enemy will be inattentive. Yes, sir, tonight.' A growl of approval sounded around the cabin.

'And how many men could you commit to such an attack?' a sharp voice asked and Wadsworth saw that it was Lieutenant-Colonel Revere who had posed the question.

Wadsworth felt the question was impertinent. It was not Revere's business to know how many infantry could be landed, but Solomon Lovell seemed unworried by the brusque demand. 'We can land eight hundred men,' the general said and Revere nodded as though satisfied with the answer.

'And how many men can the artillery train take ashore?' Wadsworth demanded.

Revere flinched, as though the question offended him. 'Eighty men, exclusive of officers,' he said resentfully.

'And I trust,' Wadsworth rather surprised himself by the defiance in his voice, 'that this time the ammunition will match the guns?'

Revere looked as if he had been slapped. He stared at Wadsworth, his mouth opened and closed, then he drew himself up as if about to launch a vicious response, but Colonel Mitchell intervened. 'More to the matter at hand,' Mitchell said, 'how many men can the enemy muster?'

William Todd who had also bridled at Revere's intervention was about to give his usual high estimate, but Peleg Wadsworth silenced him with a gesture. 'I've talked long and hard with young Fletcher,' Wadsworth said, 'and his information is not guesswork, it is not an estimate, but derives directly from the enemy paymaster.' He paused, looking about the table. 'I am persuaded that the enemy regiments can muster no more than seven hundred infantry.'

Someone gave a low whistle of surprise. Others looked dubious. 'You have confidence in that number?' Major Todd asked sceptically.

'Complete confidence,' Wadsworth said firmly.

'They possess artillerymen too,' Lovell warned.

'And they have Royal Marines,' a ship's captain spoke from the edge of the cabin.

'We have better marines,' Captain Welch insisted.

Commodore Saltonstall stirred himself, his gaze moving disinterestedly about the table as though he was faintly

196

surprised to discover himself in such company. 'We shall loan two hundred and twenty-seven marines to the militia,' he said.

'This is splendid,' Lovell said, trying to rouse the fervour of the council, 'truly splendid!' He leaned back in his chair, planted his fists wide apart on the table, and beamed at the company. 'So, gentlemen, we have a motion! And the motion is that we attack this night with all our land forces. Permit me to put a proposition to the council's vote, and may I suggest we attempt a resolution by acclamation? So, gentlemen, the motion is, do you think the force we possess sufficient to attack the enemy?'

No one responded. They were all too astonished. Even Saltonstall, who had appeared entirely disengaged from the discussion in his cabin, now gazed wide-eyed at Lovell. For a moment Wadsworth was tempted to think the general was venturing a clumsy joke, but it was apparent from Lovell's expression that he was serious. He really expected every officer present to vote on the motion as though this was a meeting of the General Assembly. The silence stretched, broken only by the footsteps of the watch-keepers on the deck above.

'In favour, aye,' Wadsworth managed to say, and his words broke the surprise in the cabin so that a chorus of voices approved the motion.

'And is anyone opposed?' Lovell asked. 'None? Good! The ayes have it.' He looked at his secretary, John Marston. 'Record in the minutes that the motion proposing that we possess sufficient force to make the assault was passed unanimously by acclamation.' He beamed at the assembled officers, then looked enquiringly at Saltonstall. 'Commodore? You will support our assault with a naval action?'

Saltonstall looked at Lovell with an expressionless face that nevertheless managed to suggest that the commodore thought the general was a witless fool. 'On the one hand,' Saltonstall finally broke the embarrassing silence, 'you wish my marines to take part in your assault, and on the other

197

you wish me to attack the enemy shipping without my marines?'

'I, well . . .' Lovell began awkwardly.

'Well?' Saltonstall interrupted harshly. 'Do you want the marines or not?'

'I would appreciate their assistance,' Lovell said weakly.

'Then we shall engage the enemy with gunfire,' Saltonstall announced loftily. There was a murmur of protest from the officers who had signed the letter condemning the commodore, but the murmur died under Saltonstall's scornful gaze.

All that was left now was to decide where and when to attack, and no one demurred from Wadsworth's proposal to assail the bluff again, but this time to attack by moonlight. 'We shall attack at midnight,' Wadsworth said, 'and assault the bluff directly.' To Wadsworth's exasperation Lovell insisted on offering both the time and place as motions for the Council's vote, but no one voted against either, though Colonel Mitchell diffidently observed that midnight left little time to make the necessary preparations.

'No time like the present,' Wadsworth said.

'You expect me to attack their shipping by night?' Saltonstall reentered the discussion. 'You want my ships grounded in the dark?'

'You can attack in the dawn, perhaps?' Lovell suggested and was rewarded with a curt nod.

The Council ended and men went back to their ships as the bright moon climbed among the stars. The rebels had voted unanimously to make their attack, to bring the enemy to battle and, with God's good help, to make a great victory.

The fog came slowly on the morning of Wednesday, July 28th, 1779. At first it was a mist that thickened imperceptibly to shroud the cloud-haunted moon with a glowing ring. The tide rippled along the anchored ships. Midnight had come and gone, and there was still no attack. The *Hunter* and *Sky*

Rocket, the two privateers that would cannonade the heights of the bluff as the rebels landed, had to be rowed upriver before anchoring close to shore and both ships arrived late. Some transport ships had too many lighters or longboats, and others too few, and the confusion had to be disentangled. Time passed and Peleg Wadsworth fretted. This was the attack that must succeed, the attack to capture the bluff and surge on to assault the fort. This was why the fleet had come to Penobscot Bay, yet one o'clock came and passed, then two o'clock, then three o'clock, and still the troops were not ready. A militia captain suggested the attack should be abandoned because the creeping fog would dampen the powder in the musket pans, a notion Wadsworth rejected with an anger that surprised him. 'If you can't shoot them, Captain,' he snapped, 'then beat them to death with your musket butts.' The captain looked at him with an aggrieved face. 'That's what you came here for, isn't it?' Wadsworth asked. 'To kill the enemy?'

James Fletcher, at Wadsworth's side, grinned, His only uniform was a white crossbelt from which hung a cartridge pouch, but most of the militia were similarly dressed. Only the marines and some militia officers wore recognizable uniforms. James's heart was throbbing palpably. He was nervous. His job was to show the attackers where paths climbed the bluff, but right now that bluff was just a moon-shadowed cliff in the mist. No light showed there. Longboats bumped and jostled alongside the transport ships, waiting to take the soldiers ashore, while on deck men sharpened knives and bayonets and obsessively checked that the flints in their musket locks were firmly embedded in the dogheads. Wadsworth and Fletcher were on board the sloop *Centurion* from which they would embark with Welch's marines. Those marines in their dark green jackets waited patiently in the *Centurion*'s waist and among them was a boy whom Wadsworth remembered from Townsend. The boy grinned at the general who tried desperately to remember the lad's name. 'It's Israel, isn't it?' Wadsworth said, the name suddenly coming to him

'Marine Fifer Trask now, sir,' the boy said in his unbroken voice.

'You joined the marines!' Wadsworth said, smiling. The lad had been provided with a uniform, the dark green coat cut down to his diminutive size, while at his waist hung a sword-bayonet. He lacked the marine's distinctive leather collar and instead had a black scarf wound tight around his scrawny neck.

'We kidnapped the little bastard, general,' a marine spoke from the dark.

'Then make sure you look after him,' Wadsworth said, 'and play well, Israel Trask.'

A rowboat banged against the *Centurion*'s side and a harried militia lieutenant scrambled over the gunwale with a message from Colonel McCobb. 'Sorry, sir, it'll be a while yet, the Colonel says he's sorry, sir.'

'God damn it!' Wadsworth could not help exclaiming.

'There still aren't enough boats, sir,' the lieutenant explained.

'Use what boats you have,' Wadsworth said, 'and send them back for the rest of the men. Send me word when you're ready!'

'Yes, sir.' The lieutenant, abashed, backed away to his boat.

'They call them minutemen?' Captain Welch appeared beside Wadsworth and asked with a hint of amusement.

Wadsworth was taken aback that the dour marine captain had even spoken. Welch was such a grim presence, so baleful, that his customary silence was welcome, yet he had sounded friendly enough in the darkness. 'Your men have food?' Wadsworth asked. It was an unnecessary question, but the tall marine made him nervous.

'They have their morsel,' Welch said, still sounding amused. General Lovell had sent a message that every man must take 'a morsel ashore to alleviate hunger', and Wadsworth had dutifully passed the order on, though he suspected hunger would be the least of their problems. 'Have you ever been to England, General?' Welch suddenly asked.

'No, no. Never.'

'Pretty place, some of it.'

'You visited it?'

Welch nodded. 'Didn't plan on it. Our ship was captured and I was taken there as a prisoner.'

'You were exchanged?'

Welch grinned, his teeth very white in the dark. 'Hell, no. I strolled out of the prison and walked all the damn way to Bristol. I signed as a deck hand on a merchantman sailing for New York. Got home.'

'And no one suspected you?'

'Not a soul. I begged and stole food. Met a widow who fed me.' He smiled at the memory. 'Glad I seen the place, but I won't ever go back.'

'I'd like to see Oxford one day,' Wadsworth said wistfully, 'and maybe London.'

'We'll build London and Oxford here,' Welch said.

Wadsworth wondered if the usually laconic Welch was talkative because he was nervous, and then, with a start, he realized that the marine was talking because Welch had divined Wadsworth's own nervousness. The general stared at the dark bluff that, in the thickening mist, was being limned by a dull lightening of the eastern sky, just a hint of grey in the black. 'Dawn's coming,' Wadsworth said.

And then, suddenly, there were no more delays. Colonel McCobb and the Lincoln County militia were ready, and so the men clambered down into the boats and Wadsworth took his place in a longboat's stern. The marines were grey-faced in the wan light, but to Wadsworth they looked reassuringly resolute, determined and frightening. Their bayonets were fixed. The *Centurion*'s sailors gave a low cheer as the boats pulled away from the transport.

A louder cheer sounded from the *Sky Rocket*, and then Wadsworth plainly heard Captain William Burke shout at his crew, 'For God and for America! Fire!'

The *Sky Rocket* split the dawn with its eight-gun broadside. Flame leaped and curled, smoke spread on the water and the first missiles crashed ashore.

The rebels were coming.

Excerpt from a letter sent by the Massachusetts Council to Brigadier-General Solomon Lovell, July 23rd, 1779:

It is the Expression of the Council . . . that you will push your Operations with all possible Vigor and dispatch and accomplish the business of the Expedition before any reinforcement can get to the enemy at Penobscot. It is also reported here and believed by many that, a Forty Gun ship and the Delaware Frigate sailed from Sandy Hook on Sixteenth Current and Stood to the Eastward; their destination was not known.

Excerpt from an Order by the State of Massachusetts Bay Council, July 27th, 1779:

Ordered that the Board of War be and they are hereby directed to furnish the two Indians of the Penobscott Tribe, now in the Town of Boston with Two Hats one of them laced two Blankets and two Shirts.

Excerpt from Brigadier-General Solomon Lovell's daily orders, Majabigwaduce, July 27th, 1779:

All Officers and Soldiers in the Army are strictly enjoin'd not to give or sell any rum to the Indians, except those who have the immediate command of them, under pain of the greatest displeasure . . . The Officers are desired to pay particular Attention that the men do not waste their Ammunition and that they keep their Arms in good Order.

SEVEN

The first shots crashed into the trees, exploding twigs, pine needles and leaves. Birds screeched and flapped into the dawn. The rebels were using chain and bar shot that whirled and slashed through branches to punch gouts of earth and shards of stone where they struck the bluff's face. 'Dear God alive,' Captain Archibald Campbell said. He was the highlander who commanded the picquets on the bluff and he stared aghast at the scores of longboats that were now emerging from the fog and pulling towards his position. In their centre, clumsily rowed by men wielding extra-long sweeps, a schooner crept towards the beach, her deck crowded with men. Two enemy warships had anchored close to the shore and those ships, still just dark shapes in the smoke and fog, were now shooting into the bluff. The *Hunter* had nine four-pounders bearing on the redcoats, while the *Sky Rocket* had eight of the small cannon in her broadside, but though the guns were small their scything missiles struck home with mind-numbing brutality. Campbell seemed frozen. He had eighty men under command, most of them scattered along the face of the bluff where the steep slope gave way to the gentler rise. 'Tell the men to lie down, sir?' a sergeant suggested.

'Yes,' Campbell said, scarcely aware that he was speaking.

The ships' guns were firing more raggedly now as the faster gun crews outpaced the slower. Each gunshot was a percussive blow to the ears, and each illuminated the bluff with a sudden flash of light that was smothered almost instantly by powder smoke. Campbell was shaking. His belly was sour, his mouth dry and his right leg quivering uncontrollably. There were hundreds of rebels coming! The fog-smothered sea was shadowed dark by the bluff, but he could make out the glimmer of oar blades beneath the gunsmoke and see the grey light reflecting from bayonets. Twigs, shattered bark, leaves, pine cones and needles showered on the picquet as the shots tore through the bluff's trees. A chain shot shattered a rotted and fallen trunk. The highlanders closest to Campbell looked nervously towards their officer.

'Send word to General McLean, sir?' the sergeant suggested stoically.

'Go,' Campbell blurted out the command, 'yes, go, go!'

The sergeant turned and a bar shot struck his neck. It severed his powdered pigtail, cut head from body and, in the grey gloom and darkness of the dawn, the spray of blood was extraordinarily bright, like ruby drops given extra brilliance by the fog-diffused sunlight that filtered through the eastern trees. A jet of blood spurted upwards and appeared to lift the head, which turned so that the sergeant seemed to be staring reproachfully at Campbell who gave a small cry of horror, then involuntarily bent double and vomited. The head, soaked in blood, thumped to earth and rolled a few feet down the slope. Another chain shot slashed overhead, scattering twigs. Birds shrieked. A redcoat fired his musket down into the cannon-smoke and fog. 'Hold your fire!' Campbell shouted too shrilly. 'Hold your fire! Wait till they're on the beach!' He spat. His mouth was sour and his right hand was twitching. There was blood on his jacket and vomit on his shoes. The sergeant's headless body was shuddering, but at last went still.

'Why in God's name hold our fire?' Lieutenant John Moore, posted on the Scottish left, wondered aloud. He led twenty-two Hamiltons positioned at Dyce's Head where the slope was the steepest. His picquet lay directly between the approaching boats and the small British battery at the bluff's top and Moore was determined to protect that battery. He watched the enemy approaching and also watched himself with a critical inward eye. An enemy chain shot slammed into a tree not five paces away and slivers of bark spattered Moore like the devil's hail, and he knew he was supposed to be frightened, yet in all truth he did not notice that fear. He sensed apprehension, yes, for no man wants to die or be wounded, but instead of a debilitating fear Moore was feeling a rising exhilaration. Let the bastards come, he thought, and then he realized that his self-examination was consuming him so that he was standing in silent absorption while his men looked to him for reassurance. Forcing himself to walk slowly along the break of the bluff, he drew his sword and flicked the slender blade at the thick undergrowth. 'Nice of the enemy to trim the trees for us,' he said. 'It improves the view, don't you think?'

'Buggers want to trim more than the trees,' Private Neill muttered.

'I don't know if you've noticed something, sir,' Sergeant McClure said quietly.

'Tell me, Sergeant. Brighten my morning.'

McClure pointed at the approaching boats that were clarifying as they emerged from the smoke-thickened fog. 'Yon bastards are in uniform, sir. I reckon they're sending their best against us. While the scoundrels up yonder,' he pointed at the more northerly longboats, 'are in any old clothes. Bunch of vagabonds, they look like.'

Moore peered westwards, then looked at the northern boats. 'You're right, Sergeant,' he said. In the nearer boats he could see the white crossbelts against the dark green coats of the marines and he assumed that the uniforms belonged to a regiment of General Washington's Continental Army. 'They're sending their best troops right here,' he said loudly, 'and you can't blame them.'

'You can't?'

'They're up against the most formidable regiment in the British Army,' Moore said cheerfully.

'Oh, aye, all twenty-two of us,' McClure said.

'If they knew what they faced,' Moore said, 'they'd turn right around and row away.'

'Permission to let them know, sir?' McClure asked, appalled at his young officer's bravado.

'Let's kill them instead, Sergeant,' Moore said, though his words were lost as a chain shot drove noisily through the branches overhead to shower the picquet with pine cones and needles.

'Don't fire yet!' Captain Archibald Campbell shouted from the bluff's centre. 'Wait till they're on the beach!'

'Bloody fool,' Moore said. And so, with drawn sword, and under the bombardment of the rebel broadsides, he walked the bluff and watched the enemy draw nearer. Battle, he thought, had come to him at last and in all his eighteen years John Moore had never felt so alive.

Wadsworth winced as the oars threw up droplets of water that splashed on his face. It might be July, but the air was cold and the water even colder. He was shivering in his Continental Army jacket and he prayed that none of the marines would mistake that shivering for fear. Captain Welch, beside him, looked entirely unconcerned, as if the boat was merely carrying him on some mundane errand. Israel Trask, the boy fifer, was grinning in the longboat's bows where he kept twisting around to stare at the bluff where no enemy showed. The bluff climbed two hundred feet from the beach, much of that slope almost perpendicular, but in the fog it

208

looked much higher. Trees thrashed under the impact of bar and chain shot, and birds circled over the high ground, but Wadsworth could see no redcoats and no puffs of smoke betraying musket fire. Fog sifted through the high branches. The leading boats were well within musket range now, but still no enemy fired.

'You stay on the beach, boy,' Welch told Israel Trask.

'Can't I . . .' the boy began.

'You stay on the beach,' Welch said again, then gave a sly glance at Wadsworth, 'with the general.'

'Is that an order?' Wadsworth asked, amused.

'Your job is to send the boats back for more men, and send those men where they're needed,' Welch said, seemingly unabashed at telling Wadsworth what he should do. 'Our job is to kill whatever bastards we find at the top of the slope.'

'If there are any there at all,' Wadsworth said. The boat was almost at the beach where small waves broke feebly, and still the enemy offered no resistance.

'Maybe they're sleeping,' Welch said, 'maybe.'

Then, as the bows of the boat grounded on the shingle, the bluff's face exploded with noise and smoke. Wadsworth saw a stab of flame high above, heard the musket-balls whip past, saw splashes of water where they struck the sea, and then the marines were shouting as they leaped ashore. Other boats scraped onto the narrow beach, which rapidly filled with green-coated men looking for a way up the bluff. A marine staggered backwards, his white crossbelt suddenly red. He fell to his knees in the small surf and coughed violently, each cough bringing more dark blood.

James Fletcher, his musket unslung, had run to a vast granite boulder that half-blocked the beach. 'There's a path here!' he shouted.

'You heard him!' Welch bellowed. 'So follow me! Come on, you rogues!'

'Start playing, boy,' Wadsworth told Israel Trask, 'give us a good tune!'

Marines were scrambling up the slope, which was steep enough to demand that they slung their muskets and used both hands to haul themselves up by gripping on saplings or rocks. A musket-ball struck a stone and ricocheted high above Wadsworth's head. A marine staggered backwards, his face a mask of red. A musket-ball had slashed through his cheek-bone and the cheek's flesh now dangled over his leather collar. Wadsworth could see the man's teeth through the ragged wound, but the marine recovered and kept climbing, making an incoherent noise as a chain-shot sighed overhead to explode a larch into splinters. Wadsworth heard a clear, high voice shouting at men to aim low and, with a start, he realized he must be hearing an enemy officer. He drew his pistol and aimed it up the steep bluff, but he could see no target, only grey-white drifts of smoke revealing that the enemy was about halfway up the slope. He shouted at the longboat crews to get back to the transports where more men waited, then he walked northwards along the beach, his boots scrunching the low ridge of dried seaweed and small flotsam that marked the high tideline. He found a dozen militia men crouching under a shelf of rock and urged them up the slope. They stared at him as if dazed, then one of them abruptly nodded and ran out of his shelter and the others followed.

More boats scraped their bows ashore and more men piled over the gunwales. The whole length of the bluff's narrow beach was now filled with men who ran into the trees and began to climb. The musket-balls buzzed, splashed or struck stone, and still the cannons of *Hunter* and *Sky Rocket* crashed and boomed and dizzied the air with their vicious missiles. The noise of cannons and muskets was deafening the foggy shore, but Israel Trask played a descant to the gun's percussion. He was trilling the jaunty 'Rogue's March' and standing exposed on the beach where, as he played, he gazed wide-eyed up the bluff. Wadsworth took hold of the boy's collar, causing a sudden hiccup in the music, and dragged him to the seaward side of the vast boulder. 'Stay there, Israel,' Wadsworth ordered, reckoning the boy would be safe in the granite's shelter.

A body, face down, was floating just by the rock. The man wore a deerskin jacket and a hole in the jacket's back showed where the killing ball had left his body. The corpse surged in on the small waves, then was sucked out. In and out it moved, relentlessly. The dead man was Benjamin Goldthwait who had elected to abandon his father's loyalties and fight for the rebels.

A militia captain had scrambled to the boulder's top and was shouting at his men to get on up the bluff. The enemy must have seen him because musket-balls crackled on the stone. 'Get up the bluff yourself!' Wadsworth shouted at the captain, and just then a ball struck the militia officer in the belly and his shout turned into a groan as he bent double and the blood seethed down his trousers. He fell slowly backwards, blood suddenly arcing above him. He slid down the boulder's side and thumped into the surf just beside Ben Goldthwait's corpse. Israel Trask's eyes widened. 'Don't mind the bodies, boy,' Wadsworth said, 'just keep playing.'

James Fletcher, ordered to stay close to Wadsworth, waded into the small waves to pull the wounded officer out of the water, but the moment he took hold of the man's shoulders a pulse of blood spurted into James's face and the injured captain writhed in agony.

'You!' Wadsworth was pointing at some sailors about to row their boat back to the transports. 'Take that wounded man back with you! There's a surgeon on the *Hunter*! Take him there.'

'I think he's dead,' James said, shuddering at the blood that had splashed on his face and spread in the small waves.

'With me, Fletcher,' Wadsworth said, 'come on!' He followed

the path by the boulder. To his left the militia were struggling through the thick undergrowth that choked the bluff, but Wadsworth sensed the marines to his right were far higher up the slope. The path slanted southwards along the bluff's face. It was not much of a path, more a vague track interrupted by roots, scrub and fallen trees and Wadsworth had to use his hands to haul himself over the most difficult parts. The track zig-zagged back north and at the turn a wounded marine was tying a strip of cloth around his bloodied thigh while just beyond him another marine lay as if asleep, his mouth open, but with no sign of a wound. Wadsworth felt a pang as he looked at the young man's face; so good-looking, so wasteful. 'He's dead, sir,' the injured marine said.

A musket-ball thumped into a tree beside Wadsworth, opening a scar of fresh wood. He pulled himself up the hill. He could hear the musketry close ahead, and he could hear Welch roaring orders above that splintering noise. The marines were still advancing, but the slope had eased now, which freed their hands to use their muskets. A scream sounded from the trees and was abruptly cut off. 'Don't let the bastards stand!' Welch shouted. 'They're running! Keep the bastards running!'

'Come on, Fletcher!' Wadsworth called. He felt a sudden exaltation. The scent of victory was redolent in the rotten egg stench of powder smoke. He saw a redcoat among the trees to his left and pointed his pistol and pulled the trigger, and though he doubted his aim at that distance, he felt a fierce delight in shooting at his country's enemies. James Fletcher fired his musket uphill, the recoil almost throwing him back off the track. 'Keep going!' Wadsworth shouted. More militia were landing, and they too sensed that they were winning this fight and scrambled upwards with a new enthusiasm. Muskets were firing all along the bluff now, American as well as British, and the shots were filling the trees with balls and smoke, but Wadsworth sensed that the heavier fire came from the Americans. Men were shouting at each other, encouraging each other and whooping with delight as they saw the redcoats retreating ever higher. 'Keep them running!' Wadsworth bellowed. My God, he thought, but they were winning!

A militiaman brought the American flag ashore and the sight of it inspired Wadsworth. 'Come on!' he shouted at a group of Lincoln County men, and he pushed uphill. A musket-ball slashed close enough to his cheek for the wind of its passage to jar his head sideways, but Wadsworth felt indestructible. To his right he could see a rough line of marines, their bayonets glinting as they climbed the shallower upper slope of the bluff while to his left the woods were thick with militiamen in their deerskin coats. He heard the distant war cries of the Indians on the American left, then the militia took up the sound to fill the trees with the eerie, high-pitched shout. The rebel fire was much denser than the enemy's musketry. The two warships had ceased firing, their broadsides more a danger to their own side than to the enemy, but the sound of American musket fire was incessant. The top of the bluff was being riddled by musketry and every moment took the attackers higher.

Rachel, one of the smallest transport schooners, had been rowed to the shore. Her bows touched the shingle and still more attackers jumped down onto the beach. They brought the flag of the Massachusetts Militia. 'Get on up!' Israel Trask paused in his playing to shout at them. 'You'll miss the fighting! Get on up!' The men obeyed him, streaming up the path to reinforce the attackers. Wadsworth realized he was close to the summit now and he reckoned he might rally the attackers there and keep them moving along Majabigwaduce's ridge as far as the fort itself. He knew the fort was unfinished, he knew it was short of guns, and with such fine men and with such impetus why should the job not be done before the sun evaporated the fog? 'Onwards,' he shouted, 'on! On! On!' He heard a cannon fire, its sound much deeper and more percussive than any musket, and for an instant he feared the British had artillery on the bluff's crest, then he saw the smoke jetting southwards and realized that the small enemy cannon on Dyce's Head must still be firing at Cross Island. No danger from those guns, then, and he shouted at the marines that the cannon-fire was not aimed at them. 'Keep going!' he bellowed, and scrambled upwards amidst a tangle of marines and militia. A man in a homespun tunic was leaning against a fallen tree, panting for breath. 'Are you wounded?' Wadsworth asked, and the man just shook his head. 'Then keep going!' Wadsworth said. 'Not far now!' A body lay sprawled across Wadsworth's path and he saw, almost with astonishment, that it was the corpse of a redcoat. The dead soldier wore a dark kilt and his hands were curled into fists and flies were crawling on the butcher's mess that had been his chest. Then Wadsworth reached the summit. Men were cheering, the British were running, the American flags were being carried uphill and Wadsworth was triumphant.

Because the bluff was taken, the redcoats were defeated, and the way to the fort lay open.

It suddenly dawned on Lieutenant John Moore that the inconceivable was happening, that the rebels were winning this fight. The realization was horrible, damning, overwhelming, and his response was to redouble his efforts to beat them back. His men had been firing down the bluff's steep slope and at first, as his green-coated enemies struggled on the steepest portion of their climb, Moore had seen his fire throw the assailants backwards. Those attackers had been following a rough and uneven path that zig-zagged up the bluff and Moore's men could fire down at them, though in the shadowed darkness the attackers were hard to see. 'Fire!' Moore shouted, then realized the call was unnecessary. His men were shooting as fast as they could reload, and all along the bluff the redcoats were hammering musket-fire down into the tangled trees. For a few moments Moore had thought they were winning, but there were scores of attackers who, as they reached less precipitous ground, began to shoot back. The bluff crackled with unending musket-fire, smoke filling the branches, heavy balls thumping into trees and flesh.

Captain Archibald Campbell, appalled by the sheer numbers of attackers, shouted at his men to retreat. 'You heard that, sir?' Sergeant McClure asked Moore.

'Stay where you are!' Moore snarled at his men.

He tried to make sense of what had happened, but the noise and smoke were chaotic. All he was certain of was that beneath him on the slope were uniformed men and Moore's duty was to throw them back to the sea and so he stayed on the bluff's upper face as the rest of Campbell's picquet retreated to the summit. 'Keep firing!' he told McClure.

'Jesus, Mary and Joseph,' McClure said, and fired his musket down into a group of attackers. The response was a crash of musketry from below, flames leaping upward in smoke, and Private McPhail, just seventeen, gave a mewing sound and dropped his musket. A sliver of rib, astonishingly white in the dawn, was protruding through his red coat and his deerskin trousers were turning red as he fell to his knees and mewed again. 'We can't stay here, sir,' McClure shouted over the musket din to Moore.

'Step back!' Moore conceded. 'Slow now! Keep firing!' He stooped beside McPhail whose teeth were chattering, then the boy gave a convulsive shudder and went still and Moore realized McPhail had died.

'Watch right, sir,' McClure warned, and Moore had a second's panic as he saw rebels climbing past him through the thick brush. Two squirrels went leaping overhead. 'Time to get the hell uphill, sir,' McClure said.

'Go back!' Moore called to his men, 'but slowly! Give them fire!' He sheathed his sword, unbuckled McPhail's belt with its cartridge pouch, then carried the belt, pouch and musket up the slope. The marines to the north had seen him and their musket-balls slashed around him, but then they veered away to attack Captain Campbell's rearward men, and that distraction gave Moore time to struggle up the last few feet to the bluff's top where he shouted at his men to form a line and stand. Some pine needles had dropped down the back of his neck and were trapped by his collar. They irritated him. He could not see Captain Campbell's men and it seemed that his small picquet was the only British presence left on the bluff, but just then a blue-coated artillery lieutenant came running from the east.

The lieutenant, one of Captain Fielding's men, commanded the three small cannon placed just behind Dyce's Head. The gunners had replaced the naval crews, releasing the sailors back to their ships, which expected an attack by the enemy fleet. The gunner lieutenant, a boy no older than Moore, stopped beside the picquet. 'What's happening?'

'An attack,' Moore said with brutal simplicity. He had looped the dead man's belt through his sword belt and now fumbled in the pouch for a cartridge, but McClure distracted him.

'We should go back, sir,' the sergeant declared.

'We stay here and keep firing!' Moore insisted. His Hamiltons were now in a single line at the bluff's top. Behind them was a small clearing, then a stand of pines beyond which the three cannon still fired across the harbour at the rebel battery on Cross Island.

'Should I take the guns away?' the artillery lieutenant asked.

'Can you fire down the bluff?' Moore asked.

'Down the bluff?'

'At them!' Moore said impatiently, pointing to where the green-coated attackers were momentarily visible in the shadowed undergrowth.

'No.'

A blast of musketry erupted on Moore's right. Two of his

men collapsed and another dropped his musket to clutch at his shoulder. One of the fallen men was writhing in agony as his blood spread on the ground. He began to scream in high-pitched yelps, and the remaining men backed away in horror. More shots came from the trees and a third man fell, dropping to his knees with his right thigh shattered by a musket-ball. Moore's small line was ragged now and, worse, the men were edging backwards. Their faces were pale, their eyes skittering in fear. 'Will you leave me here?' Moore shouted at them. 'Will the Hamiltons leave me alone? Come back! Behave like soldiers!' Moore rather surprised himself by sounding so confident, and was even more surprised when the picquet obeyed him. They had been gripped by fear and the fear had been a heartbeat away from panic, but Moore's voice had checked them. 'Fire!' he shouted, pointing towards the cloud of powder smoke showing where the enemy's destructive volley had been fired. He tried to see the enemy who had shot that volley, but the green coats of the marines melded into the trees. Moore's men fired, the heavy musket butts thumping back into bruised shoulders.

'We have to get the guns out!' the artillery lieutenant said.

'Then do it!' Moore snarled and turned away. His men's ramrods rattled in powder-fouled barrels as they reloaded.

A musket-ball hit the artillery lieutenant in the small of his back and he crumpled. 'No,' he said, more in surprise than protest, 'no!' His boots scrabbled in the leaf mould. 'No,' he said again, and another volley came, this time from the north, and Moore knew he was in danger of being cut off from the fort.

'Help me,' the artillery lieutenant said.

'Sergeant!' Moore called.

'We have to go, sir,' Sergeant McClure said, 'we're the only ones left here.'

The artillery lieutenant suddenly arched his back and gave a shriek. Another of Moore's men was on the ground, blood sheeting his bleached deerskin trousers.

'We have to go back, sir!' McClure shouted angrily.

'Back to the trees,' Moore called to his men, 'steady now!' He backed with them, stopping them again when they reached the stand of pines. The guns were just behind them now, while in front was the clearing where the dead and the dying lay and beyond which the enemy was gathering. 'Fire!' Moore shouted, his voice hoarse. The fog was much thinner and being lit by the rising sun so that the musket smoke seemed to rise into a glowing vapour.

'We have to go, sir,' McClure urged, 'back to the fort, sir.'

'Reinforcements will come,' Moore said, and a musket-ball struck Sergeant McClure's mouth, splintering his teeth, piercing his throat and severing his spine. The sergeant dropped noiselessly. His blood spattered John Moore's immaculate breeches. 'Fire!' Moore shouted, but he could have wept for frustration. He was in his first battle and he was losing it, but he would not give in. Surely the brigadier would send more men, and so John Moore, the dead man's musket still in his hand, stood his uncertain ground.

And still more rebels climbed the bluff.

Captain Welch was frustrated. He wanted to close on the enemy. He wanted to terrify, kill and conquer. He knew he led the best soldiers and if he could just lead them to the enemy then his green-jacketed marines would rip through the red ranks with a ferocious efficiency. He just needed to close on that enemy, drive him back in terror, and then keep advancing until the fort, and every damned redcoat inside it, belonged to the marines.

The slope frustrated him. It was steep and the enemy, retreating slowly, kept up a galling fire on his men, a fire the marines could scarcely return most of the time. They shot upwards when they could, but the enemy was half-hidden by trees, by shadow and by the smoke-writhing fog, and too many musket-balls were deflected by branches, or just wasted

218

in the air. 'Keep going!' Welch shouted. The higher they went the easier the slope became, but until they reached that friendlier ground good men were being killed or wounded, struck by musket-balls that plunged relentlessly from above, and every shot made Welch angrier and more determined.

He sensed, rather than saw, that he was opposed by a small group of men. They fired constantly, but because they were few their fire was limited. 'Lieutenant Dennis! Sergeant Sykes!' Welch shouted, 'take your men left!' He would outflank the bastards.

'Aye aye, sir!' Sykes roared back. Welch could hear the cannons firing above him, but no round shot or grapeshot came his way, just the damned musket-balls. He gripped a spruce branch and hauled himself up the slope, and a musket-ball smacked into the spruce's trunk and showered his face with splinters, but he was on easier ground now and he yelled at the men following to join him. He could see the enemy now, he could see they were a small group of men wearing black-faced red jackets who were stubbornly retreating across an open patch of ground. 'Kill them!' he called to his men, and the muskets of the marines belched smoke and noise, and when the smoke thinned Welch could see he had hurt the enemy. Men were on the ground, but still the rest stood and still they fired back, and Welch heard their officer shout at them. That officer annoyed him. He was a slight and elegant figure in a coat that, even in the misted dawn, looked expensively tailored. The buttons glinted gold, there was lace at the officer's throat, his breeches were snow-white and his top boots gleamed. A puppy, Welch thought sourly, a sprig of privilege, a target. Welch, in his captivity, had met a handful of supercilious Britons and they had burned a hatred of the breed into his soul. It was such men who had taken Americans to be fools, who had thought they could lord it over a despised breed, and who must now be taught a bloody lesson. 'Kill the officer,' he told his men, and the marines' muskets crashed another volley. Men bit cartridges, skinned their knuckles on the fixed bayonets as they slammed ramrods down barrels, primed locks, shot again, but still the damned puppy lived. He was holding a musket, while his sword, which hung from silver chains, was in its scabbard. He wore a cocked hat, its brim edged with silver, and beneath it his shadowed face looked very young and, Welch thought, arrogant. Goddamned puppy, Welch thought, and the goddamned puppy shouted at his men to fire and the small volley slammed into the marines, then Lieutenant Dennis's men shot from the north and that outflanking fire drove the puppy and his redcoats further back across the clearing. They left bodies behind, but the arrogant young officer still lived. He stopped his redcoats at the far trees and shouted at them to kill Americans and Welch had taken enough. He drew his heavy cutlass from its plain leather scabbard. The blade felt good in his hand. He saw the redcoats were reloading, tearing at cartridges while their muskets were butt-down on the ground. Another redcoat was struck down, his blood spattering the clean white breeches of the young officer whose men, because they were still reloading, were now defenceless. 'Use your bayonets!' Welch shouted, 'and charge!'

Welch led the charge across the clearing. He would cut the puppy down. He would slaughter these damned fools, he would take the guns behind them, then lead his green-coated killers along Majabigwaduce's spine to take the fort. The marines had reached the bluff's summit and, for Captain John Welch, that meant the battle was won.

General McLean had convinced himself that the rebel attack would be launched across the neck and so was surprised by the dawn's assault on the bluff. At first he was pleased with their choice, reckoning that Archibald Campbell's picquet was heavy enough to inflict real damage on the attackers, but the brevity of the fight told him that Campbell had achieved little.

McLean could not see the fighting from Fort George because fog shrouded the ridge, but his ears told him all he needed to know, and his heart sank because he had readied the fort for an attack from the north. Instead the assault would come from the west, and the intensity of the musket-fire told McLean that the attack would come in overwhelming force. The fog was clearing quickly now, coalescing into tendrils of mist that blew like gunsmoke across the stumps of the ridge. Once the rebels gained the bluff's summit, and McLean's ears told him that was already happening, and once they reached the edge of the trees on that high western ground, they would see that Fort George was merely a name and not yet a stronghold. It had only two guns facing the bluff, its rampart was a risible obstacle and the abatis was a frail barricade to protect the unfinished work. The rebels would surely capture the fort and Francis McLean regretted that. 'The fortunes of war,' he said.

'McLean?' Lieutenant-Colonel Campbell, the commanding officer of the highlanders, asked. Most of Campbell's regiment, those who were not on the picquet line, now stood behind the rampart. Their two colours were at the centre of their line and McLean felt a pang of sadness that those proud flags must become trophies to the rebels. 'Did you speak, McLean?' Campbell asked.

'Nothing, Colonel, nothing,' McLean said, staring west through the thinning fog. He crossed the rampart and walked towards the abatis because he wanted to be closer to the fighting. The crackling noise of musketry still rose and fell, sounding like dry thorns burning and snapping. He sent one of his aides to recall Major Dunlop's picquet, which had been guarding the isthmus, 'and tell Major Dunlop I need Lieutenant Caffrae's company! Quick now!' He leaned on his blackthorn stick and turned to see that Captain Fielding's men had already moved a twelve-pounder from the fort's north-eastern corner to the north-western bastion. Good, he thought, but he doubted any effort now would be sufficient. He looked back to the high ground where smoke and fog filtered through the trees, and from where the sound of musketry grew louder again and where the redcoats were appearing at the edge of the far trees. So his picquet, he thought regretfully, had not delayed the enemy long. He saw men fire, he saw a man fall, and then the redcoats were streaming back across the cleared land, running through the raw tree-stumps as they fled an enemy whose coats made them invisible among the distant trees. The only evidence of the rebels was the smoke of their muskets that blossomed and faded on the morning's light breeze.

There was a small gap in the abatis, left there deliberately so the defenders could negotiate the tangled branches, and the fleeing redcoats filed through that gap where McLean met them. 'Form ranks,' he greeted them. Men looked at him with startled expressions. 'Form in your companies,' he said. 'Sergeant? Dress the ranks!'

The fugitives made three ranks, and behind them, summoned from their picquet duty on the ground overlooking the neck, Major Dunlop and Lieutenant Caffrae's company arrived. 'Wait a moment, Major,' McLean said to Dunlop. 'Captain Campbell!' he shouted, indicating with his stick that he meant Archibald Campbell who had retreated just as precipitously as his men.

Campbell, nervous and lanky, fidgeted in front of McLean. 'Sir?'

'You were driven back?' McLean asked.

'There are hundreds of them, sir,' Campbell said, not meeting McLean's gaze, 'hundreds!'

'And where is Lieutenant Moore?'

'Taken, sir,' Campbell said after a pause. His eyes met McLean's and instantly looked away. 'Or worse, sir.'

'Then what is that firing about?' McLean asked.

Campbell turned and stared at the far trees from where musketry still sounded. 'I don't know, sir,' the highlander said miserably.

McLean turned to Major Dunlop. 'Quick as you can,' he said, 'take Caffrae's company and advance at the double, see if you can discover young Moore. Don't tangle with too many rebels, just see if Moore can be found.' Major Dunlop, the temporary commander of the 82nd, was an officer of rare verve and ability and he wasted no time. He shouted orders and his company, with their muskets at the trail, started westwards. It would have been suicide to advance along the cleared spine of the ridge and thus straight towards the rebels who were now gathering at the edge of the trees, so instead the company used the low ground by the harbour where they were concealed by the scatter of houses and by small fields where the maize had grown taller than a man. McLean watched them disappear, heard the fighting continue, and prayed that Moore survived. The general reckoned that young John Moore had promise, but that was not sufficient reason to rescue him, nor was it reason enough that Moore was a friend of the regiment's patron, the Duke of Hamilton, but rather it was because Moore had been given into McLean's charge. McLean would not abandon him, nor any other man under his care, and so he had sent Dunlop and the single company into danger. Because it was his duty.

Solomon Lovell landed on the narrow beach an hour after Captain Welch's marines had spearheaded the American attack. The general arrived with Lieutenant-Colonel Revere and his eighty artillerymen who, today, were armed with muskets and would serve as a reserve force to the nine hundred and fifty men who had already landed, most of whom were now at the top of the bluff. A few had never made it and their bodies lay on the steep slope, while others, the wounded, had been carried back to the beach where Eliphalet Downer, the surgeon general of the Massachusetts Militia, was organizing their treatment and evacuation. Lovell crouched beside a man whose eyes were bandaged. 'Soldier?' Lovell said. 'This is General Lovell.'

'We beat them, sir.'

'Of course we did! Are you in pain, soldier?'

'I'm blinded, sir,' the man said. A musket-ball had spattered razor-sharp splinters of beechwood into both eyes,

'But you will see your country at liberty,' Lovell said, 'I promise.'

'And how do I feed my family?' the man asked. 'I'm a farmer!'

'All will be well,' Lovell said and patted the man's shoulder. 'Your country will look after you.' He straightened, listening to the staccato rattle of musketry at the bluff's summit that told him that some redcoats must still be fighting on the heights. 'We'll need to bring artillery ashore, Colonel,' he said to Revere.

'Soon as you release us, General,' Revere said. There was an edge of resentment in his voice, suggesting that he thought it demeaning for his men to carry muskets instead of serving cannons. 'Just as soon as you release us,' he said again, though more willingly this time.

'Let's first see what we've achieved,' Lovell said. He patted the blinded man's shoulder a second time and started up the bluff, hauling himself on saplings. 'It'll be a hard job to get cannon up this slope, Colonel.'

'We'll manage that,' Revere said confidently. Taking heavy artillery up a bluff's steep face was a practical problem, and Lieutenant-Colonel Revere liked overcoming such challenges.

'I never did congratulate you on the success of your gunners at Cross Island,' Lovell said. 'You've hurt the enemy ships! A splendid achievement, Colonel.'

'Just doing our duty, General,' Revere said, but pleased all the same at the compliment. 'We killed some damned Britons!' He went on happily. 'I've dreamed of killing the damned beasts!'

'And you drove the enemy's ships back! So now there's nothing to stop our fleet from entering the harbour.'

'Nothing at all, General,' Revere agreed.

The stutter of musketry still sounded from Lovell's right, evidence that some redcoats yet remained on the high ground above the bay, but it was clear that most of the enemy had retreated because, as Lovell reached the easier slope at the top of the bluff, he found grinning militiamen who gave him a cheer. 'We beat them, sir!'

'Of course we beat them,' Lovell said, beaming, 'and all of you,' he raised his voice and lifted his hands in a gesture of benediction, 'all of you have my thanks and my congratulations on this magnificent feat of arms!'

The woods at the top of the bluff were now in rebel hands, all but for a stand of pines above Dyce's Head, which was far to the general's right and from where the musketry still sounded. Lovell's militia were thick in the woods. They had climbed the precipitous slope, they had taken casualties, but they had shot the British off the summit and all the way back to the fort. Men looked happy. They talked excitedly, recounting incidents in the fight up the steep slope, and Lovell enjoyed their happiness. 'Well done!' he said again and again.

He went to the edge of the trees and there, in front of him, was the enemy. The fog had quite gone now and he could see every detail of the fort that lay only half a mile to the east. The enemy had made a screen of branches between the woods and the fort, but from his high ground Lovell could easily see over that flimsy barricade and he could see that Fort George did not look like a stronghold at all, but instead resembled an earthen scar in the ridge's soil. The nearest rampart was thickly lined with redcoats, but he still felt relief. The fort, which in Lovell's imagination had been a daunting prospect of stone walls and sheer ramparts, now proved to be a mere scratch in the dirt.

Colonel McCobb of the Lincoln County militia hailed the general cheerfully. 'A good morning's work, sir!'

'One for the history books, McCobb! Without doubt, one

for the history books!' Lovell said. 'But not quite done yet. I think, don't you, that we should keep going?'

'Why not, sir?' McCobb answered.

Solomon Lovell's heart seemed to miss a beat. He scarcely dared believe the speed and extent of the morning's victory, but the sight of those distant redcoats behind the low rampart told him that the victory was not yet complete. He had a vision of the redcoats' muskets flaring volleys at his men. 'Is General Wadsworth here?'

'He was, sir.' McCobb said Wadsworth had been at the wood's edge where he had encouraged Colonel McCobb and Colonel Mitchell to keep their militiamen moving forward onto the cleared land, but both colonels had pleaded they needed time to reorganize their troops. Units had become scattered as they clambered up the bluff and the necessity of carrying the wounded back to the beach meant that most companies were short-handed. Besides, the capture of the high woods had seemed like a victory in itself and men wanted to savour that triumph before they advanced on Fort George. Peleg Wadsworth had urged haste, but then had been distracted by the musket-fire that still filled the trees at Dyce's Head with smoke. 'I believe he went to the right,' McCobb continued, 'to the marines.'

'The marines are still fighting?' Lovell asked McCobb.

'A few stubborn bastards are holding out there,' McCobb said.

Lovell hesitated, but the sight of the enemy's flags tipped his indecision towards confidence. 'We shall advance to victory!' he announced cheerfully. He wanted to add those arrogant enemy flags to his trophies. 'Form your fine fellows into line,' he told McCobb, then plucked at the colonel's sleeve as another doubt flickered in his mind. 'Have the enemy fired on you? With cannon, I mean?'

'Not a shot, General.'

'Well, let's stir your men from the woods! Tell them they'll

226

be eating British beef for their suppers!' The musketry from Dyce's Head suddenly intensified into an angry and concentrated crackle, and then, just as suddenly, went silent. Lovell stared towards the smoke, the only visible evidence of whatever battle was being fought among those trees. 'We should tell the marines we're advancing,' he said. 'Major Brown? Would you convey that message to Captain Welch? Tell him to advance with us as soon as he's ready?'

'I will, sir,' Major Gawen Brown, the second of Lovell's brigade majors, started off southwards.

Lovell could not stop smiling. The Massachusetts Militia had taken the bluff! They had climbed the precipitous slope, they had fought the regulars of the British Army, and they had conquered. 'I do believe,' he said to Lieutenant-Colonel Revere, 'that we may not need your cannon after all! Not if we can drive the enemy out of their works with infantry.'

'I'd still like a chance to hammer them,' Revere said. He was staring at the fort and was not impressed by what he saw. The curtain wall was low and its flanking bastions were unfinished, and he reckoned his artillery could reduce that feeble excuse for a fort into a smear of bloodied dirt.

'You zeal does you credit,' Lovell said, 'indeed it does, Colonel.' Behind him the militia sergeants and officers were rousting men from among the trees and shouting at them to form line on the open ground. The flags of Massachusetts and of the United States of America flew above them and it was time for the decisive assault.

Lieutenant Moore heard the bellowed order to charge and saw the green-uniformed men erupt out of the trees and he was aware of muskets flaming unexpectedly from his left and the chaos of the moment overwhelmed him. There was only terror in his head. He opened his mouth to shout an order, but no words came, and a hugely tall rebel in a green coat crossed by white belts, and with a long black pigtail flapping

227

behind his neck, and with a cutlass catching the morning sun in his right hand was running straight towards him and John Moore, almost without thinking, raised the musket he had rescued from Private McPhail and his finger fumbled at the trigger, and then he realized he had not even loaded or cocked the musket, but it was too late because the big rebel was almost on him and the man's face was a savagely frightening grimace of hatred and Moore convulsively pulled the trigger anyway and the musket fired.

It had been cocked and loaded and Moore had never noticed.

The ball took the rebel under the chin, it seared up through his mouth and out through his skull, lifting his hat into the air. The shock wave of the ball, compressed by the skull, drove an eye from its socket. Blood misted, blurring red in fine droplets as the rebel, dead in an instant, fell forward onto his knees. The cutlass dropped and the man's dead arms wrapped themselves around Moore's waist and then slid slowly down to his feet. Moore, aghast, noticed that the pigtail was dripping blood.

'For God's sake, young Moore, you want to win this bloody war single-handed?' Major Dunlop greeted the young lieutenant. Dunlop's men had fired a company volley from the trees to Moore's left, and that sudden volley had served to drive the momentarily outnumbered marines back to the trees.

Moore could not speak. A musket-ball plucked at the tails of his coat. He was gazing down at the dead rebel whose head was a mess of blood, red-wet hair and scraps of bone.

'Come on, lad,' Dunlop took Moore's elbow, 'let's get the devil out of here.'

The company retreated, taking Moore's surviving men with them. They withdrew along the lower ground beside the harbour as the American marines captured the three naval cannon abandoned on Dyce's Head. The rebel battery was firing from Cross Island, relentlessly thumping round shot into Captain Mowat's ships. The crest of the bluff was thick with rebels and the redcoats had no place to go now except the unfinished Fort George.

And Captain John Welch was dead.

It took time to fetch the militia from the trees, but gradually they were formed into a line. It was a rough line stretching clear across the high ground with the marines on its right, the Indians on the left and the flags at its centre. Paul Revere's men, Lovell's reserve, were in three ranks behind the two flags, one the proud starred stripes of the United States and the other the pine-tree banner of the Massachusetts Militia.

'What a magnificent morning's work,' Lovell greeted Peleg Wadsworth.

'I congratulate you, sir.'

'I thank you, Wadsworth, I thank you! But on to victory now?'

'On to victory, sir,' Wadsworth said. He decided he would not tell Lovell about Captain Welch's death, not till the battle was over and the victory gained.

'God has granted us the victory!' the Reverend Jonathan Murray announced. He had joined Lovell on the heights and, besides his brace of pistols, carried a Bible. He lifted the book high. 'God promises us "I will scatter them as with an east wind!"'

'Amen,' Lovell said. Israel Trask played his fife behind the marines, while three drummer boys and two more fifers played the 'Rogue's March' beside the two flags. Lovell's heart swelled with pride. He drew his sword, looked towards the enemy and pointed the blade forward. 'On to victory!'

A half-mile away, inside the fort, General McLean watched the rebels form at the tree-line. He had seen Major Dunlop's men climb to the battery on Dyce's Head and, with the help of a telescope, he had seen that young Moore and his men had been rescued. Those redcoats were now coming back to the fort through the low ground beside the harbour, while the remaining picquets that had guarded the neck were all inside Fort George where McLean's troops stood in three ranks behind the western rampart. Their job now was to defend that low wall with volley fire. McLean, watching the rebel line thicken, still believed he was faced by thousands, not hundreds, of enemy infantry, and now more rebels appeared to the north, showing at the trees above the neck. So he would be attacked from two sides? He glanced at the harbour and saw, to his surprise, that the enemy ships had made no aggressive move, but why should they? The fort was going to fall without their assistance. McLean limped up onto the unfinished western rampart. 'Captain Fielding!'

'Sir?' The English artillery commander hurried to join McLean.

'We'll give them a few shots, I think?'

'Wait till they advance, sir?' Fielding suggested.

'I think we might treat them now, Captain,' McLean said.

'They're too far for grape or case, sir.'

'Then give them round shot,' McLean said. He spoke wearily. He knew what must happen now. The rebels would advance and such was the length of their line they must inevitably wrap around three sides of his unfinished fort. They would take some casualties at the abatis, which was well within the effective range of the grape shot that Captain Mowat had sent ashore, but Fielding's few guns could do only limited damage and the rebels would surely surge on to assault the low walls. Then there would be chaos, panic and bayonets. His men would stand, of that McLean was sure, but they would stand and die.

So the battle was lost. Yet honour alone dictated that he showed some resistance before he surrendered the fort. No one would blame him for its loss, not when he was so outnumbered, but he would be universally despised if he yielded without showing some defiance and so McLean had determined on his course of action. He would fire round shot and keep firing as the rebels began their advance, and then, before they came into range of Captain Fielding's more lethal case and grapeshot, he would haul the flag down. It was sad, he thought, but surrender would save his men from massacre.

McLean walked to the flagpole in the south-western bastion. He had asked his aides to place a table beside the tall staff, but his slight limp and his crippled right arm made the effort of climbing onto the table difficult. 'Need a hand, sir?' Sergeant Lawrence asked.

'Thank you, Sergeant.'

'You want to see how well our guns can cut down rebels, sir?' the sergeant asked happily after he had helped McLean onto the table.

'Oh, I know you lads can defend us,' McLean lied. He stood on the table and wondered why no bagpipers had come with the two regiments. He smiled that so strange a thought should have occurred to him at such a moment. 'I do miss the pipes,' he said.

'Bagpipes, sir?' Lawrence asked.

'Indeed! The music of war.'

'Give me a good English band any day, sir.'

McLean smiled. His undignified perch on the table gave him an excellent view of the ground over which the rebels must advance. He reached into a pocket of his red coat and took out a folded penknife. 'Sergeant, would you be so kind as to open that?'

'Going to stick a rebel, General?' Lawrence asked as he extracted the blade. 'I reckon your sword will do more damage.'

McLean took the knife back. The hand of his injured right arm was too weak to loosen the halliard holding the flag and so he held the short blade in his left hand ready to cut the line when the moment came.

231

Captain Fielding came to the bastion where he insisted on laying the twelve-pounder cannon himself. 'What's the charge?' he asked Lawrence.

'Quarter charge, sir,' Lawrence said, 'three pounds.'

Fielding nodded and made some calculations in his head. The gun was cold, which meant the shot would lose some power, so he elevated the barrel just a trifle, then used the trail spike to aim the gun at a knot of men standing close to the rebels' bright flags. Satisfied that his aim and elevation were good, he stepped back and nodded to Sergeant Lawrence. 'Carry on, Sergeant,' he said.

Lawrence primed the gun, ordered the crew to cover their ears and step aside, then touched flame to the portfire. The gun roared, smoke smothered the bastion, and the round shot flew.

It flew above the abatis and over the shattered stumps, and it began to lose height as the ground rose to meet it. To Peleg Wadsworth, standing to Lovell's left, the ball appeared as a lead-grey streak in the sky. It was a flicker of grey, a pencil stroke against the sudden white-grey of powder smoke that obscured the fort, and then the streak vanished and the ball struck. It hit a militiaman in the chest, shattering ribs, blood and flesh in an explosion of butchery, and plunged on, flicking blood behind its passage, to rip a man in the groin, more blood and meat in the air, and then the ball struck the ground, bounced, and decapitated one of Revere's gunners before vanishing noisily into the woods behind.

Solomon Lovell was standing just two paces away from the first man struck by the round shot. A splinter of rib hit the general on the shoulder and a stringy splat of bloody flesh spattered wetly across his face, and just then HMS *North*, which lay closest to the fort, fired its broadside at the marines who were on the right of Lovell's lines, and the thunder of the sloop's gunfire filled the Majabigwaduce sky as Captain Fielding's second gun fired. That second ball hit a tree stump just in front of Colonel McCobb's men and struck with such violence that the stump was half-uprooted as it shattered into scraps that drove into McCobb's front rank. A man screamed in pain.

Sergeant Lawrence's crew, drilled and practised, had swabbed and reloaded the first gun, which they now levered back to the low embrasure so Lawrence could fire it a second time. The ball struck the ground just paces from Lovell and bounced harmlessly overhead, though not before it drove a shower of soil at the general's staff.

The man whose groin had been pulped by the first shot was still alive, but his belly was eviscerated and his guts coiled on the ground and he breathed in short, desperate spasms. Lovell, transfixed, watched appalled as a pulse of blood, obscenely thick, spilled out of the man's gutted trunk. The wounded man was making a pathetic noise and Lieutenant-Colonel Revere, whose uniform had been spattered by blood, was white-faced, staring wide-eyed, unmoving. Wadsworth noted the pine needles sticking to the loops of intestine on the ground. The man somehow brought up his head and looked beseechingly at Wadsworth, and Wadsworth involuntarily moved towards him, wondering what in God's name he could do or say when, with another surge of blood from his ruined guts, the man's head fell back.

'Oh dear God,' Lovell said to no one.

'God rest his soul,' the Reverend Jonathan Murray said, his voice unusually strained.

Wadsworth looked into the dead man's face. No movement there except for a fly crawling on an unshaven cheek. Behind Wadsworth a man vomited. He turned to stare at the fort where the cannon smoke lingered. 'We should advance, sir,' he said to Lovell, and was surprised that he had spoken at all, let alone sounded so detached. Lovell seemed not to have heard him. 'We should advance, sir!' Wadsworth said in a louder voice.

Solomon Lovell was gazing at the fort where another billow of smoke jetted from an unfinished bastion. The ball flew to the general's left, crashing into a tree behind the militia. 'Colonel Revere?' Lovell asked, still looking at the fort.

'General?' Revere acknowledged.

'Can your artillery reduce the fort?'

'It can,' Revere said, though without any of his usual confidence. 'It can,' he said again, unable to take his eyes from the bloody mess on the ground.

'Then we shall give your guns that chance,' Lovell said. 'The men will shelter in the trees.'

'But now's the moment to advance and . . .' Wadsworth began a protest.

'I can't attack into those guns!' Lovell interrupted shrilly. He blinked, surprised by his own tone of voice. 'I can't,' he began again, then seemed to forget what he wanted to say. 'We shall reduce their walls with artillery,' he said decisively, then frowned as another British gun hammered a ball up the ridge. 'The enemy might counter-attack,' he went on with a note of panic, 'so we must be ready to repel them. Into the trees!' He turned and waved his sword at the thick woods. 'Take the men into the trees!' he shouted at the militia officers. 'Dig defences! Here, at the tree-line. I want earthworks.' He paused, watching his men retreat, then led his staff into the cover of the high wood.

Brigadier-General McLean watched in astonishment as his enemy vanished. Was it a trick? One moment there had been hundreds of men forming into ranks, then suddenly they had all retreated into the trees. He watched and waited, but as time passed he realized that the rebels really had gone into the woods and were showing no sign of renewing their attack. He let out a long breath, took his hand from the flag's halliard and pushed the open penknife back into his pocket. 'Colonel

Campbell!' he called, 'stand down three companies! Form them into work parties to heighten the ramparts!'

'Yes, sir!' Campbell called back.

Fort George would live a few hours yet.

From Brigadier-General Lovell's despatch to Jeremiah Powell, President of the Council Board of the State of Massachusetts Bay, dated July 28th, 1779:

This morning I have made my landing good on the S.W. Head of the Peninsula which is one hundred feet high and almost perpendicular very thickly covered with Brush and trees, the men ascended the Precipice with alacrity and after a very smart conflict we put them to rout, they left in the Woods a number killed and wounded and we took a few Prisoners our loss is about thirty kill'd and wounded, we are with in 100 Rod of the Enemy's main fort on a Commanding peice of Ground, and hope soon to have the Satisfaction of informing you of the Capturing the whole Army, you will please to excuse my not being more particular, as you may Judge my situation.
Am Sir your most Obedient Humble Servant

From Brigadier-General Solomon Lovell's Journal. Wednesday July 28th, 1779:

When I returned to the Shore it struck me with admiration to see what a Precipice we had ascended, not being able to take so scrutinous a view of it in time of Battle, it is at least where we landed three hundred feet high, and almost perpendicular and the men were obliged to pull themselves up by the twigs and trees. I don't think such a landing has been made since Wolfe.

From the letter of Colonel John Brewer to David Perham, written in 1779 and published in the *Bangor Whig and Courier*, August 13th, 1846:

The General (McLean) *he received me very politely, and said . . . 'I was in no situation to defend myself, I only meant to give them one or two guns, so as not to be called a coward, and then have struck my colors, which I stood for some time to do, as I did not want to throw away the lives of my men for nothing.'*

EIGHT

Marine Captain Thomas Carnes and thirty men had been on the right flank of the marines who had fought their way up the bluff. Carnes's route lay up the steepest part of the bluff's slope and his men did not reach the summit until after Welch was shot and after the sudden counter-attack by a company of redcoats who, their volley fired, had retreated as suddenly as they had arrived. Captain Davis had taken over command of Dyce's Head and his immediate problem was the wounded marines. 'They need a doctor,' he told Carnes.

'The nearest surgeon is probably still on the beach,' Carnes said.

'Damn it, damn it,' Davis looked harried. 'Can your men carry them down? And we need cartridges.'

So Carnes took his thirty men back to the beach. They escorted two prisoners and, because they carried eight of their own wounded and did not want to cause those casualties even more pain, they descended the bluff very slowly and carefully. The injured men were laid on the shingle, joining the other men who waited for the surgeons. Carnes then led his two captives to where another six prisoners were under militia guard beside the big granite boulder. 'What happens to us, sir?' one of the prisoners asked, but the man's Scottish

239

accent was so strange that Carnes had to make him repeat the question twice before he understood.

'You'll be looked after,' he said, 'and probably a lot better than I was,' he added bitterly. Carnes had been taken captive two years earlier and had spent a hungry six months in New York before being exchanged.

The narrow strip of beach was busy. Doctor Downer, distinguished by his blood-soaked apron and an ancient straw hat, was using a probe to track a musket-ball buried in a militiaman's buttock. The injured man was held down by the doctor's two assistants, while the Reverend Murray knelt beside a dying man, holding his hand and reciting the twenty-third psalm. Sailors were landing boxes of musket ammunition, while those wounded who did not require immediate treatment were waiting patiently. A number of militiamen, too many to Carnes's eyes, seemed to have no purpose at all on the beach, but were sitting around idle. Some had even lit driftwood fires, a few of which were much too close to the newly arrived boxes of musket cartridges that were stacked above the high tideline. That ammunition belonged to the militia, and Carnes suspected the minutemen would not be generous if he requested replacement cartridges. 'Sergeant Sykes?'

'Sir?'

'How many thieves in our party?'

'Every last man, sir. They're marines.'

'Two or three of those boxes would be mighty useful.'

'So they would, sir.'

'Carry on, Sergeant.'

'What's happening on the heights, Captain?' Doctor Eliphalet Downer called from a few paces away. 'I've found the ball,' he said to his assistants as he selected a pair of blood-caked tongs, 'so hold him tight. Stay still, man, you're not dying. You've just got a British ball up your American bottom. Did the redcoats counter-attack?'

240

'They haven't yet, Doctor,' Carnes said.

'But they might?'

'That's what the general believes.'

Their conversation was interrupted by a gasp from the wounded man, then the dull boom of a British cannon firing from the distant fort. When Carnes had left the heights to bring the wounded down to the beach all the American forces had been back among the trees, but the British gunners were still sustaining a desultory fire, presumably to keep the Americans at bay. 'So what happens now?' Eliphalet Downer asked, then grunted as he forced the tongs into the narrow wound. 'Mop that blood.'

'General Lovell has called for artillery,' Carnes said, 'so I guess we batter the bastards before we assault them.'

'I've got the ball,' Downer said, feeling the jaws of his tongs scrape and close around the musket-ball.

'He's fainted, sir,' an assistant said.

'Sensible fellow. Here is comes.' The ball's extraction provoked a spurt of blood that the assistant staunched with a linen pad as Downer moved to the next patient. 'Bone saw and knife,' Downer ordered after a glance at the man's shattered leg. 'Good morning, Colonel!' This last was to Lieutenant-Colonel Revere who had just appeared on the crowded beach with three of his artillerymen. 'I hear you're moving guns to the heights?' Downer asked cheerfully as he knelt beside the injured man.

Revere looked startled at the question, perhaps because he thought it was none of Downer's business, but he nodded. 'The general wants batteries established, Doctor, yes.'

'I hope that means no more work for us today,' Downer said, 'not if your guns keep the wretches well away.'

'They will, Doctor, never you fret,' Revere said, then walked towards his white-painted barge that waited a few paces down the shingle. 'Wait here,' he called back to his men, 'I'll be back after breakfast.'

Carnes was not certain he had heard the last words correctly.

'Sir?' He had to repeat the word to get Revere's attention. 'Sir? If you need help taking the guns up the slope, my marines are good and ready.'

Revere paused at the barge to give Carnes a suspicious look. 'We don't need help,' he said brusquely, 'we've got men enough.' He had not met Carnes and had no idea that this was the marine officer who had been an artilleryman in General Washington's army. He stepped over the barge's gunwale. 'Back to the *Samuel*,' he ordered the crew.

The general wanted artillery at the top of the bluff, but Colonel Revere wanted a hot breakfast. So the general had to wait.

Lieutenant John Moore accompanied his two wounded men to Doctor Calef's barn, which now served as the garrison's hospital. He tried to comfort the two men, but felt his words were inadequate and afterwards he went into the small vegetable garden outside where, overcome with remorse, he sat on the log pile. He was shaking. He held out his left hand and saw it quivering, and he bit his lip because he sensed he was about to shed tears and he did not want to do that, not where people could see him, and to distract himself he stared across the harbour to where Mowat's ships were cannonading the rebel battery on Cross Island.

Someone came from the house and wordlessly offered him a mug of tea. He looked up and saw it was Bethany Fletcher and the sight of her provoked the tears he had been trying so hard to suppress. They rolled down his cheeks. He attempted to stand in welcome, but he was shaking too much and the gesture failed. He sniffed and took the tea. 'Thank you,' he said.

'What happened?' she asked.

'The rebels beat us,' Moore said bleakly.

'They haven't taken the fort,' Beth said.

'No. Not yet.' Moore gripped the mug with both hands.

242

The cannon smoke lay like fog on the harbour and more smoke drifted slowly from the fort where Captain Fielding's cannons shot into the distant trees. The rebels, despite their capture of the high ground, were showing no sign of wanting to attack the fort, though Moore supposed they were organizing that attack from within the cover of the woods. 'I failed,' he said bitterly.

'Failed?'

'I should have retreated, but I stayed. I killed six of my men.' Moore drank some of the tea, which was very sweet. 'I wanted to win,' he said, 'and so I stayed.' Beth said nothing. She was wearing a linen apron smeared with blood and Moore flinched at the memory of Sergeant McClure's death, then he remembered the tall American in his green coat charging across the clearing. He could still see the man's upraised cutlass blade reflecting the day's new light, the bared teeth, the intensity of hatred on the rebel's face, the determination to kill, and Moore remembered his own panic and the sheer luck that had saved his life. He made himself drink more tea. 'Why do they wear white crossbelts?' he asked.

'White crossbelts?' Beth was puzzled.

'You could hardly see them in the trees, except they wore white belts and that made them visible,' Moore said. 'Black crossbelts,' he said, 'they should be black,' and he had a sudden vision of the spray of blood from Sergeant McClure's mouth. 'I killed them,' he said, 'by being selfish.'

'It was your first fight,' Beth said sympathetically.

And it had been so different from anything Moore had expected. In his mind, for years, there had been a vision of redcoats drawn up in three ranks, their flags bright above them, the enemy similarly arrayed and the bands playing as the muskets volleyed. Cavalry was always resplendent in their finery, decorating the dream-fields of glory, but instead Moore's first battle had been a chaotic defeat in dark woods. The enemy had been in the trees and his men, ranked in

243

their red line, had been easy targets for those men in green coats. 'But why white crossbelts?' he asked again.

'Were there many dead?' Beth asked.

'Six of my men,' Moore answered bleakly. He remembered the stench of shit from McPhail's corpse and closed his eyes as if he could blot that memory away.

'Among the rebels?' Beth asked anxiously.

'Some, yes, I don't know.' Moore was too distracted by guilt to hear the anxiety in Bethany's voice. 'The rest of the picquet ran away, but they must have killed some.'

'And now?'

Moore finished the tea. He was not looking at Beth, but gazing at the ships in the harbour, noting how HMS *Albany* seemed to shiver when her guns fired. 'We did it all wrong,' he said, frowning. 'We should have moved most of the picquet to the beach and shot at them as they rowed towards the shore, then put more men halfway up the slope. We could have beaten them!' He put the mug on the logs and saw that his hand was no longer shaking. He stood. 'I'm sorry, Miss Fletcher, I never thanked you for the tea.'

'You did, Lieutenant,' Beth said. 'Doctor Calef told me to give it to you,' she added.

'That was kind of him. Are you helping him?'

'We all are,' Beth said, meaning the women of Majabigwaduce. She watched Moore, noting the blood on his finely tailored clothes. He looked so young, she thought, just a boy with a long sword.

'I must get back to the fort,' Moore said. 'Thank you for the tea.' His job, he remembered, was to burn the oaths before the rebels discovered them. And the rebels would come now, he was sure, and all he was good for was burning papers because he had failed. He had killed six of his men by making the wrong decision and John Moore was certain that General McLean would not let him lead any more men to their deaths.

He walked back to the fort where the flag still flew.

244

The harbour was a sudden cauldron of noise as more guns filled the shallow basin with smoke and, as Moore reached the fort's entrance, he saw why. Three enemy ships were under foresails and topsails, and they were sailing straight for the harbour.

They were coming to finish the job.

Commodore Saltonstall had promised to engage the enemy shipping with gunfire and so had cleared the *Warren* for action. Fog had prevented an engagement at first light and once that fog lifted there was a further delay because the *Charming Sally*, one of the privateers that would support the *Warren*, had a fouled anchor, but at last Captain Holmes solved the problem by buoying the anchor cable and casting it overboard, and so the three ships sailed slowly eastwards on the light wind. The commodore planned to sail into the harbour mouth and there use the frigate's powerful broadside to batter the three enemy sloops. The heaviest British guns on those sloops were nine-pounders, while the *Warren* had twelve and eighteen-pounders, guns that would mangle British timber and British flesh. The commodore would have liked nothing more than to have used those big guns on the thirty-two impudent men who had dared send him a letter that, though expressed in the politest words, implicitly accused him of cowardice. How dare they! He shook with suppressed anger as he recalled the letter. There were times, the commodore thought, when the notion that all men were created equal led to nothing but insolence.

He turned to see that the *Black Prince* and *Charming Sally* were following his frigate. The battery on Cross Island was already firing at the three British sloops that now barricaded the harbour's centre. There was water at either end of the British line, but the larger transport ships had been moored to block those shallow channels. Not that Saltonstall had any intention of piercing or flanking Mowat's ships; he simply

245

wanted to keep the Royal Marines on board the enemy sloops while Lovell assaulted the fort.

The wind was slight. Saltonstall had ordered battle-sails, which meant his two big courses, the mainsail and foresail, were furled onto their yards so that their canvas would not block the view forrard. He had kept the staysail furled for the same reason, so the *Warren* was being driven by flying jib, jib, and topsails. She went slowly, creeping ever closer to the narrow entrance between Cross Island and Dyce's Head, which was now in American hands. Saltonstall could see the green coats of his marines on that height. They were watching the *Warren* and evidently cheering because they waved their hats towards the frigate.

The three British sloops had been shooting towards the rebel battery on Cross Island until they saw the topsails loosed on the enemy ships, when they had immediately ceased fire so that their guns could be levered around to point at the harbour mouth. Every cannon was double-shotted so that two round shots would be fired by each gun in the first broadside. The *Warren*, by far the largest warship in the Penobscot River, looked huge as she loomed in the entrance narrows. Captain Mowat, standing on the *Albany*'s afterdeck, was surprised that only three ships were approaching, though he was more than sensible that three ships were sufficient. Still, he reckoned, if he had commanded the rebel fleet he would have sent every available vessel in an irresistible and overwhelming attack. He trained his glass on the *Warren*, noting that there were no marines on her forecastle, which suggested the frigate was not planning to try and board his sloops. Maybe the marines were hiding? The frigate's cutwater appeared huge in his glass. He collapsed the tubes and nodded to his first lieutenant. 'You may open fire,' Mowat said.

Mowat's three sloops had twenty-eight guns in their combined broadsides, a mix of nine- and six-pounders, and all of them shot two balls at the *Warren*. The noise of the guns filled the wide basin of Penobscot Bay while the Half Moon battery, which had been dug into the harbour slope west of the fort, added her four twelve-pounders. All of those round shot were aimed at the *Warren*'s bows, and the frigate shuddered under their massive blows. 'You will return the fire, Mister Fenwick!' Saltonstall shouted at his first lieutenant, and Fenwick gave the order, but the only guns that the *Warren* could use were its two nine-pounder bow-chasers, which fired together to shroud the rearing bowsprit with smoke. The *Warren*'s bows were being splintered by round shot, the impacts sending shock waves through the hull. A man was screaming in the focsle, a sound that irritated Saltonstall.

His ship palpably slowed under the constant blows. Dudley Saltonstall, standing next to the impassive helmsman, could hear timbers splintering. He was not an imaginative man, but it suddenly struck him that this vicious, concentrated gunfire was an expression of British anger against the rebels who had captured the high ground of their peninsula. Defeated on land they were revenging themselves with cannon-fire, well-aimed, brisk and efficient cannon-fire, and Saltonstall seethed with anger that his fine ship should be its victim. A twelve-pounder ball, fired from the harbour shore, struck a forrard nine-pounder, shearing its breech lines, shattering a trunnion and slaughtering two crewmen whose blood spattered twenty feet across the deck. A spew of intestines lay like an untidy rope in the ugly bloodstain. The nine-pounder sagged in its carriage. One man had lost half his head, the other had been eviscerated by the ball, which had lost its volition and come to rest by the starboard gangway.

'Swab the deck!' Saltonstall shouted. 'Be lively!' A lieutenant called for seamen to fetch buckets of water, but before they could wash the sprawling blood from the scrubbed planks, the commodore shouted again. 'Belay that order!'

Mister Fenwick, the first lieutenant, stared at Saltonstall. The commodore was famous for keeping a spanking clean ship, yet he had reversed the order to swab the deck? 'Sir?' Fenwick called uncertainly.

'Leave it be,' Saltonstall insisted. He half-smiled to himself. An idea had occurred to him and he liked it. 'Throw that offal overboard,' he gestured to the spilt intestines, 'but leave the blood.'

A twelve-pounder ball struck the mainmast with enough force to make the canvas of the big maintopsail quiver. Saltonstall watched the mast, wondering if it would fall, but the great spar held. 'Summon the carpenter, Mister Coningsby,' he ordered.

'Aye aye, sir,' Midshipman Fanning, resigned to being called Coningsby, answered.

'I want a report on the mainmast. Don't just stand there! Look lively!'

Fanning ran to a companionway to find the ship's carpenter who, he suspected, would be somewhere forrard surveying the damage that was being done to the *Warren*'s bows where most of the enemy shots were slamming into the frigate. A nine-pounder ball slashed the shrouds of the spritsail yard so that it dangled into the water, though luckily the spritsail itself was not bent onto the spar and so the canvas could not drag in the water to slow the *Warren* even more. The jib-boom was cut through and the remnant of the bowsprit was being held by only one shroud, and still the cannonballs crashed home. Lieutenant Fenwick had six men retrieving the spritsail yard and one of them suddenly turned with an astonished expression and no left arm, just a ragged bloody stump that was gushing blood. The wind of the ball buffeted Fenwick and spattered him with blood. 'Put a tourniquet on that,' he ordered, marvelling that he sounded so calm, but the wounded man, before anyone could help him, fell side-ways into the water and another six-pounder ball gouged along the gunwale to plough out long, sharp splinters that flickered across the deck. The ship shuddered again and blood oozed along the seams between the deck planking. A shot struck the waterline, spraying the forecastle with cold sea-water, and then Fenwick was aware that the *Warren* was turning, turning so slowly, lumbering around to starboard so her larboard broadside could be brought to bear on the enemy. Marines were cheering the frigate from Dyce's Head, but that was small consolation as two more shots ripped into her hull. One of the big elm pumps was working now, its crew working the long levers so that water gushed rhythmically over the *Warren*'s side. A man was whimpering somewhere, but Fenwick could not see him. 'Throw that overboard,' he snapped, pointing to the severed arm.

The frigate was turning with agonizing slowness, but her bows were at last pointed at the harbour's southern side and her powerful broadside could return the British cannonade. The commodore ordered the frigate's big guns to open fire as soon as the slow turn brought the Half Moon Battery abreast of his broadside and the noise of those cannons drowned the universe as they roared at the British emplacement. Smoke billowed as high as the furled mainyard. The guns recoiled, their trucks momentarily leaving the deck until the breech ropes took the strain. Water hissed into steam as gunners swabbed barrels. A twelve-pounder shot slashed across the poop deck, miraculously doing no damage except to a bucket that was shattered into a thousand pieces. 'Fire as you bear!' Saltonstall called, meaning that his gunners should fire as soon as the ship had turned sufficiently to bring the guns to bear on the enemy sloops, though the gunners were so obstructed by their own smoke that they could scarcely see the enemy who, in turn, were smothered by their own powder smoke, which constantly renewed itself as the flames spat through the cloud to punch more shots at the frigate.

'The carpenter says he'll look at the mainmast as soon as he can, sir!' Midshipman Fanning had to shout to make himself heard over the gunfire.

'As soon as he can?' Saltonstall repeated angrily.

'The bows are holed, sir, he says he's plugging it.'

Saltonstall grunted and a six-pounder shot, fired from HMS *Albany*, hit Fanning in the groin. He screamed and fell. Bone was showing ivory-white in the mangled remnants of his hip. He was staring up at Saltonstall, teeth bared, screaming, and his blood was sticky on the ship's wheel. 'Mother,' Fanning whimpered, 'Mother!'

'Oh, for God's sake,' Saltonstall muttered.

'You two!' the helmsman called to two crewmen crouching by the portside rail. 'Take the boy below.'

'Mother,' Fanning was crying, 'Mother.' He reached out a hand and gripped the lower wheel. 'Oh, Mother!'

'Fire!' Saltonstall shouted at his gun crews, not because they needed the order, but because he did not want to listen to the boy's pathetic crying, which, thankfully and abruptly, faded to nothing.

'He's dead,' one of the crewmen said, 'poor little bastard.'

'Watch your tongue!' Saltonstall snarled, 'and take Mister Coningsby away.'

'Take him away,' the helmsman pointed at Fanning, realizing that the seamen had been confused by the commodore's order. He stooped and prised the dead boy's grasp from the wheel.

The *Warren*'s guns were firing at the enemy sloops now, but the frigate's crew was raw. Few of the men were regular sailors, most had been pressed from the wharves of Boston and they served the guns much more slowly than the British sailors. The frigate's fire did more damage because her guns were heavier, but for every shot the *Warren* fired she received six. Another ball hit the bowsprit, almost splintering it into two long shards, then a twelve-pounder hit the mainmast again and the long spar wavered dangerously before being held by the shrouds. 'Furl the maintopsail!' Saltonstall called to the second lieutenant. He needed to take the pressure off the damaged mast or else it would go overboard and he would be a floating wreck under the pounding of the British guns. He saw smoke jet from the fort on the skyline and saw a rent appear in his foretopgallant sail. 'Take in the foresails! Mister Fenwick!' Saltonstall called through a speaking trumpet. The jibs and staysail would pull the damaged bowsprit to pieces unless they were furled. A round shot from the Half Moon Battery thumped hard into the hull, shaking the shrouds.

The two privateers had not followed the *Warren* into the harbour's mouth, but instead stood just outside the entrance and fired past the frigate at the distant sloops. So the *Warren* was taking almost all of the British cannon-fire and Saltonstall knew he could not just stay and be shot to splinters. 'Mister Fenwick! Launch two longboats! Tow the bows round!'

'Aye aye, sir!'

'We kept their marines busy,' Saltonstall muttered. That had been the arrangement, that his ships would threaten the British line and so keep the Royal Marines away from the fort, which, he assumed, General Lovell was even now attacking. It should all be over by midday, he reckoned, and there was small point in taking any more casualties and so he would retreat. He needed to turn the frigate in the narrow space and because the wind was fitful he had men tow the *Warren*'s head round. British cannonballs exploded great spouts of water about the heaving oarsmen, but none of the shots struck the longboats, which at last succeeded in turning the *Warren* westwards. Saltonstall dared not set the jib, flying jib or staysail because even this small wind would exert enough pressure on those sails to pull his damaged bowsprit to pieces, and so he relied on the longboats to tow the frigate to safety. The men hauled on their oars and slowly, persistently hammered by British round shot, the *Warren* edged her way back into the wider bay.

Saltonstall heard a cheer from the three British sloops. The commodore sneered at the sound. The fools thought they had beaten his powerful frigate, but he had never planned to engage them closely, merely to keep their marines aboard while Lovell assaulted the fort. A last shot slashed into the water to spray the quarterdeck, then the *Warren* was towed north under the lee of Dyce's Head and so out of sight of the impudent enemy. The two forrard anchors were let go, the oarsmen in the longboats rested, the guns were housed and it was time to make repairs.

Peleg Wadsworth crouched opposite the captured highlander who was sitting with his back against a bullet-scarred beech tree. The prisoner had been found hiding in a thick stand of brush, perhaps hoping to sneak his way back to Fort George, but he would have found any escape difficult because he had been struck in his calf by a musket-ball. The ball had mangled his flesh, but it had missed the bone and the doctor with the Lincoln County militia had reckoned the man would live if the wound did not turn gangrenous. 'You're to keep the wound bandaged,' Wadsworth said, 'and keep the bandage damp. You understand that?'

The man nodded. He was a tall youngster, perhaps eighteen or nineteen years old, with raven-black hair, pale skin, dark eyes and an expression of befuddlement as if he had no comprehension of what fate had just done to him. He kept looking from Wadsworth to James Fletcher, then back to Wadsworth again. He had been stripped of his red coat and wore nothing but shirt and kilt. 'Where are you from, soldier?' Wadsworth asked.

The man answered, but his accent was so strong that even when he repeated the name Wadsworth did not understand. 'You'll be properly looked after,' Wadsworth said. 'In time you'll go to Boston.' The man spoke again, though what he said was impossible to tell. 'When the war is over,' Wadsworth said slowly, as if he were talking to someone who did not speak English. He assumed the Scotsman did, but he was not

252

sure. 'When the war is over you will go home. Unless, of course, you choose to stay here. America welcomes good men.'

James Fletcher offered the prisoner a canteen of water, which the man took and drank greedily. His lips were stained by the powder from the cartridges he had bitten during the fight, and tearing the cartridges open with the teeth left a man's mouth dry as dust. He handed back the canteen and asked a question that neither Fletcher nor Wadsworth could understand or answer. 'Can you stand?' Wadsworth asked.

The man answered by standing up, though he winced when he put any weight on his injured left leg. 'Help him down to the beach,' Wadsworth ordered Fletcher, 'then find me up here again.'

It was midday. Smoke rose all along the height of the bluff where men had made camp-fires to brew tea. The British cannon still fired from the fort, but their rate of fire was much slower now. Wadsworth reckoned there were at least ten minutes between each shot, and none did any damage because the rebels were staying out of sight among the trees, which meant the enemy had nothing to aim at and their fire, Wadsworth supposed, was a mere message of defiance.

He walked southwards to where the marines held Dyce's Head. The gunfire in the harbour had died, leaving long skeins of smoke drifting slowly across the sun-rippled water. The *Warren*, her bows scarred by round shot, was seeking shelter west of the bluff where the three captured British cannon were now pointing at the fort under the guard of Lieutenant William Dennis.

Dennis smiled when his old schoolmaster appeared. 'I'm delighted to see you unscathed, sir,' he greeted Wadsworth.

'As I am you, Lieutenant,' Wadsworth said. 'Are you thinking of using these cannon?'

'I wish we could,' Dennis said, and pointed to a fire-scarred pit. 'They exploded their ready magazine, sir. They should have spiked the guns, but they didn't. So we've sent for more powder bags.'

'I'm sorry about Captain Welch,' Wadsworth said.

'It's almost too hard to believe,' Dennis said in a puzzled tone.

'I didn't know him well. Hardly at all! But he inspired confidence.'

'We thought him indestructible,' Dennis said, then made an uncertain gesture towards the west. 'The men want to bury him up here, sir, where he led the fight.'

Wadsworth looked to where Dennis pointed and saw a body shrouded by two blankets. He realized it had to be Welch's corpse. 'That seems fitting,' he said.

'When we take the fort, sir,' Dennis said, 'it should be called Fort Welch.'

'I have a suspicion,' Wadsworth replied drily, 'that we must call it Fort Lovell instead.'

Dennis smiled at Wadsworth's tone, then reached into his tail-coat pocket. 'The book I was going to give you, sir,' he said, holding out the volume by Cesare Beccaria.

Wadsworth was about to express his thanks, then saw that the book's cover had been ripped and the pages churned into a mangled mess. 'Good Lord!' he said. 'A bullet?' The book was unreadable, nothing but torn paper now.

'I hadn't finished it,' Dennis said ruefully, trying to separate the pages.

'A bullet?'

'Yes, sir. But it missed me, which is a good omen, I think.'

'I pray so.'

'I'll find you another copy,' Dennis said, then summoned a lean, hatchet-faced marine a few paces away. 'Sergeant Sykes! Didn't you say my books were only good for lighting fires?'

'True, sir,' Sykes said, 'I did.'

'Here!' Dennis tossed the ruined book to the sergeant. 'Kindling!'

Sykes grinned. 'Best use for a book, Lieutenant,' he said, then looked at Peleg Wadsworth. 'Are we going to attack the fort, General?'

'I'm certain we will,' Wadsworth said. He had encouraged Lovell to order an attack late in the day when the setting sun would be in the eyes of the fort's defenders, but so far Lovell had not committed himself. Lovell wanted to be certain that the American lines were secure from any British counter-attack before launching his troops at the fort, and so he had ordered the rebel force to dig trenches and throw up earth walls at the wood's edge. The marines had ignored the order. 'Aren't you supposed to be digging a trench here?' Wadsworth asked.

'Lord above, sir,' Dennis said, 'we don't need a trench. We're here to attack them!'

Wadsworth wholeheartedly agreed with that sentiment, but he could hardly express his agreement without seeming disloyal to Lovell. Instead he borrowed a telescope from Dennis and used it to gaze at the small British gun emplace-ment that was now the nearest enemy post. He could not see the battery clearly because it was half-hidden by a corn-field, but he could see enough. The earthwork was a semi-circle a small distance up the slope from the harbour and halfway between the marines and the fort. The battery's cannon were facing south-west, towards the harbour entrance, but Wadsworth supposed they could easily be levered around to face west and so rip into any infantry attacking from Dyce's Head. 'You think those guns are a menace, sir?' Dennis asked, seeing where Wadsworth was looking.

'They could be,' Wadsworth said.

'We can get close,' Dennis said confidently. 'They'll not see us in the corn. Fifty men could take that battery easily.'

'We may not need to capture it,' Wadsworth said. He had swung the glass to study the fort. The walls were so low that the redcoats behind it were exposed from the waist upwards, though even as he watched he could see men lifting a huge log to heighten the rampart. Then his view was blotted out by whiteness and he lowered the telescope to see that a cannon had fired, only this gun smoke was blossoming at the centre of the fort's western wall while all the previous smoke had jetted from the bastions at either end of that curtain wall. 'Is that a new cannon?'

'Must be,' Dennis said.

Wadsworth was not a man who liked curses, but he was tempted to swear. Lovell was fortifying the heights and the British, given the precious gift of time, were raising the fort's wall and placing more cannon on those ramparts, and every hour that passed would make the fort more difficult to attack. 'I trust you and your marines will stay here,' he said to Dennis, 'and join the attack.'

'I hope so too, sir, but that's the commodore's decision.'

'I suppose it is,' Wadsworth said.

'He sailed halfway into the entrance,' Dennis said, 'hammered the enemy for a half-hour and then sailed out.' He sounded disappointed, as if he had expected more from the rebels' flagship. He looked down at the British ships, which had just started firing at the rebel battery on Cross Island again. 'We need heavy guns up here,' he said.

'If we take the fort,' Wadsworth said, and wished he had said when instead of if, 'we won't need any more batteries.'

Because once the Americans captured the fort the three British sloops were doomed. And the fort was pathetic, a scar in the earth, not even half-built yet, but Solomon Lovell, after his triumph in taking the high ground, had decided to dig defences rather than make an assault. Wadsworth gave Dennis back the glass and went north to find Lovell. They must attack, he thought, they must attack.

But there was no attack. The long summer day passed and the rebels made their earthworks and the British guns pounded

256

the trees and General Lovell ordered a space cleared at the top of the bluff to be his headquarters. Lieutenant-Colonel Revere, neat in a clean shirt, discovered an easier route from the beach, one that curved about the northern end of the bluff, and his gunners cut down trees to make that track. By dusk they had hauled four guns to the summit, but it was too late to emplace the weapons and so they were parked under the trees. Mosquitoes plagued the troops who, lacking tents, slept in the open. A few made crude shelters of branches.

Night fell. The last British cannon-shot of the day lit the cleared ridge smoky red with its flash and flickered long dark shadows from the jagged stumps. The gun smoke drifted north-east and then an uneasy silence fell on Majabigwaduce.

'Tomorrow,' General Lovell spoke from beside a fire in his newly cleared headquarters, 'we shall make a grand attack.'

'Good,' Wadsworth said firmly.

'Is this beef?' Lovell asked, spooning from a pewter dish.

'Salt pork, sir,' Filmer, the general's servant, answered.

'It's very good,' Lovell said in a slightly dubious tone, 'will you take some, Wadsworth?'

'The marines were kind enough to give me some British beef, sir.'

'How thoughtful of our enemies to feed us,' Lovell said, amused. He watched as Wadsworth shrugged off his Continental Army jacket, settled by the fire and produced a needle, thread and a button that had evidently come loose. 'Don't you have a man to do that sort of thing?'

'I'm happy to look after myself, sir,' Wadsworth said. He licked the thread and managed to fiddle it through the needle's eye. 'I thought Colonel Revere did well to make the new road up the bluff.'

'Did he not do well!' Lovell responded enthusiastically. 'I wanted to tell him so, but it seems he went back to the *Samuel* at dusk.'

Wadsworth began reattaching the button and the simple

task brought a sudden memory of his wife, Elizabeth. It was a vision of her darning socks beside the evening fire, her work-basket on the wide hearthstone, and Wadsworth suddenly missed her so keenly that his eyes watered. 'I hope Colonel Revere brings howitzers,' he said, hoping no one around the fire had seen the gleam in his eyes. Howitzers, unlike cannon, lobbed their missiles in high arcs so that the gunners could shoot safely over the heads of the attacking troops.

'We only have one howitzer,' Major Todd said.

'We need it for the attack tomorrow,' Wadsworth said.

'I'm sure the colonel knows his business,' Lovell said hurriedly, 'but there won't be any attack unless I receive assurances from Commodore Saltonstall that our gallant ships will again advance through the harbour mouth.'

A small breath of wind dipped the woodsmoke to swirl around Wadsworth's face. He blinked, then frowned at the general through the fire's dancing flames. 'No attack, sir?' he asked.

'Not unless the fleet attacks at the same time,' Lovell replied.

'Do we need them to do that, sir?' Wadsworth asked. 'If we attack on land I cannot see the enemy ships interfering with us. Not if we keep our troops off the southern slope and away from their broadsides?'

'I want the British marines kept aboard their ships,' Lovell said firmly.

'I'm told the *Warren* is damaged,' Wadsworth said. He was appalled that Lovell should demand a simultaneous attack. There was no need! All the rebels had to do was attack on land and the fort would surely fall, British marines or no British marines.

'We have plenty of ships,' Lovell said dismissively. 'And I want our ships and men, our soldiers and sailors, arm in arm, advancing irresistibly to earn their laurels.' He smiled. 'I'm sure the commodore will oblige us.'

Tomorrow.

*　　*　　*

258

Thursday brought a clear sky and a gentle southerly wind that ruffled the bay. Longboats brought the skippers of all the warships to the *Warren* where Commodore Saltonstall welcomed them with an exaggerated and atypical courtesy. He had directed that all the visiting captains must board the *Warren* by the forrard starboard gangway because that entranceway allowed them a good view of the blood-smeared deck and of the cannon-shattered base of the mainmast. He wanted the visiting captains to imagine what damage the enemy could do to their own ships, none of which was as large or powerful as the *Warren*.

Once they had seen the damage they were escorted to Saltonstall's cabin where the long table was set with glasses and bottles of rum. The commodore invited the captains to sit and took amusement from the discomfort that many of them plainly felt at the unaccustomed elegance of the furnishings. The table was polished maple and at night could be illuminated by spermaceti candles that now stood unlit in elaborate silver sticks. Two of the transom windows had been broken by a British round shot and Saltonstall had deliberately left the shattered panes and splintered frames as reminders to the captains what their own ships might suffer if they insisted on an attack. 'We must congratulate the army,' Saltonstall began the Council of War, 'for their success yesterday in dislodging the enemy from the heights, though I deeply regret that Captain Welch was lost in that success.'

A few men murmured expressions of sympathy, but most watched Saltonstall warily. He was known as a supercilious, distant man, and a man to whom they had jointly sent a letter chiding him for failing to press home his attack on Mowat's ships, yet now he was apparently affable. 'Do partake of the rum,' he said, waving carelessly at the dark bottles, 'provided by our enemies. It was taken from a merchantman off Nantucket.'

'Never too early in the day for a tot,' Nathaniel West of

the *Black Prince* said, and poured himself a generous glass. 'Your health, Commodore.'

'I appreciate your sentiment,' Saltonstall said silkily, 'just as I would appreciate your advice.' He waved around the table, indicating that he sought every man's opinion. 'Our army,' he said, 'now commands the fort and may attack when and how it wishes. Once the fort has fallen, as it must, then the enemy's position in the harbour is untenable. Their ships must either sail out into our guns or else surrender.'

'Or scuttle themselves,' James Johnston of the *Pallas* said.

'Or scuttle themselves,' Saltonstall agreed. 'Now, I know there is an opinion that we should preempt that choice by sailing into the harbour and attacking the enemy directly. It is the propriety of that action I wish to discuss.' He paused and there was an embarrassed silence in the cabin, every man there remembering the letter they had jointly signed. That letter had chided Saltonstall for not sailing into the harbour and bringing on a general action with the three sloops, an action that surely would have resulted in an American victory. Saltonstall let their embarrassment stretch for an uncomfortable time, then smiled. 'Allow me to present you with the circumstances, gentlemen. The enemy have three armed ships arrayed in line facing the harbour entrance. Therefore any ship that enters the harbour will be raked by their combined broadsides. In addition, the enemy has a grand battery in the fort and a second battery on the slope beneath the fort. Those combined guns will have free play on any attacking ships. I need hardly tell you that the leading vessels will suffer considerable damage and endure grievous casualties from the enemy's cannonade.'

'As you did yesterday, sir,' Captain Philip Brown of the Continental Navy's brig, *Diligent*, said loyally.

'As we did,' Saltonstall agreed.

'But the enemy will be hurt too,' John Cathcart of *Tyrannicide* said.

'The enemy will indeed be hurt,' Saltonstall agreed, 'but are we not persuaded that the enemy is doomed anyway? Our infantry are poised to assault the fort and, when the fort surrenders, so must the ships. On the other hand,' he paused to add emphasis to what he was about to say, 'the defeat of the ships in no way forces the fort to surrender. Do I make myself plain? Take the fort and the ships are doomed. Take the ships and the fort survives. Our business here is to remove the British troops, to which end the fort must be taken. The enemy ships, gentlemen, are as dependant on the fort as are the British redcoats.'

None of the men about the table were cowards, but half of them were in business and their business was privateering. Nine captains at the table either owned the ship they commanded or else possessed a high share in the vessel's ownership, and a privateer did not make a profit by fighting enemy warships. Privateers pursued lightly armed merchantmen. If a privateer was lost then the owner's investment was lost with it, and those captains, weighing the chances of high casualties and expensive damage to their ships, began to see the wisdom of Saltonstall's suggestion. They had all seen the bloodied deck and splintered mast of the *Warren* and feared seeing worse on their own expensive ships. So why not allow the army to capture the fort? It was as good as captured anyway, and the commodore was plainly right that the British ships would have no choice but to surrender once the fort fell.

Lieutenant George Little of the Massachusetts Navy was more belligerent. 'It isn't to do with the fort,' he insisted, 'it's to do with killing the bastards and taking their ships.'

'Which ships will be ours,' Saltonstall said, miraculously keeping his temper, 'when the fort falls.'

'Which it must,' Philip Brown said.

'Which it must,' Saltonstall agreed. He forced himself to look into Little's angry eyes. 'Suppose twenty of your men are killed in an attack on the ships, and after the battle the

261

fort still survives. To what purpose, then, did your men die?'

'We came here to kill the enemy,' Little said.

'We came here to defeat the enemy,' Saltonstall corrected him, and a murmur of agreement sounded in the cabin. The commodore sensed the mood and took a leaf from General Lovell's book. 'You all expressed your sentiments to me in a letter,' he said, 'and I appreciate the zeal that letter displayed, but I would humbly suggest,' he paused, having surprised even himself by using the word 'humbly', 'that the letter was sent without a full appreciation of the tactical circumstances that confront us. So permit me to put a motion to the vote. Considering the enemy positions, would it not be more prudent to allow the army to complete its success without risking our ships in what must prove to be an attack irrelevant to the expedition's stated purpose?'

The assembled captains hesitated, but one by one the privateer owners voted against any attack through the harbour entrance and, once those men gave the lead, the rest followed, all except for George Little who neither voted for nor against, but just scowled at the table.

'I thank you, gentlemen,' Saltonstall said, hiding his satisfaction. These men had possessed the temerity to write him a letter that implicitly suggested cowardice, and yet, faced with the facts of the situation, they had overwhelmingly voted against the very sentiments their letter had expressed. The commodore despised them. 'I shall inform General Lovell,' Saltonstall said, 'of the Council's decision.'

So the warships would not attack.

And General Lovell was digging earthworks in the woods to repel a British attack.

And General McLean was strengthening the fort.

Captain Welch was buried close to where he had died on Dyce's Head. Marines dug the grave. They had already buried six of their companions lower down the slope where the soil was easier to dig, and at first they had put Welch's corpse in that common grave, but a sergeant had ordered the captain's body removed before the grave was filled with earth. 'He took the high ground,' the sergeant said, 'and he should hold it for ever.'

So a new grave had been hacked on the rocky headland. Peleg Wadsworth came to see the corpse lowered into the hole and with him was the Reverend Murray who spoke a few sombre words in the grey dawn. A cutlass and a pistol were laid on the blanket-shrouded corpse. 'So he can kill the red-coated bastards in hell,' Sergeant Sykes explained. The Reverend Murray smiled bravely and Wadsworth nodded approval. Rocks were heaped on the captain's grave so that scavenging animals could not scratch him out of the ground he had captured.

Once the brief ceremony was over Wadsworth walked to the tree-line and gazed at the fort. Lieutenant Dennis joined him. 'The wall's higher today,' Dennis said.

'It is.'

'But we can scale it,' Dennis said robustly.

Wadsworth used a small telescope to examine the British work. Redcoats were deepening the western ditch that faced the American lines and using the excavated soil to heighten the wall, but the farther wall, the eastern rampart, was still little more than a scrape in the dirt. 'If we could get behind them . . . ' he mused aloud.

'Oh we can!' Dennis said.

'You think so?'

A thunder of gunfire obliterated the marine lieutenant's reply. The semi-circular British battery on the harbour's lower slope had fired its cannon across the harbour towards Cross Island. No sooner had the sound faded than the three enemy sloops began firing. 'Is the commodore attacking?' Wadsworth asked.

The two men moved to the southern crest and saw that two privateers were firing through the harbour entrance, though neither ship was making any attempt to sail through that narrow gap. They fired at long range and the three sloops shot back. 'Gun practice,' Dennis said dismissively.

'You think we can get behind the fort?' Wadsworth asked.

'Capture that battery, sir,' Dennis said, pointing down at the semi-circle of earth that protected the British cannon. 'Once we have that we can make our way along the harbour shore. There's plenty of cover!' The route along the harbour shore wandered past cornfields, log piles, houses and barns, all of which could conceal men from the guns of the fort and the broadsides of the sloops.

'Young Fletcher would guide us,' Wadsworth said. James Fletcher had rescued his fishing boat, *Felicity*, and was using it to carry wounded men to the hospital the rebels had established on Wasaumkeag Point on the far shore of the bay. 'But I still think a direct assault would be best,' Wadsworth added.

'Straight at the fort, sir?'

'Why not? Let's attack before they make that nearer wall any higher.' A cannon fired to the north, the noise sudden, close and loud. It was an eighteen-pounder of the Massachusetts Artillery Regiment and it fired from the trees on the high ground at the redcoats working to raise the fort's curtain wall. The sound of the cannon cheered Wadsworth. 'We won't need to get behind them now,' he said to Dennis. 'Colonel Revere's guns will batter that rampart down to nothing!'

'So we attack along the ridge?' Dennis asked.

'It's the simplest way,' Wadsworth said, 'and I have a mind that simplicity is good.'

'Captain Welch would approve, sir.'

'And I shall recommend it,' Wadsworth said.

They were so close, the fort was unfinished, and all they needed to do was attack.

*   *   *

264

'I hate New York,' Sir George Collier said. He thought New York a slum; a fetid, overcrowded, ill-mannered, pestilential, humid hell on earth. 'We should just give it to the bloody rebels,' he snarled, 'let the bastards stew here.'

'Please stay still, Sir George,' the doctor said.

'Oh Christ in his britches, man, get on with it! I thought Lisbon was hell on earth and it's a goddamn paradise compared to this filthy bloody town.'

'Allow me to draw your thigh?' the doctor said.

'It's even worse than Bristol,' Sir George growled.

Admiral Sir George Collier was a small, irascible and unpleasant man who commanded the British fleet on the American coast. He was ill, which is why he was ashore in New York, and the doctor was attempting to allay the fever by drawing blood. He was using one of the newest and finest pieces of medical equipment from London, a scarifier, which he now cocked so that the twenty-four ground-steel blades disappeared smoothly into their gleaming housing. 'Are you ready, Sir George?'

'Don't blather, man. Just do it.'

'There will be a slight sensation of discomfort, Sir George,' the doctor said, concealing his pleasure at that thought, then placed the metal box against the patient's scrawny thigh and pulled the trigger. The spring-loaded blades leaped out of their slits to pierce Sir George's skin and start a flow of blood that the doctor staunched with a piece of Turkey cloth. 'I would wish to see more blood, Sir George,' the doctor said.

'Don't be a bloody fool, man. You've drained me dry.'

'You should wrap yourself in flannel, Sir George.'

'In this damned heat?' Sir George's foxlike face was glistening with sweat. Winter in New York was brutally cold, the summer was a steamy hell, and in between it was merely unbearable. On the wall of his quarters, next to an etching of his home in England, was a framed poster advertising that London's Drury Lane Theatre was presenting 'Selima and Azor, a Musical Delectation in Five Acts written by Sir George Collier'. London, he thought, now that was a city! Decent theatre, well-dressed whores, fine clubs and no damned humidity. A theatre owner in New York had thought to please Sir George by offering to present *Selima and Azor* on his stage, but Sir George had forbidden it. To hear his songs murdered by caterwauling Americans? The very thought was disgusting.

'Come!' he shouted in response to a knock on the door. A naval lieutenant entered the room. The newcomer shuddered at the blood smearing Sir George's bare thigh, then averted his eyes and stood respectfully just inside the door. 'Well, Forester?' Sir George snarled.

'I regret to inform you, sir, that the *Iris* won't be ready for sea,' Lieutenant Forester said.

'Her copper?'

'Indeed, sir,' Forester said, relieved that his bad news had not been greeted by anger.

'Pity,' Sir George grunted. HMS *Iris* was a fine 32-gun frigate that Sir George had captured two years previously. Back then she had been called the *Hancock*, an American ship, but though the Royal Navy usually kept the names of captured warships Sir George would be damned and condemned to eternal hell in New York before he allowed a British naval ship to bear the name of some filthy rebel traitor and so the *Hancock* had been renamed for a splendid London actress. 'Legs as long as a spritsail yard,' Sir George said wistfully.

'Sir?' Lieutenant Forester asked.

'Mind your own damned business.'

'Aye aye, sir.'

'Copper, you say?'

'At least two weeks' work, sir.'

Sir George grunted. '*Blonde*?'

'Ready, sir.'

'*Virginia*?'

'Fully manned and seaworthy, sir.'

'Write them both orders,' Sir George said. The *Blonde* and *Virginia* were also 32-gun frigates and the *Blonde*, usefully, had just returned from the Penobscot River, which meant Captain Barkley knew the waters. '*Greyhound*? *Camille*? *Galatea*?'

'The *Greyhound* is provisioning, Sir George. The *Galatea* and *Camille* both need crewmen.'

'I want all three ready to sail in two days. Send out the press gangs.'

'Aye aye, sir.' The *Greyhound* carried twenty-eight guns, while the *Camille* and *Galatea* were smaller frigates with just twenty guns apiece.

'The *Otter*,' Sir George said, 'to carry despatches.' The *Otter* was a 14-gun brig.

'Aye aye, sir.'

Sir George watched the doctor bandage his thigh. 'And the *Raisonable*,' he said, smiling wolfishly.

'The *Raisonable*, Sir George?' Forester asked in astonishment.

'You heard me! Tell Captain Evans she's to be ready for sea in two days. And tell him he'll be flying my flag.'

The *Raisonable* was a captured French ship, and she was also a proper warship fit to stand in the line of battle. She carried sixty-four guns, the heaviest of them thirty-two pounders, and the rebels had nothing afloat that could match the *Raisonable* even though she was one of the smallest ships of the line in the Royal Navy.

'You're going to sea, Sir George?' the doctor asked nervously.

'I'm going to sea.'

'But your health!'

'Oh, stop twittering, you imbecile. How can it be bad for me? Even the Dead Sea's healthier than New York.'

Sir George was going to sea, and he was taking seven ships led by a vast, slab-sided battleship that could blow any rebel warship clean out of the water with a single broadside.

And the fleet would sail east. To the Penobscot River and Penobscot Bay and Majabigwaduce.

Excerpts from Brigadier-General Solomon Lovell's orders to his troops, Penobscot, July 30th, 1779:

The General is much alarm'd at the loose and disorderly inattentive Behaviour of the Camp . . . As the Success of Arms under God depends principally on good Subordination the General expects that every Officer and Soldier who has the least Spark of honor left will endeavor to have his Orders put in Execution and that Colonel Revere and the Corps under his Command incamp with the Army in future on Shore, in order not only to strengthen the Lines but to manage the Cannon.

Excerpts from a letter sent by General George Washington to the Council of Massachusetts, August 3rd, 1779:

Head Quarters, West Point.
I have Just received a Letter from Lord Stirling stationed in the Jerseys dated yesterday . . . by which it appears the Ships of War at New York have all put to sea since. I thought it my duty to communicate this Intelligence that the Vessells employed in this expedition to Penobscot may be put upon their Guard, as it is probable enough that these Ships may be destined against

them and if they should be surprised the consequences would be
desagreeable. I have the honor to be with very great respect and
esteem, Gentlemen Your Most Obedient Servant

George Washington

From the deposition of John Lymburner to Justice of the
Peace Joseph Hibbert, May 12th, 1788:

(I was) *taken prisoner by the Americans at the Siege of*
Penobscot, and was in close confinement . . . we were treated
very severely for adhering to the British troops, called Tories
and Refugees, was threatened to be hanged as soon as they had
taken Fort George.

NINE

'Where the devil is Revere?' Lovell asked. He had asked the question a dozen times in the two days since he had captured the heights of Majabigwaduce and each time there had been increasing irritation in his usually calm voice. 'Has he attended a single Council of War?'

'He likes to sleep aboard the *Samuel*,' William Todd said.

'Sleep? It's broad daylight!' That was an exaggeration, for it was only a few minutes since the sun had lit the eastern fog bright.

'I believe,' Todd said carefully, 'that he finds his quarters aboard the *Samuel* more amenable to his comfort.' He was polishing his spectacles on the skirt of his coat and his face looked strangely vulnerable without them.

'We're not here for comfort,' Lovell said.

'Indeed we are not, sir,' Todd said.

'And his men?'

'They sleep on the *Samuel* too, sir,' Todd said, carefully hooking the cleaned spectacles over his ears.

'It won't do,' Lovell exploded, 'it will not do!'

'Indeed it will not, General,' Major Todd agreed, then hesitated. Fog made the treetops vague and inhibited the gunners on Cross Island and aboard the British ships so that a kind of quiet enveloped Majabigwaduce. Smoke drifted among the trees from the camp-fires on which troops boiled water for tea. 'If you approve, sir,' Todd said carefully, watching Lovell pacing up and down in front of the crude shelter made of branches and sod that was his sleeping quarters, 'I could advert to Colonel Revere's absence in the daily orders?'

'You can advert?' Lovell asked curtly. He stopped his pacing and turned to glare at the major. 'Advert?'

'You could issue a requirement in the daily orders that the colonel and his men must sleep ashore?' Todd suggested. He doubted Lovell would agree, because any such order would be recognized throughout the army as a very public reprimand.

'A very good idea,' Lovell said, 'an excellent notion. Do it. And draft me a letter to the colonel as well!'

Before Lovell could change his mind Peleg Wadsworth came to the clearing. The younger general was wearing a greatcoat buttoned against the dawn chill. 'Good morning!' he greeted Lovell and Todd cheerfully.

'An ill-fitting coat, General,' Major Todd observed with ponderous amusement.

'It belonged to my father, Major. He was a big man.'

'Did you know Revere sleeps aboard his ship?' Lovell demanded indignantly.

'I did know, sir,' Wadsworth said, 'but I thought he had your permission.'

'He has no such thing. We're not here on a pleasure cruise! You want tea?' Lovell waved towards the fire where his servant crouched by a pot. 'The water must have boiled.'

'I'd appreciate a word first, sir?'

'Of course, of course. In private?'

'If you please, sir,' Wadsworth said and the two generals walked a few paces west to where the trees thinned and from where they could gaze over the fog-haunted waters of Penobscot Bay. The topmasts of the transport ships appeared above the lowest and densest layer of fog like splinters in a snowbank. 'What would happen if we all slept aboard our ships, eh?' Lovell asked, still indignant.

'I did mention the matter to Colonel Revere,' Wadsworth said.

'You did?'

'Yesterday, sir. I said he should move his quarters ashore.'

'And his response?'

Fury, Wadsworth thought. Revere had responded like a man insulted. 'The guns can't fire at night,' he had spat at Wadsworth, 'so why man them at night? I know how to command my regiment!' Wadsworth chided himself for having let the matter slide, but at this moment he had a greater concern. 'The colonel disagreed with me, sir,' he said tonelessly, 'but I wished to speak of something else.'

'Of course, yes, whatever is on your mind.' Lovell frowned towards the topmasts. 'Sleeping aboard his ship!'

Wadsworth looked south to where the fog now lay like a great river of whiteness between the hills bordering the Penobscot River. 'Should the enemy send reinforcements, sir . . .' he began.

'They'll come upriver, certainly,' Lovell interjected, following Wadsworth's gaze.

'And discover our fleet, sir,' Wadsworth continued.

'Of course they would, yes,' Lovell said as if the point were not very important.

'Sir,' Wadsworth was urgent now. 'If the enemy come in force they'll be among our fleet like wolves in a flock. Might I urge a precaution?'

'A precaution,' Lovell repeated as if the word were unfamiliar.

'Permit me to explore upriver, sir,' Wadsworth said, pointing north to where the Penobscot River flowed into the wider bay. 'Let me find and fortify a place to which we can retreat if the enemy comes. Young Fletcher knows the upper river.

273

He tells me it narrows, sir, and twists between high banks. If it were necessary, sir, we could take the fleet upriver and shelter behind a bluff. A cannon emplacement at the river bend will check any enemy pursuit.'

'Find and fortify, eh?' Lovell said, more to buy time than as a coherent response. He turned and stared into the northern fog. 'You'd make a fort?'

'I would certainly emplace some guns, sir.'

'In earthworks?'

'The batteries must be made defensible. The enemy will surely bring troops.'

'If they come,' Lovell said dubiously.

'It's prudent, sir, to prepare for the least desirable eventuality.'

Lovell grimaced, then placed a fatherly hand on Wadsworth's shoulder. 'You worry too much, Wadsworth. That's a good thing! We should be worried about eventualities.' He nodded sagely. 'But I do assure you we shall capture the fort long before any more redcoats arrive.' He saw Wadsworth was about to speak so hurried on. 'You'd require men to make an emplacement and we cannot afford to detach men to dig a fort we may never need! We shall require every man we have to make the assault once the commodore agrees to enter the harbour.'

'If he agrees,' Wadsworth said drily.

'Oh, he will, I'm sure he will. Haven't you seen? The enemy's been driven back yet again! It's only a matter of time now!'

'Driven back?' Wadsworth asked.

'The sentries say so,' Lovell exulted, 'indeed they do.' Mowat's three ships, constantly battered by Colonel Revere's cannon on Cross Island, had moved still farther eastwards during the night. Their topmasts, hung with the British flags, were all that were presently visible and the sentries on Dyce's Head reckoned that those topmasts were now almost a mile away from the harbour entrance. 'The commodore doesn't have to

274

fight his way into the harbour now,' Lovell said happily, 'because we've driven them away. By God, we have! Almost the whole harbour belongs to us now!'

'But even if the commodore doesn't enter the harbour, sir . . .' Wadsworth began.

'Oh, I know!' the older man interrupted. 'You think we can take the fort without the navy's help, but we can't, Wadsworth, we can't.' Lovell repeated all his old arguments, how the British ships would bombard the attacking troops and how the British marines would reinforce the garrison, and Wadsworth nodded politely though he believed none of it. He watched Lovell's earnest face. The man was eminent now, a landowner, a selectman, a churchwarden and a legislator, but the schoolmaster in Wadsworth was trying to imagine Solomon Lovell as a boy, and he conjured an image of a big, clumsy lad who would earnestly try to be helpful, but never be a rule-breaker. Lovell was declaring his belief that Brigadier McLean's men outnumbered his own. 'Oh, I realize you disagree, Wadsworth,' Lovell said, 'but you young men can be headstrong. In truth we face a malevolent and a mighty foe, and to overcome him we must harness all our oxen together!'

'We must attack, sir,' Wadsworth said forcefully.

Lovell laughed, though without much humour. 'One minute you tell me to prepare ourselves for defeat, and the next moment you wish me to attack!'

'The one will happen without the other, sir.'

Lovell frowned as he worked out what Wadsworth meant, then shook his head dismissively. 'We shall conquer!' he said, then described his grand idea that the commodore's ships should sail majestically into the harbour, their cannons blazing, while all along the ridge the rebel army advanced on a fort being hammered by naval gunfire. 'Just imagine it,' he said enthusiastically, 'all our warships bombarding the fort! My goodness, but we'll just stroll across those ramparts!'

'I'd rather we attacked in tomorrow's dawn,' Wadsworth said, 'in the fog. We can close on the enemy in the fog, sir, and take them by surprise.'

'The commodore can't shift in the fog,' Lovell said dismissively. 'Quite impossible!'

Wadsworth looked eastwards. The fog seemed to have thickened so that the topmasts of only one ship were visible, and it had to be a ship because there were three topmasts, each crossed by a topgallant yard. Three crosses. Wadsworth did not think it mattered whether the commodore attacked or not, or rather he thought it should not matter because Lovell had the men to assault the fort whether the commodore attacked or not. It was like chess, Wadsworth thought, and had a sudden image of his wife smiling as she took his castle with her bishop. The fort was the king, and all Lovell had to do was move one piece to achieve checkmate, but the general and Saltonstall insisted on a more complex plan. They wanted bishops and knights zig-zagging all over the board and Wadsworth knew he could never persuade either man to take the simple route. So, he thought, make their complicated moves work, and make them work soon before the British brought new pieces to the board. 'Has the commodore agreed to enter the harbour?' he asked Lovell.

'Not exactly agreed,' Lovell said uncomfortably, 'not yet.'

'But you believe he will, sir?'

'I'm sure he will,' Lovell said, 'in time he will.'

Time was precisely what the rebels lacked, or so Wadsworth believed. 'If we control the harbour entrance . . .' he began and was again interrupted by Lovell.

'It's that wretched battery on the harbour foreshore,' the general said, and Wadsworth knew he was referring to the semi-circular earthwork the British had dug to cover the harbour entrance. That battery was now the closest enemy post.

'So if the battery were captured, sir,' Wadsworth suggested, 'then the commodore would take advantage?'

'I would hope he would,' Lovell said.

'So why don't I prepare a plan to capture it?' Wadsworth asked.

Lovell stared at Wadsworth as though the younger man had just wrought a miracle. 'Would you do that?' the general asked, immensely pleased. 'Yes, do that! Then we can advance together. Soldier and sailor, marine and militia, together! How soon can you have such a plan? By noon, perhaps?'

'I'm sure I can, sir.'

'Then I shall propose your plan at this afternoon's Council,' Lovell said, 'and urge every man present to vote for it. My goodness, if we capture that battery then the commodore . . .' Lovell checked whatever he might have said because there was an abrupt crackle of musketry. It rose in intensity and was answered by a cannon shot. 'What the devil are those rogues doing now?' Lovell asked plaintively and hurried away eastwards to find out. Wadsworth followed.

As gunfire splintered the morning.

'You can't give the enemy any rest,' Brigadier McLean had said. The Scotsman had been astonished that the rebels had not assaulted the fort, and even more surprised when it became clear that General Lovell was digging defences on the high ground. McLean now knew his opponent's name, learned from an American deserter who had crept across the ridgetop at night and called aloud to the sentries from the abatis. McLean had questioned the man who, trying to be helpful, expressed his belief that Lovell had brought two thousand troops to the peninsula. 'It may be even more, sir,' the man said.

'Or fewer,' McLean retorted.

'Yes, sir,' the miserable wretch had said, 'but it looked like plenty enough at Townsend, sir,' which was no help at all. The deserter was a man in his forties who claimed he had been pressed into the militia ranks and had no wish to fight. 'I just want to go home, sir,' he said plaintively.

'As do we all,' McLean had said and put the man to work in the hospital's cookhouse.

The rebel guns had opened fire the day after the high ground was lost. The rate of fire was not high, and many of the balls were wasted, but the fort was a big target and a near one, and so the big eighteen-pounder balls thrashed into the newly made rampart, scattering dirt and timber. The new storehouse was hit repeatedly until its gabled roof was virtually demolished, but so far no shot had managed to hit any of McLean's own cannon. Six were now mounted on the western wall and Captain Fielding was keeping up a steady fire at the distant tree-line. The rebels, rather than mount their cannon at the edge of the woods, had emplaced them deep inside the trees, then cut down corridors to give the cannons avenues of fire. 'You might not hit much,' McLean had told Fielding, 'but you'll keep them worried and you'll hide us in smoke.'

It was not enough just to worry the enemy, McLean knew they had to be kept off-balance and so he had ordered Lieutenant Caffrae to assemble forty of the liveliest men into a skirmishing company. Caffrae was a sensible and intelligent young man who liked his new orders. He added a pair of drummer boys to his unit and four fife players, and the company used the fog, or else the trees to the peninsula's north, to get close to the enemy lines. Once there the small band played 'Yankee-Doodle', a tune that for some reason annoyed the rebels. The skirmishers would shout orders to imaginary men and shoot at the rebel trenches, and whenever a large party of the enemy came to challenge Caffrae's company he would withdraw under cover, only to reappear somewhere else to taunt and to shoot again. Caffrae, temporarily promoted to captain, danced in front of Lovell's men. He provoked, he challenged. He would sometimes go at night to disturb the rebel sleep. Lovell's men were to be given neither rest nor comfort, but be constantly harassed and alarmed.

'Let me go, sir,' Lieutenant Moore pleaded with McLean.

'You will, John, you will,' McLean promised. Caffrae was out in the ground between the lines and his men had just fired a volley to wake the morning. The skirmishers' fifes were trilling their mocking tune, which always provoked a wild response of ill-aimed musketry from the trees where the rebels sheltered. McLean stared westwards in an attempt to discover Caffrae's position among the wisps of fog that slowly cleared from the heights, and instead saw the rebels' gun corridors choke with sudden smoke as the enemy guns began their daily fire. The first shots fell short, ploughing into the ridge to throw up plumes of soil and wood chips.

The rebel gunfire was a nuisance, but McLean was grateful that it was no more than that. If the Scotsman had been commanding the besiegers he would have ordered his gunners to concentrate the balls at one point of the defences and, when that place had been thoroughly destroyed, to move their aim slightly left or right and so demolish the fort systematically. Instead the enemy gunners fired at whatever they pleased, or else they just aimed generally at the fort, and McLean was finding it a simple enough task to repair whatever damage the balls did to the western curtain wall and its flanking bastions. Yet, if the gunfire was not proving as destructive as he had feared, it was still eroding his men's confidence. Sentries had to stand with their heads exposed above the rampart if they were to watch the enemy and, on the very first day of the rebel bombardment, one such sentry had been hit by a cannonball that had shattered his head into a mess of blood, bone and brains. The ball had then struck the remnants of the storehouse gable and come to rest, still plastered with bloody hair, against a water butt. Other men had been injured, mostly by stones or splinters jarred from the rampart by a cannonball. The rebels were using an howitzer too, a weapon McLean feared more than their largest cannon, but the gunners were inexpert and the howitzer dropped its exploding shot randomly across the ridge-top.

'I have a job for you now, Lieutenant,' McLean said to Moore.

'Of course, sir.'

'Come with me,' McLean said and walked towards the fort's gate, stabbing his blackthorn stick into the soil with each step. He knew that the day's onset of rebel cannon-fire would make his men nervous and he wanted to allay their fears. 'Captain Fielding!'

'Sir?' the English artilleryman called back.

'Bide your fire a short while!'

'I will, sir.'

Mclean went outside the fort, then led Moore west and north until they were standing some twenty paces in front of Fort George's ditch and in full view of the rebel lines. 'Our task is just to stand here, Lieutenant,' McLean explained.

Moore was amused. 'It is, sir?'

'To show the men they have nothing to fear.'

'Ah, and if we're killed, sir?'

'Then they will have something to fear,' McLean said. He smiled. 'But this is a large part of an officer's responsibility, Lieutenant.'

'To die very visibly, sir?'

'To set an example,' McLean said. 'I want our men to see that you and I don't fear the cannonade.' He turned and looked towards the distant trees. 'Why in God's name don't they attack us?'

'Maybe we should attack them, sir?' Moore suggested.

McLean smiled. 'I'm thinking we could do that,' he said slowly, 'but to what end?'

'To defeat them, sir?'

'They're doing that to themselves, Lieutenant.'

'They'll wake up to that knowledge, sir, won't they?'

'Aye, they will. And when they realize by how many they

280

outnumber us then they'll come swarming across that land,' he waved the stick at the ridge, 'but we've a good few guns emplaced now, and the wall's higher, and they'll find us a more difficult nut to crack.' The brigadier was still convinced the rebels numbered at least three thousand men. Why else would they have needed so many transport ships? 'But they needs do it quickly, Lieutenant, because I dare hope there are reinforcements on their way to us.' He handed Moore the blackthorn stick. 'Hold that for me, will you?' he asked, then took a tinder-box and a tobacco-filled clay pipe from his pocket. Moore, knowing the general's wounded right arm made McLean clumsy, took the tinder-box and struck a flame from the charred linen. McLean bent forward to light the pipe, then took back his tinder-box and stick. 'Thank you, John,' he said, puffing contentedly as a cannon-ball churned up soil fifteen paces away and bounced to fly above the fort. 'And I daresay we could attack them,' McLean continued his earlier train of thought, 'but I've no mind to do that. Fighting gets very confused among trees, and once they see how few we are, they're likely to rally and counter-charge. It could all get lamentably messy. No, for now it's better to make them die on Captain Fielding's guns, eh? And every day that passes, Lieutenant, is worth a thousand men to us. The ditch gets deeper and the wall gets higher. See?' He had turned to watch an ox dragging another oak trunk up the slope from the village. The big trunk would be used to heighten the western rampart.

McLean turned back as a renewed crescendo of musketry sounded from where Captain Caffrae was evidently poking the wasps' nest. 'Please let me accompany Caffrae, sir,' Moore pleaded again.

'He knows when to retreat, Lieutenant,' McLean said sternly.

Moore smarted from that gentle reprimand. 'I'm sorry, sir.'

'No, no, you learned your lesson. And you showed the right instinct, I grant you that. A soldier's job is to fight, God help him, and you fought well. So aye, I'll let you go, but you take your orders from Caffrae!'

'Of course I will, sir. And, sir . . .' Whatever Moore had been about to say went unexpressed, because a sudden blow threw him backwards. It felt as though he had been punched in the belly. He staggered a half-pace and instinctively clutched a hand to where the blow had landed, but discovered he was unwounded and his uniform undamaged. McLean had also been thrown backwards, held upright only by his blackthorn stick, but the brigadier was also untouched. 'What . . .' Moore began. He was aware that his ears rang from a gigantic noise, but what had caused it he did not know.

'Don't move,' McLean said, 'and look cheerful.'

Moore forced a smile. 'That was a cannon-ball?'

'It was indeed,' McLean said, 'and it went between us.' He looked towards the fort where the ox was bellowing. The round shot, that had flown clean between the two redcoats, had struck the ox's haunches. The fallen animal was bleeding and bellowing on the track just a few paces from Fort George's entrance. A sentry ran from the gate, cocked his musket and shot the animal just above the eyes. It twitched and was still. 'Fresh beef!' McLean said.

'Dear God,' Moore said.

'You brushed with death, Mister Moore,' McLean said, 'but I do believe you were born under a lucky star.'

'You too, sir.'

'Now we wait for four more shots,' McLean said.

'Four, sir?'

'They play four cannon on us,' McLean said, 'two eighteen-pounders, a twelve-pounder,' he paused while a rebel gun fired, 'and an howitzer.' The shot rumbled high overhead to fall somewhere far to the east. 'So the fourth shot, John, will almost certainly be from the same gentlemen who so narrowly missed killing us and I wish to see if they shoot at us again.'

'A quite natural curiosity, sir,' Moore said, making the brigadier laugh.

The howitzer fired next, and its shell landed short of the fort where it lay trickling smoke from its fuse until it exploded harmlessly. The twelve-pounder slammed a ball into the south-western bastion, and then the eighteen-pounder that had come so close to killing McLean and Moore fired again. The ball skimmed the abatis well to the general's north, bounced short of the ditch and flew over the ramparts to crash into a spruce on Doctor Calef's property. 'You see,' McLean said, 'they're not aiming true. There's no consistency in their aim. Captain Fielding!'

'Sir?'

'You may engage the enemy again!' McLean called as he led Moore back to the fort.

The British guns opened fire. All day long the opposing artillery duelled, Captain Caffrae taunted the enemy, Fort George's ramparts grew higher and General Lovell waited for Commodore Saltonstall.

Peleg Wadsworth wanted a force of marines, sailors and militia for his attack on the Half Moon Battery. He had decided to attack under cover of darkness, and to do it that very night. The rebels had already captured the British batteries on Cross Island and on Dyce's Head, now they would take the last of the British outworks and once that was taken there would only be the fort left to conquer.

'What you don't understand,' Commodore Saltonstall had told Wadsworth, 'is that the fort is formidable.'

Wadsworth, seeking the help of the marines, had gone that afternoon to the *Warren* where he discovered Saltonstall examining four iron hoops that had been strapped about the frigate's damaged mainmast. The commodore had greeted Wadsworth with a grunt, then invited him to the quarterdeck. 'I presume you want my marines again?' the commodore asked.

'I do, sir. The army's council voted to make an attack tonight, sir, and to request the assistance of your marines.'

'You can have Carnes, Dennis and fifty men,' Saltonstall said briskly, as if by agreeing quickly he could rid himself of Wadsworth's company.

'And I'd also be grateful for your advice, Commodore,' Wadsworth said.

'My advice, eh?' Saltonstall sounded suspicious, but his tone had softened. He looked cautiously at Wadsworth, but the younger man's face was so open and honest that the commodore decided there was nothing underhand in the request. 'Well, advice is free,' he said with heavy humour.

'General Lovell is convinced the fort will not fall while the enemy ships remain,' Wadsworth said.

'Which is not your opinion?' Saltonstall guessed shrewdly.

'I am General Lovell's deputy, sir,' Wadsworth said tactfully.

'Ha.'

'Can the enemy ships be taken, sir?' Wadsworth asked, broaching the subject directly.

'Oh, they can be taken!' Saltonstall said dismissively. He disconcerted Wadsworth by looking just past the brigadier's left ear rather than into his eyes. 'Of course they can be taken.'

'Then . . .'

'But at what price, Wadsworth? Tell me that! At what price?'

'You must tell me, sir.'

Saltonstall deigned to look directly at Wadsworth for a moment as if deciding whether his answer would be wasted on such a man. He evidently decided it would not be, because he sighed heavily as though he was weary of explaining the obvious. 'The wind sets from the south-west,' he said, looking past Wadsworth again, 'which means we can sail into the harbour, but we cannot sail out. Once inside the harbour we lay under the enemy's guns. Those guns, Wadsworth, as you may have observed, are efficiently manned.' He paused, plainly tempted to make a comparison with the militia's artillery, but he managed to suppress the comment. 'The harbour is constricted,' he went on, 'which dictates that we must enter in file, which in turn means the lead ship must inevitably sustain heavy damage from the enemy's fire.' He waved briskly towards the *Warren*'s bows, which still showed evidence of hasty repairs to her bowsprit and forecastle. 'Once inside we have no room to manoeuvre so we must anchor to preserve our position opposite the enemy ships. Either that or sail directly at them and board them. And all that while, Wadsworth, we are under the cannon of the fort, and what you don't understand is that the fort is formidable.'

Wadsworth wondered whether to argue, but decided argument would merely goad Saltonstall into stubbornness. 'It seems that what you're saying, sir,' he said, 'is that the ships will not fall till the fort is taken?'

'Precisely!' Saltonstall sounded relieved, as if Wadsworth was a dim pupil who had at last grasped the simplest of propositions.

'Whereas General Lovell is convinced the fort cannot be taken until the ships are destroyed.'

'General Lovell is entitled to his opinion,' Saltonstall said loftily.

'If we succeed in capturing the enemy's remaining shore battery,' Wadsworth suggested, 'it will make your task easier, sir?'

'My task?'

'Of capturing the enemy ships, sir.'

'My task, Wadsworth, is to support your forces in the capture of the fort.'

'Thank you, sir,' Wadsworth said, hiding his exasperation, 'but might I assure General Lovell that you will attack their shipping if we mount an assault on the fort?'

'This presupposes that you have disposed of the enemy's shore battery?'

'It does, sir.'

'A joint attack, eh?' Saltonstall still sounded suspicious, but after a brief hesitation, nodded cautiously. 'I would consider a joint attack,' he said grudgingly, 'but you do realize, I trust, that the position of Mowat's ships becomes untenable once the fort is taken?'

'I do, sir.'

'But that McLean's position is still formidable whether the ships are taken or not?'

'I understand that too, sir.'

Saltonstall turned to glower at the waist of the *Warren*, but saw nothing to provoke a complaint. 'The Congress, Wadsworth, has spent precious public money building a dozen frigates.'

'Indeed it has, sir,' Wadsworth said, wondering what that had to do with the fort on Majabigwaduce's peninsula.

'The *Washington*, the *Effingham*, the *Congress* and the *Montgomery* are all scuttled, Wadsworth. They are lost.'

'Sadly, sir, yes,' Wadsworth said. The four frigates had been destroyed to prevent their capture.

'The *Virginia*, taken,' Saltonstall went on remorselessly, 'the *Hancock*, taken. The *Raleigh*, taken. The *Randolph*, sunk. Do you wish me to add the *Warren* to that sad record?'

'Of course not, sir,' Wadsworth said. He glanced up at the snake-embossed flag flying at the *Warren*'s stern. It bore the proud motto 'Don't Tread on Me', but how could the British even try if the snake's only ambition was to avoid battle?

'Capture the shore battery,' Saltonstall said in his most lordly voice, 'and the fleet will reconsider its opportunities.'

'Thank you, sir,' Wadsworth said.

He had been silent as he was rowed ashore from the frigate. Saltonstall was right, Wadsworth did disagree with Lovell. Wadsworth knew the fort was the king on Majabigwaduce's chess board, and the three British ships were pawns. Take the fort and the pawns surrendered, but take the pawns and the king remained, yet Lovell would not be persuaded to attack the fort any more than Saltonstall could be persuaded to throw caution to the south-west wind and destroy Mowat's three sloops. So now the battery must be attacked in hope that a successful assault would persuade the two commanders to greater boldness.

And time was short and it was shrinking, so Peleg Wadsworth would attack that night. In the dark.

James Fletcher tacked the *Felicity* south from Wasaumkeag Point where the rebels had taken over the remaining buildings of Fort Pownall, a decayed wooden and earth-banked fortress erected some thirty years before to deter attacks upriver by French raiders. There was no adequate shelter for wounded men on the heights of Majabigwaduce so the house and storerooms of the old fort were now the rebels' hospital. Wasaumkeag Point lay on the far bank of Penobscot Bay, just south of where the river opened from being a narrow and fast-flowing channel between high wooded banks. James, when he was not needed by Wadsworth, used the *Felicity* to carry wounded men to the hospital and now he did his best to hurry back, eager to join Wadsworth before dusk and the attack on the British battery.

The *Felicity*'s course was frustrating. She made good enough progress on each starboard tack, but inevitably the wind drove the small boat nearer and nearer the eastern bank and then James had to endure a long port tack that, in the flooding tide, seemed to take him farther and farther from Majabigwaduce's bluff beneath which he wanted to anchor the *Felicity*. But James was used to the south-west wind. 'You can't hurry the breeze,' his father had said, 'and you can't change its mind, so there's no point in getting irritated by it.' James wondered what his father would think of the rebellion. Nothing good, he supposed. His father, like many who lived about the river, had been proud to be an Englishman.

It did not matter to him that the Fletchers had lived in Massachusetts for over a hundred years, they were still Englishmen. An old, yellowing print of King Charles I had hung in the log house throughout James's childhood, and was now tacked above his mother's sickbed. The king looked haughty, but somehow sad, as if he knew that one day a rebellion would topple him and lead him to the executioner's block. In Boston, James had heard, there was a tavern called the Cromwell's Head that hung its inn-sign so low above the door that men had to bow their heads to the king-killer every time they entered. That story had angered his father.

He tacked the *Felicity* in the cove just north of the bluff. The sound of the cannonade between the fort and the rebel lines was loud now, the smoke from the guns drifting like a cloud above the peninsula. He was on a port tack again, but it would be a short one and he knew he would reach the shore well before nightfall. He sailed under the stern of the *Industry*, a transport sloop, and waved to its captain, Will Young, who shouted some good-natured remark that was lost in the sound of the cannons.

James tacked to run down the *Industry*'s flank where a longboat was secured. Three men were in the longboat while above them, at the sloop's gunwale, two men threatened the trio with muskets. Then, with a shock, James recognized the three captives: Archibald Haney, John Lymburner and William Greenlaw, all from Majabigwaduce. Haney and Lymburner had been friends of his father, while Will Greenlaw had often accompanied James on fishing trips downriver and had paid court to Beth once or twice, though never successfully. All three men were Tories, Loyalists, and now they were evidently prisoners. James let his sheets go so that the *Felicity* slowed and shivered. 'What the devil are you doing with the bastards?' Archibald Haney called. Haney was like an uncle to James.

Before James could say a word in response a sailor appeared at the gunwale above the longboat. He carried a wooden pail.

'Hey, Tories!' the sailor called, then upended the bucket to cascade urine and turds onto the prisoners' heads. The two guards laughed.

'What the hell did you do that for?' James shouted.

The sailor mouthed some response and turned away. 'They put us here one hour a day,' Will Greenlaw said miserably, 'and pour their slops on us.'

The tide was taking the *Felicity* north and James tightened the jib sheet to get some way on her. 'I'm sorry,' he called.

'You'll be sorry when the king asks who was loyal to him!' Archibald Haney shouted angrily.

'The English treat our prisoners far worse!' Will Young bellowed from the *Industry*'s stern.

James had been forced onto a port tack again and the wind took him away from the sloop. Archibald Haney shouted something, but the words were lost on the breeze, all but one. Traitor.

James tacked the boat again and ran her towards the beach. He dropped her anchor, furled her mainsail and stowed the foresails, then hailed a passing lighter to give him a dry-ride ashore. Traitor, rebel, Tory, Loyalist? If his father were still alive, he wondered, would he dare be a rebel?

He climbed the bluff, retrieved the musket from his shelter and walked south to Dyce's Head to find Peleg Wadsworth. The sun was low now, casting a long shadow over the ridge and along the harbour's foreshore. Wadsworth's men were gathering in the trees where they could not be seen from the fort. 'You look pensive, young James,' Wadsworth greeted him.

'I'm well enough, sir,' James said.

Wadsworth looked at him more closely. 'What is it?'

'You know what they're doing to the prisoners?' James asked, then blurted out the whole tale. 'They're my neighbours, sir,' he said, 'and they called me traitor.'

Wadsworth had been listening patiently. 'This is war, James,' he said gently, 'and it creates passions we didn't know we possessed.'

'They're good men, sir!'

'And if we released them,' Wadsworth said, 'they'd work for our enemies.'

'They would, yes,' James allowed.

'But that's no reason to maltreat them,' Wadsworth said firmly, 'and I'll talk to the general, I promise,' though he knew well enough that whatever protest he made would change nothing. Men were frustrated. They wanted this expedition finished. They wanted to go home. 'And you're no traitor, James,' he said.

'No? My father would say I am.'

'Your father was British,' Wadsworth said, 'and you and I were both born British, but that's all changed now. We're Americans.' He said the word as though he were not used to it, but felt a pang of pride because of it. And tonight, he thought, the Americans would take a small step towards their liberty. They would attack the battery.

In the dark.

The Indians joined Wadsworth's militia after sunset. They appeared silently and, as ever, Wadsworth found their presence unsettling. He could not lose the impression that the dark-skinned warriors judged him and found him wanting, but he forced a welcome smile in the dark night. 'I'm glad you're here,' he told Johnny Feathers who was apparently the Indian's leader. Feathers, who had been given his name by John Preble who negotiated for the State with the Penobscot tribe, neither answered nor even acknowledged the greeting. Feathers and his men, he had brought sixteen this night, squatted at the edge of the trees and scraped whetstones over the blades of their short axes. Tomahawks, Wadsworth supposed. He wondered if they were drunk. The general's order that no liquor was to be given to the Indians had met with small success, but so far as Wadsworth could tell these men were sober as churchwardens. Not that he cared, drunk or sober the Indians were among his best warriors, though Solomon Lovell was more sceptical of their loyalties. 'They'll want something in exchange for helping us,' he had told Wadsworth, 'and not just wampum. Guns, probably, and God knows what they'll do with those.'

'Hunt?'

'Hunt what?'

But the Indians were here. The seventeen braves had muskets, but had all chosen to carry tomahawks as their primary weapon. The militia and marines had muskets with fixed bayonets. 'I don't want any man firing prematurely,' Wadsworth told his militiamen and saw, in the small light of the waning moon, the look of incomprehension on too many faces. 'Don't cock your muskets till you need to shoot,' he told them. 'If you stumble and fall I don't want a shot alerting the enemy. And you,' he pointed to a small boy who was armed with a sheathed bayonet and an enormous drum, 'keep your drum silent till we've won!'

'Yes, sir.'

Wadsworth crossed to the boy who looked scarcely a day over eleven or twelve. 'What's your name, boy?'

'John, sir.'

'John what?'

'John Freer, sir.' John Freer's voice had not broken. He was rake-thin, nothing but skin, bones and wide eyes, but those eyes were bright and his back was straight.

'A good name,' Wadsworth said, 'free and Freer. Tell me, John Freer, do you have your letters?'

'My letters, sir?'

'Can you read or write?'

The boy looked shifty. 'I can read some, sir.'

'Then when this is all over,' Wadsworth said, 'we must teach you the rest, eh?'

291

'Yes, sir,' Freer said unenthusiastically.'

'He brings us luck, General,' an older man put in. He placed a protective hand on the boy's shoulder. 'We can't lose if Johnny Freer is with us, sir.'

'Where are your parents, John?' Wadsworth asked.

'Both dead,' the older man answered, 'and I'm his grandfather.'

'I want to stay with the company, sir!' John Freer said eagerly. He had divined that Wadsworth was contemplating an order that he stay behind.

'We'll look after him, sir,' the grandfather said, 'we always do.'

'Just keep your drum quiet till we've beaten them, John Freer,' Wadsworth said and patted the boy on the head. 'After that you can wake the dead for all I care.'

Wadsworth had three hundred militiamen, or rather two hundred and ninety-nine militiamen and one small drummer boy. Saltonstall had kept his word and sent fifty marines and had added a score of the *Warren*'s sailors who were armed with cutlasses, boarding pikes and muskets. 'The crew wants to fight,' Carnes explained the presence of the seamen.

'They're most welcome,' Wadsworth had said.

'And they will fight!' Carnes said enthusiastically. 'Demons, they are.'

The seamen were on the right. The militiamen and Indians were in the centre and Captain Carnes and his marines on the left. Lieutenant Dennis was second in command of the marines. They were all lined at the edge of the trees by Dyce's Head, close to Captain Welch's grave, and to the east the ground dropped gently away towards the Half Moon Battery. Wadsworth could see the enemy earthwork in the small moonlight, and even if it had been dark its position would have been betrayed by two small camp-fires that burned behind the emplacement. The fort was a dark silhouette on the horizon.

Just beyond the enemy battery were the westernmost houses of the village. The closest, which was dwarfed by a large barn, lay only a few paces beyond the British guns. 'That's Jacob Dyce's house,' James Fletcher told Wadsworth, 'he's a Dutchman.'

'So no love for the British?'

'Oh, he loves the British, Jacob does. Like as not old Jacob will shoot at us.'

'Let's hope he's asleep,' Wadsworth said and hoped all the enemy were sleeping. It was past midnight, a Sunday now, and the peninsula was moonlit black and silver. Small wisps of smoke drifted from chimneys and camp-fires.

The British sloops were black against the distant water and no lights showed aboard.

Two of the transport ships had been beached at Majabigwaduce's eastern tip, while the third had been added to the line of sloops because, in their new position, the British were trying to blockade a much greater width of water. The transport ship, which was anchored at the southern end of the line, looked much bigger than the three sloops, but Carnes, who had used a telescope to examine the ship in daylight, reckoned it carried only six small cannon. 'It looks big and bad,' he said now, watching the enemy ships in the dark, 'but it's feeble.'

'Like the fort,' Lieutenant Dennis put in.

'The fort gets more formidable every day,' Wadsworth said, 'which is why we must use haste.' He had been appalled when, at the afternoon's Council of War, General Lovell had toyed with the idea of starving the British out of Fort George. The council's sentiment had been against such a plan, swayed by Wadsworth's insistence that the British would surely be readying a relief force for the besieged garrison, but Lovell, Wadsworth knew, would not give up the idea easily. That made tonight's action crucial. A clear victory would help persuade Lovell that his troops could outfight the redcoats, and Wadsworth, looking at the marines, had no doubt that they could. The green-coated men looked grim, lean and frightening as they waited. With such troops, Wadsworth thought, a man might conquer the world.

The militia were not so threatening. Some looked eager, but most appeared frightened and a few were praying on their knees, though Colonel McCobb, his moustache very white against his tanned face, was confident of his men. 'They'll do just fine,' he said to Wadsworth. 'How many enemy do you reckon?'

'No more than sixty. At least we couldn't see more than sixty.'

'We'll twist their tails right and proper,' McCobb said happily.

Wadsworth clapped his hands to get the militiamen's attention again. 'When I give the word,' he called to the men crouching at the edge of the wood, 'we advance in line. We don't run, we walk! When we get close to the enemy I'll give the order to charge and then we run straight at their works.' Wadsworth reckoned he sounded confident enough, but it felt unnatural and he was assailed by the thought that he merely play-acted at being a soldier. Elizabeth and his children would be sleeping. He drew his sword. 'On your feet!' Let the enemy be sleeping too, he thought as he waited for the line to stand. 'For America!' he called. 'And for liberty, forward!'

And all along the wood's edge men walked into the moonlight. Wadsworth glanced left and right and was astonished at how visible they were. The silvery light glittered from bayonets and lit the white crossbelts of the marines. The long line was walking raggedly downhill, through pastureland and scattered trees. The enemy was silent. The glow of the camp-fires marked the battery. The guns there faced the harbour entrance, but how soon could the British turn them to face the approaching patriots? Or were the gunners fast asleep?

Wadsworth's thoughts skittered, and he knew that was caused by nervousness. His belly felt empty and sour. He gripped his sword as he looked up at the fort, which appeared formidable from this lower ground. That is what we should be attacking, Wadsworth thought. Lovell should have every man under his command assaulting the fort, one screaming attack in the dark and the whole business would be over. But instead they were attacking the battery and perhaps that would hasten the campaign's end. Once the battery was taken then the Americans could mount their own guns on the harbour's northern shore and hammer the ships, and once the ships were gone then Lovell would have no excuse not to attack the fort.

Wadsworth leaped a small ditch. He could hear the waves breaking on the shingle to his right. The long line of attackers was very ragged now, and he remembered the children on the common at home and how he had tried to rehearse manoeuvring them from column to line. Maybe he should have advanced in column? The gun emplacement was only two hundred yards away now, so it was too late to try and change the formation. James Fletcher walked beside Wadsworth, his musket held in clenched hands. 'They're sleeping, sir,' Fletcher said in a tight voice.

'I hope so,' Wadsworth said.

Then the night exploded.

The first gun was fired from the fort. The flame leaped and curled into the night sky, the lurid flash lighting even the southern shore of the harbour before the powder smoke obscured the fort's silhouette. The cannon-ball landed somewhere to Wadsworth's right, bounced and crashed into the meadows behind and then two more guns split the night, and Wadsworth heard himself shouting. 'Charge! Charge!'

Ahead of him a flame showed, then he was dazzled as he heard the sound of the gun and the whistle of grapeshot. A man screamed. Other men were cheering and running.

Wadsworth stumbled over the rough ground. Marines were dark shapes to his left. Another round shot slammed into the turf, bounced and flew on. A splinter of light came from an enemy musket in the gun emplacement, then another cannon sounded and grapeshot seethed around Wadsworth. James Fletcher was with him, but when Wadsworth glanced left and right he saw very few militiamen. Where were they? More muskets shot flame, smoke and metal from the battery. There were men standing on the rampart, men who vanished behind a rill of smoke as still more muskets punched the night. The marines were ahead of Wadsworth now, running and shouting, and the sailors were coming from the beach and the battery was close now, so close. Wadsworth had no breath to shout, but his attackers needed no orders. The Indians overtook him and a cannon fired from the emplacement and the sound deafened Wadsworth, it punched the air about him, it dizzied him, it wreathed him in the foul egg stench of powder smoke that was thick as fog and he heard the screaming just ahead and the clash of blades, and a shouted order that was abruptly cut off, and then he was at the earthwork and he saw a smoking cannon muzzle just to his right as Fletcher pushed him upwards.

The devil's work was being done inside the emplacement where marines, Indians and sailors were slaughtering redcoats. A gun fired from the fort, but the ball went high to splash harmlessly into the harbour. Lieutenant Dennis had stabbed a sword into a British sergeant who was bent over, trapping the steel in his flesh. A marine clubbed the man on the head with a musket butt. The Indians were making a high-pitched shrieking sound as they killed. Wadsworth saw blood bright as a gun-flame spurt from a skull split by a tomahawk. He turned towards a British officer in a red coat whose face was a mask of terror and Wadsworth slashed his sword at the redcoat, the blade hissing in empty air as a marine drove a bayonet deep into the man's lower belly and ripped the blade upwards, lifting the redcoat off his feet as an Indian chopped a hatchet into the man's spine. Another redcoat was backing towards the fires, his hands raised, but a marine shot him anyway, then smashed the stock of his musket across the man's face. The rest of the British were running. They were running! They were vanishing into Jacob Dyce's cornfield, fleeing uphill towards the fort.

'Take prisoners!' Wadsworth shouted. There was no need for more killing. The gun emplacement was taken and, with a fierce joy, Wadsworth understood that the battery was too low on the shore to be hit by the fort's guns. Those guns were trying, but the shots were flying just overhead to splash uselessly into the harbour. 'Let's hear your drum now, John Freer!' Wadsworth shouted. 'You can sound the drum as loud as you like now!'

But John Freer, aged twelve, had been clubbed to death by a redcoat's brass-bound musket butt. 'Oh dear God,' Wadsworth said, gazing down at the small body. The bloodied skull was black in the moonlight. 'I should never have let him come,' he said, and felt a tear in one eye.

'It was that bastard,' a marine said, indicating the twitching body of the redcoat who had tried to surrender and who had been shot before having his face beaten in by the marine. 'I saw the bastard hit the lad.' The marine stepped to the fallen redcoat and kicked him in the belly. 'You yellow bastard.'

Wadsworth stooped beside Freer and put a finger on the drummer's neck, but there was no pulse. He looked up at James Fletcher. 'Run back to the heights,' he said, 'and tell General Lovell we're in possession of the battery.' He held out a hand to check Fletcher. Wadsworth was gazing eastwards at the British ships. The dark shapes seemed so close now. 'Tell the general we need to put our own guns here,' he said. Wadsworth had captured the British guns, but they were smaller than he had expected to find. The twelve-pounder cannons must have been moved back to the fort and replaced with six-pounders. 'Tell the general we need a pair of eighteen-pounders,' he said, 'and tell him we need them here by dawn.'

'Yes, sir,' Fletcher said, and ran back towards the high ground and Wadsworth, watching him go, saw militiamen scattered on that long slope leading to Dyce's Head. Too many militiamen. At least half had refused to attack, evidently terrified by the British cannon-fire. Some had kept going and now stood in the battery watching the fifteen prisoners being searched, but most had simply run away and Wadsworth shuddered with anger. The marines, Indians and sailors had done the night's work, while most of the minutemen had hung back in fear. John Freer had been braver than all his comrades, and the boy had a crushed skull to prove it.

'Congratulations, sir,' Lieutenant Dennis smiled at Wadsworth.

'You and your marines achieved this,' Wadsworth said, still looking at the militia.

'We beat their marines, sir,' Dennis said cheerfully. The gun emplacement had been protected by Royal Marines. Dennis sensed Wadsworth's unhappiness and saw where the general was looking. 'They're not soldiers, sir,' he said, nodding towards the militiamen who had refused to attack. Most of those laggards were now walking towards the battery, chivvied by their officers.

'But they are soldiers!' Wadsworth said bitterly. 'We all are!'

'They want to get back to their farms and families,' Dennis said.

'Then how do we take the fort?' Wadsworth asked.

'They have to be inspired, sir,' Dennis said.

'Inspired!' Wadsworth laughed, though not with any amusement.

'They'll follow you, sir.'

'Like they did tonight?'

'Next time you'll give them a speech, sir,' Dennis said, and

298

Wadsworth felt his former pupil's gentle chiding. Dennis was right, he thought. He should have given them a rousing encouragement, he should have reminded the militia why they fought, but then a strange ripping noise interrupted his regrets and he turned to see an Indian crouching by a corpse. The dead marine had been stripped of his red coat, now he was being scalped. The Indian had cut the skin across the crown and was tearing it loose by the hair. The man sensed Wadsworth's gaze and turned, his eyes and teeth bright in the moonlight. Four other corpses had already been scalped. Marines were searching among the billets, discovering tobacco and food. The militiamen just watched. Colonel McCobb was haranguing the three hundred men, telling them they should have behaved better. A marine knocked the top from one of two huge hogsheads that stood at the back of the emplacement and Wadsworth wondered what they contained, then was diverted by a dog barking fiercely from the battery's southern edge. A sailor tried to calm the dog, but it snapped at him and a marine casually shot the animal. Another marine laughed.

That was the last gunfire of the night. Mist thickened on the harbour. James Fletcher returned to the captured battery just before dawn to say that General Lovell wanted Wadsworth back on the heights. 'Is he going to send the guns?' Wadsworth asked.

'I think he wants you to arrange that, sir.'

Meaning Lovell wanted Wadsworth to deal with Lieutenant-Colonel Revere. The sailors had already gone back to their ships and Captain Carnes had been instructed to return with his marines as soon as possible, but Wadsworth was unhappy leaving the militia to guard the captured battery and Carnes agreed that a dozen marines should stay under Lieutenant Dennis's command. 'I'll leave a good sergeant with young Dennis,' Carnes said.

'He needs that?'

'We all need that, sir,' Carnes said, and shouted at Sergeant Sykes to pick a dozen good men.

Colonel McCobb was officially in charge of the battery. 'You might start by throwing up a rampart,' Wadsworth suggested to him. The existing semi-circular rampart looked towards the harbour entrance and Wadsworth wanted an earthwork that faced the fort. 'I'll be bringing the guns as soon as I can,' he said.

'I'll be waiting, sir,' McCobb promised.

Three hundred men now guarded the captured battery that could be used to destroy the ships. Then Lovell might attack the fort. And then the British would be gone.

Brigadier McLean appeared in a nightcap. He was in uniform and had a grey greatcoat, but had been given no time to dress his hair and so wore the red cap with its long blue tassel. He stood on Fort George's south-western bastion and stared down at the low ground where the Half Moon emplacement was mostly hidden by the cornfield. 'I think we're wasting our cannon-fire,' he told Fielding, who himself had been woken by the sudden eruption of firing.

'Cease fire!' Fielding called.

An alert gunner sergeant had seen the rebels attacking down the open slope from Dyce's Head and had opened fire. 'Give the man an extra ration of rum,' McLean said, 'and my thanks.'

The gunners had done well, McLean thought, yet their efforts had not saved the Half Moon Battery. The Royal Marines and gunners evicted from the emplacement were straggling into the fort and telling their tale of rebels swarming over the ramparts. They claimed there had been hundreds of attackers, and the defenders had numbered just fifty. 'Tea,' McLean said.

'Tea?' Fielding asked.

'They should brew some tea,' McLean gestured at the defeated men.

Hundreds? He wondered. Maybe two hundred. The sentries on Fort George's ramparts had been given a clear view of the attackers, and the most reliable men reckoned they had seen two or three hundred rebels, many of whom had not pressed home the attack. Now a growing fog was obscuring all the lower ground.

'You sent for me, sir?' Captain Iain Campbell, one of the 74th's best officers, now joined the brigadier on the rampart.

'Good morning, Campbell.'

'Good morning, sir.'

'Only it's not a good morning,' McLean said. 'Our enemy has shown initiative.'

'I heard, sir.' Iain Campbell had dressed hurriedly and one of his coat buttons was undone.

'Have you ever captured an enemy earthwork, Campbell?'

'No, sir.'

'Unless your men are very well-disciplined it leads to disorganization,' McLean said 'which leads me to believe that our enemy are rather disorganized right now.'

'Yes, sir,' the highlander said, smiling as he understood what the brigadier insinuated.

'And Captain Mowat won't like it if the enemy holds the Half Moon Battery, he won't like it at all.'

'And we must help the Royal Navy, sir,' Campbell said, still smiling.

'Indeed we must, it is our God-given duty. So take your good lads down there, Captain,' McLean said, 'and shoo the rogues away, will you?'

Fifty marines had been surprised and driven from the Half Moon Battery so McLean would send fifty Scotsmen to take it back.

McLean went to have his hair dressed.

Excerpt of a letter from Brigadier-General Solomon Lovell to Jeremiah Powell, President of the Council Board of the State of Massachusetts Bay, August 1st, 1779:

. . . that with the Troops that now constitute my Army it is not practicable to gain a Conquest by a storm and not probable without length of time to reduce them by a regular siege. To Effect the First I must request a few regular disciplined troops and Five Hundred hand Grenades . . . at least four Mortars of Nine Inches or as near as your Ordnance will admit with an ample supply of Fire Shells.

Excerpt of a letter from the Board of War to the Council Board of Massachusetts, August 3rd, 1779:

The Board of War would represent to your Honors that by the great expence incurred by the Penobscot expedition they are so draind of Money that they are under the greatest embarrasments in the execution of the Common business of the Office, and are now calld upon for the payment of £100,000 due to persons for provision sent upon that expedition. The present scarcity of bread in the publick magazines both state and continental is alarming and may be attended with fatal consequences . . .

Excerpt of a letter from Samuel Savage, President of the Board of War, Boston, to Major-General Nathaniel Gates, August 3rd, 1779:

Reports say that our Forces at Penobscot have, after a most vigorous resistance, obliged the Enemy to surrender themselves both Naval and Land Forces, Prisoners of War, and that this glorious event took place on Saturday last.

TEN

The sun had not risen when Peleg Wadsworth roused Lieutenant-Colonel Revere who, publicly ordered to sleep ashore, had erected the tents captured on Cross Island and made them his new quarters. They were the only tents in Lovell's army and some men wondered why they had not been offered to the general himself.

'I only just got to sleep,' Revere grumbled as he pushed the tent flap aside. Like most of the army he had watched the gunflashes in the night.

'The enemy battery is taken, Colonel,' Wadsworth said.

'I saw that. Very satisfying.' Revere pulled a wool blanket around his shoulders. 'Friar!'

A man crawled from a turf and timber shelter. 'Sir?'

'Rouse the fire, man, it's chilly.'

'Yes, sir.'

'Very satisfying,' Revere said, looking at Wadsworth again.

'The captured battery is being entrenched,' Wadsworth said, 'and we need to move our heaviest guns there.'

'Heaviest guns,' Revere echoed. 'And boil some tea, Friar.'

'Tea, sir, yes, sir.'

'Heaviest guns,' Revere said again, 'I suppose you mean the eighteens?'

'We have six of them, do we not?'

'We do.'

'The new battery is close to the enemy ships. I want them hit hard, Colonel.'

'We all want that,' Revere said. He went close to the camp-fire that, newly revived, flamed bright. He shivered. It might have been high summer, but the nights in eastern Massachusetts could be surprisingly cold. He stood by the blaze that lit his blunt face. 'We're scarce of eighteen-pounder round shot,' he said, 'unless the commodore can provide some?'

'I'm certain he will,' Wadsworth said. 'The shot is intended for the enemy ships, he can't possibly object.'

'Possibly,' Revere said with evident amusement, then he shook his head as if clearing his mind of some unwelcome thought. 'Do you have children, General?'

Wadsworth was taken aback by the question. 'Yes,' he said after a pause, 'I have three. Another coming very soon.'

'I miss my children,' Revere said tenderly, 'I do miss them dearly.' He gazed into the flames. 'Teapots and buckles,' he said ruefully.

'Teapots and buckles?' Wadsworth asked, wondering if they were nicknames for Revere's children.

'How a man earns his living, General. Teapots and buckles, cream jugs and cutlery.' Revere smiled, then shrugged his home thoughts away. 'So,' he sighed, 'you want to take two of the eighteens from our lines here?'

'If they're the closest, yes. Once the ships are sunk they can be returned.'

Revere grimaced. 'If I put two eighteens down there,' he said, 'the British are not going to like it. How do we defend the guns?'

It was a good question. Brigadier McLean would hardly stand idly by while two eighteen-pounders knocked splinters off the three sloops. 'Colonel McCobb has three hundred men at the battery,' he told Revere, 'and they'll stay there till the ships are destroyed.'

'Three hundred men,' Revere said dubiously.

'And you may place smaller cannon for your defence,' Wadsworth suggested, 'and by now the entrenchments should be well begun. I believe the battery will be safe.'

'I could take guns down in the fog,' Revere suggested. The air felt clammy and wisps of mist were already showing among the high trees.

'Then let's do it,' Wadsworth said energetically. If the guns could be emplaced by midday then the enemy ships might be cruelly hurt by dusk. The range was short and the eighteen-pounder balls would strike with a savage force. Sink the ships and the harbour would belong to the patriots, and after that Lovell would have no reason not to storm the fort. Wadsworth, for the first time since the rebels had taken the heights of Majabigwaduce, felt optimistic.

Get it done, he thought. Pull down the enemy flag. Win.

And then the muskets sounded.

Captain Iain Campbell led his fifty highlanders down to the village, then followed a cart track westwards till the company reached the edge of Jacob Dyce's land. A small light flickered from behind the Dutchman's shutters, suggesting he was awake.

The highlanders crouched by the corn and Campbell stood above them. 'Are you all listening well?' he asked them, 'because I have a thing to tell you.'

They were listening. They were youngsters, most not yet twenty, and they trusted Iain Campbell because he was both a gentleman and a good officer. Many of these men had grown up on the lands of Captain Campbell's father, the laird, and most of them bore the same surname. Some, indeed, were the captain's half-brothers, though that was not a truth admitted on either side. Their parents had told them that the

Campbells of Ballaculish were good people and that the laird was a hard man, but a fair one. Most had known Iain Campbell since before he became a man, and most supposed they would know him till they followed his coffin to the kirk. One day Iain Campbell would live in the big house and these men, and their children, would doff their hats to him and beg his help when they were in trouble. They would tell their children that Iain Campbell was a hard man, but a fair one, and they would say that not because he was their laird, but because they would remember a night when Captain Campbell took all the risks he asked them to take. He was a privileged man and a brave man and a very good officer.

'The rebels,' Campbell spoke low and forcefully, 'captured the Half Moon Battery last night. They're there now, and we're going to take it back. I talked to some of the men they drove away, and they heard the rebels shouting at each other. They learned the name of the rebel leader, their officer. He's a MacDonald.'

The crouching company made a noise like a low growl. Iain Campbell could have given them a rousing speech, a blood and thunder and fight-for-your-king speech, and if he had been given the tongue of an angel and the eloquence of the devil that speech would not have worked as well as the name MacDonald.

He had invented MacDonald's existence, of course. He had no idea who led the rebels, but he did know that the Campbells hated the MacDonalds and the MacDonalds feared the Campbells, and by telling his men that a MacDonald was their enemy he had roused them to an ancient fury. It was no longer a war to suppress a rebellion, it was an ancestral blood feud.

'We're going through the corn,' Captain Campbell said, 'and we'll form line at the other side and you charge with your bayonets. We go fast. We win.'

He said no more, except to give the necessary orders, then

he led the fifty men past the field of corn that grew taller than a bonneted highlander's head. Fog was spreading from the water, thickening over the battery and hiding the dark shapes of the highlanders.

The sky behind Campbell was lightening to a wolf-grey, but the tall corn shadowed his men as they spread into a line. Their muskets were loaded, but not cocked. Metal scraped on metal as men slotted and twisted their bayonets onto gun muzzles. The bayonets were seventeen-inch spikes, each sharpened to a wicked point. The battery was only a hundred paces away, yet the rebels had still not seen the kilted highlanders. Iain Campbell drew his broadsword and grinned in the half-darkness. 'Let's teach the Clan Donald who is master here,' he said to his men, 'and now let's kill the bastards.'

They charged.

They were highlanders from the hard country on Scotland's west coast. War was in their blood, they had suckled tales of battle with their mother's milk, and now, they believed, a MacDonald was waiting for them and they charged with all their clan's ferocity. They screamed as they charged, they raced to be first among the enemy and they had the advantage of surprise.

Yet even so Iain Campbell could not believe how quickly the enemy broke. As he neared the battery and could see more through the dark fog he had a moment of alarm because there seemed to be hundreds of rebels, they were far more numerous than his company, and he thought what a ridiculous place this was to meet his death. Most of the rebels were in the battery itself, which was as crowded as a Methodist meeting. Only about twenty men were working on the entrenchments and it was evident they had set no sentries or, if they had placed picquets, those sentries were asleep. Astonished faces turned to stare at the shrieking highlanders. Too many faces, Campbell thought. There would be a marble plaque in the kirk with his name and this day's date and a dignified epitaph, then that vision vanished because the enemy was already running. 'Kill!' Campbell heard himself shout. 'Kill!' And the shout spurred even more of the enemy to flee westwards. They dropped their picks and spades, they scrambled over the west-facing rampart and they ran. A few, very few, fired at the approaching highlanders, but most forgot they were carrying muskets and just abandoned the battery to run towards the heights.

One group of men was dressed in dark uniforms crossed by white belts and those men did not run. They tried to form a line and they presented muskets and they fired a ragged volley at Campbell's men as the highlanders leaped the newly dug scratch of a ditch. Iain Campbell felt the wind of a ball whip past his cheek, then he was swinging his heavy blade at a smoking musket, knocking it aside as he brought the sword back to stab low and fast. The steel punctured cloth, skin, flesh and muscle, and then his Campbells were all around him, screaming hatred and lunging with bayonets, and the outnumbered enemy broke. 'Give them a volley!' Campbell shouted. He twisted his blade in the enemy's belly and thumped his left fist into the man's face. Corporal Campbell added his bayonet and the rebel went down. Captain Campbell kicked the musket from the enemy's grasp and dragged his blade free of the clinging flesh. Musket flashes cast sudden stark light on blood, chaos and Campbell fury.

A lone American officer tried to rally his men. He slashed his sword at Campbell, but the laird's son had learned his fencing at Major Teague's Academy on Edinburgh's Grassmarket and he parried the swing effortlessly, reversed, turned his wrist and lunged the blade into the American officer's chest. He felt the sword scrape on a rib, he grimaced and lunged harder. The man choked, gasped, spewed blood and fell. 'Give them a volley!' Campbell shouted again. He had hardly needed to think to defeat the rebel officer, it had all been instinctive. He dragged his sword free and saw an American sergeant in a green uniform coat stagger and fall. The sergeant was not wounded, but a highlander had thumped the side of his head with a musket stock and he was half-dazed. 'Take his musket!' Campbell called sharply. 'Don't kill him! Just take him prisoner!'

'He could be a MacDonald,' a Campbell private said, quite ready to thrust his bayonet into the sergeant's belly.

'Take him prisoner!' Campbell snapped. He turned and looked towards the heights where the dawn was lighting the slope, but the fog hid the fleeing rebels. Scottish muskets coughed smoke, stabbed flame into the fog and shot balls uphill to where the Americans retreated. 'Sergeant MacKellan!' Campbell called. 'You'll set a picquet! Smartly now!'

'You sure this bastard's not a MacDonald?' the private standing above the dazed rebel sergeant asked.

'He's called Sykes,' a voice said, and Campbell turned to see it was the wounded rebel officer who had spoken. The man had propped himself on an elbow. His face, very white in the dawn's wan light, was streaked with blood that had spilled from his mouth. He looked towards the green-coated sergeant. 'He's not called MacDonald,' he managed to say, 'he's called Sykes.'

Campbell was impressed that the young officer, despite his chest wound, was trying to save his sergeant's life. That sergeant was sitting now, guarded by Jamie Campbell, the youngest son of Ballaculish's blacksmith. The wounded officer spat more blood. 'He's called Sykes,' he said yet again, 'and they were drunk.'

Campbell crouched beside the injured officer. 'Who was drunk?' he asked.

'They found barrels of rum,' the man said, 'and I couldn't stop them. The militia.' The highlanders were still shooting into the fog, hastening the retreat of the rebels who had now vanished into the fog that spread inexorably up the long slope. 'I told McCobb,' the wounded officer said, 'but he said they deserved the rum.'

'Rest,' Campbell said to the man. There were two great

311

hogsheads at the back of the battery and they had evidently been full of naval rum and the rebels, celebrating their victory, had celebrated too hard. Campbell found a discarded knapsack that he put beneath the wounded officer's head. 'Rest,' he said again. 'What's your name?'

'Lieutenant Dennis.'

The blood on Dennis's coat looked black and Campbell would not even have known it was blood except that it reflected a sheen in the weak light. 'You're a marine?'

'Yes,' Dennis choked on the word and blood welled at his lips and ran down his cheek. His breath rasped. 'We changed sentries,' he said, and whimpered with sudden pain. He wanted to explain that the defeat was not his fault, that his marines had done their job, but the militia picquet that had replaced his marine sentries had failed.

'Don't speak,' Campbell said. He saw the fallen sword nearby and slid the blade into Dennis's scabbard. Captured officers were allowed to keep their swords, and Campbell reckoned Lieutenant Dennis deserved it as a reward for his bravery. He patted Dennis's blood-wet shoulder and stood. Robbie Campbell, a corporal, and almost as great a fool as his father who was a drunken drover, had found a drum that was painted with an eagle and the word 'Liberty' and he was beating it with his fists and capering like the fool he was. 'Stop that noise, Robbie Campbell!' Campbell shouted, and was rewarded with silence. The drummer boy's corpse was lying beside a newly dug grave. 'Jamie Campbell! You and your brother will make a stretcher. Two muskets, two jackets!' The quickest way to fashion a stretcher was to thread the sleeves of two jackets onto a pair of muskets. 'Carry Lieutenant Dennis to the hospital.'

'Did we kill the MacDonald, sir?'

'The MacDonald ran away,' Campbell said dismissively. 'What do you expect of a MacDonald?'

'The yon bastards!' a private said angrily and Campbell

312

turned to see the bloodied heads of the Royal Marine corpses, their scalps cut and torn away. 'Bloody heathen savage god-damned bastards,' the man growled.

'Take Lieutenant Dennis to the surgeons,' Campbell ordered, 'and the prisoner to the fort.' He found a rag in a corner of the battery and wiped his broadsword's long blade clean. It was almost full light now. Rain began to fall, heavy rain that splashed on the battery's wreckage and diluted the blood.

The Half Moon Battery was back in British hands, and on the high ground Peleg Wadsworth despaired.

'They're patriots!' General Lovell complained. 'They must fight for their liberty!'

'They're farmers,' Wadsworth said wearily, 'and carpenters and labourers and they're the men who didn't volunteer for the Continental Army, and half of them didn't want to fight anyway. They were forced to fight by press gangs.'

'The Massachusetts Militia,' Lovell said in a hurt voice. He was standing beneath the cover of a sail that had been strung and pegged between two trees to make a headquarter's tent. The rain pattered on the canvas and hissed in the camp-fire just outside the tent.

'They're not the same militia who fought at Lexington,' Wadsworth said, 'or who stormed Breed's Hill. Those men are all gone into the army,' or their graves, he thought, 'and we have the leavings.'

'Another eighteen deserted last night,' Lovell said despairingly. He had set a picquet on the neck, but that post did little to stop men sneaking away in the darkness. Some, he supposed, deserted to the British, but most went north into the wild woods and hoped to find their way home. Those who were caught were condemned to the Horse, a brutal punishment whereby a man was sat astride a narrow beam with muskets tied to his legs, but the punishment was evidently not brutal

313

enough, because still the militiamen deserted. 'I am ashamed,' Lovell said.

'We still have enough men to assult the fort,' Wadsworth said, not sure he believed the words.

Lovell ignored them anyway. 'What can we do?' he asked helplessly.

Wadsworth wanted to kick the man. You can lead us, he thought, you can take command, but in fairness, and Peleg Wadsworth was a man given to honesty about himself, he did not think he was showing great leadership either. He sighed. The dawn's fog had cleared to reveal that the British had abandoned the recaptured Half Moon Battery, leaving the earthwork empty, and there was something insulting in that abandonment. They seemed to be saying that they could retake the battery whenever they wished, though Lovell showed no desire to accept the challenge. 'We can't hold the battery,' the general said despairingly.

'Of course we can, sir,' Wadsworth insisted.

'You saw what happened! They ran! The rascals ran! You want me to attack the fort with such men?'

'I think we must, sir,' Wadsworth said, but Lovell said nothing in return. The rain was coming down harder, forcing Wadsworth to raise his voice. 'And, sir,' he continued, 'at least we've rid ourselves of the enemy battery. The commodore might sail into the harbour?'

'He might,' Lovell said in a tone that suggested pigs might take wings and circle the heights of Majabigwaduce singing hallelujahs. 'But I fear . . . ' he began, and stopped.

'Fear, sir?'

'We need disciplined troops, Wadsworth. We need General Washington's men.'

Praise the Lord, Wadsworth thought, but did not betray his reaction. He knew how hard it had been for Lovell to make that admission. Lovell wanted the glory of this expedition to shine on Massachusetts, but the general must now share that renown with the other rebellious states by calling in troops from the Continental Army. That army had real soldiers, disciplined men, trained men.

'A single regiment would be enough,' Lovell said.

'Let me convey the request to Boston,' the Reverend Jonathan Murray suggested.

'Would you?' Lovell asked eagerly. He had become more than slightly tired of the Reverend Murray's pious confidence. God might indeed wish the Americans to conquer here, but even the Almighty had so far failed to move the commodore's ships past Dyce's Head. The clergyman was no military man, but he possessed persuasive powers and Boston would surely listen to his pleas. 'What will you tell them?'

'That the enemy is too powerful,' Murray said, 'and that our men, though filled with zeal and imbued with a love of liberty, nevertheless lack the discipline to bring down the walls of Jericho.'

'And ask for mortars,' Wadsworth said.

'Mortars?' Lovell asked.

'We don't have trumpets,' Wadsworth said, 'but we can rain fire and brimstone on their heads.'

'Yes, mortars,' Lovell said. A mortar was even more deadly for siege work than an howitzer and, anyway, Lovell possessed only one howitzer. The mortars would fire their shells high in the sky so that they fell vertically into the fort and, as the fort's walls grew higher, so those walls would contain the explosions and spread death among the redcoats. 'I shall write the letter,' Lovell said heavily.

Because the rebels needed reinforcements.

Next day Peleg Wadsworth tied a large piece of white cloth to a long stick and walked towards the enemy fort. Colonel Revere's guns had already fallen silent and, soon after, the British guns went quiet too.

Wadsworth went alone. He had asked James Fletcher to accompany him, but Fletcher had begged off. 'They know me, sir.'

'And you like some of them?'

'Yes, sir.'

'Then stay here,' Wadsworth had said, and now he walked down the ridge's gentle slope, between the shattered tree stumps, and he saw two red-coated officers leave the fort and come towards him. He thought that they would not want him to get too close in case he saw the state of the fort's walls, but he was evidently wrong because the two men waited for him inside the abatis. It seemed they did not care if he had a good view of the ramparts. Those ramparts were under constant bombardment from Revere's guns yet, to Wadsworth's eyes, they looked remarkably undamaged. Maybe that was why the British officers did not mind him seeing the walls. They were mocking him.

It had rained again that morning. The rain had stopped, but the wind felt damp and the clouds were still low and threatening. The wet weather had soaked the men encamped on the heights, it had drenched the stored cartridges and increased the militia's misery. Some men had hissed at Lovell as the general accompanied Wadsworth to the tree-line and Lovell had pretended not to hear the sound.

The abatis had been knocked about by gunfire and it was not difficult to find a way through the tangled branches. Wadsworth felt foolish holding the flag of truce above his head so he lowered it as he approached the two enemy officers. One of them, the shortest, had grey hair beneath his cocked hat. He leaned on a stick and smiled as Wadsworth approached. 'Good morning,' he called genially.

'Good morning,' Wadsworth responded.

'Not really a good morning, though, is it?' the man said. His right arm was held unnaturally. 'It's a chill and wet morning. It's raw! I am Brigadier-General McLean, and you are?'

'Brigadier-General Wadsworth,' Wadsworth said, and felt entirely fraudulent in claiming the rank.

'Allow me to name Lieutenant Moore to you, General,' McLean said, indicating the good-looking young man who accompanied him.

'Sir,' Moore greeted Wadsworth by standing briefly to attention and bowing his head.

'Lieutenant,' Wadsworth acknowledged the politeness.

'Lieutenant Moore insisted on keeping me company in case you planned to kill me,' McLean said.

'Under a flag of truce?' Wadsworth asked sternly.

'Forgive me, General,' McLean said, 'I jest. I would not think you capable of such perfidy. Might I ask what brings you to see us?'

'There was a young man,' Wadsworth said, 'a marine officer called Dennis. I have a connection with his family,' he paused, 'I taught him his letters. I believe he is your prisoner?'

'I believe he is,' McLean said gently.

'And I hear he was wounded yesterday. I was hoping . . .' Wadsworth paused because he had been about to call McLean 'sir', but managed to check that foolish impulse just in time, 'I was hoping you could reassure me of his condition.'

'Of course,' McLean said and turned to Moore. 'Lieutenant, be a good fellow and run to the hospital, would you?'

Moore left and McLean gestured at two tree stumps. 'We might as well be comfortable while we wait,' he said. 'I trust you'll forgive me if I don't invite you inside the fort?'

'I wouldn't expect it,' Wadsworth said.

'Then please sit,' McLean said, and sat himself. 'Tell me about young Dennis.'

Wadsworth perched on the adjacent stump. He talked awkwardly at first, merely saying how he had known the Dennis family, but his voice became warmer as he spoke of William Dennis's cheerful and honest character. 'He was always a fine boy,' Wadsworth said, 'and he's become a fine man. A good young man,' he stressed the 'good', 'and he hopes to be a lawyer when this is all over.'

'I've heard there are honest lawyers,' McLean said with a smile.

'He will be an honest lawyer,' Wadsworth said firmly.

'Then he will do much good in the world,' McLean said, 'and yourself, General? I surmise you were a schoolteacher?'

'Yes.'

'Then you have done much good in the world,' McLean said. 'As for me? I went to be a soldier forty years ago and twenty battles later here I still am.'

'Not doing good for the world?' Wadsworth could not resist enquiring.

McLean took no offence. 'I commanded troops for the King of Portugal,' he said, smiling, 'and every year there was a great procession on All Saints' Day. It was magnificent! Camels and horses! Well, two camels, and they were poor mangy beasts,' he paused, remembering, 'and afterwards there was always dung on the square the king needed to cross to reach the cathedral, so a group of men and women were detailed to clean it up with brooms and shovels. They swept up the dung. That's the soldier's job, General, to sweep up the dung the politicians make.'

'Is that what you're doing here?'

'Of course it is,' McLean said. He had taken a clay pipe from a pocket of his coat and put it between his teeth. He held a tinder-box awkwardly in his maimed right hand and struck the steel with his left. The linen flared up and McLean lit the pipe, then snapped the box closed to extinguish the flame. 'Your people,' he said when the pipe was drawing, 'had a disagreement with my people, and you or I, General, might well have talked our way to an accord, but our lords and masters failed to agree so now you and I must decide their arguments a different way.'

318

'No,' Wadsworth said. 'To my mind, General, you're the camel, not the sweeper.'

McLean laughed at that. 'I'm mangy enough, God knows. No, General, I didn't cause this dung, but I am loyal to my king and this is his land, and he wants me to keep it for him.'

'The king might have kept it for himself,' Wadsworth said, 'if he had chosen any rule except tyranny.'

'Oh, he's such a tyrant!' McLean said, still amused. 'Your leaders are wealthy men, I believe? Landowners, are they not? And merchants? And lawyers? This is a rebellion led by the wealthy. Strange how such men prospered so under tyranny.'

'Liberty is not the freedom to prosper,' Wadsworth said, 'but the freedom to make choices that affect our own destiny.'

'But would a tyranny allow you to prosper?'

'You have restricted our trade and levied taxes without our consent,' Wadsworth said, wishing he did not sound so pedagogic.

'Ah! So our tyranny lies in not allowing you to become wealthier still?'

'Not all of us are wealthy men,' Wadsworth said heatedly, 'and as you well know, General, tyranny is the denial of liberty.'

'And how many slaves do you keep?' McLean asked.

Wadsworth was tempted to retort that the question was a cheap jibe, except it had stung him. 'None,' he said stiffly. 'The keeping of Negroes is not common in Massachusetts.' He felt acutely uncomfortable. He knew he had not argued well, but he had been surprised by his enemy. He had anticipated a pompous, supercilious British officer, and instead found a courteous man, old enough to be his father, who seemed very relaxed in this unnatural encounter.

'Well, here the two of us are,' McLean said happily, 'a tyrant and his downtrodden victim, talking together.' He pointed his pipe stem towards the fort where John Moore had gone on his way to the hospital. 'Young Moore reads his history. He's a fine young man, too. He likes history, and here he is, here we both are, writing a new chapter. I sometimes wish I could peer into the future and read the chapter we write.'

'You might not like it,' Wadsworth said.

'I think it certain that one of us will not,' McLean said.

The conversation faltered. McLean drew on his pipe and Wadsworth gazed at the nearby ramparts. He could see the timber spikes in the ditch and, above them, the earth and log wall that was now higher than a man's head. No one could leap the ramparts now, the wall would need to be climbed and fought for. It would be hard and bloody work and he wondered if even Continental Army troops could manage it. They could if the wall were breached and Wadsworth looked for evidence that Colonel Revere's guns were having any effect, but other than the mangled roof of the storehouse inside the fort there was little sign of the cannonade. There were places where the wall had been battered by round shot, but those places had all been repaired. Mortars, he thought, mortars. We need to turn the interior of the fort into a cauldron of shrieking metal and searing flame. The curtain wall between the protruding corner bastions was lined with redcoats who gazed back at Wadsworth, intrigued by the proximity of a rebel. Wadsworth tried to count the men, but there were too many.

'I'm keeping most of my men hidden,' McLean said.

Wadsworth felt guilty, which was ridiculous because it was his duty to examine the enemy. Indeed, General Lovell had only agreed to this enquiry about Lieutenant Dennis's fate because it offered Wadsworth an opportunity to examine the enemy's defences. 'We're keeping most of ours hidden too,' Wadsworth said.

'Which is sensible of you,' McLean said. 'I see from your uniform you served in Mister Washington's army?'

320

'I was an aide to the general, yes,' Wadsworth said, offended by the British habit of referring to George Washington as 'mister'.

'A formidable man,' McLean said. 'I'm sorry young Moore is taking so long.' Wadsworth made no answer and the Scotsman smiled wryly. 'You very nearly killed him.'

'Lieutenant Moore?'

'He insisted on fighting the war single-handed, which I suppose is a good fault in a young officer, but I'm profoundly grateful he survived. He has great promise.'

'As a soldier?'

'As a man and as a soldier. Like your Lieutenant Dennis, he is a good young man. If I had a son, General, I should wish him to be like Moore. Do you have children?'

'Two sons and a daughter, and another child coming very soon.'

McLean heard the warmth in Wadsworth's voice. 'You're a fortunate man, General.'

'I think so.'

McLean drew on the pipe, then blew a stream of smoke into the damp air. 'If you will allow an enemy's prayers, General, then let me pray you will be reunited with your family.'

'Thank you.'

'Of course,' McLean said blandly, 'you could effect that reconciliation by withdrawing now?'

'But we have orders to capture you first,' Wadsworth said with some amusement in his voice.

'I shall not pray for that,' McLean said.

'I think, perhaps, we should have attempted it a week ago,' Wadsworth said ruefully, and immediately wished he had left the words unspoken. McLean said nothing, merely inclined his head, which small gesture might have been interpreted as agreement. 'But we shall attempt it again,' Wadsworth finished.

'You must do your duty, General, of course you must,'

McLean said, then turned because Wadsworth had looked towards the fort's south-western corner. John Moore had appeared there and now walked towards them with a scabbarded sword held in one hand. The lieutenant glanced at Wadsworth, then bent and whispered in McLean's ear and the general winced and closed his eyes momentarily. 'I am sorry, General Wadsworth,' he said, 'but Lieutenant Dennis died this morning. You may be assured that he received the best treatment we could offer, but, alas, the ministrations were not sufficient.' McLean stood.

Wadsworth stood too. He looked at McLean's grave face and then, to his shame, tears rolled down his cheeks. He turned away abruptly.

'There is nothing to be ashamed of,' McLean said.

'He was a fine man,' Wadsworth said, and he knew he was not crying because of Dennis's death, but because of the waste and indecision of this campaign. He sniffed, composed himself and turned back to McLean. 'Please thank your doctor for whatever he attempted.'

'I will,' McLean said, 'and please be assured we shall give Lieutenant Dennis a Christian burial.'

'Bury him in his uniform, please.'

'We shall do that, of course,' McLean promised. He took the scabbarded sword from Moore. 'I presume you brought this because it belonged to the lieutenant?' he asked Moore.

'Yes, sir.'

McLean handed the sword to Wadsworth. 'You might wish to return that to his family, General, and you may tell them from his enemy that their son died fighting heroically. They can be proud of him.'

'I shall,' Wadsworth said and took the sword. 'Thank you for indulging my enquiry,' he said to McLean.

'I enjoyed most of our conversation,' McLean said and held a hand towards the abatis as though he were a host conducting an honoured guest towards his front door. 'I am truly sorry about your Lieutenant Dennis,' he said, walking westwards beside the much taller American. 'Maybe one day, General, you and I can sit in peace and talk about these things.'

'I'd like that.'

'As would I,' McLean said, stopping just short of the abatis. He smiled mischievously. 'And do please give my regards to young James Fletcher.'

'Fletcher,' Wadsworth said as if the name were new to him.

'We have telescopes, General,' McLean said, amused. 'I regret he chose the allegiance he did. I regret that very much, but do tell him his sister is well, and that the tyrants give her and her mother rations.' He held out his hand. 'We won't resume our cannon practice till you're back among the trees,' he said.

Wadsworth hesitated, then shook the offered hand. 'Thank you, General,' he said, then began the long, lonely walk back up the ridge's spine.

McLean stayed at the abatis, watching Wadsworth's solitary walk. 'He's rather a good man, I think,' he said when the American was well out of earshot.

'He's a rebel,' Moore said disapprovingly.

'And if you or I had been born here,' McLean said, 'then like as not we would be rebels too.'

'Sir!' John Moore sounded shocked.

McLean laughed. 'But we were born across the sea, and it's not so many years since we had our own rebels in Scotland. And I did like him.' He still watched Wadsworth. 'He's a man who wears his honesty like a badge, but luckily for you and me he's no soldier. He's a schoolmaster and that makes us fortunate in our enemies. Now let's get back inside before they start shooting at us again.'

At dusk, that same day, Lieutenant Dennis was buried in his green uniform. Four highlanders shot a volley into the fading light, then a wooden cross was hammered into the soil.

The name Dennis was scratched on the cross with charcoal, but two days later a corporal took the cross for kindling.

And the siege went on.

The three redcoats slipped out of the tented encampment at mid-afternoon on the day that the enemy officer had come to the fort under a flag of truce. They had no idea why the rebel had come, nor did they care. They cared about the sentries placed to stop men sneaking out of the camp and into the woods, but that picquet was easy enough to avoid, and the three men vanished into the trees and then turned west towards the enemy.

Two were brothers called Campbell, the third was a Mackenzie. They all wore the dark kilt of Argyle and carried their muskets. Off to their left the cannons were firing, the sound sporadic, sudden, percussive and now a part of their daily lives. 'Down there,' Jamie Campbell said, pointing, and the three followed a vague track that led downhill through the trees. All three were grinning, excited. The day was grey and a light rain spat from the south-west.

The track led to the marshy isthmus that connected Majabigwaduce's peninsula to the mainland. Jamie, the oldest of the brothers and the acknowledged leader of the three men, did not want to reach the isthmus, rather he was hoping to work his way along the wooded slope just above the marsh. The rebels patrolled that ground. He had seen them there. Sometimes Captain Caffrae's company went to the same land and ambushed a rebel patrol, or else mocked the Americans with fife-music and jeers. This afternoon, though, the wood above the marsh seemed empty. The three crouched in the brush and gazed west towards the enemy lines. To their right the trees were thinner, while ahead was a small clearing in which a spring bubbled. 'Not a bloody soul here,' Mackenzie grumbled.

'They come here,' Jamie said. He was nineteen, with dark

eyes, black hair and a hunter's watchful face. 'Watch up the slope,' he told his brother, 'we don't want bloody Caffrae finding us.'

They waited. Birds, now as accustomed to the cannon-fire as the troops, sang harshly in the trees. A small animal, strangely striped, flitted across the clearing. Jamie Campbell stroked the stock of his musket. He loved his musket. He treated the stock with oil and boot-blacking so that the wood was smooth like silk, and the caress of the weapon's dark curves put him in mind of the sergeant's widow in Halifax. He smiled.

'There!' his brother Robbie hissed.

Four rebels had appeared at the clearing's far side. They were in dull brown coats, trews and hats, and festooned with belts, pouches and bayonet scabbards. Three of the men carried two pails apiece, the fourth had a musket in his hands. They shambled to the spring where they stooped to fill their buckets.

'Now!' Jamie said, and the three muskets flamed loud. One of the men at the spring was thrown sideways, his blood a flicker of red in the grey rain. The fourth rebel shot back at the smoke among the trees, but Mackenzie and the Campbell brothers were already running away, whooping and laughing.

It was sport. The general had forbidden it, and had threatened a dire punishment to any man who left the lines to take a shot at the enemy without permission, but the young Scotsmen loved the risk. If the rebels would not come to them then they would go to the rebels, whatever the general wanted. Now all they needed to do was get back safe to the tents without being found.

Then, tomorrow, do it again.

Samuel Adams reached Major-General Horatio Gates's headquarters at Providence in Rhode Island late in the afternoon. Swollen clouds were heaping, and off to the west the thunder already grumbled. It was hot and humid and Adams was shown into a small parlour where, despite the open windows, no hint of wind brought relief. He wiped his face with a big spotted handkerchief. 'Would you like tea, sir?' a pale lieutenant in Continental Army uniform asked.

'Ale,' Samuel Adams said firmly.

'Ale, sir?'

'Ale,' Samuel Adams said even more firmly.

'General Gates will be with you directly, sir,' the lieutenant said distantly and, Adams suspected, inaccurately, then vanished into the nether regions of the house.

The ale was brought. It was sour, but drinkable. Thunder sounded louder, though no rain fell and still no wind blew through the open sash windows. Adams wondered if he was hearing the sound of the siege guns pounding the British in Newport, but all reports said the attempts to evict that garrison had proven hopeless, and a moment later a distant flash of lightning confirmed that it was indeed thunder. A dog howled and a woman's voice was raised in anger. Samuel Adams closed his eyes and dozed.

He was woken by the sound of nailed boots on the wooden floor of the hallway. He sat upright just as Major-General Horatio Gates came into the parlour. 'You rode from Boston, Mister Adams?' the general boomed in greeting.

'Indeed I did.'

Despite the heat Gates had been wearing a greatcoat that he now threw to the lieutenant. 'Tea,' he said, 'tea, tea, tea.'

'Very good, your honour,' the lieutenant said.

'And tea for Mister Adams!'

'Ale!' Adams called in correction, but the lieutenant was already gone.

Gates unstrapped the scabbarded sword he wore over his Continental Army uniform and slammed it onto a table heaped with paperwork. 'How are matters in Boston, Adams?'

'We do the Lord's work,' Adams said gently, though Gates entirely missed the irony. The general was a tall man a few years younger than Samuel Adams who, after his long ride

326

down the Boston Post Road, was feeling every one of his fifty-seven years. Gates glared at the papers resting under his sword. He was, Adams thought, an officer much given to glaring. The general was heavy-jowled with a powdered wig that was not quite large enough to hide his grey hairs. Sweat trickled from under the wig. 'And how do you fare in this fair island?' Adams asked.

'Island?' Gates asked, looking suspiciously at his visitor. 'Ah, Rhode Island. Damn silly name. It's all the fault of the French, Adams, the French. If the damned French had kept their word we'd have evicted the enemy from Newport. But the French, damn their eyes, won't bring their ships. Damned fart-catchers, every last one of them.'

'Yet they are our valued allies.'

'So are the damned Spanish,' Gates said disparagingly.

'As are the damned Spanish,' Adams agreed.

'Fart-catchers and papists,' Gates said, 'what kind of allies are those, eh?' He sat opposite Adams, long booted legs sprawling on a faded rug. Mud and horse dung were caked on the soles of his boots. He steepled his fingers and stared at his visitor. 'What brings you to Providence?' he asked. 'No, don't tell me yet. On the table. Serve us.' The last five words were addressed to the pale lieutenant who placed a tray on the table and then, in an awkward silence, poured two cups of tea. 'You can go now,' Gates said to the hapless lieutenant. 'A man cannot live without tea,' he declared to Adams.

'A blessing of the British empire?' Adams suggested mischievously.

'Thunder,' Gates said, remarking on a clap that sounded loud and close, 'but it won't get here. It'll die with the day.' He sipped his tea noisily. 'You hear much from Philadelphia?'

'Little you cannot read in the news prints.'

'We're dilly-dallying,' Gates said, 'dilly-dallying, shilly-shallying and lolly-gagging. We need a great deal more energy, Adams.'

'I am sure your honour is right,' Adams said, taking his cue for the honorific from the lieutenant's mode of address. Gates was nicknamed 'Granny', though Adams thought that too kind for a man so touchy and sensible of his dignity. Granny had been born and raised in England and had served in the British Army for many years before a lack of money, slow promotion and an ambitious wife had driven him to settle in Virginia. His undoubted competence as an administrator had brought him high rank in the Continental Army, but it was no secret that Horatio Gates thought his rank should be higher still. He openly despised General Washington, believing that victory would only come when Major-General Horatio Gates was given command of the patriot armies. 'And how would your honour suggest we campaign?' Adams asked.

'Well, it's no damned good sitting on your fat backside staring at the enemy in New York,' Gates said energetically, 'no damned good at all!'

Adams gave a flutter of his hands that might have been construed as agreement. When he rested his hands on his lap again he saw the slight tremor in his fingers. It would not go away. Age, he supposed, and sighed inwardly.

'The Congress must come to its senses,' Gates declared.

'The Congress, of course, pays close heed to the sentiments of Massachusetts,' Adams said, dangling a great fat carrot in front of Gates's greedy mouth. The general wanted Massachusetts to demand George Washington's dismissal and the appointment of Horatio Gates as commander of the Continental Army.

'And you agree with me?' Gates asked.

'How could I possibly disagree with a man of your military experience, General?'

Gates heard what he wanted to hear in that answer. He stood and poured himself more tea. 'So the State of Massachusetts wants my help?' he asked.

'And I had not even stated my purpose,' Adams said with feigned admiration.

'Not difficult to grasp, is it? You've sent your pillow-biters off to Penobscot Bay and they can't get the job done.' He turned a scornful face on Adams. 'Sam Savage wrote to tell me the British had surrendered. Not true, eh?'

'Alas, not true,' Adams said with a sigh. 'The garrison appears to be a more difficult nut to crack than we had supposed.'

'McLean, right? A competent man. Not brilliant, but competent. You wish for more tea?'

'This is as sufficient as it is delicious,' Adams said, touching a finger to the untasted cup.

'You sent your militia. How many?'

'General Lovell commands around a thousand men.'

'What does he want?'

'Regular troops.'

'Ah ha! He wants real soldiers, does he?' Gates drank his second cup of tea, poured a third, then sat again. 'Who pays for this?'

'Massachusetts,' Adams said. God knew Massachusetts had already spent a fortune on the expedition, but it seemed another fortune must now be expended and he prayed that Brigadier-General McLean had a vast chest of treasure hidden in his toy fort or else the State's debt would be crippling.

'Rations, transport,' Gates insisted 'both must be paid for!'

'Of course.'

'And how do you convey my troops to the Penobscot River?'

'There is shipping in Boston,' Adams said.

'You should have asked me a month ago,' Gates said.

'Indeed we should.'

'But I suppose Massachusetts wanted the battle honour for itself, eh?'

Adams gently inclined his head to indicate assent and tried to imagine this irascible, touchy, resentful Englishman in charge of the Continental Army and was profoundly grateful for George Washington.

'Lieutenant!' Gates barked.

The pale lieutenant appeared at the door. 'Your honour?'

'My compliments to Colonel Jackson. His men are to march for Boston at daybreak. They march with arms, ammunition and a day's rations. Full orders will follow tonight. Tell the colonel he is to keep a detailed, mark that, detailed, list of all expenditures. Go.'

The lieutenant went.

'No good shilly-shallying,' Gates said to Adams. 'Henry Jackson's a good man and his regiment is as fine as any I've seen. They'll finish McLean's nonsense.'

'You are very kind, General,' Adams said.

'Not kind at all, efficient. We have a war to win! No good sending fart-catchers and pillow-biters to do a soldier's job. You'll do me the honour of dining with me?'

Samuel Adams sighed inwardly at that prospect, but liberty had its price. 'It would be a distinct privilege, your honour,' he said.

Because, at last, a regiment of trained American soldiers was going to Penobscot Bay.

Letter from Brigadier-General Lovell to Commodore Saltonstall, August 5th, 1779:

I have proceded as far as I Can on the present plan and find it inafectual for the purpose of disloging or destroying the Shiping I must therefore request an ansure from you wether you will venter your Shiping up the River in order to demolish them or not that I may conduct my Self accordingly.

From the Minutes of Brigadier-General Lovell's Council of War, Majabigwaduce, August 11th, 1779:

Great want of Discipline and Subordination many of the Officers being so exceedingly slack in their Duty, the Soldiers so averse to the Service and the wood in which we encamped so very thick that on an alarm or any special occasion nearly one fourth part of the Army are skulked out of the way and conceal'd.

From the Journal of Sergeant Lawrence, Royal Artillery, Fort George, Majabigwaduce, August 5th and August 12th, 1779:

The General was very much surprised to see so many Men leave the Fort today to take shots at the Enemy without leave. He assures them that any who may be Guilty of this again shall be most severely punished for disobedience of orders.

ELEVEN

Wednesday, August 11th, started with a thick fog and still airs. Small waves slapped wearily on the harbour shore where a lone gull cried. Peleg Wadsworth, standing on Dyce's Head, could see neither the enemy fort nor their ships. Fog blanketed the world. No cannon fired because the whiteness concealed targets from rebel and king's men alike.

Colonel Samuel McCobb had brought two hundred men from his Lincoln County militia to the meadow just beneath Dyce's Head. These were the same men who had fled from the Half Moon Battery and now they waited for General Lovell who had decided to send them back to the battery. 'If you fall off a horse,' Lovell had asked Peleg Wadsworth the previous night, 'what do you do?'

'Climb back into the saddle?'

'My sentiments, my sentiments,' Lovell had declared. The general, who had been in despair just a couple of days before, had apparently climbed back into his own saddle of confidence. 'You dust yourself down,' Lovell had said, 'and scramble back up! Our fellows need to be shown they can beat the enemy.'

James Fletcher was waiting with Peleg Wadsworth. Fletcher would guide McCobb's men down to Jacob Dyce's cornfield, which lay a hundred or so paces up the slope from the deserted battery. There the militia would hide. It was a trap devised by Lovell who was certain that McLean would not be able to resist the lure. Wadsworth had urged Lovell to assault the fort directly, but the general had insisted that McCobb's men required heartening. 'They need a victory, Wadsworth,' Lovell had declared.

'Indeed they do, sir.'

'As things are,' Lovell had admitted with bleak honesty, 'we're not ready to assault the fort, but if the militia's confidence is restored, if their patriotic fervour is aroused, then I believe there is nothing they cannot achieve.'

Peleg Wadsworth hoped that was true. A letter had arrived from Boston warning that a fleet of British warships had left New York harbour and it was presumed, no one could say for certain, that the fleet's destination was Penobscot Bay. Time was short. It was possible that the enemy fleet was sailing elsewhere, to Halifax or maybe down the coast toward the Carolinas, but Wadsworth worried that any day now he would see topsails appear above the seaward islands in the Penobscot River. Some men were already urging abandonment of the siege, but Lovell was unwilling to contemplate failure, instead he wanted his militia to win a small victory that would lead to the greater triumph.

And so this ambush had been devised. McCobb was to take his men down to the concealment of the cornfield from where he would send a small patrol to occupy the deserted battery. Those men would carry picks and spades so that they appeared to be making a new rampart to face the British, a defiance that Lovell was certain would provoke a response from Fort George. McLean would send men to drive the small patrol away and the ambush would be sprung. As the British attacked the men heightening the earthwork, so McCobb's men would erupt from the cornfield and assault the enemy's flank. 'You'll give them a volley,' Lovell had encouraged McCobb the night before, 'then drive them away at the point of bayonets. Balls and bayonets! That'll do the job.'

General Lovell now appeared in the dawn fog. 'Good morning, Colonel!' the general cried cheerfully.

'Good morning, sir,' McCobb answered.

'Good morning, good morning, good morning!' Lovell called to the assembled men who mostly ignored him. One or two returned the greeting, though none with any enthusiasm. 'Your men are in good heart?' the general asked McCobb.

'Ready and raring for the day, sir,' McCobb answered, though in truth his men looked ragged, sullen and dispirited. Days of camping in the woods had left them dirty and the rain had rotted their shoe leathers, though their weapons were clean enough. McCobb had inspected the weapons, tugging at flints, drawing bayonets from sheaths or running a finger inside a barrel to make certain no powder residue clung to the metal. 'They'll do us proud, sir,' McCobb said.

'Let us hope the enemy plays his part!' Lovell declared. He looked upwards. 'Is the fog thinning?'

'A little,' Wadsworth said.

'Then you should go, Colonel,' Lovell said, 'but let me say a word or two to the men first?'

Lovell wanted to inspire them. He knew spirits were dangerously low, he heard daily reports of men deserting the lines or else hiding in the woods to evade their duties, and so he stood before McCobb's men and told them they were Americans, that their children and children's children would want to hear of their prowess, that they should return home with laurels on their brows. Some men nodded as he spoke, but most listened with expressionless faces as Lovell moved to his carefully prepared climax. 'Let after ages say,' he declared with an orator's flourish, 'that there they did stand like men inspired, there did they fight, and fighting some few fell, the rest victorious, firm, inflexible!'

He stopped abruptly, as if expecting a cheer, but the men

just gazed blankly at him, and Lovell, discomfited, gestured that McCobb should take them down the hill. Wadsworth watched them pass. One man had tied his boot-soles to the uppers with twine. Another man limped. A few were bare-footed, some were grey-headed and others looked absurdly young. He wished Lovell had thought to ask Saltonstall for a company of marines, but the general and the commodore were barely on speaking terms now. They communicated by stiff letters, the commodore insisting that the ships could not be attacked while the fort existed, and the general certain that the fort was impregnable so long as the British ships still floated.

'I think that went very well,' Lovell said to Wadsworth, 'don't you?'

'Your speech, sir? It was rousing.'

'Just a reminder of their duty and our destiny,' Lovell said. He watched the last of the militia disappear into the fog. 'When the day clears,' he went on, 'you might look to those new batteries?'

'Yes, sir,' Wadsworth said unenthusiastically. Lovell wanted him to establish new gun batteries that could bombard the British ships. Those new batteries, Lovell now insisted, were the key to the army's success, but the idea made little sense to Wadsworth. Building more batteries would take guns from their primary job of cannonading the fort and, besides, the gunners had already warned Lovell that they were running short of ammunition. The twelve-pounder shot was almost entirely expended, and the eighteen-pounders had fewer than two hundred rounds between them. Colonel Revere was being blamed for that shortage of powder and shot, but in all fairness everyone had expected the British to be defeated within a week of the fleet's arrival, and now the army had been encamped before Fort George for almost three weeks. There was even a lack of musket cartridges because the spare ammunition had not been properly protected from the rain.

336

General McLean, Wadsworth thought bitterly, would never have allowed his cartridges to deteriorate. He had been unsettled by his meeting with the Scotsman. It was strange to feel such a liking for an enemy and McLean's air of easy confidence had gnawed at Wadsworth's hopes.

Lovell had heard the lack of enthusiasm in Wadsworth's voice. 'We must rid ourselves of those ships,' he said energetically. The topmasts of the four British ships were visible above the fog now, and Wadsworth instinctively glanced southwards to where he feared to see enemy reinforcements arriving, but the Penobscot's long sea-reach was entirely shrouded by the fog. 'If we can establish those new batteries,' Lovell went on, still sounding as though he addressed an election meeting rather than confiding in his deputy, 'then we can so damage the enemy that the commodore will feel it safe to enter the harbour.'

Wadsworth suddenly wanted to commit murder. The responsibility for capturing the fort was not Saltonstall's, but Lovell's, and Lovell was doing anything except fulfil that obligation.

The violent sensation was so strange to Peleg Wadsworth that, for a moment, he said nothing. 'Sir,' he finally said, mastering the urge to be bitter, 'the ships are incapable—'

'The ships are the key!' Lovell contradicted Wadsworth before the objection was even articulated. 'How can I throw my men forward if the ships exist on their flank?' Easily, Wadsworth thought, but knew he would get nowhere by saying so. 'And if the commodore won't rid me of the ships,' Lovell went on, 'then we shall have to do the business ourselves. More batteries, Wadsworth, more batteries.' He pushed a finger at his deputy. 'That's your task today, General, to make me cannon emplacements.'

It was clear to Wadsworth that Lovell would do anything rather than assault the fort. He would nibble about the edges, but never bite the centre. The older man feared failure in the great endeavour and so sought for smaller successes, and in doing so he risked defeat if British reinforcements arrived before any American troops came. Yet Lovell would not be persuaded to boldness and so Wadsworth waited for the fog to clear, then went down to the beach where he discovered Marine Captain Carnes standing beside two large crates. The guns on the heights had started firing and Wadsworth could hear the more distant sound of the British guns returning the fire. 'Twelve-pounder ammunition,' Carnes greeted Wadsworth cheerfully, pointing at the two crates, 'courtesy of the *Warren*.'

'We need it,' Wadsworth said, 'and thank you.'

Carnes nodded towards his beached longboat. 'My fellows are carrying the first boxes up to the batteries, and I'm guarding the rest to make sure no rascally privateer steals them.' He kicked at the shingle. 'I hear your militiamen are planning to surprise the enemy?'

'I hope the enemy haven't heard that,' Wadsworth said.

'The enemy's probably content to do nothing,' Carnes said, 'while we twiddle our fingers.'

'We do more than that,' Wadsworth said, bridling at the implied criticism, which, if he were honest, he would agree with.

'We should be attacking the fort,' Carnes said.

'We should indeed.'

Carnes gave the taller man a shrewd glance. 'You reckon the militia can do it, sir?'

'If they're told the quickest way home is through the fort, yes. But I'd like some marines to lead the way.'

Carnes smiled at that. 'And I'd like your artillery to concentrate their fire.'

Wadsworth remembered his close-up look at Fort George's western wall and knew the marine was right. Worse, Carnes had been a Continental Army artillery officer, so knew what he was talking about. 'Have you talked to Colonel Revere about that?' he asked.

'You can't talk to Colonel Revere, sir,' Carnes said bitterly.

'Maybe we should both talk to him,' Wadsworth said, much as he dreaded such a conversation. Lieutenant-Colonel Revere reacted to criticism with belligerence, yet if the remaining ammunition was to be used wisely then the guns had to be laid skilfully. Wadsworth felt a pang of guilt at his part in appointing Revere to the expedition, then suppressed the rueful thoughts. There was already far too much blame being spread through the expedition. The army was blaming the navy, the navy was scornful of the army, and almost everyone was complaining about the artillery.

'We can talk to him,' Carnes said, 'but with respect, sir, you'd be better off just replacing him.'

'Oh, surely not,' Wadsworth said, trying to head off the disparagement he knew was coming.

'He watches the fire a hundred paces away from his guns,' Carnes said, 'and he reckons a shot is good if it merely hits the fort. I haven't seen him correct the aim once! I told him he should be hammering the same length of wall with every damn gun he's got, but he just told me to stop my impertinence.'

'He can be prickly,' Wadsworth said sympathetically.

'He's given up hope,' Carnes said bleakly.

'I doubt that,' Wadsworth said loyally. 'He detests the British.'

'Then he should damn well kill them,' Carnes said vengefully, 'but I hear he votes to abandon the siege in your Councils of War?'

'So does your brother,' Wadsworth said with a smile.

Carnes grinned. 'John stands to lose his ship, General! He's not making money at anchor in this river. He wants the *Hector* out at sea, snapping up British cargoes. What does Colonel Revere have to lose by staying?' He did not wait for an answer, but nodded out to the anchorage where the white-painted Castle Island barge had just left the *Samuel*. 'And talk of the devil,' he said grimly. Lieutenant-Colonel Revere might have obeyed the order to sleep ashore, but he was still visiting the *Samuel* two or three times a day and now he was evidently being rowed ashore after one such visit. 'He goes to the *Samuel* for his breakfast,' Carnes said.

Wadsworth stayed quiet.

'Then again for his dinner,' Carnes continued relentlessly.

Wadsworth still said nothing.

'And usually for his supper too,' Carnes said.

'I need a boat,' Wadsworth said abruptly, trying to avert yet more carping, 'and I'm sure the colonel will oblige me.' There were usually a half-dozen longboats on the shingle, their crews dozing above the high-tide line, but the only boat now on the beach was the one that had brought Carnes and the ammunition, and its oarsmen were carrying that ammunition up the bluff and so Wadsworth walked to where Revere's barge would come ashore. 'Good morning, Colonel!' he called as Revere approached. 'You have fresh twelve-pounder ammunition!'

'Has McCobb gone?' was Revere's response.

'He has indeed, an hour and a half since.'

'We should have sent a four-pounder with him,' Revere said. His barge grounded on the shingle and he stepped forward over the rowers' benches.

'Too late now, I'm afraid,' Wadsworth said and extended a hand to steady Revere as he climbed over the barge's bows. Revere ignored the gesture. 'Are you ashore for a while now?' Wadsworth asked.

'Of course,' Revere said, 'I have work here.'

'Then would you be good enough to allow me the use of your boat? I need to visit Cross Island.'

Revere bridled at the request. 'This barge is for the artillery!' he said indignantly, 'it can't be spared for other people.'

Wadsworth could scarce believe what he heard. 'You won't lend its use for an hour or so?'

'Not for one minute,' Revere said curtly. 'Good day to you.'

Wadsworth watched the colonel walk away. 'If this war goes on another twenty years,' he said, his bitterness at last expressing itself, 'I will not serve another day with that man!'

'My crew will be back soon,' Captain Carnes said. He was smiling, having overheard Wadsworth's remark. 'You can use my boat. Where are we going?'

'The channel south of Cross Island.'

Carnes's marines rowed Wadsworth and the captain south into the channel behind Cross Island. That island was one of a necklace of rocks and islets that bounded a cove to the south of Majabigwaduce Harbour. A narrow isthmus separated the cove from the harbour itself and Wadsworth went ashore on its strip of stony beach where he unfolded the crude map James Fletcher had drawn for him. He pointed across the placid waters of Majabigwaduce's inner harbour towards the thickly wooded eastern shore. 'A man called Haney farms land over there,' he told Carnes, 'and General Lovell wants a battery there.'

A battery on Haney's land would hammer the British ships from the east. Wadsworth climbed one of the steep, overgrown hillocks that studded the isthmus and, once at the summit, used Captain Carnes's powerful telescope to gaze at the enemy. At first he examined the four British ships. The closest vessel was the transport, *Saint Helena*, which dwarfed the smaller sloops, yet those three smaller ships were far more heavily armed. Their east-facing gunports were closed, but Wadsworth reckoned there were no guns hidden behind those blank wooden squares. The rebels had seen British sailors taking cannon ashore, and the verdict had been that Captain Mowat had offered his ships' portside broadsides to the fort's defence. If Wadsworth needed any confirmation of that suspicion he gained it from seeing that the sloops were very slightly keeled over to starboard. He gave the telescope to Carnes and asked him to examine the ships. 'You're right, sir,' the marine said, 'they are listing.'

'Guns on one side only?'

'That would explain the list.'

So any guns on Haney's land would have no opposition, at least until Mowat managed to shift some cannon from his west-facing broadsides. Place guns on Haney's land and the rebels would be just a thousand yards from the sloops, a range at which the eighteen-pounders would be lethal. 'But how do we get men and guns there?' Wadsworth wondered aloud.

'Same way we came, sir,' Carnes said. 'We carry the boats across this strip of land and relaunch them.'

Wadsworth felt a dull anger at the sheer waste of effort. It would take a hundred men two days to make a battery on Haney's land, and what then? Even if the British ships were sunk or taken, would it make it any easier to capture the fort? True, the American ships could sail safe into the harbour and their guns could fire up at the fort, but what damage could their broadsides do to a wall so high above them?

Wadsworth trained the telescope on Fort George. At first he mis-aimed the tubes and was amazed that the fort looked so small, then he took his eye from the glass and saw that a new fort was being constructed and it was that second work he was seeing. The new fort, much smaller than Fort George, lay on the ridge to the east of the larger work. He trained the telescope again and saw blue-coated naval officers while the men digging the soil were not in any kind of uniform. 'Sailors,' he said aloud.

'Sailors?'

'They're making a new redoubt. Why?'

'They're making a refuge,' Carnes said.

'A refuge?'

'If their ships are defeated the crews will go ashore. That's where they'll go.'

'Why not go to the main fort?'

'Because McLean wants an outwork,' Carnes said. 'Look at the fort, sir.'

Wadsworth edged the telescope westwards. Trees and houses skidded past the lens, then he steadied the glass to examine Fort George. 'Bless me,' he said.

He was gazing at the fort's eastern wall that was hidden to anyone on the high ground to the west. And that eastern curtain wall was unfinished. It was still low. Wadsworth could see no cannon there, only a shallow ridge of earth that he supposed was fronted by a ditch, but the important thing, the thing that made his hopes rise and his heart beat faster, was that the wall was still low enough to be easily scaled. He lowered the glass's aim, examining the village with its cornfields, thickets, barns and orchards. If he could reach that low ground then he reckoned he could conceal his men from both the ships and the fort. They could assemble out of sight, then attack that low wall. The impudent flag above the fort might yet be pulled down.

'McLean knows he's vulnerable from the east,' Carnes said, 'and that new redoubt protects him. He'll put cannon there.'

'Or he will when it's finished,' Wadsworth said, and it was clear the new redoubt was far from completion. We should attack from the east, he thought, because that was where the British were weak.

Wadsworth aimed the telescope towards Dyce's Head, but the British ships obstructed his view and he could see nothing of the ambush, if indeed it had been sprung. No powder smoke showed in the sky above the abandoned battery. Wadsworth edged the telescope right again to stare across the low eastern tail of Majabigwaduce's peninsula. He was looking at the land north of the peninsula. He stared for a long time, then gave the glass back to Carnes. 'Look there,' he pointed. 'There's a meadow at the waterside. You can just see a house above it. It's the only house I can see there.'

Carnes trained the glass. 'I can see it.'

'The house belongs to a man called Westcot. General Lovell

wants a battery up there too, but will its guns reach the British ships?'

'Eighteen-pounder shot will,' Carnes said, 'but it's too far for anything smaller. Must be a mile and a half, so you'll need your eighteens.'

'General Lovell insists the ships must be defeated,' Wadsworth explained, 'and the only way we can do that is by sinking them with gunfire.'

'Or by taking our ships in,' Carnes said.

'Will that happen?'

Carnes smiled. 'The commodore is so high above me, sir, that I never hear a word he says. But if you weaken the British ships? I think in the end he'll go in.' He swung the glass to examine the sloops. 'That shoreward sloop? She hasn't stopped pumping her bilges from the day we arrived. She'll sink fast enough.'

'Then we'll build the batteries,' Wadsworth said, 'and hope we can riddle them with round shot.'

'And General Lovell's right about one thing, sir,' Carnes said. 'You do need to get rid of the ships.'

'The ships will surrender if we capture the fort,' Wadsworth said.

'No doubt they will,' Carnes said, 'but if a British relief fleet arrives, sir, then we want all our ships inside the harbour.'

Because then the tables would be turned and it would be the British who would have to fight their way through cannon-fire to attack the harbour, but only if the harbour belonged to the rebels, and the only way that the Americans could capture the harbour was by storming the fort.

It was all so simple, Wadsworth thought, so very simple, and yet Lovell and the commodore were making it so complicated.

Wadsworth and Carnes were rowed back to the beach beneath Majabigwaduce's bluff. As the longboat threaded the anchored warships Wadsworth stared south towards the sea-reach, south to where the reinforcements, either British or American, would arrive.

And the river was empty.

'I do believe,' McLean was staring south through a telescope, 'that is my friend, Brigadier Wadsworth.' He was gazing at two men, one in a green coat, who were on the harbour's southern shore. 'I doubt they're taking the air. You think they're contemplating new batteries?'

'It would be sensible of them, sir,' Lieutenant Moore answered.

'I'm sure Mowat's seen them, but I'll let him know.' McLean lowered the glass and turned westwards. 'If the rascals dare to build a battery on the harbour shore we'll lead them a merry dance. And what steps are those rogues doing?' He pointed down towards the abandoned Half Moon Battery where a score of rebels appeared to be digging a ditch. It was difficult to see, because Jacob Dyce's house, barn and cornfield were partly in the way.

'May I, sir?' Moore asked, holding a hand for the telescope.

'Of course. Your eyes are younger than mine.'

Moore stared at the men. 'They're not working particularly hard, sir,' he said, after watching for a while. Six men were digging, the others were lounging amidst the wreckage of the battery.

'So what are they doing?'

'Making the battery defensible, sir?'

'And if they wanted to do that,' McLean asked, 'why not send a hundred men? Two hundred! Three! Throw up a wall fast. Why send so few men?'

Moore did not reply because he did not know the answer. McLean took the glass back and used the lieutenant's shoulder as a rest. He took a swift look at the lackadaisical work-party, then raised the telescope to stare at the trees on Dyce's Head. 'Ah,' he said after a while.

345

'Ah, sir?'

'There are a score of men on the high ground. They're not usually there. They're watching and waiting.' He collapsed the telescope's tubes. 'I do believe, Lieutenant, that our enemy has prepared a trap for us.'

Moore smiled. 'Really, sir?'

'What are those fellows watching? They can't be there to watch a ditch being dug!' McLean frowned as he gazed westwards. A rebel cannonball flew overhead. The sound of the guns was now so normal that he scarcely noticed it, though he took careful note of the effect of the rebel gunfire, most of which was wasted and it amused McLean that Captain Fielding was so offended by that. As an artilleryman the English captain expected better of the enemy gunners, though McLean was delighted that the rebel cannoneers were being so wasteful. If they had spent an extra minute laying each gun they could have demolished most of Fort George's western wall by now, but they seemed content to fire blind. So what were those men doing on Dyce's Head? They were plainly staring towards the fort, but to see what? And why were there so few men at the Half Moon Battery? 'They're there to draw us out,' McLean decided.

'The ditch-diggers?'

'They want us to attack them,' McLean said, 'and why would they want that?'

'Because they have more men there?'

McLean nodded. He reckoned half of warfare was reading the enemy's mind, a skill that was now ingrained in the Scotsman. He had fought in Flanders and in Portugal, he had spent a lifetime watching his enemies and learning to translate their every small movement, and to translate what he saw in the knowledge that very often those movements were calculated to deceive. At first, when the rebels had arrived, McLean had been puzzled by these enemies. They had so nearly captured the fort, then they had decided on a siege instead of a storm, and he had worried about what cleverness that tactic concealed, but now he was almost certain that there was no cleverness at all. His enemy was simply cautious, and the best way to keep him cautious was to hurt him. 'We're being invited to dance to a rebel tune, Lieutenant.'

'And we decline the honour, sir?'

'Oh good Lord, no, no! Not at all!' McLean said, enjoying himself. 'Somewhere down there is a much larger body of the enemy. I think we must take the floor with them!'

'If we do, sir, then might . . .'

'You want to dance?' McLean interrupted Moore. 'Of course, Lieutenant.' It was time to let Moore off the leash, the general decided. The young man still blamed himself, and rightly, for his brave stupidity on the day when the rebels had captured the high ground, but it was time Moore was offered redemption for that mistake. 'You'll go with Captain Caffrae,' McLean said, 'and you shall dance.'

Commodore Saltonstall declared he would be responsible for constructing the battery on Haney's land if General Lovell was prepared to send a pair of eighteen-pounder cannons to the new work. Saltonstall did not communicate directly with Lovell, but sent Hoysteed Hacker, captain of the Continental sloop *Providence*, with the offer. He carried Lovell's consent back to the commodore, and so that afternoon eight longboats left the anchored warships and rowed south of Cross Island to land on the narrow isthmus. The boats were manned by over a hundred sailors equipped with spades and picks, which they carried, with the boats, across the narrow neck of land. They relaunched the boats and rowed across to the eastern side of Majabigwaduce Harbour. They were led by Commodore Saltonstall who wanted to site the battery himself.

He discovered the perfect place for a battery, a low headland that pointed like a finger directly at the British ships and with space enough for two guns to pound the enemy sloops.

'Dig here,' he ordered. He would raise a rampart around the headland. Eventually, he knew, Mowat would haul guns across the sloops' decks to return the fire, so the rampart needed to be high and stout enough to protect the gunners.

Mowat was evidently busy because Saltonstall could see boats rowing constantly between the sloops and the shore. A new and smaller fort was being built east of Fort George and Saltonstall suspected it was there to add firepower to the harbour defences. 'We bring our ships in here,' he told his first lieutenant, 'and they'll pour shot down on us.'

'They will, sir,' Lieutenant Fenwick said loyally.

Saltonstall pointed to the new earthwork that the British were making. 'They're putting more guns up there. They can't wait to have our ships under their cannons. It's a death trap.'

'Unless Lovell captures the fort, sir.'

'Captures the fort!' Saltonstall said scathingly. 'He couldn't capture a dribble of piss with a chamberpot. The man's a damned farmer.'

'What are they doing?' Fenwick pointed to the British sloops from which four longboats, each crammed with red-coated Royal Marines, were rowing north-east towards the Majabigwaduce River.

'They're not coming this way,' Saltonstall said.

'I presume we'll post marines here, sir?' Fenwick asked.

'We'll need to.' The new battery was isolated and, if the British had a mind to it, easily attacked. Yet the guns did not have to be here for long. Whenever the rebel fire had become too warm the British ships had moved their position and Saltonstall was convinced that a battery here on Haney's land and another to the north would drive Mowat away from his present position. The Scotsman would either take his sloops north into the narrow channel of the Majabigwaduce River or else seek refuge in the southernmost reaches of the harbour, but in either place he would be unable to support the fort with his broadsides and, once the sloops had been driven away, Saltonstall could contemplate bringing his ships into the harbour and using their guns to bombard the fort on the ridge. But only if Lovell attacked at the same time. He watched the Royal Marines rowing steadily up the Majabigwaduce River. 'Foraging, maybe?' he guessed. The boats vanished behind a distant point of land.

The sailors were having a hard time because the soil was thin. The commodore, feeling restless and bored by the dull work, left Lieutenant Fenwick to supervise the diggers while he walked up a trail towards a farm. It was a miserable farm too, little more than a lichen-covered log cabin with a field-stone chimney, a ramshackle barn, some cornfields and a stony pasture with two thin cows, all of it hacked out of the forest. The log pile was bigger than the house and the dung-heap even bigger. Smoke seeped from the chimney, suggesting someone was home, but Saltonstall had no wish to engage in a conversation with some dirt-poor peasant and so he avoided the house, walking instead around the margin of the cow pasture and climbing towards the summit of the hill east of the house from where, he thought, he might get a fine view of the new enemy fort.

He knew Solomon Lovell was blaming him for not attacking the British ships and Saltonstall despised Lovell for that blame. The man was a Massachusetts farmer, not a soldier, and he had no conception whatever of naval matters. To Solomon Lovell it all seemed so easy. The American ships should sail boldly through the harbour entrance and use their broadsides to shatter the enemy ships, but Saltonstall knew what would happen if he attempted that manoeuvre. The wind and tide would carry the *Warren* slowly, and her bows would be exposed to all Mowat's guns, and the cannon from the fort would pour their heavy shot down into her hull and the scuppers would be dripping blood by the time he hauled into the wind to bring his own broadside to bear. Then, true enough, he might batter one of the sloops into submission,

349

and the larger rebel ships would be there to help, but even if all the British ships were taken the fort would still be hammering shot down the slope. And probably heated shot. McLean was no fool and by now he must surely have built a furnace to heat shot red, and such shot, lodged in a frigate's timbers, could start a fire to reach the magazine and then the *Warren* would explode, scattering her precious timbers all across the harbour.

So Saltonstall was not minded to attack, not unless the fort was being distracted by a land assault at the same time and General Lovell showed no appetite for such a storm. And no wonder, the commodore thought, because in his opinion Lovell's militia was little more than a rabble. Perhaps, if real soldiers arrived, the assault would be possible, but until such a miracle happened Saltonstall would keep his precious fleet well outside the range of enemy cannons. By now the commodore had reached the hill's low summit where he took the telescope from his tail-pocket. He wanted to count the guns in Fort George and look for the telltale shimmer of heat coming from a shot-furnace.

He steadied the glass against a spruce. It took a moment to bring the lenses into focus, then he saw redcoats leaving the fort and straggling down the track into the village. He lifted the tubes to bring the fort into view. The glass was powerful, giving Saltonstall a close-up glimpse of a cannon firing. He saw the carriage jump and slam back, saw the eruption of smoke and watched the gunners close on the weapon to ready it for the next shot. He waited for the sound to reach him.

And heard musket-fire instead.

Captain Caffrae's men had not left the fort together, but instead had gone down to the village in small groups so that no rebel watching from the western heights would be forewarned that the company was deploying.

Caffrae assembled them by the Perkins's house where the new-born Temperance was crying. He inspected weapons, told his two drummers and three fifers to keep their instruments quiet, then led the company westwards. They kept to the paths that were hidden from the heights and so reached Aaron Banks's house where a large barn offered concealment. 'Take a picquet into the corn,' Caffrae ordered Lieutenant Moore, 'and I want no heroics, Mister Moore!'

'We're just there to watch,' John Moore said.

'To watch,' Caffrae confirmed, 'and to pray if you like, but not with your eyes closed.'

Moore took six men. They went past the barn and through a small turnip patch beside the house. Aaron Banks's two pretty daughters, Olive and Esther, stared wide-eyed from a window and Moore, seeing them, put a finger to his lips. Olive grinned and Esther nodded.

The picquet went into the concealing corn. 'No smoking,' Moore told his men because he did not want the telltale wisps of pipe smoke to reveal their presence. The men crouched and slid forward, trying their best not to disturb the tall stalks. Once at the field's western edge they lay still. Their job was to watch for any rebel movement that might threaten Caffrae's concealed men, though for now the rebels showed no sign of energy. Moore could clearly see sixteen militiamen at the Half Moon Battery. What enthusiasm they had shown for trenching had dissipated and they now sat in a group inside the old earthwork. A couple were fast asleep.

To Moore's left was Jacob Dyce's house while to his right, a hundred paces higher up the slope, was the Dutchman's cornfield. In front of him the long hill climbed to the distant bluff. There were men at the very top, evidently waiting to watch whatever drama occurred at the battery. The rebel guns were hidden among the trees beyond the skyline, but their noise pounded the afternoon and their smoke whitened the sky.

After a while Jacob Dyce came out of his house. He was a squat, middle-aged man with a prophet's beard. He carried a hoe that he now used to weed some beans. He worked slowly, gradually getting nearer and nearer to his neighbour's cornfield. 'De rascals are in my corn,' he suddenly spoke without looking up from his work. He stooped to tug at a weed. 'Lots of rascals hiding there. You hear me?' He still did not look towards Moore and his men.

'I hear you,' Moore said quietly, 'how many?'

'Lots,' the Dutchman said. He chopped the hoe's blade savagely. 'Lots! They are *de duivelsgebroed*!' He glanced briefly towards where Moore was hiding. '*De duivelsgebroed*!' he said again, then ambled back to his house.

Moore sent Corporal MacRae, a reliable man, to tell Caffrae that the devil's brood were indeed hiding uphill. Moore peered at the Dutchman's cornfield and thought he saw the stalks moving, but he could not be sure. Caffrae himself came to join Moore and peered up at the maize. 'The bastards want to take us in the flank,' he said.

'If we advance,' Moore said.

'Oh, we must advance,' Caffrae said wolfishly, 'why else did we come here?'

'There could be three hundred men hidden there,' Moore warned.

'Probably no more than a hundred who need a good thrashing.'

That was Brigadier McLean's tactic. Whenever the rebels attempted a manoeuvre they had to be slapped so hard that their morale fell even lower. McLean knew he was mostly opposed by militiamen and he had drummed that fact into his officers. 'You're professionals, you're soldiers,' he said repeatedly, 'and they're not. Make them scared of you! Think of them as fencibles.' The fencibles were the civilian soldiers in Britain, enthusiastic amateurs who, in McLean's view, merely played at soldiering. 'They may have their marines,' Moore warned now.

'Then we thrash them too,' Caffrae said confidently, 'or rather you will.'

'I will?'

'I'll bring the company forward and you command it. Advance on the battery, but watch your right. If they're there, they're going to charge you, so wheel when you're ready, give them a volley and counter-charge.'

Moore's heart gave a leap. He knew McLean must have suggested that Caffrae allow him to command the company, and he knew, too, that this was his chance for redemption. Do this right and he would be forgiven for his sins on the day the rebels landed.

'We'll do it noisily,' Caffrae said, 'with drums and squeals. Let 'em know we're the cocks on this dunghill.'

So what could go wrong? Moore supposed that it would be a disaster if the enemy did number a couple of hundred men, but what McLean would be watching for was evidence that Moore demonstrated good sense. His job was to smack the enemy, not win the war. 'Drums and squeals,' he said.

'And bayonets,' Caffrae said with a smile. 'And enjoy yourself, Lieutenant. I'll fetch the hounds, and you can flush the covert.'

It was time to dance.

The muskets were close, so close that Saltonstall involuntarily jumped in shock. He almost dropped the telescope.

At the foot of the hill, between him and the harbour, were redcoats. They were running in loose order. They had evidently fired a volley because the smoke lingered behind them. They had not stopped to reload, but now followed that volley with a bayonet charge, and Saltonstall understood that these men had to be the Royal Marines he had seen vanishing up the Majabigwaduce River. He had thought they must be foraging to the north, but instead they had landed on the river's eastern bank then worked their way southwards through the woods and now they drove off the men who had been making the battery on Haney's land. They were cheering. Sunlight glinted off their long bayonets. Saltonstall had a glimpse of his men running southwards, then the closest British marines saw the commodore at the hill's top and a half-dozen of them turned towards him. A musket banged and the ball skittered through the leaves.

Saltonstall ran. He went east down the hill, leaping the steeper sections, blundering through brush, pelting as fast as he could. A white-scutted deer ran ahead of him, alarmed by the shouts and shots. Saltonstall stumbled through a stream, cut southwards and kept running until he found a thick patch of undergrowth. There was a stitch in his left side, he was panting, and he crouched among the dark leaves and tried to calm himself.

His pursuers were silent. Or else they had abandoned the hunt. More muskets sounded, their distinctive crackling an unmistakable noise, but they seemed far away now, a wicked descant to the deeper bass rhythm of the big cannons beyond the harbour.

Saltonstall did not dare move till the light faded. Then, alone except for the cloud of mosquitoes, he worked his cautious way westwards. He went very slowly, ever alert to an enemy, though when he reached the harbour shore he saw that the redcoats were all gone.

And so were his longboats. He could see them. Every one had been captured and taken back to the enemy sloops. The British had not even bothered to slight the new earthworks of the battery Saltonstall's men had thrown up. They knew they could recapture it whenever they wished and leaving the low wall was an invitation to the rebels to return and be chased away again.

Saltonstall was stranded now. The enemy-filled harbour lay between him and his fleet, and no rescue would be coming. There was no choice but to walk. He recalled the chart in his cabin on board the *Warren* and knew that if he followed the harbour's shore he must eventually come back to the Penobscot River. Five miles? Maybe six, and the light was almost gone and the mosquitoes were feasting and the commodore was unhappy.

He started walking.

To the north, beyond the neck, Peleg Wadsworth had found a shelf of pastureland in Westcot's farm. He had not needed to make any earthworks to defend the shelf because it was edged by a sudden steep slope that was defence enough. Fifty militiamen, goaded and commanded by Captain Carnes of the marines, had manhandled one of Colonel Revere's eighteen-pounder cannon onto a lighter that had been rowed northwards. The gun was landed, then dragged over a mile through the woods until it reached the farm. There had been a few moments of worry when, shortly after Wadsworth and Carnes had discovered the site, four longboats filled with British marines had rowed up the Majabigwaduce River and Wadsworth had feared they would land close by, but instead they had gone to the farther bank of the river where they offered no threat to the big cannon that, at last, was dragged onto the pastureland. The militiamen had carried thirty rounds for the gun, which Carnes laid in the fading light. 'The barrel's cold,' he told the gun's crew, 'so she'll shoot a little low.'

The range looked much too long to Peleg Wadsworth's untutored eye. In front of him was a strip of shallow water and then the low marshy tail of Majabigwaduce's peninsula. The cannon was pointed across that tail at the British ships just visible in the harbour beyond. Carnes was aiming at the central sloop, HMS *Albany*, though Wadsworth doubted he could be sure of hitting any of the ships at such a distance.

Peleg Wadsworth walked a long way to the east until he was far enough from the big cannon to be sure that its smoke would not blot his view. He had borrowed Captain Carnes's

355

good telescope again and now he sat on the damp ground and propped his elbows on his knees to hold the long tubes steady. He saw a large group of empty longboats tethered to the *Albany* and a sailor leaning on the rail above. The sloop quivered every time she fired one of her cannon at the battery on Cross Island, which still kept up its harassing fire. The splintering sound of musketfire crackled far away, but Wadsworth resisted the temptation to swing the glass. If that was Lovell's ambush it would be hidden from him by the loom of the ridge. He kept watching the enemy sloop.

Carnes took a long time aiming the cannon, but at last he was satisfied. He had brought wooden pegs with him and he pushed three into the turf, one beside each wheel, and the third next to the gun's trail. 'If it's aimed right,' he told the crew, 'those pegs will guide us back. If it's wrong, we know where to start our corrections.' He warned the crew to step back and cover their ears. He blew on the tip of the linstock to brighten the glowing fuse, then leaned over to touch fire to the powder-filled reed thrust down the touch-hole.

The gun leaped back. Its thunder cracked the sky. Smoke jetted out beyond the shelf to spread across the nearer water. A flame curled and vanished inside the smoke. The noise was so sudden and loud that Wadsworth jumped and momentarily lost his focus, then he steadied the glass and found the *Albany* and saw a sailor smoking a pipe at the rail, and then, to his astonishment and joy, he saw the sailor leap back as a bright gouge of newly shattered timber showed in the sloop's hull just above the waterline. 'A direct hit!' he shouted. 'Captain! Well done! A direct hit!'

'Reload and run back!' Carnes shouted.

He was a marine. He did not miss.

Solomon Lovell thought his careful ambush must have failed. He waited and waited, and morning passed into afternoon, and the afternoon melded into the early evening, and still the British offered no challenge to the men who had occupied the deserted battery close to the harbour shore. A small crowd had gathered on the eastward side of Dyce's Head, many of them skippers of the anchored ships who had heard that the British were about to be given a thorough trouncing and so had rowed ashore to enjoy the spectacle. Commodore Saltonstall was not present, he had evidently gone to make a new battery on the harbour's farther shore and Peleg Wadsworth was similarly employed north and east of the neck. 'New batteries!' Lovell exulted to Major Todd, 'and a victory today! We shall be in a fine position tomorrow.'

Todd glanced south to where new ships might appear, but nothing showed in the river's seaward reach. 'General Wadsworth sent for an eighteen-pounder,' he told Lovell. 'It should have reached him by now.'

'Already?' Lovell asked, delighted. He felt that the whole expedition had turned a corner and hope was renewed. 'Now we only need McLean to snap at our bait,' Lovell said anxiously. He gazed down at the battery where the militiamen who were supposed to be pretending to raise a defensive rampart were instead sitting in the fading sunlight.

'He won't take the bait if we're all watching,' a harsh voice said.

Lovell turned to see Colonel Revere had come to the bluff. 'Colonel,' he said in wary greeting.

'You've got a crowd gawping up here like Boston nobs watching the town on Pope Night,' Revere said. He pointedly ignored Todd.

'Let us hope the destruction equals Pope Night,' Lovell responded genially. Every November 5th the townsfolk of Boston made giant effigies of the Pope, which were paraded through the streets. The supporters of the rival effigies fought each other, a superb brawl that left bones broken and skulls bloodied, and at the end the effigies were burned into the night as the erstwhile foes drank themselves insensible.

'McLean's not a fool,' Revere said. 'He'll know something's amiss with this crowd up here!'

Lovell feared his artillery commander was right, indeed the thought had already occurred to him that the presence of so many spectators might signal something extraordinary to the British, but he wanted these men to witness the success of the ambush. He needed word to spread through the army and the fleet that McLean's redcoats could be thrashed. The men seemed to have forgotten their great victory in taking the bluff, the whole expedition had become mired in pessimism and it needed to be whipped into enthusiasm again.

'So McLean's no fool, is he?' Todd asked caustically.

Because at the foot of the hill, between a barn and a cornfield, the redcoats had appeared.

And Solomon Lovell had his ambush.

'They're all yours, Mister Moore!' Captain Caffrae called. Fifty men, two drummer boys and three fifers were now Moore's responsibility. The company had formed just north of Jacob Dyce's house. They were in three ranks with the musicians behind. Caffrae, before leading his men from concealment, had ordered them to load their muskets and fix their bayonets. 'Let's hear the "British Grenadier"!' Moore called. 'Smartly now!'

The drums gave a roll, the fifers found the rhythm and began the sprightly tune. 'No man is to fire until I give the command!' Moore said to the company. He walked along the short front rank, then turned to see that the rebels in the Half Moon Battery had scrambled to their feet. They were watching him. He drew his sword and his heart gave a lurch as he heard the long blade scrape in the scabbard's throat. He was nervous and he was excited and he was frightened and he was elated. Captain Caffrae had positioned himself beside the musicians, ready no doubt to take over command of the company if Moore did the wrong thing. Or if he died,

Moore thought, and felt a lump in his throat. He suddenly needed to piss very badly. Oh God, he thought, let me not wet my breeches. He walked towards the company's right-hand side. 'We're going to drive those scoundrels away,' he said, trying to sound casual. He took post at the right and sloped his sword blade over his shoulder. 'Company will advance! By the right! March!'

The fifes played, the drums rattled and the redcoats went at a steady pace to trample down Jacob Dyce's newly weeded bean patch. The front rank held their muskets low, their bayonets making a line of glinting oiled steel. Guns boomed on the ridge above and other cannons crashed their sound across the harbour, but those conflicts seemed far away. Moore deliberately did not look to his right because he did not want to give the hidden rebels any hint that he knew they were present. He walked towards the Half Moon Battery and the handful of rebels there watched him come. One levelled a musket and fired, the ball flying high. 'You'll hold your fire!' Moore called to his men. 'Just drive them away with steel!'

The few rebels backed away. They were outnumbered by the advancing company and their orders were to draw the redcoats on till they could be trapped by McCobb's two hundred men hidden in the corn and so they retreated across the semi-circular rampart and up the slope beyond.

'Steady!' Moore called. He could not resist a quick glance to his right, but nothing moved on that higher ground. Had the rebels abandoned the idea of an ambush? Maybe the Dutchman had been wrong and there were no rebels hidden in the corn. A gun bellowed at the ridgetop to make a sudden cloud of smoke above which white gulls flew like paper scraps in a gale. Moore's mind was skittering like the gulls. What if there were two hundred rebels? Three hundred? What if the green-coated marines were there?

Then there was a shout from the right, the corn was being trampled, there were more shouts and Lieutenant Moore felt

359

a strange calm. 'Company will halt!' he heard himself call. 'Halt!' He turned his back on the enemy to look at his redcoats. They had kept their dressing and their ranks were orderly and tight. 'By the right!' he commanded loudly. 'Right wheel! Half!' He stood motionless while the three short ranks swung about like a gate until they faced northwards. Moore turned to look up the slope where, from out of the high corn, a horde of enemies was appearing. Dear God, Moore thought, but there were far more than he had expected. 'I want to hear the drum and fifes!' he shouted. 'Company will advance! By the right! March!'

And now go straight for them, he thought. No hesitation. If he hesitated then the enemy must smell his fear and that would give them courage. So just march with levelled bayonets and the "British Grenadier" filling the air with its defiance, and the enemy was in no order, just a mass of men appearing from the corn and too far away for a volley to have any effect and so Moore just marched up the slope towards them and the thought flickered through his mind that the enemy was far too numerous and his duty now was to retreat. Was that what McLean would want? Caffrae was offering no advice, and Moore sensed that he did not need to retreat. The enemy had begun to fire their muskets, but the range was still too long. A ball flicked through the grass beside Moore, another whipped overhead. One rebel shot his ramrod by mistake, the long rod circling in the air to fall on the grass. The enemy was obscured by patches of powder smoke that drifted back into the trampled maize, but Moore could see their disorganization. The rebels glanced left and right, looking to see what their friends did before they obeyed their officers' shrill cries. One man had white hair falling almost to his waist, another was white-bearded, and some looked like schoolboys given muskets. They were plainly nervous.

And suddenly Moore understood that the discipline of his men was a weapon in itself. The rebels, tired and hungry after a long day in the cornfield, were frightened. They did not see fifty equally nervous young men, they saw a red-coated killing machine. They saw confidence. And though they had burst out of the corn they had not charged down the hill, but were now being chivvied into ranks by officers and sergeants. They had made a mistake, Moore thought. They should have charged. Instead he was attacking and they were on the defensive, and it was time to frighten them even more. But not too close, Moore thought. He decided he would not wait till the enemy was inside easy musket range. Get too close and the enemy might realize just how easily his fifty men could be overwhelmed and so, when he gauged he was about eighty paces from the rebels, he called a halt.

'Front rank, kneel!' Moore shouted.

A man in the rear rank fell backwards, his face a sudden blossom of red where a musket ball had struck his cheek. 'Close ranks!' Caffrae called.

'Company!' Moore drew out the last syllable. He was watching the enemy. 'Take aim!' The muskets were levelled. The muzzles wavered slightly because the men were not accustomed to aiming while the heavy bayonets hung from the barrels. 'Fire!' Moore shouted.

The muskets flamed and smoked. Wadding, shot from the barrels, started small fires in the grass. The volley crashed into rebels and corn. 'Company will advance at the double!'

Moore would not waste time reloading. 'March!' There were bodies at the corn's edge. Blood in the evening. A man was crawling back into the high stalks to leave a trickle of blood on the grass. Smoke was thick as fog.

'Bayonets!' Moore shouted. It was not an order, for his men already had fixed bayonets, but rather a word to frighten an already frightened enemy. 'Scotland for ever!' he shouted, and his men cheered and hurried through the remnants of their own powder smoke. They were driven by drums, defiance and pride, and the rebels were running. The enemy militia were running back towards the bluff. All of them, like men running a race. Some even threw away their muskets so that they could run faster. No green uniforms, Moore noted. His Scotsmen were whooping, losing cohesion, and Moore wanted them to keep their discipline. 'Company will halt,' he shouted, 'halt!' His sharp voice checked the redcoats. 'Sergeant Mackenzie! Dress the ranks if you please. Let's at least try to look like His Majesty's soldiers, and not like His Majesty's royal ragamuffins!' Moore sounded stern, but he was grinning. He could not help it. His men were grinning too. They knew they had done well and the more experienced among them knew they had been well led. Moore waited for the ranks to be properly formed. 'Company will wheel to the left!' he called. 'By the left, left wheel, half!'

The Scotsmen were still grinning as they marched about to face the spectators who watched from Dyce's Head. Distant cheers sounded from Fort George. The slope ahead of Moore was full of rebels who ran, limped or walked away. The rebel dead or wounded, four men, lay sprawled on the grass. Moore put the point of his sword into the scabbard and thrust the blade home. He gazed up the slope. You bastards want our fort, he thought, then you just bloody well come and take it.

'Congratulations, Moore,' Caffrae said, but for once the courteous Moore did not offer a polite reply. He was in urgent need of something else and so he went to the edge of the Dutchman's corn, unbuttoned the flap of his breeches and pissed long and hard. The company laughed, and Moore felt happier than he had ever felt. He was a soldier.

Excerpts from General Solomon Lovell's Proclamation to his troops, August 12th, 1779:

We have now a Portion of our Enterprise to compleat, in which if we are successful, and I am confident we must be, being in superior numbers and having that Liberal Characteristic 'Sons of Liberty and Virtue' I again repeat, we must ride triumphant over the rough diabolical Torrent of Slavery, and the Monsters sent to rivet its Chains . . . Is there a man able to bear Arms in this camp? that would hide his Face in the day of Battle; is there an American of this Character? is there a man so destitute of Honor? . . . Let each man stand by his Officer, and each Officer animated, press forward to the Object in view, then shall we daunt the vaunting Enemy, who wishes to intimidate us by a little Parade, then shall we strike Terror to the Pride of Britain.

From a Despatch to Commodore Saltonstall from the Continental Navy Department, August 12th, 1779:

Our Apprehensions of your danger have ever been from a Reinforcement to the Enemy. You can't expect to remain much longer without one . . . It is therefore our orders that as soon as you receive this you take the Most Effectual Measures for the Capture or Destruction of the Enemies Ships and with the greatest dispatch the nature and Situation of things will Admit of.

From an Order In Council, Boston, August 8th, 1779:

Ordered that Thomas Cushing and Samuel Adams Esqrs be a Committee to wait upon the Capt of the French Frigate to know of him whether he should be willing to proceed to Penobscot with his Ship for the purpose of reinforcing the American fleet – who reported that they had waited upon his Excellency the Chevalier De la Luzerne who informed them that he would speak with the Capt of said Frigate and if possible influence his proceeding to Penobscot.

From a report received in Boston, August 9th, 1779:

Gilbert Richmond first Mate, of the Argo – declares that on the 6th Instant, off Marthas Vineyard – he fell in with eight sail of Vessels – supposed to be of force – steering So Et with a view of weathering the S. Shoal of Nantucket – The Commodore carried a poop light. The informant thinks – they were about 40 Miles So of the West end of the Vineyard.

TWELVE

And, suddenly, there was hope.

After the disappointment of the previous day, after the ignominious flight of the militia from an enemy force scarce a quarter its size, there was suddenly a new spirit, a second chance, an expectation of success.

Hoysteed Hacker was the cause. Captain Hacker was the tall naval captain who had captured HMS *Diligent*, and he was rowed ashore at first light and climbed to the clearing in the woods that served as Lovell's headquarters. 'The commodore has vanished,' he told Lovell who was taking breakfast at a trestle table.

'Vanished?' Lovell gazed up at the naval captain. 'How do you mean? Vanished?'

'Gone,' Hacker said in his expressionless, deep voice, 'vanished. He was with the sailors who were attacked yesterday, and I suppose he was captured.' Hacker paused. 'Maybe killed.' He shrugged as if he did not much care.

'Sit down, Captain. Have you eaten?'

'I've eaten.'

'Have some tea, at least. Wadsworth, did you hear this news?'

'I just did, sir.'

'Sit, do,' Lovell said. 'Filmer? A cup for Captain Hacker.'

Wadsworth and Todd were sharing the bench opposite Lovell. Hacker sat beside the general who gazed at the big, impassive naval officer as if he were Gabriel bringing news from heaven. Fog drifted through the high trees. 'Dear me,' Lovell finally comprehended the news, 'so the commodore is captured?' He did not sound in the least dismayed.

'Or killed,' Hacker said.

'Does that make you the senior naval officer?' Lovell asked.

'It does, sir.'

'How did it happen?' Wadsworth asked, and listened as Hacker described the unexpected attack by the British marines who had driven the sailors southwards from the battery on Haney's land. The commodore had been separated from the rest who had all made it safely back to the river's bank south of Cross Island. 'So no casualties?' Wadsworth asked.

'None, sir, except perhaps the commodore. He might have been hurt.'

'Or worse,' Lovell said, then added hastily, 'pray God it isn't so.'

'Pray God,' Hacker said equally dutifully.

Lovell flinched as he bit into some twice-baked bread. 'But you,' he asked, 'you are now in command of the fleet?'

'I reckon so, sir.'

'You've taken command of the *Warren*?' Wadsworth asked.

'Not formally, sir, no, but I'm the senior naval officer now, so I'll move to the *Warren* this morning.'

'Well, if you command the fleet,' Lovell said sternly, 'I must make a request of you.'

'Sir?' Hacker asked.

'I must ask you, Captain, to attack the enemy shipping.'

'That's why I came here,' Hacker said stolidly.

'You did?' Lovell seemed surprised.

'Seems to me, sir, we should attack soon. Today.' Hacker pulled a ragged piece of paper from his pocket and spread it on the table. 'Can I suggest a method, sir?'

'Please,' Lovell said.

The paper was a pencil-drawn chart of the harbour, which marked the enemy's four ships, though Hacker had put a cross over the hull of the *Saint Helena*, the transport that lay at the southern end of Mowat's line. She was only there to stop the Americans sailing around Mowat's flank and her armament of six small guns was too light to be a cause of concern. 'We have to attack the three sloops,' Hacker said, 'so I propose taking the *Warren* in to attack the *Albany*.' He tapped the chart, indicating the central sloop of Mowat's three warships. 'I'll be supported by the *General Putnam* and the *Hampden*. They'll anchor abreast of the *North* and *Nautilus*, sir, and give them fire. The *General Putnam* and *Hampden* will be hit hard, sir, it's unavoidable, but I believe the *Warren* will crush the *Albany* quickly enough and then we can use our heavy guns to force the surrender of the other two sloops.' Hacker spoke in an expressionless tone that gave the impression of a slow mind, an impression that Wadsworth realized was quite false. Hacker had given the problem a great deal of impressive thought. 'Now, sir,' the naval captain continued, 'the commodore's concern was always the fort and its guns. They can plunge shot down into our ships and for all we know they might have heated shot, sir.'

'Heated?' Lovell asked.

'Not a pleasant thought, sir,' Hacker said. 'If a red-hot shot lodges in a ship's timber, sir, it can start a fire. Ships and fire aren't the best of friends, so I want to keep the enemy's shots away from the leading ships as far as that's possible. I'm proposing that the *Sally, Vengeance, Black Prince, Hector, Monmouth, Sky Rocket* and *Hunter* should follow us into the harbour and make a line of battle here.' He indicated a dotted line that he had drawn parallel to the harbour's northern shore. 'They can shoot up at the fort, sir. They'll do little enough damage, but they should distract the enemy gunners, sir, and draw their fire away from the *Warren*, the *General Putnam* and *Hampden*.'

'This is feasible?' Lovell asked, scarcely daring to believe what he was hearing.

'Tide's right this afternoon,' Hacker said in a very matter-of-fact voice. 'I reckon it will take an hour and a half to get the first three ships into position and an hour's work to destroy their sloops. But I'm worried that we'll have the best part of our fleet in the harbour, sir, and even after we've taken the enemy vessels we'll still be under the cannons in their fort.'

'So you want us to attack the fort?' Wadsworth guessed.

'I think that's advisable, sir,' Hacker said respectfully, 'and I plan to put one hundred marines ashore, sir, to aid your endeavour. Might I suggest they occupy the lower ground with some of your militia?' He put a broad, tar-stained finger on the map, indicating the land between the fort and the British ships.

'Why that ground?' Lovell asked.

'To prevent the enemy's marines coming ashore from the defeated ships,' Hacker explained, 'and if our marines assault the fort from the south, sir, then the rest of your forces can attack from the west.'

'Yes,' Peleg Wadsworth said enthusiastically, 'yes!'

Lovell was silent. The fog was too thick to allow any gunner to shoot accurately so the cannons of both sides were quiet. A gull called. Lovell was remembering the shame of the previous day, the sight of McCobb's militia running away. He flinched at the memory.

'It will be different this time,' Wadsworth said. He had been watching Lovell's face and had divined the general's thoughts.

'In what manner?' Lovell asked.

'We've never used all our men to attack the fort, sir,' Wadsworth said. 'We've only attacked the enemy piecemeal. This time we use all our strength! How many cannon will we take into the harbour?' This question was put to Hoysteed Hacker.

'Those ships,' Hacker put a tar-stained finger on his chart, 'will carry over two hundred cannon, sir, so say a hundred guns in broadside.'

'A hundred cannon, sir,' Wadsworth said to Lovell. 'A hundred cannon filling the harbour! The noise alone will distract the enemy. And the marines, sir, leading the way. We hurl a thousand men against the enemy, all at once!'

'It should get the business done,' Hacker said in much the same tone he might have used to describe striking down a topmast or shifting a ton of ballast.

'A hundred marines,' Lovell said in a plaintive voice that made it clear he would have preferred to have all the marines ashore.

'I need some to board the enemy ships,' Hacker said.

'Of course, of course,' Lovell conceded.

'But the marines are begging for a good fight,' Hacker growled. 'They can't wait to prove themselves. And just as soon as the enemy ships are taken or destroyed, sir, I'll order the rest of the marines and every sailor I can spare to join your assault.'

'Ships and men, sir,' Wadsworth said, 'fighting as one.'

Lovell's gaze flicked uncertainly between Wadsworth and Hacker. 'And you think it can be done?' he asked the naval captain.

'Soon as the tide floods,' Hacker, said, 'which it will this afternoon.'

'Then let it be done!' Lovell decided. He planted both fists on the table. 'Let us finish the job! Let us take our victory!'

'Sir? Captain Hacker, sir?' A midshipman appeared at the edge of the clearing. 'Sir?'

'Boy!' Hacker acknowledged the breathless lad. 'What is it?'

'Commodore Saltonstall's compliments, sir, and will you return to the *Providence*, sir.'

The men at the table all stared at the boy. 'Commodore Saltonstall?' Lovell eventually broke the silence.

'He was discovered this morning, sir.'

'Discovered?' Lovell asked in a hollow voice.

'On the river bank, sir!' The midshipman appeared to believe he had brought good news. 'He's safe on board the *Warren*, sir.'

'Tell him . . . ' Lovell said, then could not think what he wanted to say to Saltonstall.

'Sir?'

'Nothing, lad, nothing.'

Hoysteed Hacker slowly crumpled the hand-drawn chart and tossed it onto the camp-fire. The first gun of the new day fired.

Lieutenant John Moore, paymaster to His Majesty's 82nd Regiment of Foot, knocked nervously on the house door. A cat watched him from the log pile. Three chickens, carefully penned by laced withies, clucked at him. In the garden of the next door house, the one nearer the harbour, a woman beat a rug that was hanging from a line suspended between two trees. She watched him as suspiciously as the cat. Moore raised his hat to the woman, but she turned away from the courtesy and beat dust from the rug even more energetically. A gun fired from the fort, its sound muffled by the trees surrounding the small log houses.

Bethany Fletcher opened the door. She was wearing a shabby brown dress beneath a white apron on which she wiped her hands, which were red from scrubbing clothes. Her hair was disarrayed and John Moore thought she was beautiful. 'Lieutenant,' she said in surprise, blinking in the daylight.

'Miss Fletcher,' Moore said, bowing and removing his hat.

'You bring news?' Beth asked, suddenly anxious.

'No,' Moore said, 'no news. I brought you this.' He held a basket towards her. 'It's from General McLean, with his compliments.' The basket contained a ham, a small bag of salt and a bottle of wine.

'Why?' Beth asked, without taking the gift.

'The general is fond of you,' Moore said. He had discovered the courage to face four times as many rebels as the men he led, but he had no courage to add 'as am I'. 'He knows life is hard for you and your mother, Miss Fletcher,' he explained instead, 'especially with your brother absent.'

'Yes,' Beth said, but still did not take the proffered gift. She had never refused the simpler rations offered by the garrison to the inhabitants of Majabigwaduce, the flour, salted beef, dried peas, rice and spruce beer, but McLean's generosity embarrassed her. She walked a few paces further from the house so that her neighbour could see her clearly. She wanted to give no excuse for any gossip.

'The wine is port wine,' Moore said. 'Have you ever tasted port wine?'

'No,' Beth said, flustered.

'It is stronger than claret,' Moore said, 'and sweeter. The general is fond of it. He served in Portugal and acquired a taste for the wine which is said to be a tonic. My father is a doctor and he frequently prescribes port wine. Can I put it here?' Moore placed the basket on the threshold of the house. Inside, beyond an open inner door, he had a glimpse of Beth's mother. Her face was sunken, still and white, her open mouth dark, and her hair straggling white on a pillow. She looked like a corpse and Moore turned away quickly. 'There,' he said, for lack of anything else to say.

Beth shook her head. 'I cannot accept the gift, Lieutenant,' she said.

'Of course you can, Miss Fletcher,' Moore said with a smile.

'The general would not . . . ' Beth began, then evidently thought better of whatever she had been about to say and checked herself. She brushed away a stray lock of hair and tucked it under her cap. She looked anywhere but at Moore.

'General McLean would be hurt if you refused the gift,' Moore said.

'I'm grateful to him,' Beth said, 'but . . . ' Again she fell silent.

371

She took a thimble from the pocket of her apron and turned it in her fingers. She shrugged. 'But . . . ' she said again, still not looking at Moore.

'But your brother fights for the rebels,' Moore said.

She turned her eyes on him, and those eyes widened with surprise. Blue eyes, Moore noted, blue eyes of extraordinary vitality. 'The general knows?' she asked.

'That your brother fights for the rebels? Yes, of course he knows,' Moore said with a reassuring smile. He stooped and recovered the thimble, which had fallen from her hands. He held it out to her, but Beth made no move to take it and so, very deliberately, he placed it in the basket. Beth turned to look at the harbour through the trees. The fog was gone and Majabigwaduce's water sparkled beneath a summer sun. She stayed silent. 'Miss Fletcher . . .' Moore began.

'No!' she interrupted him. 'No, I can't accept.'

'It is a gift,' Moore said, 'nothing more, nothing less.'

Beth bit her lower lip, then turned defiantly back to the red-coated lieutenant. 'I wanted James to join the rebels,' she said, 'I encouraged him! I carried news of your guns and men to Captain Brewer! I betrayed you! Do you think the general would offer me a gift if he knew I'd done all that? Do you?'

'Yes,' Moore said.

That answer startled her. She seemed to crumple and crossed to the log pile where she sat and absent-mindedly stroked the cat. 'I didn't know what to think when you all came here,' she said. 'It was exciting at first.' She paused, thinking. 'It was new and different, but then there were just too many uniforms here. This is our home, not yours. You took our home away from us.' She looked at him for the first time since she had sat down. 'You took our home away from us,' she said again.

'I'm sorry,' Moore said, not knowing what else to say.

She nodded.

'Take the gift,' Moore said, 'please.'

'Why?'

'Because the general is a decent man, Miss Fletcher. Because he offers it as a token of friendship. Because he wants you to know that you can depend on his protection whatever your opinion. Because I don't want to carry the basket back to the fort.' Beth smiled at that last reason and Moore stood, waiting. He could have added that the gift had been given because McLean was as vulnerable as any other man to a fair-haired girl with an enchanting smile, but instead he just shrugged. 'Because,' he finished.

'Because?'

'Please accept it,' Moore said.

Beth nodded again, then wiped her eyes with a corner of the apron. 'Thank the general from me.'

'I will.'

She stood and crossed to the door where she turned. 'Goodbye, Lieutenant,' she said, then picked up the basket and was gone inside.

'Goodbye, Miss Fletcher,' Moore said to the closed door.

He walked slowly back to the fort and felt defeated.

The three ships dipped to the wind, they swooped on the long waves, the seas broke white at their cutwaters, their sails were taut and the wind was brisk at their sterns. Away to port was Cape Anne where the breakers fretted at the rocks. 'We must stay inshore,' Captain Abraham Burroughs told Colonel Henry Jackson.

'Why?'

'Because the bastards are out there somewhere,' the captain said, nodding to starboard where the fog bank had retreated south-eastwards to lie like a long dun cloud over the endless ocean. 'We run into a British frigate, Colonel, and you can say goodbye to your regiment. If I see a frigate out there I run for port.' He waved a hand at the other two ships. 'We ain't men-of-war, we're three transports.'

But the three transport ships carried Henry Jackson's regiment, as fine a regiment as any in the world, and it was on its way to Majabigwaduce.

And in the distant fog, out to sea, in a place where there were no marks, a fishing boat from Cape Cod watched other ships loom from the whiteness. The fishermen feared the big vessels would capture them, or at least steal their catch, but not one of the British ships bothered with the small gaff-rigged fishing boat. One by one the great ships slid past, the bright paint on their figureheads and the gilding on their sterns dulled by the fog. They all flew blue ensigns.

The vast *Raisonable* led, followed by five frigates; the *Virginia*, the *Blonde*, the *Greyhound*, the *Galatea* and the *Camille*. The last of the relief fleet, the diminutive *Otter*, had lost touch and was somewhere to the south and east, but her absence scarcely diminished the raw power of Sir George Collier's warships. The fishermen watched in silence as the blunt-bowed battleship and her five frigates ghosted past. They could smell the stench of the fleet and the stink of hundreds of men crammed into the cannon-freighted hulls. One hundred and ninety-six cannon, some of them ship-slaughtering thirty-two-pounders, were on their way to Majabigwaduce.

'Sons of goddamned bastard bitches,' the fishing boat's captain spat when the *Camille*'s gilded stern gallery had been swallowed by the fog.

And the ocean was empty again.

The rebels had been in Penobscot Bay for nineteen days, and in possession of the high ground for sixteen of those days. There had been more than twenty Councils of War, some just for the naval captains, some for the senior army officers and a few for both. Votes had been taken, motions had been passed, and still the enemy was neither captivated nor killed.

The resurrection and return of the commodore had dampened Lovell's spirits. Of late he and Saltonstall had only communicated by letter, but Lovell thought it incumbent on him to visit the *Warren* and congratulate Saltonstall on his survival, though the commodore, whose long face was blotched red with mosquito bites, did not appear grateful for the general's concern. 'It is a providence of God that you were spared capture or worse,' Lovell said awkwardly.

Saltonstall grunted.

Lovell nervously broached the subject of entering the harbour. 'Captain Hacker was hopeful . . .' he began.

'I am aware of Hacker's sentiments,' Saltonstall interrupted.

'He thought the manoeuvre feasible,' Lovell said.

'He may think what he damn well likes,' Saltonstall said hotly, 'but I'm not taking my ships into that damned hole.'

'And unless the ships are taken,' Lovell forged on anyway, 'I do not think the fort can be attacked with any hope of success.'

'You may depend upon one thing, General,' Saltonstall said, 'which is that my ships cannot be risked in the harbour while the fort remains in enemy hands.'

The two men stared at each other. The guns were at work again, though the rebel rate of fire was much slower now because of the shortage of ammunition. There was powder smoke at Cross Island, and on the heights of Majabigwaduce and across the inlet north of the peninsula. Even more smoke rose from the low ground close to the Half Moon Battery. Lovell, angered that the Banks's house and barn had provided cover for the Scottish troops that had driven his men away so ignominiously, had ordered that the buildings should be burned as a punishment. 'And the Dutchman's house too,' he had insisted, and so forty men had gone downhill at first light and set fire to the houses and barns. They had not lingered on the low ground, fearing a counter-attack by McLean's men, but had just set the fires and retreated again.

'I shall present the circumstances to my officers,' Lovell

now said stiffly, 'and we shall discuss the feasibility of an attack on the fort. You may depend upon it that I shall convey their decision to you promptly.'

Saltonstall nodded. 'My compliments, General.'

That afternoon Lovell went to the *Hazard*, one of the ships belonging to the Massachusetts Navy and from where he summoned his brigade majors, the commanders of the militia, Colonel Revere and General Wadsworth. The Council of War would be held in the comfort of the brig's stern cabin where gawking soldiers could not linger nearby to overhear the discussions. Captain John Williams, the *Hazard*'s commanding officer, had been invited to attend as a courtesy and Lovell asked him to explain the navy's reluctance to enter the harbour. 'Not everyone's reluctant,' Williams said, thinking of his own first lieutenant, George Little, who was ready to mutiny if that meant he could sail the diminutive brig into Majabigwaduce's harbour and take on the British. 'But the commodore is being prudent.'

'In what way?' Wadsworth asked.

'You can get a ship in easy enough,' Williams said, 'but it would be a devilish business to get her out again.'

'The object,' Wadsworth pointed out quietly, 'is to stay in the harbour. To occupy it.'

'Which means you have to destroy those guns in the fort,' Williams said, 'and there's another thing. The fleet is running short of men.'

'We impressed men in Boston!' Lovell complained.

'And they're deserting, sir,' Williams said. 'And the privateer captains? They're not happy. Every day they spend here is a day they can't capture prizes at sea. They're talking of leaving.'

'Why did we bring all these ships?' Wadsworth asked. He had put the question to Williams, who just shrugged. 'We brought a fleet of warships and we don't use them?' Wadsworth asked more heatedly.

'You must put that question to the commodore,' Williams said evenly. There was silence, broken only by the endless clanking of the *Hazard*'s pump. The damage the brig had taken when Lieutenant Little had sailed her so close to Mowat's sloops was still not properly repaired. The brig would need to be hauled ashore for those timbers to be replaced, caulked and made tight, but the pump was keeping her afloat easily enough.

'So we must capture the fort,' Peleg Wadsworth said, breaking the gloomy silence, and then overrode the chorus of voices that complained that such a feat was impossible. 'We must take men to the rear of the fort,' he explained, 'and assault from the south and east. The walls there are unfinished and the eastern rampart, so far as I can see, has no cannon.'

'Your men won't attack,' Revere said scornfully. For a week now, in every Council of War, Lieutenant-Colonel Revere had urged abandonment of the siege, and now he pressed the point. 'The men won't face the enemy! We saw that yesterday. Three-quarters of the small arms cartridges have gone and half the men are hiding in the woods!'

'So you'd run away?' Wadsworth asked.

'No one accuses me of running away!'

'Then, damn it, stay and fight!' Wadsworth's anger at last exploded and his use of a swear word alone was sufficient to silence the whole cabin. 'Goddamn it!' he shouted the words and hammered Captain Williams's table so hard that a pewter candlestick fell over. Men stared at him in astonishment, and Wadsworth surprised even himself by his sudden vehemence and coarse language. He tried to calm his temper, but it was still running high. 'Why are we here?' he demanded. 'Not to build batteries or shoot at ships! We're here to capture their fort!'

'But . . .' Lovell began.

'We demand marines of the commodore,' Wadsworth overrode his commanding officer, 'and we assemble every man, and we attack! We attack!' He looked around the cabin, seeing

377

the scepticism on too many faces. Those who favoured aban-donment of the expedition, led by Colonel Revere, were fervent in their view, while those still willing to prosecute the siege were at best lukewarm. 'The commodore,' Wadsworth went on, 'is unwilling to enter the harbour while the guns are there to harass his shipping. So we assure him that we will silence the guns. We will take men to the rear of the enemy's work and we shall attack! And the commodore will support us.'

'The commodore . . .' Lovell began.

Wadsworth again interrupted him. 'We have never offered the commodore our whole-hearted support,' he said emphati-cally. 'We've asked him to destroy the ships before we attack and he has asked us to destroy the fort before the attacks. Then why not make a compromise? We both attack. If he knows our land force is making an assault then he will have no choice but to support us!'

'Perhaps the regular troops will arrive,' McCobb put in.

'The *Diligent* has sent no word,' Lovell said. The *Diligent*, the fast Continental Navy brig captured from the British, had been posted at the mouth of the Penobscot River to serve as a guard boat that could give warning of the approach of any shipping, but her captain, Philip Brown, had sent no messages, which suggested to Lovell that any reinforcements, for either side, were at least a day away.

'We can't wait to see if Boston sends us troops,' Wadsworth insisted, 'and besides, British reinforcements are just as likely! We were sent here to perform a task, so for God's sake, let us do it! And do it now before the enemy is strengthened.'

'I doubt we can do it now,' Lovell said, 'tomorrow, maybe?'

'Then tomorrow!' Wadsworth said, exasperated. 'But let us do it! Let us do what we came here to do, to do what our country expects of us! Let us do it!'

There was silence, broken by Lovell who looked brightly about the cabin. 'We certainly have something to discuss,' he said.

'And let us not discuss it,' Wadsworth said harshly, 'but make a decision.'

Lovell looked startled at his deputy's forcefulness. For a moment it seemed as if he would try to wrest back the command of the cabin, but Wadsworth's face was grim and Lovell acceded to the demand. 'Very well,' he said stiffly, 'we shall make a decision. Would all those in favour of General Wadsworth's proposal please so indicate now?' Wadsworth's hand shot up. Lovell hesitated, then raised his own hand. Other men followed Lovell's lead, even those who usually supported an end to the siege. All but one.

'And those opposed?' Lovell asked. Lieutenant-Colonel Revere raised his hand.

'I declare the motion carried,' Lovell said, 'and we shall beg the commodore to support us in an attack tomorrow.'

The next day would be Friday, August the thirteenth.

Friday the thirteenth dawned fair. The wind was light and there was no fog, which meant the rebel battery on Cross Island opened fire at first light, as did the more distant eighteen-pounder on the northern shore beyond the peninsula. The balls slammed hard into the hulls of the British sloops.

Captain Mowat was resigned to the bombardment. He had moved his ships twice, but there was no other anchorage to which he could retreat now, not unless he moved the sloops far away from the fort. The pumps on all three sloops worked continually, manned by sailors who chanted shanties as they drove the great handles up and down. The *Albany*'s carpenter was patching the hull as well as he was able, but the big eighteen-pounder shots tore up the oak planking with savage force. 'I'll keep her afloat, sir,' the carpenter promised Mowat at dawn. He had plugged three horrible gashes at the sloop's waterline, but a proper repair would have to wait till the sloop could be beached or docked.

'Luckily they're still shooting high,' Mowat said.

'Pray God they go on doing that, sir.'

'I hope you are bloody praying!' Mowat said.

'Day and night, sir, night and day.' The carpenter was a Methodist and kept a well-thumbed copy of the Bible in his carpenter's apron. He frowned as a rebel ball struck the taffrail and showered splinters across the afterdeck. 'I'll mend the topsides when we've done the lower strakes, sir.'

'Topsides can wait,' Mowat said. He did not care how ragged his ship looked so long as she floated and could carry her guns. Those guns were silent for now. Mowat reckoned his nine-pounders could do little damage to the battery on Cross Island and none of his guns was powerful enough to reach the new battery to the north and so he did not waste powder and shot on the rebels. One of Captain Fielding's twelve-pounders, up at the fort, slammed shots into Cross Island, a fire that merely served to keep the rebels hidden deep among the trees. A crackle of muskets sounded ashore. In the last few days that noise had been constant as McLean's men infiltrated the trees by the neck or else hunted through the fields and barns of the settlement in search of rebel patrols. They were doing it without orders and McLean, though he approved the sentiments behind such rebel hunting, had commanded that it be stopped. Mowat guessed that the flurry of shots came from Captain Caffrae's Light Company, which had kept up its harassment of the enemy lines.

'Deck ahoy!' a lookout called from the foremast. 'Swimmer!'

'Do we have a man overboard?' Mowat demanded of the officer of the watch.

'No, sir.'

Mowat went forrard to see that a man was indeed swimming towards the *Albany* from the direction of the harbour mouth. He looked exhausted. He swam a few strokes, then trod water before feebly trying to swim again, and Mowat shouted at the bosun to heave the man a line. It took a moment for the man to find the line, then he was hauled to the sloop's side and dragged up on deck. He was a seaman with a long pigtail hanging down his bare back and pictures of whales and anchors tattooed onto his chest and forearms. He stood dripping and then, exhausted and shivering, sat on one of the nine-pounder trucks. 'What's your name, sailor?' Mowat asked.

'Freeman, sir, Malachi Freeman.'

'Fetch him a blanket,' Mowat ordered, 'and some tea. Put a tot of rum in the tea. Where are you from, Freeman?'

'Nantucket, sir.'

'A fine place,' Mowat said. 'So what brought you here?'

'I was pressed, sir. Pressed in Boston.'

'Onto what vessel?'

'The *Warren*, sir.'

Freeman was a young man, scarce twenty years old Mowat judged, and he had swum from the *Warren* in the night's dark. He had reached the beach beneath Dyce's Head where he had shivered and waited for the guard boats to retreat in the dawn. Then he had swum for the sloops.

'What are you, Freeman?' Mowat asked. He saw how Freeman's hands were stained black from continually climbing tarred rigging. 'A topman?'

'Aye aye, sir, four years now.'

'His Majesty always appreciates a good topman,' Mowat said, 'and are you willing to serve His Majesty?'

'Aye aye, sir.'

'We'll swear you in,' Mowat said, then waited as a blanket was draped about the deserter's shoulders and a can of hot rum-laced tea thrust into his hands. 'Drink that first.'

'They're coming for you, sir,' Freeman said, his teeth chattering.

'Coming for me?'

'The commodore is, sir. He's coming today, sir. They told us last night. And he's making bulwarks on the *Warren*'s bow, sir.'

'Bulwarks?'

'They're strengthening the bows, sir, and putting three layers of logs across the focsle, sir, to protect the marines.'

Mowat looked at the shivering man. He played with the idea that the rebels had sent Freeman with deliberately misleading information, but that made little sense. If Saltonstall wished to mislead Mowat he would surely pretend he was withdrawing, not attacking. So the rebels were coming at last? Mowat gazed westwards to where he could just see the anchored warships beyond Dyce's Head. 'How many ships will come?' he asked.

'Don't know, sir.'

'I don't suppose you do,' Mowat said. He walked to the main shrouds and propped a glass on one of the ratlines. Sure enough he could see men working on the bows of the *Warren*. They appeared to be roving new lines to the bowsprit, while others were hauling logs up from a longboat. So, at long last, they were coming? 'It won't be till the afternoon flood,' he said to his first lieutenant.

'That gives us most of the day to get ready, sir.'

'Aye, it does.' Mowat collapsed the glass and looked up at the sky. 'The glass?' he asked.

'Still falling, sir.'

'So there's dirty weather coming as well, then,' Mowat said. The sky was pellucid now, but he reckoned there would be clouds, fog and rain before nightfall by when, he knew, he would either be dead or captured. He was under no illusions. His small flotilla could do grievous damage to the American ships, but he could not defeat them. Once the *Warren* turned her broadside onto the sloops she could pound them with guns that were twice as heavy as the British cannon, and defeat was inevitable. The *Warren* would be hurt, but the *Albany* would die. That was unavoidable, so the most Mowat could hope for was to hurt the *Warren* badly, then get his men safe on land where they could help McLean defend the fort. 'All marines are to be brought back aboard,' he told his first lieutenant, 'and all guns double-shotted. Sand the decks. Tell the surgeon to sharpen his damn knives. We'll go down snarling, but by God, they'll know they've been fighting against the Royal Navy.'

Then he sent a message to McLean.

The rebels are coming.

Peleg Wadsworth asked for volunteers. The militia, in truth, had been disappointing and, except for the first day ashore when they had climbed the bluff to throw back the strong enemy picquet, they had not fought with spirit. But that did not mean there were no brave men among them, and Wadsworth only wanted the brave. He walked around the woods and talked to groups of men, he spoke to the picquets manning the earthworks that edged the woods, and he told all of them what he planned. 'We're going along the harbour shore,' he said, 'and once we're behind the enemy, between him and his ships, we shall make an assault. We won't be alone. The commodore will enter the harbour and fight the enemy, and his ships will bombard the fort while we attack. I need men willing to make that attack, men willing to climb the hill with me and storm the enemy ramparts. I need brave men.'

Four hundred and forty-four men volunteered. They assembled among the trees at the top of Dyce's Head where Lieutenant Downs and fifty marines waited, and where Wadsworth divided the militia volunteers into four companies. The Indian braves formed their own small company. It was early afternoon. The day had dawned so bright, but now the sky clouded and a late fog drifted up the sea-reach.

'The fog will help hide us,' Wadsworth remarked.

'So God is an American,' Lieutenant Downs said, making Wadsworth smile, then the marine lieutenant looked past Wadsworth. 'General Lovell coming, sir,' he said softly.

Wadsworth turned to see Solomon Lovell and Major Todd approaching. Was this bad news? Had Commodore Saltonstall changed his mind? 'Sir,' he greeted the general cautiously.

Lovell looked pale and drawn. 'I have decided,' he said slowly, 'that I should go with you.'

Wadsworth hesitated. He had thought to lead this attack and that Lovell would make a separate advance with the remaining men along the ridge's spine, but something in Lovell's face told him to accept the older man's decision. Lovell wanted to be in this assault because he needed to prove to himself he had done all that he could. Or perhaps, Wadsworth thought less generously, Lovell had an eye to posterity and knew that fame would attend the man who led the successful assault on Fort George. 'Of course, sir,' he said.

Lovell looked heartbroken. 'I just ordered the big guns off the heights,' he said, gesturing north towards the woods where Revere's cannon had been emplaced.

'You ordered . . .' Wadsworth began in puzzlement.

'There's no ammunition,' Lovell interrupted him bleakly.

Wadsworth was about to point out that more ammunition could be supplied, if not from Boston then perhaps from the *Warren*'s magazine, then he understood why Lovell had given the apparently defeatist order to remove the guns. It was because the general at last understood that this was the rebels' final chance. If this attack failed then nothing else would work, at least not till American reinforcements arrived and, until that day, there would be no more need of heavy guns. 'Colonel McCobb and Colonel Mitchell will lead the attack along the ridge,' Lovell went on. Neither Lovell nor Wadsworth expected much from the second attack, which would be made by the men who had not volunteered, yet their visible presence on the ridge must keep some British defenders on the western side of their fort, and that was why the second attack was planned.

'We're honoured you're here, sir,' Wadsworth said generously.

'I won't interfere with your deployments,' Lovell promised.

Wadsworth smiled. 'We're all at God's mercy now, sir.'

And if God was merciful the rebels would go down the long hill in full sight of the fort and under the fire of its cannons. They would pass the smoking remnants of the burned houses and barns, then make their way through cornfields and orchards, and through the small yards where vegetables grew. Once sheltered by the village they would make for a group of houses that lay between the fort and the British ships, and there Wadsworth would wait until the commodore's attack diverted the fort's defenders and filled the harbour with noise, smoke and flame.

With the marines and Indians added to his force Wadsworth now led five hundred men. The best men. Was it enough? McLean had at least seven hundred in the fort, but the troops led by Colonel McCobb and Colonel Mitchell would keep some of those defenders facing west, and once the British ships were taken or sunk the rest of the American marines would come ashore. The numbers would be about equal, Wadsworth thought, then decided that he could not win this battle by an exercise of mental arithmetic. He could plan his moves as far as the harbour's edge, but after that the devil would roll his dice and it would be smoke and flame, screams and steel, the chaos of anger and terror, and what use was mathematics then? If Wadsworth's grandchildren were to learn of this day and of this victory they must learn of courage and of men doing a great deed. And if the deed was not great it would not be memorable. So at some point he must let go of calculation and throw himself on anger and resolve. There was no easy way. Both Lovell and Saltonstall had shirked the fight because they sought a sure solution, and no such easy answer existed. The expedition would only succeed when it rose above prudence and challenged men to perform great deeds. So yes, he thought, five hundred men was enough, because that was all he had to do this thing, and this thing had to be done in the name of American liberty. 'James?' he spoke to Fletcher. 'Let's go.'

Forty of the volunteers were manning drag-ropes attached to two of the four-pounder cannons that, so far, had scarcely been used. They were too small to be effective at anything except close range, but on this day they might be battle-winners. Lieutenant Marett, one of Revere's officers, commanded the two pieces that had an ample supply of round shot, though Captain Carnes, before returning to the *General Putnam*, had insisted that the two small guns were also equipped with grape. He had made the missiles himself, collecting stones from the beach that the *General Putnam*'s sailors had sewn into rough bags of sail canvas. The bags could be rammed on top of a round shot so that when the guns were fired the stones would spread like lethal duckshot. Lieutenant Marett had nervously protested that the stones would ruin the guns' barrels, but had fallen silent under Carnes's baleful stare. 'Damn the barrels,' Carnes had said, 'it's the ruin they'll do to British guts that matters.'

The first tendrils of fog curled over the slope as the men went down to the shore. They went in open order, hurrying across the meadows and through the scattered trees. A round shot fired from Fort George gouged a scar across grassland. A second gun fired, then a third, but all the balls ricocheted harmlessly from the ground. That was a good omen, Wadsworth thought, and was surprised that he sought omens. He had prayed in the dawn. He liked to think that faith and prayer were sufficient to themselves, and that he was now in God's hands, but he found himself watching every phenomena for any sign that this attack would succeed. The British sloops, though their guns would bear on the harbour shore, did not fire and that was surely the hand of provi-dence. The smoke from the burning houses was blown towards Fort George and, though Wadsworth's rational mind told him that was merely because the wind persisted from the south-west, he wanted to believe it was a sign that God desired to blind and choke the enemy. He saw six of the Indians crouching beside the cornfield where he had ordered the men to gather. They formed a circle, their dark heads close together, and he wondered what God they prayed to. He remembered a man named Eliphalet Jenkins who had founded a mission to the Wampanoag tribe and whose body, gutted empty by knives and blanched pale by the sea, had been washed ashore at Fairhaven. Why was he remembering that old tale? And then he thought of the story James Fletcher had told him about a man and boy, both English, who many years before had been gelded then burned alive by the Indians of Majabigwaduce. Was that another omen?

The two guns arrived safely. Each was attached to a caisson that held their ammunition and on the nearer of those wagons was painted a slogan, 'Liberty or Death'. That was easily said, Wadsworth thought, but death seemed more imminent now. Imminent and immanent. The words batted in his head. Why did the enemy sloops not fire? Were they asleep? A shell from the fort landed in the smouldering remnants of Jacob Dyce's house and exploded harmlessly with a dull, impotent boom and an eruption of ash and smouldering timbers. Imminent, immanent and impotent. For some reason Wadsworth thought of a text that had been the foundation of a sermon that the Reverend Jonathan Murray had preached on the first Sunday after the expedition had landed, 'where the worm dieth not and the fire is not quenched'. The worm, Murray said, was the evil of British tyranny and the fire the righteous anger of men who fought for liberty. But why did we burn these houses, Wadsworth wondered, and how many men of Majabigwaduce had been enraged by that arson and, even now, manned the ramparts of the fort? 'The worm will shrivel,' Murray had promised, 'it will shrivel and hiss as it burns!' Yet the scripture,

Wadsworth thought, did not promise that punishment, only that the worm dieth not. Was that an omen?

'Do we go on, sir?' Fletcher asked.

'Yes, yes.'

'You look as if you're dreaming, sir,' Fletcher said, grinning.

'I was wondering how many civilians will be helping the garrison.'

'Oh, some will,' Fletcher said dismissively. 'Old Jacob for one, but he can't shoot straight. Doctor Calef, of course.'

'I knew Calef in Boston,' Wadsworth said.

'He's not a bad fellow. A bit pompous. But he'll be doctoring, not soldiering.'

'On we go,' Wadsworth said, and it seemed unreal now. The ships still did not fire and the bombardment from the fort fell silent because the Americans were on the low ground and protected from the guns on the fort's southern wall by a shoulder of land that ran parallel to the ridge. They were concealed too by houses, cornfields and trees. Lilies blossomed in yards. A woman hurriedly took in some drying washing because the sky was still darkening and promised rain. The marines, in a double file, advanced on the left ready to turn and oppose any sally by the fort's garrison, but McLean sent none. A chained dog barked at the passing soldiers until a woman called for it to be silent. Wadsworth looked up to his left, but all he could see of the fort was the slow-stirring flag at the top of its pole. He crossed the newly made track that led from the beach to the fort's gate. If I were McLean, Wadsworth thought, I would send men down to fight, but the Scotsman did no such thing, nor did Mowat fire from his sloops, though he must be seeing the rebels file through the settlement. 'He's not going to waste shot on us,' Lieutenant Downs suggested when Wadsworth expressed surprise that the British ships had been silent.

'Because we can't hurt him?'

'Because he's double-shotted his guns to welcome our ships. That's all he's worried about, sir, the ships.'

'He can't know they're planning to attack him,' Wadsworth pointed out.

'If they saw our focsle's being strengthened,' Downs said, 'they'll have guessed.'

And suppose the ships did not come? Saltonstall had very reluctantly agreed to make an attack, and suppose he changed his mind? Wadsworth's men were now in line with the ships, meaning they were between Mowat and McLean, and Wadsworth could see the red uniforms of the Royal Marines on the deck of HMS *North*. The fog was thickening and a first slow spatter of rain fell.

Then a fair-haired girl came running from a house to throw her arms around James Fletcher's neck, and Wadsworth knew they had arrived. He ordered the two guns to face the harbour, their job to open fire if any Royal Marines came from the ships. The rest of his men crouched in yards and orchards. They were a quarter-mile from the fort's south-eastern bastion and hidden from it by a large cornfield. They were in place. They were ready. If McLean could see them he took no apparent heed because none of the fort's guns fired, while the sloops' broadsides were now facing well away from the rebels. We go uphill from here, Wadsworth thought. Through the cornfield and across the open ground and over the ditch and up the wall and so to victory, and that sounded easy, but there would be round shot and grapeshot, screams and blood, smoke and volleys, death squirming in agony, men shrieking, steel slithering in guts, shit-soiled breeches and the devil laughing as he rattled his dice.

'They know we're here,' Solomon Lovell had not spoken since they left the high ground, but now, looking up at the flag flying above the fort, he sounded nervous.

'They know,' Wadsworth said. 'Captain Burke!' William Burke, the skipper of the privateer *Sky Rocket*, had come with the soldiers and his duty now was to return and tell Commodore Saltonstall that the assault force was in position. Saltonstall had insisted that a seaman carry him that news, an insistence that amused Wadsworth because it suggested the naval officer did not trust the army. 'Are you satisfied we're in position, Mister Burke?' Wadsworth asked.

'I'm well satisfied, General.'

'Then pray tell the commodore we shall attack as soon as he opens fire.'

'Aye aye, sir,' Burke said, and set off westwards, escorted by four militiamen. A longboat waited for him beneath Dyce's Head. It would take an hour, Wadsworth thought, for the message to be delivered. It began to rain harder. Fog and rain on Friday the thirteenth, but at least Wadsworth was confident that, at long last, the ships would come.

And the fort, with God's good help, would fall.

'We do nothing, of course,' McLean said.

'Nothing?' John Moore asked.

'We could have a late luncheon, I suppose? I'm told there's oxtail soup.'

Moore gazed down from the fort's south-eastern bastion. The rebels, at least four hundred of them, were hidden somewhere close to the Fletcher house. 'We could send two companies to rout them, sir,' the lieutenant suggested.

'They have a company of marines,' McLean said, 'you saw that.'

'Then four companies, sir.'

'Which is exactly what they want us to do,' McLean said. Rainwater dripped from the peaks of his cocked hat. 'They want us to weaken the garrison.'

'Because then they'll attack from the heights?'

'I must assume so,' McLean said. 'I do like an oxtail soup, especially seasoned with a little sherry wine.' McLean went cautiously down the short flight of steps from the bastion, helping himself with the blackthorn stick. 'You'll serve with Captain Caffrae,' he told Moore, 'but do remember your other duty if the rebels should break through.'

'To destroy the oaths, sir?'

'Exactly that,' McLean said, 'but I assure you they won't break through.'

'No?' Moore asked with a smile.

'Our enemies have made a mistake,' McLean said, 'and divided their force, and I dare believe that neither of their contingents has the strength to break through our defence.' He shook his head. 'I do like it when the enemy does my work. They're not soldiers, John, they're not soldiers, but that doesn't mean the fight will be easy. They have a cause, and they're ready to die for it. We'll win, but it will be hard work.'

The brigadier knew that the crisis had come and was just grateful that it had taken so long to arrive. Captain Mowat's message had said that the rebel ships were at last determined to enter the harbour, and McLean now knew that the naval assault would be accompanied by a land attack. He expected the main body of the rebels to come from the heights, and so he had posted the majority of his men on the western side of the fort, while three companies of the 82nd were placed to defend against the attack by the men who had worked their way along the shore to conceal themselves in the low ground. Those three companies were reinforced by naval cannon already loaded with grapeshot that could turn the ditch beyond the low eastern wall into a trench slopping with blood. And it would be bloody. In another hour or two McLean knew that Majabigwaduce would be besieged by noise, by the smoke of cannon and by the spite of musket-fire. Mowat's sloops would put up a stalwart defence, but they would surely be destroyed or taken, and that was sad, yet their loss would not mean defeat. The important thing was to hold the fort, and that McLean was determined to do, and so, though his officers yearned to make a sally and attack the concealed rebels, he would keep his redcoats inside Fort George's walls and let the rebels come to die on his guns and bayonets.

Because that was why he had built Fort George, to kill the king's enemies, and now those enemies were obliging him. And so he waited.

It began to rain harder, a steady rain, pelting down almost vertically because the wind was so light. The fog moved in bands, thick sometimes, then thinning, and at times whole swathes of the river were clear of the fog to reveal a sullen grey water being dimpled by rain. The rainwater dripped from yards and rigging to darken the warships' decks.

'You trust the army, Mister Burke?' Saltonstall asked.

'They're in position, Commodore, and ready to go. Yes, sir, I trust them.'

'Then I suppose we must indulge them.'

Five rebel ships would sail into Majabigwaduce Harbour. The *General Putnam* would lead the attack, closely followed by the *Warren* and the New Hampshire ship, *Hampden*. The *Charming Sally* and the *Black Prince* would come behind those three leading vessels.

It had been Saltonstall's idea to send the *General Putnam* first. She was a large, well-built ship that carried a score of nine-pounder cannons, and her orders were to sail directly at Mowat's line and then turn upwind to anchor opposite the southernmost sloop, the *Nautilus*. Once anchored, the *General Putnam* would hammer the *Nautilus* with her broadside while the *Warren*, with her much larger guns, came into line opposite the British flagship, the *Albany*. The *Hampden*, with her mix of nine-pounder and six-pounder cannon, would then take on the *North* while the two remaining ships would use their broadsides to pound the fort.

'He wants us dead,' Thomas Reardon, first lieutenant of the *General Putnam*, commented.

'But it makes sense to send us in first,' Daniel Waters, the skipper, said bleakly.

'To kill us?'

'The *Warren*'s our most powerful ship. No point in having her half-beaten to death before she opens fire.'

'So we're to be half-beaten to death instead?'

'Yes,' Waters said, 'because that's our duty. Hands to the capstan.'

'He's saving his skin, that's the only sense it makes.'

'That's enough! Capstan!'

Capstans creaked as the anchors were hauled. The topgallantsails were released first, showering water onto the decks that had been scattered with sand to give the gunners firm footing on planks that would become slippery with blood. The guns were double-shotted. The three leading vessels all carried marines whose muskets would harry the enemy gunners.

The crews of the other ships cheered as the five attacking vessels got underway. Commodore Saltonstall watched approvingly as his flying jib was raised and backed to turn the *Warren* away from the wind, then as the jib and foretopmast staysail were hoisted and sheeted hard home. The topgallants caught the small wind, and Lieutenant Fenwick ordered the other topsails released. Men slid down rigging, ran along yards and fought with rain-tightened bindings to loose the big sails that scattered more gallons of rainwater that had been trapped within the canvas folds. 'Sheet them hard!' Fenwick called.

And the *Warren* was moving. She even heeled slightly to the fitful wind. At her stern the snake ensign flew from the mizzen gaff, while the Stars and Stripes were unfurled at her maintop, the proud colours bright in the drab rain and drifts of fog. Israel Trask, the boy fifer, played on the frigate's forecastle. He began with 'The Rogue's March' because it was a jaunty tune, a melody to make men dance or fight. The gunners had scarfs tied about their ears to dull the sound of the cannon and most, even though it was a chill day, were stripped to the waist. If they were wounded they did not want a musket-ball or timber splinter to drive cloth into the flesh, for every man knew that invited gangrene. The cannon were black in the rain. Saltonstall liked a spick and span ship, but he had nevertheless permitted the gunners to chalk the guns' barrels. 'Death to Kings,' one said, 'Liberty forever,' was written on another, while a third, somewhat mysteriously, just said 'Damn the Pope', a sentiment that seemed irrelevant to the day's business, but which so accorded with the commodore's own prejudices that he had allowed the slogan to stay.

'A point to starboard,' Saltonstall said to the helmsman.

'Aye aye, sir, point to starboard it is,' the helmsman said, and made no correction. He knew what he was doing, and he knew too that the commodore was nervous, and nervous officers were prone to give unnecessary orders. The helmsman would keep the *Warren* behind the *General Putnam*, close behind, so close that the frigate's jib-boom almost touched the smaller ship's ensign. The harbour entrance was now a quarter-mile away. Men were waving from the top of Dyce's Head. Other men watched from Cross Island where the American flag flew. No guns fired. A rift of fog drifted across the harbour centre, half-shrouding the British ships. The fort was not visible yet. There was a whisper of wind, just enough so that the ships picked up speed and the sea at the *Warren*'s cutwater made a small splashing noise. Two knots, maybe two and a half, Saltonstall thought, and one nautical mile to go before the wheel spun to lay the frigate's broadside opposite the *Albany*. The forecastle of the *Warren* looked ugly because the marines had erected barricades of logs to protect themselves against the enemy's fire. And that fire would begin as soon as the frigate passed Dyce's Head, but most of it would be aimed at the *General Putnam* and for half a nautical mile the *General Putnam* must endure that fire without being able to answer it. At two knots that half nautical mile would be covered in fifteen minutes. Each British gun would fire six or seven shots in that time.

So at least three hundred shots would beat the *General Putnam*'s bows, which Captain Waters had reinforced with heavy timbers. Saltonstall knew that some men despised him for letting the *General Putnam* take that beating, but what sense did it make to sacrifice the largest ship in the fleet? The *Warren* was the monarch of this bay, the only frigate and the only ship with eighteen-pounder cannons, and it would be foolish to let the enemy cripple her with three hundred round shot before she was capable of unleashing her terrifying broadside.

And what good would this attack do anyway? Saltonstall felt a pulse of anger that he was being asked to do this thing. Lovell should have attacked and taken the fort days ago! The Continental Navy was having to do the Massachusetts Militia's job, and Lovell, damn him, must have complained to his masters in Boston who had persuaded the Navy Board there to send Saltonstall a reprimand. What did they know? They were not here! The task was to capture the fort, not sink three sloops that, once the fort was taken, were doomed anyway. So good marines and fine sailors must die because Lovell was a nervous idiot. 'He's not fitted to be elected town Hog Reeve,' Saltonstall sneered.

'Sir?' the helmsman asked.

'Nothing,' the commodore snapped.

'By the mark three!' a seaman called from the beakhead, casting a lead-weighted line to discover the depth.

'We've plenty of water, sir,' the helmsman said encouragingly. 'I remember from the last time we poked our nose in.'

'Quiet, damn your eyes,' Saltonstall snapped.

'Quiet it is, sir.'

The *General Putnam* was almost abreast of Dyce's Head now. The wind faltered, though the ships kept their way. On board the British ships the gunners would be crouching behind their barrels to make sure their aim was true.

'Commodore, sir!' Midshipman Ferraby shouted from the taffrail.

'What is it?'

'Signal from the *Diligent*, sir. Strange sail in sight.'

Saltonstall turned. There, far to the south, just emerging from a band of fog that half-obscured Long Island, was his guard ship, the *Diligent*, with signal flags bright at a yardarm. 'Ask how many sail,' he ordered.

'It says three ships, sir.'

'Why the hell didn't you say so the first time, you damned fool? What ships are they?'

'He doesn't know, sir.'

'Then send an order telling him to find out!' Saltonstall barked, then took the speaking trumpet from its hook on the binnacle. He put the trumpet to his mouth. 'Wear ship!' he bellowed, then turned back to the signal midshipman. 'Mister Ferraby, you damned fool, make a signal to the other attack ships that they are to return to the anchorage!'

'We're going back, sir?' Lieutenant Fenwick was driven to ask.

'Don't you be a damned fool as well. Of course we're going back! We do nothing till we know who these strangers are!'

And so the attack was suspended. The rebel ships turned away, their sails flapping like monstrous wet wings. Three strange ships were in sight, which meant reinforcements had arrived.

But reinforcements for whom?

From Lieutenant George Little's deposition to the Massachusetts Court of Enquiry, sworn on September 25th, 1779:

By order of Capt Williams I went with 50 Men on Board the Hamden to man her as I suppos'd to grand Attack the Enem'y About the Same time the Comodore Boats being Imploy'd In Bringing off Loggs to Build a Brest Work on his fore Castle – I have Offten Herd Capt Williams say that from the first Counsell of war that the Comodore being always preaching Terro Against going in the Harbour to Attack the Enemeys Shiping.

From Brigadier-General Lovell's despatch to Jeremiah Powell, President of the Council Board of the State of Massachusetts Bay, dated August 13th, 1779:

I receiv'd your favour of Augt 6th this day wherein you mention your want of intelligence of the State of the army under my Command . . . The Situation of my Army at present I cannot but say is very critical . . . Many of my Officers and Soldiers are dissatisfied with the Service tho' there are some who deserve the greatest credit for their Alacrity and Soldier

397

like conduct . . . Inclosed you have the Proceedings of five Councils of War, You may Judge my Situation when the most important Ship in the Fleet and almost all the private property Ships are against the Seige.

THIRTEEN

A Royal Marine at the taffrail of HMS *North* fired his musket at the small group of Americans who had gathered at the top of the beach. The musket-ball fluttered close above their heads to bury itself in the trunk of a spruce. None of the Americans seemed to notice, but kept gazing fixedly towards the harbour entrance. A marine sergeant shouted at the man to save his ammunition. 'The range is too long, you stupid bastard.'

'Just saying hello to them, Sergeant.'

'They'll be saying hello to you soon enough.'

Captain Selby, the commanding officer of HMS *North*, was watching the approaching rebel ships. His view was veiled by wisps of fog and sheets of rain, but he recognized the meaning of the enemy's furled mainsails. The rebels wanted a clear view forrard, they were ready for battle. He walked along the sloop's deck, talking to his gunners. 'You'll hit them hard, lads. Make every shot count. Aim at their waterline, sink the bastards before they can board us! That's the way to beat them!' Selby doubted the three sloops could sink an enemy warship, at least not before the rebels opened fire. It was astonishing how much punishment a ship could take before it began to sink, but it was his duty to sound confident. He could see five enemy ships approaching the harbour entrance and all of them looked bigger than his sloop. He reckoned the enemy would try to board and capture the *North* and so he had readied the boarding pikes, axes and cutlasses with which his crew would fight the attackers.

He stopped at the *North*'s bows beside a great samson post that held one of the seventeen-inch hawsers linking his sloop to the *Albany*. He could see Captain Mowat at the *Albany*'s stern, but he resisted the temptation to make small talk across the gap. A fiddler was playing aboard Mowat's sloop and the crew was singing, and his own men took up the song.

We'll rant and we'll roar like true British sailors,
We'll range and we'll roam over all the salt seas,
Until we strike soundings in the Channel of old England
From Ushant to Scilly 'tis thirty-five leagues.

Was it thirty-five leagues, he wondered? He remembered the last time he had beat up northwards from Ushant, the sea a grey monster and the Atlantic gale singing in the shrouds. It had seemed further than thirty-five leagues. He watched the enemy and distracted himself by converting thirty-five land leagues to nautical miles. The numbers fluttered in his head and he forced himself to concentrate. A touch under ninety-one and a quarter nautical miles, say an easy dawn to dusk run in a sloop of war given a fresh wind and a clean hull. Would he ever see Ushant again? Or would he die here, in this fog-haunted, rain-drenched, God-forsaken harbour on a rebel coast? He still watched the enemy. A fine dark-hulled ship led them, and close behind her was the larger bulk and taller masts of the *Warren*. The thought of that frigate's big guns gave Selby a sudden empty feeling in his belly and, to disguise his nervousness, he levelled his glass towards the approaching ships. He saw green-jacketed marines in the frigate's fighting tops and he thought of the musket-fire that would rain onto his deck and then, inexplicably, he saw some of the enemy's sails flutter and begin to turn away from view. He lowered the glass, still staring. 'Good God,' he said.

The American frigate was turning. Had she lost her rudder? Selby gazed in puzzlement and then saw that all the rebel ships were following the frigate's example. They were falling off the wind, their sails shivering as the crews loosened sheets. 'They surely aren't going to open fire from there?' he wondered aloud. He watched, half-expecting to see the hull of the leading ship vanish in a sudden cloud of powder smoke, but none showed. She just turned sluggishly and kept on turning.

'The bastards are running away!' Henry Mowat called from the *Albany*. The singing on the sloops faltered and died as men stared at their enemy turning away. 'They've got no belly for the fight!' Mowat shouted.

'Dear God,' Selby said in astonishment. His telescope showed him the name on the stern of the ship that had been leading the attack, and which was now the rearmost vessel of the retreating fleet. '*General Putnam*,' he read aloud, 'and who the devil is General Putnam?' he asked. But whoever he was, the ship named for General Putnam was now sailing away from the harbour, as was the rebel frigate and the three other ships. They were all stemming the flooding tide to return to their anchorage. 'Well, I'll be damned,' Selby said, collapsing his glass.

On board the *North* and on board the *Albany* and on the sanded deck of the *Nautilus* the seamen cheered. Their enemy had run away without firing a shot. Mowat, usually so grim and purposeful, was laughing. And Captain Selby ordered an immediate extra issue of rum.

Because it seemed he might see Ushant again.

The Americans on the beach were Generals Lovell and Wadsworth, Lieutenant Downs of the Continental Marines and the four majors who would lead the militia companies uphill. Only now it seemed there was not going to be any attack because Commodore Saltonstall's ships were turning away. General Lovell stared open-mouthed as the ships slowly wore around just beyond the harbour entrance. 'No,' he protested to no one in particular.

Wadsworth said nothing. He just stared through his telescope.

'He's turned away!' Lovell said in apparent disbelief.

'Attack now, sir,' Downs urged.

'Now?' Lovell asked, bemused.

'The British will be watching the harbour mouth,' Downs said.

'No,' Lovell said, 'no, no, no.' He sounded heartbroken.

'Attack, please!' Downs pleaded. He looked from Lovell to Wadsworth. 'Avenge Captain Welch, attack!'

'No,' Peleg Wadsworth supported Lovell's decision. He closed the telescope and stared bleakly at the harbour mouth. He could hear the British crews cheering aboard the sloops.

'Sir,' Downs began to appeal.

'We need every man to attack,' Wadsworth explained, 'we need men attacking along the ridge and we need cannon-fire from the harbour.' The signal for Colonel Mitchell and Colonel McCobb to begin their advance was the sight of the American ships engaging the British and it seemed that signal was not going to be sent now. 'If we attack alone, Captain,' Wadsworth went on, 'then McLean can concentrate his whole force against us.' There was a time for heroics, a time for the desperate throw that would write bright glory on a new page of American history, but that time was not now. To attack now would be to kill men for nothing and give McLean another victory.

'We must go back to the heights,' Lovell said.

'We must go back,' Wadsworth echoed.

It began to rain even harder.

It took over two hours to get the men and the pair of four-pounder cannons back to the heights by which time dark had

402

fallen. The rain persisted. Lovell sheltered under the sail-canvas tent that had replaced his earlier shelter. 'There must be an explanation!' he complained, but no news had come from the fleet. Saltonstall had sailed towards the enemy and then, at the last moment, had turned away. Rumour said that strange ships had been sighted on the river's sea-reach, but no one had confirmed that report. Lovell waited for an explanation, but the commodore sent none and so Major William Todd was sent in search of the answer. A longboat was hailed from the nearest transport and Todd was rowed southwards to where the lanterns of the warships glimmered through the wet dark. '*Warren* ahoy!' the steersman called from the longboat that banged against the frigate's hull. Hands reached down from the gunwale to help Major Todd aboard.

'Wait for me,' Todd ordered the longboat's crew, then he followed Lieutenant Fenwick down the frigate's deck, past the big guns that still bore their chalked inscriptions, and so to the commodore's cabin. Water dripped from Todd's coat and hat, and his boots squelched on the chequered canvas carpet.

'Major Todd,' Saltonstall greeted Todd's arrival. The commodore was seated at his table with a glass of wine. Four spermaceti candles in fine silver sticks lit a book he was reading.

'General Lovell sends his compliments, sir,' Todd began with the politic lie, 'and asks why the attack did not take place?'

Saltonstall evidently thought the question brusque, because he jerked his head back defiantly. 'I sent a message,' he said, looking just past Todd's shoulder at the panelled door.

'I regret to say none arrived, sir.'

Saltonstall marked his place in the book with a strip of silk, then turned his attention back to the cabin door. 'Strange ships were sighted,' he said. 'You could hardly expect me to engage the enemy with strange ships at my rearward.'

'Ships, sir?' Todd asked and hoped that they were the reinforcements from Boston. He wanted to see a regiment of trained soldiers with their flags flying and drums beating, a regiment that could assault the fort and wipe it from the face of Massachusetts.

'Enemy ships,' Saltonstall said bleakly.

There was a short silence. Rain pattered on the deck above and a boxed chronometer made an almost indiscernible ticking. 'Enemy ships?' Todd repeated feebly.

'Three frigates in their van,' Saltonstall went on relentlessly, 'and a ship of the line with two more frigates coming behind.' He turned back to his book, removing the silk marker.

'You're sure?' Todd asked.

Saltonstall spared him a pitying glance. 'Captain Brown of the *Diligent* is capable of recognizing enemy colours, Major.'

'So what . . . ?' Todd began, then thought that there was no use in asking the commodore what should happen now.

'We retreat, of course,' Saltonstall divined the unasked question. 'We have no choice, Major. The enemy has anchored for the night, but in the morning? In the morning we must go upriver to find a defensible place.'

'Yes, sir.' Todd hesitated. 'You'll forgive me, sir, I must report back to General Lovell.'

'Yes, you must. Goodnight,' Saltonstall said, turning a page.

Todd was rowed back to the beach. He stumbled up the slippery path in the darkness, falling twice so that when he appeared in Lovell's makeshift tent he was muddied as well as wet. His face told Lovell the news, news that Todd related anyway. Rain beat on the canvas and hissed in the fire outside as the major told of the newly arrived British fleet that was anchored to the south. 'It seems they've come in force, sir,' Todd said, 'and the commodore believes we must retreat.'

'Retreat,' Lovell said bleakly.

'In the morning,' Todd said, 'if there's wind enough, the enemy will come here, sir.'

'A fleet?'

'Five frigates and a ship of the line, sir.'

404

'Dear God.'

'He seems to have abandoned us, sir.'

Lovell looked as if he had been slapped, but suddenly he straightened. 'Every man, every gun, every musket, every tent, every scrap of supply, everything! On the ships tonight! Call General Wadsworth and Colonel Revere. Tell them we will leave the enemy nothing. Order the guns evacuated from Cross Island. You hear me? We will leave the enemy nothing! Nothing!'

There was an army to be saved.

It rained. The night was windless and so the rain fell hard and straight, turning the rough track that zig-zagged up the northern end of the bluff into a chute of mud. There was no moonlight, but Colonel Revere had the idea to light fires at the track's edge, and by their light the supplies were carried down to the beach where more fires revealed the longboats nuzzling the shingle.

The guns had to be manhandled down the track. Fifty men were needed for each eighteen-pounder. Teams hauled on drag-ropes to stop the huge guns running away, while other men wrenched at the huge carriage wheels to guide the weapons down to the beach where lighters waited to take the artillery back to the *Samuel*. Lights glimmered wet from the ships. The rain seethed. Tents, musket cartridges, barrels of flour, boxes of candles, picks, spades, weapons, everything was carried down to the beach where sailors loaded their boats and rowed out to the transports.

Peleg Wadsworth blundered through the dark wet trees to make sure everything was gone. He carried a lantern, but its light was feeble. He slipped once and fell heavily into a deserted trench at the edge of the woods. He picked up the lantern that, miraculously, had stayed alight, and gazed east into the darkness that surrounded Fort George. A few tiny rain-diffused splinters of light showed from the houses below the fort, but McLean's defences were invisible until a cannon fired and its sudden flame lit the whole ridge before fading. The cannonball ploughed through trees. The British fired a few guns every night, not in hope of killing rebels, but rather to disturb their sleep.

'General? General?' It was James Fletcher's voice.

'I'm here, James.'

'General Lovell wants to know if the guns are taken off Cross Island, sir.'

'I told Colonel Revere to do that,' Wadsworth said. Why had Lovell not asked Revere directly? He walked along the trench and saw that it was empty. 'Help me out, James,' he said, holding up a hand.

They went back through the trees. General Lovell's table was being carried away, and men were pulling down the shelter under which Wadsworth had slept so many nights. Two militiamen were piling the shelter's brush and branches onto the camp-fire that blazed bright in a billow of smoke. All the camp-fires were being fed fuel so the British would not guess the rebels were leaving.

The rain eased towards dawn. Somehow, despite the darkness and the weather, the rebels had managed to rescue everything from the heights, though there was a sudden alarm when McCobb realized the Lincoln County militia's twelve-pounder gun was still at Dyce's Head. Men were sent to retrieve it as Wadsworth went carefully down the rain-slicked track. 'We've left them nothing,' Major Todd greeted him on the beach. Wadsworth nodded wearily. It had been a considerable achievement, he knew, but he could not help wonder at the enthusiasm men had shown to rescue the expedition's weapons and supplies, an enthusiasm that had not been evident when they had been asked to fight. 'Did you see the pay chest?' Todd asked anxiously.

'Wasn't it in the general's tent?'

'It must be with the tent, I suppose,' Todd said.

The rain stopped altogether and a grey, watery dawn lit the eastern sky. 'Time to go,' Wadsworth said. But where? He looked southwards, but the seaward reach of Penobscot Bay was shrouded by a mist that hid the enemy ships. A lighter waited to take away the missing twelve-pounder, but the only other boat on the beach was there to carry Todd and Wadsworth to the *Sally*. 'Time to go,' Wadsworth said again. He stepped into the boat and left Majabigwaduce to the British.

No guns fired in the dawn. The night's rain had stopped, the clouds had cleared, the sky was limpid, the air was still and no fog obscured Majabigwaduce's ridge. Yet no guns fired from the rebel batteries and there was not even the smaller sound of rebel picquets clearing night-dampened powder from their muskets. Brigadier McLean stared at the heights through his glass. Every few moments he swung the glass southwards, but mist still veiled the lower river and it was impossible to tell what ships lay there. The garrison had seen the strange ships appear in the twilight, but no one was certain whether they were British or American. McLean looked back to the woods. 'They're very quiet,' he said.

'Buggered off, maybe,' Lieutenant-Colonel Campbell, commanding officer of the 74th, suggested.

'If those ships are ours?'

'Then our enemies will have their tails between their legs,' Campbell said, 'and they'll be scampering for the hills.'

'My goodness, and maybe you're right.' McLean lowered the glass. 'Lieutenant Moore?'

'Sir?'

'My compliments to Captain Caffrae, and ask him to be so good as to take his company for a look at the enemy lines.'

'Yes, sir, and, sir?'

'And yes, you may accompany him, Lieutenant,' McLean said.

The fifty men filed through the abatis and went west along

407

the ridge, keeping close to the northern side where the trees were dark from the previous day's rain. To their left were the stumps of the felled pines, many scarred by cannon shot that had fallen short. About halfway between the fort and the rebel trenches Caffrae led the company into the trees. They went cautiously now, still going westwards, but slowly, always alert for rebel picquets among the leaves. Moore wished he wore a green coat like the enemy marines. He stopped once, his heart pounding because of a sudden noise to his right, but it was only a squirrel scrabbling up a trunk. 'I think they've gone,' Caffrae said softly.

'Or perhaps they're being clever,' Moore suggested.

'Clever?

'Luring us into an ambush?'

'We'll find out, won't we?' Caffrae said. He peered ahead. These woods had been his playground where he came to alarm the rebels, but he had rarely advanced this far down the ridge. He listened, but heard nothing untoward. 'Staying here won't put gravy on the beefsteak, will it?' he said. 'Let's move on.'

They threaded the wet trees, still going at snail's pace. Caffrae now edged back to the left so he could see the cleared ground and he realized he had advanced well beyond the rebels' foremost trenches, and those trenches were empty. If this was an ambush then it would surely have been sprung by now. 'They've gone,' he said, trying to convince himself.

They went faster now, advancing ten or fifteen paces at a time, then came to a clearing that had plainly been a rebel encampment. Felled logs surrounded the wet ashes of three camp-fires, rough shelters of branches and sod stood at the clearing's edges, and a latrine pit stank in the woods behind. Men peered into the shelters, but found nothing, then followed Caffrae along a track that led towards the river. Moore saw a piece of paper caught in the under-growth and fished it out with his sword. The paper was wet and disintegrating, but he could still see that someone had written a girl's name in pencil. Adelaide Rebecah. The name was written again and again in a round and childish hand. Adelaide Rebecah.

'Anything interesting?' Caffrae asked.

'Just mis-spelt love,' Moore said and threw the paper away.

At the side of the path between two of the encampments was a row of graves, each marked with a wooden cross and heaped with stones to stop animals clawing up the corpses. Names were written in charcoal on the crosses. Isaac Fulsome, Nehemiah Eldredge, Thomas Snow, John Reardon. There were seventeen names and seventeen crosses. Someone had written the words 'for Liberty' after Thomas Snow's name, except they had run out of space and the 'y' was awkwardly cramped into a corner of the crosspiece.

'Sir!' Sergeant Logie called. 'Sir!' Caffrae ran to the sergeant. 'Listen, sir,' Logie said.

For a moment all Caffrae could hear was the water dripping from the leaves and the small susurration of feeble waves on the bluff's beach, but then he heard voices. So the rebels were not gone? The voices appeared to come from the foot of the bluff and Caffrae led his men that way to discover a road hacked into the steep face. The road was rutted by wheels because this was how the guns had been hauled to the heights and then hauled down again, and one gun was still on shore. Caffrae, reaching the bluff's edge, saw a boat on the shingle and saw men struggling with a cannon at the road's end. 'We'll have that gun, lads,' he said, 'so come on!'

A dozen rebels were manhandling the twelve-pounder onto the beach, but the ruts in the road were waterlogged and the gun was heavy, and the men were tired. Then they heard the noises above them and saw the redcoats bright among the trees. 'Lift the barrel!' the rebel officer ordered. They gathered around the gun and lifted the heavy barrel out of its carriage and staggered with their burden across the shingle.

The redcoats were whooping and running. The rebels almost swamped the lighter as they dumped the barrel on its stern, but the boat stayed afloat and they clambered aboard and the sailors pulled on the oars as the first Scotsmen arrived on the beach. One rebel stumbled as he tried to shove the boat offshore. He lost his footing and fell full-length into the water just as the oars bit and carried the craft away. His companions stretched arms towards him as he waded and thrashed his way towards the receding boat, but it pulled further away and a Scottish voice ordered the man back to the beach. He was a prisoner, but the cannon barrel was saved. The lighter was rowed still further offshore as the remainder of Caffrae's men streamed onto the shingle where one of them, a corporal, raised his musket. 'No!' Caffrae called sharply. 'Let them be!' That was not mercy but caution because some of the transport ships carried small cannon and the beach was well inside their range. To fire a musket was to invite the reply of a grape-loaded cannon. The musket dropped.

Moore stopped by the abandoned gun carriage. Ahead of him was Penobscot Bay and the rebel fleet. There was no wind so the fleet was still anchored. The sun was well above the horizon now and the day was crystal clear. The dawn mist had vanished so that Moore could now see the second fleet, a smaller fleet, which lay far to the south, and at the heart of that smaller fleet was a big ship, a ship with two decks of guns, a ship far bigger than anything the rebels possessed, and Moore knew from the size of the ship that the Royal Navy had arrived.

And the rebels were gone from Majabigwaduce.

Peleg Wadsworth had pleaded with General Lovell to prepare themselves for just this emergency. He had wanted to take men upriver and find a point of land where gun batteries could be prepared and then, if the British did send a fleet, the rebels could withdraw behind their new defences and pound the pursuing ships with gunfire, but Lovell had refused every such plea.

Now Lovell wanted exactly what Wadsworth had asked for so often. James Fletcher was summoned to the *Sally's* stern-deck and asked what lay upriver. 'There's about six, seven mile of bay, General,' Fletcher told Lovell, 'then it's a narrow river after that. She goes twenty mile before you can go no further.'

'And the river winds over those twenty miles?' Lovell asked.

'In places she does,' James said. 'There's some straight channels and there are twists as tight as Satan's tail.'

'The banks are hilly?'

'All the way, sir.'

'Then our objective,' Lovell said, 'is to find a bend in the river that we can fortify.' The rebel fleet could shelter upriver of the bend, and every gun that could be carried ashore would be dug into the high ground to shatter the pursuing British ships. The fleet would thus be saved and the army preserved. Lovell gave Wadsworth a rueful smile. 'Don't chide me, Wadsworth,' he said, 'I know you foresaw this might happen.'

'I hoped it would not, sir.'

'But all will be well,' Lovell said with sublime confidence. 'Some energy and application will preserve us.'

Little could be done while there was no wind to move the ships. Yet Lovell was pleased with the night's work. Everything that could be saved from the heights, all except for one gun carriage, had been embarked and that achievement, in a night of rain and chaos, had been remarkable. It boded well for the army's survival. 'We have all our guns,' Lovell said, 'all our men and all our supplies!'

'Almost all our guns,' Major Todd corrected the general.

'Almost?' Lovell asked indignantly.

'The cannon were not recovered from Cross Island,' Major Todd said.

'Not recovered! But I gave distinct orders that they were to be withdrawn!'

'Colonel Revere claimed he was too busy, sir.'

Lovell stared at the major. 'Busy?'

'Colonel Revere also claimed, sir,' Todd went on, taking some pleasure in describing the failings of his enemy, 'that your orders no longer applied to him.'

Lovell gaped at his brigade major. 'He said what?'

'He averred that the siege had been abandoned, sir, and that therefore he was no longer obliged to accept your orders.'

'Not obliged to accept my orders?' Lovell asked in disbelief.

'That is what he claimed, sir,' Todd said icily. 'So I fear those guns are lost, sir, unless we have time to retrieve them this morning. I also regret to tell you, sir, that the pay chest is missing.'

'It'll turn up,' Lovell said dismissively, still brooding over Lieutenant-Colonel Revere's brazen insolence. Not obliged to accept orders? Who did Revere think he was?

'We need the pay chest,' Todd insisted.

'It will be found, I'm sure,' Lovell said testily. There had been chaos in the dark and it was inevitable that some items would have been carried to the wrong transport ship, but that could all be sorted out once a safe anchorage was discovered and protected. 'But first we must haul those guns off Cross Island,' Lovell insisted, 'I will leave nothing for the British. You hear me? Nothing!'

But there was no time to rescue the cannon. The first catspaws of wind had just begun to ruffle the bay and the British fleet was already hauling its anchors and loosing sails. The rebel fleet had to move and one by one the anchors were raised, the sails released and the ships, assisted by the flood tide, retreated northwards. The wind was weak and fickle, scarce enough to stir the fleet, so some smaller ships used their long ash oars to help their progress while others were towed by longboats.

The cannon on Cross Island were abandoned, but everything else was saved. All the rebel guns and supplies had been carried down the muddy track in the rainy dark, then rowed out to the transport ships, and now those ships edged northwards, northwards to the river narrows, and northwards to safety.

And behind them, between the transport ships and Sir George Collier's flotilla, the rebel warships cleared for action and spread slowly across the bay. If the transports were sheep then Saltonstall's warships were the dogs.

And the wolves were coming.

Redcoats gathered at Dyce's Head to watch the unfolding drama. Brigadier McLean's servant had thoughtfully brought a milking stool all the way to the bluff and McLean thanked the man and sat down to watch the unfolding battle. It would be a privileged view of a rare sight, McLean thought. Seventeen rebel warships waited for six Royal Navy vessels. Three British frigates led the way, while the big two-decker and the remaining two frigates came on more slowly. 'I do believe that's the *Blonde*,' McLean said, staring at the nearest frigate through his telescope. 'It's our old friend Captain Barkley!' Off to McLean's right the nineteen rebel transports were inching northwards. From this distance it looked as if their sails hung limp and powerless, but minute by minute they drew further away.

The *Blonde* fired her bow-chasers. To the watchers ashore it looked as if her bowsprit was blotted out by blossoming smoke. A moment later the sound of the two guns pounded the bluff. A pair of white fountains showed where the round shots had splashed well short of the *Warren* that lay at the centre of the rebel line. The smoke thinned and drifted ahead of the British ships.

'Look at that!' Lieutenant-Colonel Campbell exclaimed. He was pointing at the harbour mouth where Mowat's three sloops had appeared. They were kedging out of the harbour against the prevailing wind. Ever since he had heard that the rebels had abandoned the siege Mowat had been retrieving his ships' guns from their shore emplacements. His men had worked hard and fast, desperate to join the promised fight in the bay, and now, with their portside broadsides restored, the three sloops were on their way to join Sir George's flotilla. Longboats took turns to carry anchors far forrard of the sloops' bows, the anchors were dropped, then the sloops were hauled forward on the anchor rode as a second anchor was rowed still further ahead for the next leg of the journey. They leapfrogged anchor by anchor out of the harbour and the *North*'s pumps still clattered and spurted, and all three ships showed damage to their hulls from the long rebel bombardment, but their guns were loaded and their tired crews eager. The *Blonde* fired again, and once again the shots dropped short of the rebel ships.

'They do say,' McLean remarked, 'that firing the guns brings on the wind.'

'I thought it was the other way round,' Campbell said, 'that gunfire stills the wind?'

'Well, it's one or the other,' McLean said happily, 'or maybe neither? But I do remember a nautical fellow assuring me of it.' And perhaps firing the two chasers on HMS *Blonde* had brought on a small wind because the British ships seemed to be making better speed as they approached the rebel fleet. 'It will be bloody work,' McLean said. The foremost three frigates would be far outgunned by the rebels, though the big *Raisonable* was not that far behind and her massive lower guns were sufficient to blow each of the rebel warships out of the water with a single broadside. Even the *Warren*, with her eighteen-pounders, would be far outmatched by the two-decker's thirty-two-pounders. 'Mind you,' McLean went on, 'sailors do tell us the strangest things! I had a skipper on the

Portugal run who swore blind the world was flat. He claimed to have seen the rainbows at its edge!'

'The fellow who took us to Halifax,' Campbell said, 'told us tales of mermaids. He said they flocked together like sheep, and that down in the southern seas it's tits and tails from horizon to horizon.'

'Really?' Major Dunlop asked eagerly.

'That's what he said! Tits and tails!'

'Dear me,' McLean said, 'I see I must sail south.' He straightened on the stool, watching the three sloops. 'Oh, well done, Mowat!' he said enthusiastically. The three sloops had laboriously used their anchors to haul themselves out of the harbour and now loosed their sails.

'And what does that signify?' Major Dunlop asked. His question had been prompted by a string of bright signal flags that had appeared at the *Warren*'s mizzen mast. The flags meant nothing to the watchers on the bluff who had now been joined by most of Majabigwaduce's inhabitants, curious to watch an event that would surely make their village famous.

'He's taking them into battle, I suppose,' Campbell suggested.

'I suppose he must be,' McLean agreed, though he did not see what the rebels could do other than what they were already doing. Commodore Saltonstall's seventeen ships were in a line with all their broadsides pointing at the oncoming ships, and that gave the rebels a huge advantage. They could shoot and shoot, secure in the knowledge that only the bow-chasers on the three leading frigates could return the fire. The Royal Navy, the brigadier thought, must take some grievous casualties before the big two-decker battleship could demolish the American defiance.

Except the Americans were not defiant. 'What on earth?' McLean asked.

'Bless me,' Campbell said, equally astonished.

Because the meaning of Saltonstall's signal was suddenly clear. There would be no fight, at least no fight of the

415

commodore's making because, one by one, the rebel warships were turning away. They had loosed their sheets and were running before the small wind. Running northwards. Running away. Running for the safety of the river narrows.

Six ships and three sloops chased thirty-seven vessels.

All running away.

Three rebel ships decided to make a break for the open sea. The *Hampden*, with her twenty guns, was the largest, while the *Hunter* had eighteen guns and the *Defence* just fourteen. The commodore's orders had required every ship to do its best to evade the enemy, and so the three ships tacked westwards across the bay, aiming to take the less used western channel past Long Island and so downriver to the ocean that lay twenty-six nautical miles to the south. The *Hunter* was a new ship and reputed to be the fastest sailor on the coast, while Nathan Brown, her captain, was a canny man who knew how to coax every last scrap of speed from his ship's hull. There was precious little wind, not nearly as much as Brown would have liked, yet even so his sleek hull moved perceptibly faster than the *Hampden*, which, being larger, should have been the quicker vessel.

Signal flags fluttered from a yardarm on HMS *Raisonable*. For a time it was hard to tell what those flags portended, because nothing seemed to change in the British fleet, then Brown saw the two rearmost British frigates turn slowly westwards. 'Bastards want a race,' he said.

It was an unequal race. The two smaller rebel ships might be quick and nimble sailors, but they had the disadvantage of sailing closer to the wind and the two frigates easily closed the gap through which the rebels needed to tack. Two guns fired from HMS *Galatea* were warning enough. The shots were fired at long range, and both blew past the *Defence*'s bows, but the message of the two near misses was clear. Try to sail through the gap and your small ships will receive the full broadsides of two frigates, and to escape past those frigates the rebels needed to tack through the channel where the frigates waited. They would be forced to sail within pistol shot and John Edmunds, the *Defence's* captain, had an image of his two masts falling, of his deck slicked with blood and of his hull quivering under the relentlessly heavy blows. His guns were mere four-pounders and what could four-pounders do against a frigate's full broadside? He might as well throw bread-crusts at the enemy. 'But I'll be damned before the bastards take my ship,' he said.

He knew his attempt to sail the *Defence* past the frigates had failed and so he let his brig's bows fall off the wind and then drove her, all sails standing, straight towards the Penobscot's western shore. 'Joshua!' he called to the first mate. 'We're going to burn her! Break open the powder barrels.'

The *Defence* ran ashore. Her masts bowed forrard as the bows grated on the shingle beach. Edmunds thought the masts would surely fall, but the backstays held and the sails slatted and banged on the yards. Edmunds took the flag from her stern and folded it. His crew was spilling powder and splashing oil on the decks. 'Get ashore, boys,' Edmunds called, and he went forrard, past his useless guns, and paused in the bows. He wanted to weep. The *Defence* was a lovely ship. Her home was the open ocean where she should have been living up to her martial name by chasing down fat British merchantmen to make her owners rich, but instead she was caught in an enclosed seaway and it was time to bid her farewell.

He struck flint on steel and spilled the burning linen from his tinder-box onto a powder trail. Then he climbed over the gunwale and dropped down to the beach. His eyes were wet when he turned to watch his ship burn. It took a long time. There was more smoke than fire at first, but then the flames flickered up the tarred rigging and the sails caught the blaze, and the masts and yards were outlined by fire so that the *Defence* looked like the devil's own vessel, a flame-rigged brigantine, a defiant fighting-ship sailing her way into hell. 'Oh God damn the bastards,' Edmunds said, brokenhearted, 'the sons of goddamned bitch bastards!'

The *Hunter* sought shelter in a narrow cove. Nathan Brown, her skipper, ran her gently aground in the tight space and ordered an anchor lowered and the sails furled and, once the ship was secure, he told his crew to find shelter ashore. The *Hunter* might be a quick ship, but even she could not outsail the broadsides of the two enemy frigates and her four-pounder cannon were no match for the British guns, yet Nathan Brown could not bring himself to burn the ship. It would have been like murdering his wife. The *Hunter* had magic in her timbers, she was fast and nimble, a charmed ship, and Nathan Brown dared to hope that the British would ignore her. He prayed that the pursuers would continue north and that once the Royal Navy ships had passed he might extricate the *Hunter* from the narrow cove and sail her back to Boston, but that hope died when he saw two longboats crammed with sailors leave the British frigates.

Brown had ordered his men ashore in case the British tried to destroy the *Hunter* with cannon-fire, but now it seemed the enemy was intent on capture rather than destruction. The crowded longboats drew nearer. At least half the *Hunter*'s crew of a hundred and thirty men were armed with muskets and they began shooting as the longboats approached the grounded ship. Water spouted around the oarsmen as musket-balls struck, and at least one British sailor was hit and the boat's oars momentarily tangled, but then the longboats vanished behind the *Hunter*'s counter. A moment later the enemy sailors were aboard the ship and attaching tow-lines to her stern. The treacherous tide lifted her off the shingle and a strange flag, the hated flag, broke at her mizzen gaff's peak as she was towed back to the river. She was now His Majesty's ship, the *Hunter*. Just to the south, hidden from Brown's crew by a shoulder of wooded land, the powder

418

magazine in the *Defence* exploded, sending a dark smoke-cloud boiling above the land and a shower of burning timbers that fell to hiss in the bay and start small fires ashore.

The *Hampden* was the largest of the three ships that tried to reach the sea, and she saw the fate of the *Hunter* and *Defence* and so her captain, Titus Salter, turned back to make the safety of the river narrows. The *Hampden* had been donated by the State of New Hampshire and she was well-found, well-manned and expensively equipped, yet she was not a fast sailor and late in the afternoon HMS *Blonde* came within range of her and opened fire. Titus Salter turned the *Hampden* so that her portside broadside of ten guns faced the enemy and he returned the fire. Six nine-pounder cannon and four six-pounders spat at the much larger *Blonde*, which hammered back with twelve- and eighteen-pounders. HMS *Virginia* came behind the *Blonde* and added her broadside. The guns boomed across the bay as dense smoke rose to shroud the lower rigging. Fire twisted from the cannon barrels. Men sweated and hauled on guns, they swabbed and rammed and ran the guns out and the gunners touched linstocks to portfires and the great guns leaped back and the round shot slammed remorselessly into the *Hampden*'s hull. The shots shattered the timbers and drove wicked-edged splinters into men's bodies. Blood spilled along the deck seams. Chain shot whistled in the smoke, severing shrouds, stays and lines. The sails twitched and tore as bar shot shredded the canvas. The foremast went first, toppling across the *Hampden*'s bows to smother ripped sails across the forrard cannon, but still the American flag flew and still the British pounded the smaller ship. The frigates drifted closer to their helpless prey. Their biggest guns were concentrated on the rebel hull and the smoke from their eighteen-pounders shrouded the *Hampden*. The rebel fire became slower and slower as men were killed or wounded. A ribcage, shattered by an eighteen-pounder shot, was scattered across the deck. A man's severed hand lay in the scuppers. A cabin boy was trying not to cry as a seaman tightened a tourniquet around his bloody, ragged thigh. The rest of his leg was ten feet away, reduced to a pulp by twelve pounds of round shot. Another eighteen-pounder ball hit a nine-pounder cannon and the noise, like a great bell, was heard on Majabigwaduce's distant bluff, and the barrel was struck clean off its carriage to fall onto a gunner who lay screaming, both legs crushed, and another ball slammed through the gunwale and struck the mainmast, which first swayed, then fell towards the stern, the sound splintering and creaking, stays and shrouds parting, men screaming a warning, and still the relentless shots came.

Fifteen minutes after the *Blonde* had begun the fight Titus Salter ended it. He pulled down his flag and the guns went silent and the smoke drifted across the sun-dappled water and a prize crew came from the *Blonde* to board the *Hampden*.

The remainder of the rebel fleet still sailed north.

Towards the river narrows.

The rebels had occupied no buildings in Majabigwaduce and Doctor Eliphalet Downer, the expedition's surgeon general, had complained about keeping badly wounded men in make-shift shelters constructed from branches and sail-cloth, and so the rebels had established their hospital in what remained of the buildings of Fort Pownall at Wasaumkeag Point, which lay some five miles upriver and on the opposite bank from Majabigwaduce. Now, as the guns boomed flat across the bay, Peleg Wadsworth took forty men to evacuate the patients to the sloop *Sparrow* that lay just offshore. The men, most with bandaged stumps, either walked or were carried on stretchers made from oars and coats. Doctor Downer stood next to Wadsworth and watched the distant frigates pound the *Hampden*. 'So what now?' he asked bleakly.

'We go upriver,' Wadsworth said.

'To the wilderness?'

'You take the *Sparrow* as far north as you can,' Wadsworth said, 'and find a suitable house for the hospital.'

'These arrangements should have been made two weeks ago,' Downer said angrily.

'I agree,' Wadsworth said. He had tried to persuade Lovell to make those arrangements, but the general had regarded any preparations for a retreat as defeatism. 'But they weren't made,' he went on firmly, 'so now we must all do the best we can.' He turned and pointed at the small pasture. 'Those cows must be slaughtered or driven away,' he said.

'I'll make sure it's done,' Downer said. The cows were there to give the patients fresh milk, but Wadsworth wanted to leave nothing that could be useful to the enemy. 'So I become a herdsman and a slaughterer,' Downer said bitterly, 'then find a house upstream and wait for the British to find me?'

'It's my intention to make a stronghold,' Wadsworth explained patiently, 'and so keep the enemy to the lower river.'

'If you're as successful at that as you've been at everything else in the last three weeks,' Downer said vengefully, 'we might as well all shoot ourselves now.'

'Just obey orders, Doctor,' Wadsworth said testily. He had snatched a couple of hours' sleep as the *Sally* drifted northwards, but he was tired. 'I'm sorry,' he apologized.

'I'll see you upriver,' Downing said, his tone indicating regret for the words he had spoken before. 'Go and do your work, General.'

The transport ships were in the northern part of the bay now. Most had anchored during the ebb tide and now used the evening flood and the small wind to crawl towards the river narrows. James Fletcher had explained that the entrance to the narrows was marked by an obstacle, Odom's Ledge, that lay in the very centre of the stream. There were navigable channels to either side of the rock, but the ledge itself was a ship-killer. 'It'll rip the bottom out of a boat,' James had told Wadsworth, 'and the British won't try and get past in the dark. No one could try and pass Odom's in the dark.'

Wadsworth was using the *Sally*'s longboat and he and Fletcher were being rowed northwards from Wasaumkeag Point. The oarsmen were silent, as were the enemy frigates' guns, which meant the *Hampden* was taken. Wadsworth turned to gaze at the view. It was a summer evening and he was in the middle of the largest fleet the rebels had ever gathered, a huge fleet, their sails beautifully catching the lowering sun, and they were all fleeing from the much smaller fleet. The rebel ships converged towards the ledge. The British frigates fired an occasional bow-chaser, the balls splashing short of the rearmost rebels. The wolves were herding the sheep, Wadsworth thought bitterly, and the *Warren*, taller and more beautiful than all the surrounding vessels, was running like the rest when her duty, surely, was to turn and fight her way into legend.

'There's the *Samuel*, sir,' James Fletcher pointed to the brig that had almost reached the narrows' entrance.

'Get me close to the *Samuel*,' Wadsworth ordered the boatswain.

The brig was towing both Revere's barge and a flat-bottomed lighter. Wadsworth stood and cupped his hands as his longboat closed on the *Samuel*. 'Is Colonel Revere on board?'

'I'm here,' a voice boomed back.

'Keep rowing,' Wadsworth said to the boatswain, then cupped his hands again. 'Put a cannon on the lighter, Colonel!'

'You want what?'

Wadsworth spoke more distinctly. 'Put a cannon on the lighter! I'll find a place to land it!' Revere shouted something back, but Wadsworth did not catch the words. 'Did you hear me, Colonel?' he shouted.

'I heard you!'

'Put a cannon on the lighter! We need to get guns ashore when we find a place to defend!'

Again Revere's answer was indistinct, but the longboat had now passed the *Samuel* and Wadsworth was confident that Revere had understood his orders. He sat and watched the broken water above the ledge where the riverbanks, steep and tree-covered, narrowed abruptly. The tide was slackening and the hills robbed the small wind of much of its power. A schooner and a ship had anchored safely upstream of the ledge while, behind them, many of the other ships were still being towed by tired men in longboats.

'What we do,' Wadsworth spoke to himself as much as to the men in his boat, 'is discover a place we can defend.' He had been told the river twisted and in his mind's eye was a sharp turn where he could land guns on the upstream bank. He would begin with one of Revere's cannon, because once that was emplaced it would mark the new rebel position and as the ships passed upstream they could donate cannons, crewmen and ammunition so that, by morning, Wadsworth would command a formidable battery of artillery that pointed directly downstream. The approaching British would be forced to sail straight at those guns. The river was far too narrow to allow them to turn and use their broadsides, so instead they must either sail into the furious bombardment or, much more likely, anchor and so refuse the offered fight. The rebel fleet could shelter behind the new fortress while the army could camp ashore and recover its discipline. A road could be hacked westwards through the woods so that new men, new ammunition and new guns could be brought to renew the assault on Majabigwaduce. As a child Wadsworth had loved the story of Robert the Bruce, the great Scottish hero who had been defeated by his English enemies and who had fled to a cave where he watched a spider try to make a web. The spider failed repeatedly, but repeatedly tried again until at last it was successful, and that spider's persistence had inspired the Bruce to try again and so achieve his great victory. So now the rebels must play the

423

spider, and try again, and keep trying until at last the British were gone from Massachusetts.

But, as the crew rowed him steadily upstream, it seemed to Wadsworth that the river hardly twisted at all. An island, Orphan Island, divided the river into two channels and Odom's Ledge was in the navigable western branch. Once past Orphan Island the river's bends seemed gentle. The flooding tide helped the oarsmen. They were now far ahead of the ships, travelling in a summer's gentle evening up a swirling, silent river edged by tall, dark trees. 'Where are these sharp bends?' Wadsworth asked James Fletcher nervously.

'Up ahead,' James Fletcher said. The oar blades dipped, pulled and dripped, and then, suddenly, there was the perfect place. Ahead of Wadsworth the river twisted abruptly to the east, making almost a right-angled bend, and the slope above the bend was steep enough to deter any attack, but not so steep that guns could not be placed there.

'What's this place called?' Wadsworth asked.

Fletcher shrugged. 'The river bend?'

'It will have a name,' Wadsworth said vehemently, 'a name for the history books. Spider Bend.'

'Spider?'

'It's an old story,' Wadsworth said, but he did not elaborate. He had found the place to make his stand, and now he must gather troops, guns and resolve. 'Back down the river,' he told the crew.

Because Peleg Wadsworth would fight back.

The rebel warships were faster than the transports and they gradually overhauled the slower vessels and passed Odom's Ledge into the river narrows. All the warships and almost half of the transports passed that bottleneck, but a dozen slower boats were still stranded in the bay where the tide was slackening, the wind dying and the enemy approaching. Every sailor knew that there was more wind at the top of a

424

mast than at the bottom, and the masts of the British ships were taller than the transports' masts, and the frigates were flying all their topgallant sails and so had the benefit of what small breeze remained in the limpid evening. The sun was low now so that the frigates' hulls were in shadow, but their high sails reflected the bright sun. They crept northwards, ever closer to the transports crammed with men, guns and supplies, and looming behind them, queen of the river, was the towering *Raisonable* with her massive cannon.

Just short of Odom's Ledge, on the western bank, was a cove. It was called Mill Cove because a sawmill had been built where a stream emptied into the cove, though the mill was long gone now, leaving just a skeleton of rafters and a stone chimney overgrown with creepers. The dozen transports, almost becalmed and increasingly threatened by the frigates, turned towards the cove. They were being towed, but the river's current had now overpowered the last of the flood tide and they could not force their way through the narrow channels either side of the ledge and so they hauled themselves across the current to the shallow waters of Mill Cove and used the last of the wind to drive their bows ashore. Men dropped over the gunwales. They carried their muskets and haversacks, they waded ashore, they gathered disconsolate beside the mill's ruins and they watched their ships burn.

One by one the transports burst into flames. Each and every ship was valuable. The boat-builders of Massachusetts were famous for their skills and it was said that a ship built in New England could outsail any vessel from the old world and the British would love to capture these ships. They would be taken to Canada, or perhaps back to Britain, and the ships would be sold at auction and the prize money distributed among the sailors of the ships that had captured them. The warships might be purchased by the Admiralty, as the captured frigate *Hancock* had been bought, so the *Hampden* would end its days as the HMS *Hampden*, and HMS *Hunter* would be

425

using her New England given speed and her New England cast guns to chase smugglers in the English channel.

But now the American transport skippers would deny their enemies a similar victory. They would not yield their ships to a British prize court. Instead they burned the transports and the banks of Mill Cove flickered with the light of the flames. Two of the burning hulls drifted towards the river's centre. Their sails and rigging and masts were alight. When a mainmast fell it was a curving collapse of bright fire, sparks exploding into the evening as the lines and yards and spars cascaded into the river.

And the fire did what the *Warren* and the other warships had failed to do. It stopped the British. No captain would take his ship near a burning hull. Sails, tarred rigging and wooden hulls were dangerously flammable and a wind-driven spark could turn one of His Majesty's proud ships into a charred wreck, and so the British fleet dropped anchor as the last of the evening wind died.

Upstream, beyond Odom's Ledge, the rest of the rebel fleet struggled northwards until the current and the dying light forced them to anchor. At Mill Cove hundreds of men, with no orders and no officers confident of what should be done, started walking westwards. They headed across a wilderness towards their distant homes.

While in Fort George Brigadier-General Francis McLean raised a glass and smiled at the guests who had gathered about his table. 'I give you the Royal Navy, gentlemen,' he said, and his officers stood, lifted their glasses of wine and echoed the brigadier's toast. 'The Royal Navy!'

From a letter by General Artemas Ward, commander of the Massachusetts Militia, to Colonel Joseph Ward, September 8th, 1779:

The commander of the fleet is cursed, bell, book, and candle . . . Lieutenant-Colonel Paul Revere is now under an arrest for disobedience of orders, and unsoldierlike behaviour tending to cowardice.

From Brigadier-General Solomon Lovell's journal, August 14th, 1779:

The British Ships coming up the Soldiers were obliged to take to the Shore, and set fire to their Vessels, to attempt to give a description of this terrible Day is out of my Power it would be a fit Subject for some masterly hand to describe it in its true colours, to see four Ships pursuing seventeen Sail of Armed Vessells nine of which were stout Ships, Transports on fire, Men of War blowing up, Provision of all kinds, and every kind of Stores on Shore (at least in small Quantities) throwing about, and as much confusion as can possibly be conceived.

Excerpt from Brigadier-General Francis McLean's letter to Lord George Germaine, His Majesty's Secretary of State for the American Colonies, August, 1779:

It only remains for me to endeavour to do justice to the cheerfulness and spirit with which all ranks of our little garrison underwent the excessive fatigue required to render our post tenable. The work was carried on under the enemy's fire with a spirit that would have done credit to the oldest soldiers; from the time the enemy opened their trenches, the men's spirits increased daily, so that our last chief difficulty was in restraining them.

FOURTEEN

Peleg Wadsworth slept ashore, or rather he lay awake on the river's bank and must have dozed, because he twice awoke with a start from vivid dreams. In one he was cornered by the Minotaur, which appeared with Solomon Lovell's head crowned with a pair of blood-dripping horns out of nightmare. He finally sat with his back against a tree and a blanket about his shoulders, and watched the dark river swirl slow and silent towards the sea. To his left, to seaward, there was a glow in the sky and he knew that red light was cast by the ships still burning in Mill Cove. It looked like an angry dawn, and it filled him with an immense lassitude, so he closed his eyes and prayed to God that he was given the strength to do what was needed. There was still a fleet and an army to rescue, and an enemy yet to be defied, and long before first light he roused James Fletcher and his other companions. Those companions were now Johnny Feathers and seven of his Indians who possessed two birch-bark canoes. The canoes slipped through the water with much greater ease than the heavy longboats and the Indian had happily agreed to let Wadsworth use the canoes in his attempt to organize a defence. 'We must go downriver,' he told Feathers.

The tide was flooding again and the ships were using that

tide to escape upriver. Their topsails were set, though no wind powered the vessels, which either floated upstream on the tide or were being towed by longboats. The canoes passed six vessels and Wadsworth shouted to each crew that they should take their ship past the place where the river turned sharply eastwards and then anchor. 'We can defend the river there,' he called, and sometimes a captain responded cheerfully, but mostly the sullen crews received his orders in silence.

Wadsworth found the *Warren* aground where the river widened briefly to resemble a lake. Three other warships were anchored nearby. The frigate was evidently waiting for the tide to float her free of a mud bank.

'You want to go on board?' Johnny Feathers asked.

'No.'

Wadsworth had no stomach for a confrontation with Commodore Saltonstall, which, he suspected, would be fruitless. Saltonstall already knew what his duty was, but Wadsworth reckoned pointing out that duty would merely provoke a sneer and obfuscation. If the fleet and army were to be saved it would be by other men, and Wadsworth was looking for the means of that salvation.

He found it a quarter-mile downstream of the *Warren* where the *Samuel*, the brig that carried the expedition's artillery, was being pulled northwards by two longboats. Wadsworth's canoe went alongside the brig and he scrambled up and across the *Samuel*'s gunwale. 'Is Colonel Revere here?'

'He went away in his barge, sir,' a seaman answered.

'I hope that's good news,' Wadsworth said, and walked aft to where Captain James Brown stood by his wheel. 'Did Colonel Revere ship a cannon onto the lighter?' he asked Brown.

'No,' Brown answered curtly, nodding to the ship's waist where the cannons were now parked wheel to wheel.

'So where is he?'

430

'Damned if I know. He took his baggage and left.'

'He took his baggage?' Wadsworth asked.

'Every last box and bundle.'

'And his men?'

'Some are here, some went with him.'

'Oh dear God,' Wadsworth said. He stood irresolute for a moment. The *Samuel* was inching upstream. The river was so narrow here that branches of trees sometimes brushed against the brig's lower yards. Wadsworth had hoped that Revere's one cannon, placed at Spider Bend, would be a marker for the rest of the fleet and the first of many cannon that could hold the British pursuers at bay. 'You'll keep going upstream?' he suggested to Brown.

The *Samuel*'s captain gave a mirthless bark of laughter. 'What else do you suggest I do, General?'

'Ten miles upstream,' Wadsworth said, 'the river turns sharply to the right. I need the guns there.'

'We'll be lucky to make two miles before the tide turns,' Brown said, 'or before the damned English catch us up.'

'So where is Colonel Revere?' Wadsworth demanded and received a shrug in answer. He had not passed Revere's white-painted barge as he descended the river, which meant the colonel and his artillerymen must be further downriver, and that gave Wadsworth a glimmer of hope. Had Revere decided to fortify a place on the Penobscot's bank? Was he even now finding a place where a battery could hammer the British ships? 'Did he give you instructions for the cannon?' Wadsworth asked.

'He asked for his breakfast.'

'The cannon, man! What does he want done with the cannon?'

Brown turned his head slowly, spat a stream of tobacco juice onto the portside scupper, then looked back to Wadsworth. 'He didn't say,' Brown said.

Wadsworth went back to the canoe. He needed Revere!

He needed artillery. He wanted a battery of eighteen-pounder cannon, the largest in the rebel army, and he wanted ammunition from the *Warren*, then he wanted to see the round shot crunching into the bows of the British frigates. He thought briefly of returning to the *Warren*, which also had the big guns he needed, but first, he decided, he would discover what Colonel Revere planned. 'That way, please,' he told Feathers, pointing downstream. He would go to the *Warren* afterwards and demand that Saltonstall give the artillery all the eighteen-pounder shot they needed.

The sun was up now, the light clear and crisp, the river sparkling, and the sky spoiled only by the smear of smoke from the ships still burning south of Odom's Ledge. A quarter-mile beyond the *Samuel* there was a whole group of anchored ships, both transports and warships, all chaotically clustered where the river divided around the northern tip of Orphan Island. On the eastern bank, just upstream of the island, was a small settlement about half the size of Majabigwaduce. 'What's that place?' Wadsworth called to James Fletcher who was in the second canoe.

'Buck's plantation,' James called back.

Wadsworth gestured that the Indians should stop paddling. The river bent here, and Wadsworth wondered why he had not chosen this as a place to defend. True, the curve was not so pronounced as the sharp turn higher up the river, but in the early morning light the river's twist looked sharp enough and on the western bank, opposite Buck's plantation, was a high bluff about which the Penobscot curled. He needed a place on the western bank so that supplies could come from Boston without being ferried across the river, and the bluff looked a likely enough spot. There were already men ashore at the bluff's foot, and there were plenty of guns aboard the nearby ships. Everything Wadsworth needed was here, and he pointed to the narrow beach at the base of the bluff. 'Put me ashore there, please,' he said, then called across to James

Fletcher again. 'You're to go back upstream and find the *Samuel*,' he shouted. 'Ask Captain Brown to bring her back downriver. Tell him I need the cannons here.'

'Yes, sir.'

'And after that go to the *Warren*. Tell the commodore I'm making a battery here,' he pointed at the western bluff, 'and say I'm expecting his ship to join us. Tell him we need his eighteen-pounder ammunition!'

'He won't like me saying that.'

'Tell him anyway!' Wadsworth called. The canoe scraped onto the beach and Wadsworth jumped ashore. 'Wait for me, please,' he asked the Indians, then strode down the beach towards the men who sat disconsolate at the high tide line. 'Officers!' he shouted. 'Sergeants! To me! Officers! Sergeants! To me!'

Peleg Wadsworth would pluck order from chaos. He was still fighting.

Lieutenant Fenwick was obeying Commodore Saltonstall's orders, though with a heavy heart. The *Warren*'s main magazine had been half-emptied, and the powder charges were being carried down to the bilge and up to the maindeck. There was a growing pile of powder bags on the ballast stones at the foot of the main mast in the bilge's darkness, another under the forecastle and a third beneath Saltonstall's cabin. On deck there were heaps of bags around each mast. White trails of slow-match were laid from each pile, the snaking canvas ropes meeting in a tangle on the foredeck. 'What we cannot do,' Saltonstall told Fenwick, 'is allow the enemy to capture the ship.'

'Of course not, sir.'

'I will not allow British colours to fly from my ship.'

'Of course not, sir,' Fenwick said again, 'but we could go upriver, sir?' he added nervously.

'We are aground,' Saltonstall said sarcastically.

'The tide is flooding, sir,' Fenwick said. He waited, but Saltonstall made no comment. 'And there are French ships, sir.'

'There are French ships, Lieutenant?' Saltonstall asked caustically.

'A French flotilla might arrive, sir.'

'You are privy to the French fleet's movements, Lieutenant?'

'No, sir,' Fenwick said miserably.

'Then kindly obey my orders and prepare the ship for burning.'

'Aye aye, sir.'

Saltonstall walked to the taffrail. The early light was pellucid and the air still. The slow tide gurgled at the *Warren*'s waterline. He was gazing downstream to where a gaggle of ships was clustered by a bluff. Two sloops were using the tide to come upriver, but it seemed most of the ships had decided to stay by the bluff where longboats and lighters were carrying supplies to the western bank. The British ships were out of sight, presumably still below Odom's Ledge where the smoke rose to tarnish the sky. The smoke rose vertically, but Saltonstall knew that as soon as that pillar of smoke was ruffled by the wind the enemy sloops and frigates would start upstream.

It had been a shambles, he thought angrily. From start to finish, a goddamned shambles, and to the commodore's mind the only successes had been achieved by the Continental Navy. It had been the marines who captured Cross Island and the marines who had led the fight up the bluff at Dyce's Head, and after that Lovell had quivered like a sick rabbit and demanded that Saltonstall do all the fighting. 'And what if we had captured the sloops?' the commodore demanded angrily.

'Sir?' a sailor within earshot asked.

'I'm not talking to you, damn your eyes.'

'Aye aye, sir.'

Would Lovell have captured the fort if the sloops had been

taken? Saltonstall knew the answer to that question. Lovell would have found another obstacle to prevent a fight. He would have whined and moaned and tarried. He would have demanded a battery on the moon. He would have dug more trenches. It was a shambles.

The *Warren* trembled as the tide lifted her. She shifted a few inches, settled again, then trembled once more. In a moment she would swing her stern upstream and tug at her anchor rode. Lieutenant Fenwick looked at the commodore with a hopeful expression, but Saltonstall ignored him. Fenwick was a good officer, but he had little comprehension of what was at stake here. The *Warren* was a precious piece of equipment, a well-found, well-armed frigate, and the British would love to hang their damned flag from her stern and take her into their fleet, but Saltonstall would be damned to the deepest circle of hell before he allowed that to happen. That was why Saltonstall had declined battle the previous day. Oh, he could have sacrificed the *Warren* and most of the other rebel warships to give the transports more time to escape the enemy, but in making that sacrifice he might well have been boarded and then the *Warren* would become His Majesty's frigate. And it was all very well for Fenwick to suggest sailing upriver, but the *Warren* had the deepest draught of all the fleet and she would not get far before she grounded again and the British, seeing her, would do their utmost to capture her.

'Boat approaching, sir!' a bosun called from the *Warren's* waist.

Saltonstall grunted an acknowledgement. He went and stood by the ship's wheel as the longboat pulled across the tide. He watched the *Pidgeon*, a transport schooner, being towed upstream and noted that the river's current was fighting the tide and giving the oarsmen a hard time. Then the longboat banged into the frigate's hull and a man climbed onto the deck and hurried aft towards the commodore. 'Lieutenant

Little, sir,' he introduced himself, 'first lieutenant of the *Hazard*.'

'I know who you are, Lieutenant,' Saltonstall said coolly. In the commodore's opinion Little was a firebrand, an impetuous, unthinking firebrand from the so-called Massachusetts Navy, which, so far as the commodore was concerned, was nothing but a toy navy. 'Where is the *Hazard*?' Saltonstall asked.

'Upstream, sir. I was lending a hand to the *Sky Rocket*, sir.' The *Sky Rocket*, a fine sixteen-gun privateer, was aground by the bluff and waiting for the tide. 'Captain Burke sends his compliments, sir,' Little said.

'You may return them, Lieutenant.'

Little looked about the deck. He saw the powder bags, the slow-matches and the combustibles stacked around the masts. Then he looked back to the immaculate commodore in his black shining top-boots, white breeches, blue waistcoat, blue tail-coat, and with his brushed cocked hat glinting with gold braid. 'Captain Burke wants orders, sir,' Little said in a curt voice.

'Captain Burke is ordered to deny his ship to the enemy,' Saltonstall said.

Little shuddered, then turned so suddenly that Saltonstall instinctively put a hand to his sword's hilt, but the lieutenant was merely pointing to the place where the river swirled around the bluff. 'That's where you should be, sir!'

'Are you presuming to give me orders, Lieutenant?' Saltonstall's voice was icy.

'You haven't even fired a gun!' Little protested.

'Lieutenant Little . . .' Fenwick began.

'Lieutenant Little is returning to his ship,' Saltonstall interrupted Fenwick. 'Good day to you, Lieutenant.'

'Damn you!' Little shouted and sailors stopped working to listen. 'Put your ship at the bend,' he snapped, still pointing to where the river swirled around the western bluff. 'Anchor her fore and aft. Put springs on the anchors so your broadside points downstream and fight the bastards!'

'Lieutenant . . .' Saltonstall began.

'For God's sake, fight!' Little, an officer of the Massachusetts Navy, was now screaming into the commodore's face, spattering it with spittle. 'Move all your big eighteens to one side! Let's hurt the bastards!' Little's face was just two inches from Saltonstall when he bellowed the last four words. Neither Saltonstall nor Fenwick said anything. Fenwick plucked feebly at Little's arm and Saltonstall merely looked disgusted, as though a turd had suddenly appeared on his holy-stoned deck. 'Oh, for God's sake,' Little said, struggling to control his anger, 'the river below the bend is narrow, sir! A ship can't turn in the width of that channel! The British will be forced to come single file, bows to our guns, and they can't answer our shots. They can't answer! They can't bring their big ships up here, they have to send frigates, and if we put guns there we can slaughter the bastards!'

'I am grateful for your advice, Lieutenant,' Saltonstall said with utter disdain.

'Oh, you cowardly bastard!' Little spat.

'Lieutenant!' Fenwick seized Little's arm. 'You don't know who you're speaking to!'

Little shook off the lieutenant's hand. 'I know who I'm speaking to,' he sneered, 'and I know where I am and I damned well know where the enemy is too! You can't just burn this ship without a fight! Give her to me! I'll damn well fight her!'

'Good day, Lieutenant,' Saltonstall said icily. Fenwick had beckoned two crewmen who now stood menacingly close to the furious Little. James Fletcher had evidently come aboard during the argument. 'Get off my ship!' Saltonstall snarled at Fletcher, then turned back to Little. 'I command here! On this ship you take my orders! And my orders are for you to leave before I have you put in irons.'

'Come ashore,' Little invited the commodore, 'come ashore, you yellow bastard, and I'll fight you there. Man on man, and the winner takes this ship.'

437

'Remove him,' Saltonstall said.

Little was dragged away. He turned once and spat at Saltonstall, then was pushed down to his waiting longboat.

The *Warren* lurched and came free of the sandbank. A breath of wind touched Commodore Saltonstall's cheek and lifted the snake ensign at the frigate's stern. The smoke in the clear sky wavered and started to drift north-west.

Which meant the British were coming.

The men on the beach beneath the bluff had come from the transports that were anchored or grounded in the river. They now sat disconsolate and leaderless on the shingle. 'What are your orders?' Wadsworth asked one sergeant.

'Don't have any orders, sir.'

'We're going home!' a man shouted angrily.

'How?' Wadsworth demanded.

The man had hefted a haversack sewn from sail-canvas. 'Any way we can. Walk, I guess. How far is it?'

'Two hundred miles. And you're not going home, not yet.' Wadsworth turned on the sergeant. 'Get your men in order, we still have a war to fight.'

Wadsworth strode down the beach, shouting at officers and sergeants to assemble their men. If the British could be stopped at this bend then there was a good chance to reorganize the army upriver. Trees could be felled, a camp made, and guns placed to deter any British assault. All it needed was a firm defence on this sun-drenched morning. As Wadsworth followed the bank further downstream he saw how the river narrowed into a valley that ran almost straight southwards to Odom's Ledge about four miles away. The river itself was about three hundred paces wide, but that was deceptive because the navigable channel was much narrower and the British ships must creep up that channel in single file, the leading ship's vulnerable bows pointing straight at the bluff. Four guns would do the job! He ordered militia captains to clear a ledge on the bluff's slope and when they complained that they had no axes or shovels he snapped at them to find a boat and search the transport ships for the necessary tools. 'Just do some work! You want to go home and tell your children you ran away from the British? Have any of you seen Colonel Revere?'

'He went downriver, sir,' a surly militia captain answered.

'Downriver?'

The captain pointed to the long, narrow valley where the rearmost American ship, a schooner, was trying to reach the rest of the fleet still gathered by the bluff. Her big mizzen sail was poled out to port to catch the tiny wind that had at last started to scurry catspaws across the river's surface. Four of the schooner's crew were using huge oars to try and hasten her passage, but the oars dipped and pulled pathetically slowly. Then Wadsworth saw why they were using the long sweeps. Behind the schooner was a much larger ship, a ship with more sails and higher masts, a ship that suddenly fired her bow-chasers to fill the valley with smoke and with the echo of her two cannon shots. The balls had not been aimed at the schooner, but rather to either side of her hull as a signal that she should haul down her ensign and let the pursuing British take her as a prize.

Wadsworth ran down the beach. There were men on the schooner's bows waving frantically. They had no longboat, no boat of any sort, and they wanted a rescue, and there, not fifty paces away, was Revere's white-painted barge with its crew of oarsmen. It was rowing upriver ahead of the schooner, suggesting that Revere had gone downstream, maybe hoping to escape past the British ships, but, discovering the futility of such a hope, had been forced back northwards. Wadsworth could see Lieutenant-Colonel Revere himself in the barge's sternsheets and he stopped at the water's edge and cupped his hands, 'Colonel Revere!'

Revere waved to show he had heard the hail.

439

Wadsworth pointed at the schooner that he now recognized as the *Nancy*. 'The *Nancy*'s crew needs rescuing! Take your barge and pick them up!'

Revere twisted on his bench to look at the *Nancy*, then turned back to Wadsworth. 'You've no right to give me commands now, General!' Revere called, then said something to his crew who kept rowing upstream, away from the doomed *Nancy*.

Wadsworth wondered if he had misheard. 'Colonel Revere!' He shouted slowly and clearly so there could be no misunderstanding. 'Take your barge and get those crewmen off the *Nancy*!' The schooner was lightly crewed and there was plenty of room in the barge's bows for all of her seamen.

'I was under your command so long as there was a siege,' Revere called back, 'but the siege is over, and with it your authority has ended.'

For a heartbeat Wadsworth did not believe what he had heard. He gaped at the stocky colonel, then was overcome with rage and indignation. 'For God's sake, man, they're Americans! Go and rescue them!'

'I've got my baggage here,' Revere called back and pointed to a heap of boxes covered by sailcloth. 'I'm not willing to risk my baggage! Good day to you, Wadsworth.'

'You . . . ' Wadsworth began, but was too angry to finish. He turned and walked up the beach to keep pace with the barge. 'I am giving you an order!' he shouted at Revere. Men on the beach watched and listened. 'Rescue that crew!'

The British frigate astern of the *Nancy* fired her bow-chasers again and the balls seared past the hull to throw up great fountains of river-water. 'You see?' Revere called when the echo of the gunfire had faded. 'I can't risk my baggage!'

'I promise you an arrest, Colonel!' Wadsworth called savagely. 'Unless you obey my orders!'

'You can't give me orders now!' Revere said, almost cheerfully. 'It's over and done with. Good day, General!'

'I want your guns on the bluff ahead!'

Revere waved a negligent hand towards Wadsworth. 'Keep rowing,' he told his men.

'I shall have you arrested!' Wadsworth bellowed.

But the barge kept going and Lieutenant-Colonel Paul Revere's baggage was safe.

HMS *Galatea* led the British frigates. At her bows was a figure-head of Galatea, her painted skin as white as the marble from which her mythical statue had been carved. In that myth she had sprung to life from the marble and now she came upriver, naked except for a wisp of silk covering her hips, and with her defiant head raised to look straight ahead with startling blue eyes. The frigate was flying topsails and topgallantsails only, the high canvas catching what small wind came from the south. Ahead of her was chaos, and the *Galatea* made the chaos worse. The schooner *Nancy* had been abandoned, but a British prize crew secured the vessel and used the captured schooner's anchors to drag her to the eastern bank of the river so that the *Galatea* and HMS *Camille*, which followed the *Galatea*, could pass. The nymph and her blue eyes vanished in a sudden billow of smoke as the two long-barrelled nine-pounder bow-chasers fired from the frigate. The balls skipped across the water towards the mass of rebel shipping. Red-coated Royal Marines on the *Galatea*'s forecastle waited for the cannon smoke to drift away, then began shooting muskets at the distant men on the river's western bank. They fired at very long range, and none of the balls found a target, but the beach emptied fast as men sought shelter among the trees.

And there was more smoke now, far more smoke. It did not come from British cannons, but from fires aboard the rebel ships. Captains struck flint against steel and lit their slow-matches, or else thrust fire into the kindling of the combustibles stacked below decks and around masts. Longboats pulled for the shore as smoke poured out of companionways.

441

The *Galatea* and the *Camille* both dropped stern anchors and took in their topsails. No ship would risk itself by sailing into an inferno. Fire loved timber, tar and linen, and every sailor feared fire much more than he feared the sea, and so the two frigates lay in the river, rising gently on the incoming tide, and their crews watched an enemy destroy itself.

The proud ships burned. The sleek privateers and the heavy transports burned. Smoke thickened to a dense thunder-dark cloud that boiled into the summer sky, and amidst the smoke were savage tongues of flame leaping and spreading. When the hungry fire found new timber it would sometimes explode and the light would glimmer across the water and new flame would erupt into the rigging. That rigging was ablaze, each ship and brig and sloop and schooner outlined by fire until a mast burned through and then, so slowly, a blazing lattice would topple, sparks rushing upwards as the spars and lines arced downwards, and the river would hiss and steam as the masts collapsed.

The *Sky Rocket*, a sixteen-gun ship-privateer, was aground just beyond the bluff and in the haste to evacuate the bluff she had taken the remainder of the ammunition from the abandoned rebel batteries. Her hold was filled with powder, and the fire found the hold and the *Sky Rocket* exploded. The force of the blast shivered the smoke from the other burning ships, it blew timber and burning sails high into the air where, like sky rockets, they flew to leave a myriad smoke trails curving far above the river. The noise was physical, a pounding of sound that was heard in Fort George, and then other magazines exploded, as if copying the *Sky Rocket*'s example, and the hulls lurched, steam mixed with the churning smoke, and rats screamed in the filthy bilges as the consuming fire roared like furnaces run wild. Men ashore wept for their lost ships, and the oven-heat of the blaze touched the faces of the seamen staring in wonder from the *Galatea*'s foredeck. Flaming yards, their halliards burned through, dropped onto

442

fiery decks and more hulls shattered as more gunpowder caught the fire and ripped the wooden ships apart. Anchor rodes parted and fire ships drifted and hulls collided, their flames mingling and growing, the smoke thickening and rising ever higher. Some ships had left their guns charged with shot and those guns now fired into the burning fleet. Gun-barrels collapsed through burning decks. The furnace roared, the cannon hammered, and the river hissed as the wrecks sank in ash-filthy water where charred debris drifted.

Beyond the bluff, still anchored even though she was well afloat now, the *Warren* was abandoned. She was bigger than either the *Galatea* or the *Camille*. She carried thirty-two guns to their twenty each, though she had no naked nymph protecting her bows. She had been built at Providence, Rhode Island, and was named for Joseph Warren, the Boston doctor who had sparked the rebellion by sending the horsemen to warn Lexington and Concord that the British were coming. Warren had been a patriot and an inspiration. He was appointed a general in the rebellious militia but, because his commission had not arrived, he had fought as a private at Bunker Hill and there he had died and the frigate was named in tribute to him, and since her launch she had captured ten rich British merchantmen. She was a lethal machine, heavily armed by the standards of other frigates, and her big eighteen-pounders were larger than any cannon aboard the smaller British frigates.

But now, as the last of her crew rowed ashore, the *Warren* burned. Dudley Saltonstall did not look behind to see the smoke and, once ashore, he struck straight into the woods so that the trees would hide the sight of the burning frigate, of the flames rippling fast up her rigging, of the furled sails bursting into fire, of the sparks flying and falling.

All along the river the ships burned. Not one was left.

Peleg Wadsworth watched in silence. The guns that should have kept the British at bay were being sunk to the river's bed and the men who should have rallied and fought were scattered and leaderless. Panic had struck before Wadsworth could inspire resistance and now the great fleet was burning and the army was broken.

'What now?' James Fletcher asked. Smoke covered the sky like a pall.

'Do you remember the story of Shadrach, Meshach and Abednego?' Wadsworth asked. 'From the Bible?'

James had not expected that answer and was puzzled for a moment, then he nodded his head. 'Mother told us that tale, sir,' he said. 'Weren't they the men who were thrown into the fire?'

'And all the king's men watched them, and saw they were not harmed by the fiery furnace,' Wadsworth said, remembering the sermon he had heard in Boston's Christ Church the day before the fleet sailed. 'The scripture tells us the fire had no power over those men.' He paused, watching the frigate burn. 'No power,' he said again and he thought of his dear wife and of the child waiting to be born, then smiled at James. 'Now come,' he said, 'you and I have work to do.'

The remaining powder in the *Warren*'s magazine exploded. The foremast flew upwards, spewing smoke and sparks and fire, the hull burst apart along its flame-bright seams, the sudden light seared the shivering river red and the frigate disappeared. It was over.

From an Order in Council, Boston, dated September 6th, 1779:

Therefore Ordered that Lieutenant Colonel Paul Revere be and he hereby is directed Immediately to Resign the Command of Castle Island and the other Fortresses in the Harbour of Boston to Captain Perez Cushing, and remove himself from the Castle and Fortresses aforesaid and repair to his dwelling house in Boston and there continue untill the matter complained of can be duly inquired into . . .

From a Petition of Richard Sykes to the Massachusetts House of Representatives, September 28th, 1779:

Your Petitioner was . . . a Sergeant of Marines on board the Ship General Putnam when an attack was made on one of the Redoubts . . . your Petitioner was made a Prisoner and was carried from Penobscot to New York in the Reasonable Man of War was stript of almost all his Clothing . . . Your Petitioner prays your Honors would allow him Pay for the cloathing he lost . . . viz 2 Linnen Shirts 3 Pair Stockings 1 pair Buck Skin Breeches 1 pair Cloth Breeches 1 Hat I Knapsack 1 Handkerchief 1 pair Shoes.

HISTORICAL NOTE

The Penobscot Expedition, of July and August 1779, is an actual event and I have tried, within the constraints of fiction, to describe what happened. The occupation of Majabigwaduce was intended to establish a British province that would be called New Ireland and would serve as a naval base and as a shelter for loyalists fleeing rebel persecution. The government of Massachusetts decided to 'captivate, kill or destroy' the invaders and so launched the expedition that is often described as the worst naval disaster in United States history before Pearl Harbor. The fleet that sailed to the Penobscot River was the largest assembled by the rebels during the War of Independence. The lists of ships in the various sources differ in detail, and I assume that two or three transport ships must have left before Sir George Collier's arrival, but the bulk of the fleet was present, which made it a terrible disaster both for the Continental Navy and for Massachusetts. The fourteen-gun brig *Pallas* had been sent to patrol beyond the mouth of the Penobscot River and so was absent when Sir George Collier's relief ships arrived and she alone survived the debacle. Two American ships, the *Hunter* and the *Hampden*, were captured (some sources add the schooner *Nancy* and nine other transports), and the remaining ships were burned.

447

Doctor John Calef, in his official position as the Clerk of the Penobscot Council (appointed by the British), listed thirty-seven rebel ships as taken or burned, and that seems broadly correct.

The blame for the disaster has been almost universally placed on the shoulders of Commodore Dudley Saltonstall. Saltonstall was no hero at Penobscot, and he appears to have been an awkward, unsociable man, but he certainly does not bear the full responsibility for the expedition's failure. Saltonstall was court-martialled (though no record of the trial exists, so it might never have convened), and was dismissed from the Continental Navy. The only other man to be court-martialled for his conduct at Majabigwaduce was Lieutenant-Colonel Paul Revere.

It is an extraordinary coincidence that two men present at Majabigwaduce in the summer of 1779 were to be the subjects of famous poems. Paul Revere was celebrated by Henry Longfellow, and it is Revere's presence at Majabigwaduce that gives the expedition much of its interest. Few men are so honoured as a hero of the American Revolution. There is a handsome equestrian statue to Revere in Boston and, in New England at least, he is regarded as the region's paramount patriot and revolutionary hero, yet he does not owe his extraordinary fame to his actions at Majabigwaduce, nor even to his midnight ride, but to Henry Longfellow's poem, which was published in *The Atlantic Monthly* magazine in 1861.

Listen, my children, and you shall hear
Of the midnight ride of Paul Revere.

And Americans have been hearing of the midnight ride ever since, mostly oblivious that the poem plays merry-hell with the true facts and ascribes to Revere the heroics of other men. This was deliberate; Longfellow, writing at the outbreak of the American Civil War, was striving to create a patriotic legend, not tell an accurate history. Revere did indeed ride to warn Concord and Lexington that the British regulars were marching from Boston, but he did not complete the mission. Many other men rode that night and have been forgotten while Paul Revere, solely thanks to Henry Longfellow, gallops into posterity as the undying patriot and rebel. Before the poem was published Revere was remembered as a regional folk-hero, one among many who had been active in the patriot cause, but in 1861 he entered legend. He was indeed a passionate patriot, and he was vigorous in his opposition to the British long before the outbreak of the revolution, but the *only* time Revere ever fought the British was at Majabigwaduce, and there, in General Artemas Ward's words, he showed 'unsoldierlike behaviour tending to cowardice'. The general was quoting Marine Captain Thomas Carnes who closely observed Revere during the expedition and Carnes, like most others in the expedition, believed Revere's behaviour there was disgraceful. Revere's present reputation would have puzzled and, in many cases, disgusted his contemporaries.

A second man at Majabigwaduce was to have a famous poem written about him. This man died at Corunna in Spain and the Irish poet Charles Wolfe began his tribute thus:

Not a drum was heard, not a funeral note,
As his corse to the rampart we hurried;
Not a soldier discharged his farewell shot
O'er the grave where our hero was buried.

We buried him darkly at the dead of night,
The sods with our bayonets turning . . .

The poem, of course, is *The Burial of Sir John Moore after Corunna*. Lieutenant John Moore went on to revolutionize the British Army and is the man who forged the famed Light Division, a weapon that Wellington used to such devastating

449

effect against the French in the Napoleonic Wars. Lieutenant-General Sir John Moore died in 1809 defeating Marshal Soult at Corunna, but Lieutenant John Moore's first action was fought on the fogbound coast of Massachusetts. Moore did leave a brief account of his service at Majabigwaduce, but I invented much for him. His extraordinary ability to load and fire a musket five times a minute is recorded, and he was in command of the picquet closest to Dyce's Head on the morning of the successful American assault. Lieutenant Moore, alone among the picquets' officers, attempted to stem the attack and lost a quarter of his men. I doubt that Moore did kill Captain Welch (though Moore was carrying a musket and must have been very close to Welch when the marine captain died), but it is certain that it was Moore's bad luck to be faced by the American marines who were, by far, the most effective troops on the rebel side. Those first marines did wear green coats and it is tempting, though unproven, to think that those uniforms influenced the adoption of green jackets for the 60th and 95th Rifles, regiments that Moore nurtured and that served Britain so famously in the long wars against France. Welch's death on the heights was one of the strokes of ill-fortune that beset the expedition. John Welch was an extraordinary man who had escaped from imprisonment in England and had made his way back across the Atlantic to rejoin the rebellion.

Peleg Wadsworth, in his long statement to the official Court of Enquiry, offered three reasons for the disaster: 'the Lateness of our Arival before the Enemy, the Smallness of our Land Forces, and the uniform Backwardness of the Commander of the Fleet.' History has settled on the third reason and Commodore Dudley Saltonstall has been made to carry the whole blame. He was dismissed from the Continental Navy and it has even been suggested, without a shred of supporting evidence, that he was a traitor in British pay. He was no traitor, and it seems egregious to single out his performance

450

as the primary reason for the expedition's failure. In 2002 the Naval Institute Press (Annapolis, Maryland) published George E. Buker's fine book, *The Penobscot Expedition*. George Buker served as a naval officer and his book is a spirited defence of a fellow naval officer. The main accusation against the commodore was that he refused to take his ships into Majabigwaduce Harbour and so eliminate Captain Mowat's three sloops, and Saltonstall's description of the harbour, 'that damned hole', is often quoted as the reason for his refusal. George Buker goes to great lengths to show the difficulties Saltonstall faced. The British naval force might have been puny compared to the rebels' naval strength, but they held a remarkably strong position, and any attack past Dyce's Head would have taken the American ships into a cauldron of cannon-fire from which it would have been almost impossible to escape without the unlikely help of an easterly wind (which, of course, would have prevented them from entering). George Buker is persuasive, except that Nelson faced a roughly similar situation at Aboukir Bay (and against an enemy stronger than himself) and he sailed into the bay and won, and John Paul Jones (who had served under Saltonstall and had no respect for the man) would certainly have sailed into the harbour to sink Mowat's sloops. It is grossly unfair to condemn a man for not being a Nelson or a John Paul Jones, yet despite George Buker's arguments it is still hard to believe that any naval commander, given the vast preponderance of his fleet over the enemy, declined to engage that enemy. The thirty-two naval officers who signed the round-robin urging Saltonstall to attack certainly did not believe that the circumstances were so dire that no attack was feasible. Saltonstall's ships would have suffered, but they would have won. The three British sloops would have been captured or sunk, and then what?

That question has never been answered, and it was not in the interest of Massachusetts to answer it. George Buker's book is subtitled *Commodore Saltonstall and the Massachusetts Conspiracy of 1779*, and its main argument is that the government of Massachusetts conspired to place all the blame on Saltonstall, and in that ambition they were brilliantly successful. The expedition was a Massachusetts initiative, undertaken without consultation with the Continental Congress, and almost wholly funded by the State. Massachusetts insured all the private ships, paid the crews, supplied the militia, provided weapons, ammunition and stores, and lost every penny. British money was still in use in Massachusetts in 1779 and the official enquiry was told that the loss amounted to £1,588,668 (and ten pence!) and the real figure was probably much closer to two million pounds. Discovering the equivalency of historic monetary sums to present values is a difficult and uncertain task, but at a most conservative estimate that loss, in 2010 US dollars, amounts to around $300,000,000. This enormous sum effectively bankrupted the State. However, Massachusetts was lucky. The *Warren* had been in Boston Harbour when the news of the British incursion arrived, and it had made sense to use that powerful warship, and the two other Continental Navy vessels at Boston, and so permission to deploy them had been sought and received from the Continental Navy Board. This meant that a small portion of the defeated forces had been Federal and if the blame could be placed on that Federal component then the other states might be made to recompense Massachusetts for the loss. That required, in turn, for Saltonstall to be depicted as the villain of the piece. Massachusetts argued that it had been Saltonstall's behaviour that had betrayed the whole expedition and, supported by mendacious evidence (especially from Solomon Lovell), that argument prevailed. It took many years, but in 1793 the Federal Government of the United States of America largely reimbursed Massachusetts for the financial loss. So placing the entire blame on Saltonstall was politically motivated and very successful as the American taxpayer ended up paying for the mistakes of Massachusetts.

So why did Saltonstall not attack? He left no account, and if his court-martial ever took place then the records have been lost and so we do not possess his testimony. It was certainly not cowardice that stayed his hand because he proved his courage elsewhere in the war, and the suggestion that he was in British pay is unsupportable. My own belief is that Saltonstall was unwilling to sacrifice his men and, quite possibly, one of the few frigates left to the Continental Navy in an operation that, though successful, would not have advanced the aim of the expedition. Yes, he could have taken the three sloops, but would Lovell have matched his achievement on land? I suspect Saltonstall believed that the Massachusetts Militia was inadequate, for which belief he had much evidence, and that destroying the sloops was irrelevant to the expedition's purpose, which was the capture of Fort George. If the sloops were taken or sunk, the fort would have survived, albeit in a less advantageous situation, whereas the capture of the fort irrevocably doomed the sloops. Saltonstall understood that. This is not to exonerate the commodore. He was a difficult, prickly man and he was obdurate in his relations with Lovell, and he failed miserably to stop or even attempt to slow the British pursuit during the retreat upriver, but he was not the man who ruined the expedition. Lovell was.

Solomon Lovell has been forgiven for the expedition's failure, yet it was Lovell who did not press the attacks on Fort George that, on the day his troops landed, was scarcely defensible. It does seem true that McLean was fully prepared to surrender rather than provoke a ghastly hand-to-hand fight over his inadequate ramparts (at that moment McLean still believed, probably based on the number of rebel transport ships, that he was outnumbered by at least four to one). But Lovell held back. And went on holding back. He refused Peleg Wadsworth's eminently sensible suggestion that the rebels should prepare a fortification upriver to which they could withdraw if the British should send reinforcements. He made no attempt, ever, to storm the fort, but instead called endless Councils of War (which made decisions by votes) and insisted, in increasingly petulant tones, that Saltonstall attack the sloops before the militia moved against the fort. It is evident that the Massachusetts Militia were poor soldiers, yet that too was Lovell's responsibility. They needed discipline, encouragement and leadership. They received none of those things and so they camped forlornly on the heights until the order came to retreat. It is true that once Fort George's walls were raised sufficiently high Lovell's chances of capturing the work were almost non-existent because he did not have enough men and his artillery had failed to blast a way through the ramparts, but certainly he had every hope of a successful storm in the first week of the siege. My belief is that Dudley Saltonstall understood perfectly well that his destruction of the sloops would not lead to the fort's capture, and that therefore any attack on the British ships would simply result in unneccessary naval casualties. He was finally persuaded to enter the harbour on Friday, August 13th, but abandoned that attack because of the arrival of Sir George Collier's relief fleet. The aborted land-sea attack might well have eliminated Mowat's sloops, but Lovell's forces would surely have been decimated by the fort's defenders. It was all too little too late, a fiasco caused by atrocious leadership and lack of decision.

The British, on the other hand, were very well led by two professionals who trusted each other and co-operated closely. McLean's tactics, which were simply to go on strengthening Fort George while constantly irritating his besiegers with Caffrae's Light Company, worked perfectly. Mowat donated guns and men whenever needed. The British, after all, only had to survive until reinforcements arrived, and they were fortunate that Sir George Collier (who really did write the musical presented at the Drury Lane Theatre) beat Henry Jackson's regiment of Continental Army regulars to the

Penobscot River. Brigadier-General Francis McLean was a very good soldier and, even by the estimate of his enemies, a very good man, and he served his king well at Majabigwaduce. Once the whole affair was over McLean went out of his way to ensure that the wounded rebels, stranded far up the river, were supplied with medical necessities and had a ship to convey them back to Boston. There are rebel accounts of encounters with McLean and in all of them he is depicted as a humane, generous and decent man. The two regiments he led at Majabigwaduce were every bit as inexperienced as the militia they faced, yet his young Scotsmen received leadership, inspiration and example. Peleg Wadsworth did not meet Francis McLean during the siege, so their conversation is entirely fictional, though the cause of it, Lieutenant Dennis's injury and capture, was real enough. It was Captain Thomas Thomas, master of the privateer *Vengeance*, and Lovell's secretary, John Marston, who approached the fort under a flag of truce to discover Dennis's sad fate, but I wanted McLean and Wadsworth to meet and so changed the facts.

I changed as little as I could. So far as I know, Peleg Wadsworth was not asked to investigate the charge of peculation against Revere, an accusation that faded away into the larger mess of Penobscot. I telescoped some events of the siege. Brigadier McLean spent a couple of days exploring Penobscot Bay before deciding on Majabigwaduce as the site for his fort, a reconnaissance I ignored. There were two attempts to lure the British into ambushes at the Half Moon Battery, both of them disastrous, but for fictional purposes one seemed sufficient, and I have no evidence that John Moore was involved in either action. The final immolation of the rebel fleet stretched over three days, which I shrank to two.

The total casualties incurred at Penobscot are very hard to establish. Lovell, in his journal, reckoned the rebels lost only fourteen dead and twenty wounded in their assault on the bluff, while Peleg Wadsworth, in his written recollection of the same action, estimated the number of rebels killed and wounded at a hundred. The militia returns are not helpful. Lovell's men were reinforced by some local volunteers (though Lovell noted a general reluctance among the militia of the Penobscot valley to take up arms against the British) so that, on the eve of Sir George Collier's arrival, the rebel army numbered 923 men fit for duty as against 873 three weeks before, and this despite combat losses and the regrettably high rate of desertion. The best evidence suggests that total British losses were twenty-five killed, between thirty and forty seriously wounded, and twenty-six men taken prisoner. Rebel casualties are much harder to estimate, but one contemporary source claims fewer than 150 killed and wounded, though another, adding in the men who did not survive the long journey home through thickly forested country, goes as high as 474 total casualties. My own conclusion is that rebel casualties were about double the British figures. That might be a low estimate, but certainly the Penobscot Expedition, though a disaster for the rebels, was blessedly not a bloodbath.

Lieutenant George Little's angry confrontation with Saltonstall at the end of the expedition is attested by contemporary evidence, as is Peleg Wadsworth's encounter with Paul Revere during the retreat upriver. Revere, asked to rescue the schooner's crew, refused on the personal grounds that he did not wish to risk his baggage being captured by the British and on the more general grounds that, the siege being over, he was no longer obliged to obey the orders of his superior officers. Some sources claim that he landed the baggage, then sent the barge back for the schooner's crew. That may well be true, and the crew was rescued even though the schooner itself probably became a third British prize, but afterwards Revere simply left the river without orders and, abandoning most of his men, made his way back to Boston. Once home he was suspended from his command of the Artillery Regiment, placed under house arrest and, eventually, court-martialled.

Peleg Wadsworth had threatened Revere with arrest, and it was Revere's truculent insolence on the day that Wadsworth ordered him to rescue the schooner's crew that was to cause Revere the most trouble, but other major charges were levelled by Brigade Major William Todd and by Marine Captain Thomas Carnes. Those accusations were investigated by the Committee of Enquiry established by the General Court of Massachusetts that was convened to discover the reasons for the expedition's failure.

Todd and Revere, as the novel suggests, had a long history of animosity that certainly coloured Todd's accusations. Brigade Major Todd claimed that Revere was frequently absent from the American lines, a charge that is supported by other witnesses and by Lovell's General Order of July 30th, 1779 (quoted at the top of Chapter Nine), and he cited various times when Revere had disobeyed orders, specifically during the retreat. Thomas Carnes echoed some of those complaints. I know of no reason why Carnes, unlike Todd, should have harboured a personal dislike of Revere, though perhaps it is significant that Carnes had been an officer in Gridley's Artillery and Richard Gridley, the regiment's founder and commanding officer, had fallen out with Revere over Masonic business. Carnes complained that when the Americans landed, Revere was supposed to be leading his artillerymen as a reserve corps of infantry, but instead went back to the *Samuel* for breakfast. Carnes's basic charges, though, concerned Revere's fitness as a gunner, a subject on which Carnes was expertly equipped to comment. Revere, Carnes said, was not present to supervise the construction of the batteries and gave his gunners no instruction or proper supervision. In cross-examination Carnes, an experienced artilleryman, claimed it was extraordinary that Revere 'should make such a bad shot and know no more about artillery'. It was Carnes's written deposition that accused Revere of behaviour 'which tends to cowardice'. Wadsworth testified that Revere was frequently absent from

457

the rebel lines and described Revere's refusal to obey orders during the eventual retreat. Wadsworth also noted that Revere, when offered a chance to vote on whether or not to continue the siege, consistently chose against continuance. That is not evidence of cowardice, but the minutes of those councils do reveal that Revere was by far the most vehement of the men urging abandonment of the siege.

The Court of Enquiry published its findings in October, 1779. It concluded that Commodore Saltonstall bore the entire blame for the expedition's failure and specifically exonerated Generals Lovell and Wadsworth, yet, despite all the evidence, it gave no judgement on Paul Revere's behaviour. George Buker convincingly argues that the committee did not want to dilute its absurd charge that the Continental Navy, in the person of Dudley Saltonstall, was solely responsible for the disaster.

Revere was dissatisfied. He had not been condemned, but neither had his name been cleared and Boston was rife with rumours of his 'unsoldierlike' behaviour. He demanded to be court-martialled. Revere, it seems to me, was a difficult man. One of his most sympathetic biographers admits that it was Revere's 'personality traits' that weakened his chances of gaining a Continental Army commission. He was quarrelsome, exceedingly touchy about his own reputation and prone to pick fights with anyone who criticized him. He had a separate spat with John Hancock who, inspecting Castle Island during Revere's absence at Penobscot, dared to find fault with its defences. The General Court, however, did not grant him a court-martial, but instead reconvened the Committee of Enquiry, which was now charged with investigating Revere's behaviour and a crucial piece of evidence was the 'diary' Revere had ostensibly kept at Majabigwaduce and that, unsurprisingly, shows him to be a model of military diligence. I have no proof that this 'diary' was manufactured for the enquiry, but it seems very likely. Revere also produced many witnesses to counter the charges against him and his vigorous defence was largely successful because, when the committee reported in November, 1779, it cleared Revere of the charge of cowardice, though it did mildly condemn him for leaving Penobscot without orders and for 'disputing the orders of Brigadier-General Wadsworth respecting the Boat'. Revere's only defence against the latter charge was that he had misunderstood Wadsworth's orders.

Yet, though he had been cleared of cowardice, Revere was still dissatisfied and once again he petitioned for a court-martial. That court finally convened in 1782 and Revere at last received what he wanted, exoneration. The suspicion is that people were tired of the whole affair and that, in February, 1782, four months after the great rebel triumph at Yorktown, no one wanted to resurrect unhappy memories of the Penobscot Expedition and so, though the court-martial weakly chided Revere for his refusal to rescue the schooner's crew, they acquitted him 'with equal Honor as the other Officers', which, in the circumstances, was very faint praise indeed. The controversy over Revere's behaviour at Majabigwaduce persisted with a bitter exchange of letters in the Boston press, but it was long forgotten by 1861 when Revere was abruptly elevated to the heroic status he enjoys today. Other offences such as Revere's delay of the fleet's departure, his petty refusal to allow anyone else to use the Castle Island barge and his failure to withdraw the guns from Cross Island are all attested by various sources.

Dudley Saltonstall was dismissed from the navy, but was able to invest in a privateer, the *Minerva*, with which, in 1781, he captured one of the richest prizes of the whole Revolutionary War. After the war Saltonstall owned trading ships, some of them used for slaving, and he died, aged fifty-eight in 1796. Paul Revere was also successful after the war, opening a foundry and becoming a prominent Boston industrialist. He died in 1818, aged eighty-three. Solomon Lovell's political career was not harmed by the Penobscot fiasco. He remained a Selectman for Weymouth, Massachusetts, a Representative in the General Court, and he helped devise the State's new constitution. He died aged sixty-nine in 1801. A memorialist wrote that Solomon Lovell was 'esteemed and honored . . . respected and trusted in the counsels of the State . . . his name has been handed down through the generations.' A better judgement was surely made by a young marine at Majabigwaduce who wrote, 'Mister Lovell would have done more good, and made a much more respectable appearance in the deacon's seat of a country church, than at the head of an American army.'

Captain Henry Mowat remained in the Royal Navy, his last command a frigate on which he died, probably of a heart attack, off the coast of Virginia in 1798. He is buried in St John's churchyard, Hampton, Virginia. Brigadier-General Francis McLean returned to his command at Halifax, Nova Scotia, where he died, aged sixty-three just two years after his successful defence of Fort George. John Moore far transcended his old commander in fame and is now celebrated as one of the greatest, and most humane, generals ever to serve in the British army. He died aged forty-eight at Corunna just as he had fought at Majabigwaduce, leading from the front.

In 1780, a year after the expedition, Peleg Wadsworth was sent back to eastern Massachusetts as commander of the Penobscot region's militia. The British garrison at Fort George learned of his presence and sent a raiding party that, after a brief fight in which Wadsworth was wounded, captured him. Wadsworth was imprisoned in Fort George where his wife, allowed to visit her husband, was told of a plan to move Wadsworth to a prison in Britain. Wadsworth and a second prisoner, Major Burton, then devised and executed a daring escape that was wholly successful, and today the bay north of Castine (as Majabigwaduce is now called) and west of the neck is named Wadsworth Cove after the place where the two escapees found a boat. Peleg Wadsworth remained in eastern Massachusetts. After the war he opened a hardware store and built a house in Portland that can still be seen (as can Paul Revere's house in Boston), and he served in the Massachusetts Senate and as a representative for the Province of Maine in the US Congress. He became a farmer in Hiram, and was a leader in the movement to make Maine a separate state, an ambition realized in 1820. He and his wife Elizabeth had ten children, and he died in 1829, aged eighty-one. George Washington held Peleg Wadsworth in the highest esteem and one of the Wadsworth family's treasured heirlooms was a lock of Washington's hair that was a gift from the first president. Peleg Wadsworth was, to my mind, a true hero and a great man.

The British stayed at Majabigwaduce, indeed it was the very last British post to be evacuated from the United States. Many of the Loyalists moved to Nova Scotia when the British left, some taking their houses with them, though interestingly a number of British soldiers, including Sergeant Lawrence of the Royal Artillery, settled in Majabigwaduce after the war and, by all accounts, were warmly welcomed. Most of the sunken cannon from the rebel fleet were retrieved and put into British service, which explains why commemorative gun-barrels bearing the Massachusetts state seal are found as far afield as Australia. Then, in the War of 1812, the British returned and captured Majabigwaduce again, and again garrisoned the fort where they stayed till the war's end. It was during this second occupation that the fort's walls were strengthened with masonry and the British Canal, which is now a marshy ditch, was dug as a defensive work across the neck. Fort George still exists, a national monument now. It stands on the ridge above the Maine Maritime Academy in Castine, and is a peaceful, beautiful place. The ramparts are mostly overgrown with grass, and legend in Castine says that on still nights the ghost of a drummer-boy can be heard

461

beating his drum in the old fort. One version claims the ghost is a British boy who was inadvertently locked into a magazine when the garrison evacuated in 1784, others say it is an American lad killed in the fighting of 1779. The earliest reference I can discover is in William Hutchings's recollections where he avers that the boy, a rebel drummer, was killed at the Half Moon Battery. There is a footpath that twists up and down the bluff by Dice Head (as Dyce's Head is now called), giving the visitor a chance to admire the achievement of those Americans who, on July 28th, 1779, assaulted and won that position. The large boulder on the beach is called Trask's Rock after the boy fifer who played there throughout the assault. Castine prospered during the 19th century, mostly because of the timber trade, and is now a picturesque and tranquil harbour town, and very mindful of its fascinating history. During one of my visits I was told that Paul Revere had stolen the expedition's pay chest, an allegation that is not supported by any direct evidence, but indicative of the scorn that some in this part of New England feel for a man revered elsewhere in the region.

The quotations that head each chapter are, as far as possible, reproduced with their original spelling and capitalization. I took most of those quotations from the *Documentary History of the State of Maine*, Volumes XVI and XVII, published by the Maine Historical Society in 1910 and 1913 respectively. Both those collections of contemporary documents were of enormous value, as was C.B. Kevitt's book, *General Solomon Lovell and The Penobscot Expedition*, published in 1976, which contains an account of the expedition along with a selection of original sources. I also used Solomon Lovell's journal of the expedition, published by The Weymouth Historical Society in 1881, and John E. Cayford's *The Penobscot Expedition*, published privately in 1976. I have already mentioned George Buker's invaluable book, *The Penobscot Expedition*, which persuasively argues that the enquiries into the disaster were part of a successful Massachusetts conspiracy to shift both blame and financial responsibility onto the federal government. Without doubt the liveliest and most readable description of the whole expedition is found in Charles Bracelen Flood's book, *Rise, and Fight Again*, published by Dodd Mead and Company in 1976, which deals with four instances of rebel disaster on the road to independence. David Hackett Fischer's fascinating book, *Paul Revere's Ride*, Oxford University Press, 1994, does not touch on the expedition of 1779, but is a superb guide to the events leading to the revolution and to Paul Revere's influential role in that period. Readers curious about the origin of and reactions to Longfellow's poem (which Fischer describes as 'grossly, systematically, and deliberately inaccur -ate') will find his essay 'Historiography' (printed in the book's end matter) invaluable. The best biography of Revere is *A True Republican, the Life of Paul Revere*, by Jayne E. Triber, published by the University of Massachusetts, Amherst, 1998. The famous *Life of Colonel Paul Revere*, by Elbridge Goss, published in 1891, is short on biographical details, but contains a long treatment of the Penobscot Expedition. A new biog- raphy of Sir John Moore is badly needed, but I found a useful source in his brother's two-volume biography, *The Life of Lieutenant-General Sir John Moore, K.B.* by James Carrick Moore, published by John Murray, London, in 1834. I dis-covered many details about 18th-century Majabigwaduce in George Wheeler's splendid *History of Castine, Penobscot and Brookville*, published in 1875, and in the Wilson Museum Bulletins, issued by the Castine Scientific Society. The Wilson Museum, on Perkins Street in Castine, is well worth a visit as, of course, is Castine itself. I must thank Rosemary Begley and the other citizens of Castine who took the time to guide me through their town and its history, Garry Gates of my hometown, Chatham, Massachusetts, for drawing the map of Majabigwaduce, Shannon Eldredge who combed through a daunting number of log-books, letters and diaries to produce an invaluable timeline, Patrick Mercer, MP (and a talented historical novelist himself), for generous advice on late 18th-century drill, and most of all my wife, Judy, who endured my Penobscot obsession with her customary grace.

A final note, and this strikes me as the supreme irony of the Penobscot Expedition: Peleg Wadsworth, who promised to have Paul Revere arrested and who was undoubtedly angered by Revere's behaviour at Majabigwaduce, was the maternal grandfather of Henry Wadsworth Longfellow, the man who single-handedly made Revere famous. Wadsworth's daughter Zilpha, who makes a fleeting appearance at the beginning of this book, was the poet's mother. Peleg Wadsworth would have been appalled, but, as he surely knew better than most men, history is a fickle muse and fame her unfair offspring.

The SHARPE series
(in chronological order)

SHARPE'S TIGER
SHARPE'S TRIUMPH
SHARPE'S FORTRESS
SHARPE'S TRAFALGAR
SHARPE'S PREY
SHARPE'S RIFLES
SHARPE'S HAVOC
SHARPE'S EAGLE
SHARPE'S GOLD
SHARPE'S ESCAPE
SHARPE'S FURY
SHARPE'S BATTLE
SHARPE'S COMPANY
SHARPE'S SWORD
SHARPE'S ENEMY
SHARPE'S HONOUR
SHARPE'S REGIMENT
SHARPE'S SIEGE
SHARPE'S REVENGE
SHARPE'S WATERLOO
SHARPE'S DEVIL

I then told the Commodore that …
he might in half an hour make
everything his own. *In* reply to which
he hove up his long chin, and said,
'*I* am not risking my shipping
in that damned hole.'